NAOMI'S HOPE

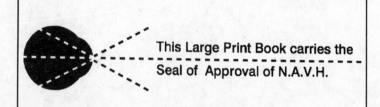

This Large Print Book carries the
Seal of Approval of N.A.V.H.

JOURNEY TO PLEASANT PRAIRIE, BOOK 3

NAOMI'S HOPE

JAN DREXLER

THORNDIKE PRESS

A part of Gale, a Cengage Company

Farmington Hills, Mich • San Francisco • New York • Waterville, Maine
Meriden, Conn • Mason, Ohio • Chicago

GALE
A Cengage Company

Copyright © 2017 by Jan Drexler.
Scripture used in this book, whether quoted or paraphrased by the characters, is taken from the King James Version of the Bible.
Scripture quotations labeled ESV are from The Holy Bible, English Standard Version® (ESV®), copyright© 2001 by Crossway, a publishing ministry of Good News Publishers. Used by permission. All rights reserved. ESV Text Edition: 2011
Thorndike Press, a part of Gale, a Cengage Company.

LIBRARY OF CONGRESS CATALOGING-IN-PUBLICATION DATA

Names: Drexler, Jan, author.
Title: Naomi's hope / by Jan Drexler.
Description: Large print edition. | Waterville, Maine : Thorndike Press, a part of Gale, a Cengage Company, 2017. | Series: Journey to Pleasant Prairie ; #3 | Series: Thorndike Press large print Christian historical fiction
Identifiers: LCCN 2017021612| ISBN 9781432842048 (hardcover) | ISBN 1432842048 (hardcover)
Subjects: LCSH: Large type books. | GSAFD: Christian fiction. | Love stories.
Classification: LCC PS3604.R496 N36 2017b | DDC 813/.6—dc23 LC record available at https://lccn.loc.gov/2017021612

Published in 2017 by arrangement with Revell Books, a division of Baker Publishing Group

Printed in the United States of America
1 2 3 4 5 6 7 21 20 19 18 17

To my children:
Jacob, Carrie, Benjamin, and Michael.
Through you, I learned what it means
to be a mother.

Soli Deo Gloria

In this you rejoice, though now for a little while, if necessary, you have been grieved by various trials, so that the tested genuineness of your faith — more precious than gold that perishes though it is tested by fire — may be found to result in praise and glory and honor at the revelation of Jesus Christ. Though you have not seen him, you love him. Though you do not now see him, you believe in him and rejoice with joy that is inexpressible and filled with glory, obtaining the outcome of your faith, the salvation of your souls.

1 Peter 1:6–9 ESV

1

Lagrange County, Indiana
April 1846

"Davey!"

Only the echoing chop of a felling ax answered Naomi Schrock's call. The new neighbor to their north must be working. *Daed* had said someone had bought the last quarter section still remaining between their land at the edge of the Haw Patch and the marshes surrounding the Little Elkhart River.

Naomi shaded her eyes against the setting sun. The late afternoon light was bright, a last burning gasp before night fell. Where was that boy?

"Davey!"

He must be out of hearing distance again, but which direction had he gone this time? The regular *chop-chop* of the ax drew her attention, just as it would have drawn Davey's curious mind. Gathering her skirts in her hands, Naomi plunged into the forest at the north edge of the clearing. The path was easy enough to follow. Davey liked to stick to the narrow deer trails through the underbrush.

In the three years since her family had arrived in the Haw Patch in northern Indiana, Daed had made some progress in clearing the trees around their house and barnyard. The log home he had built that first summer was comfortable, although *Mamm* still missed the white frame house in Somerset County, Pennsylvania, that they had left behind when they made this move.

But most important, Daed's dream of being part of a new Amish settlement had been realized. More than thirty families had bought land in the northern Indiana forests, and additional settlers still appeared each spring and summer.

Like this unknown owner of the felling ax. The faint trail Naomi followed was leading directly toward the sound. She could only hope that Davey wasn't making a pest of himself with their new neighbor.

Naomi emerged from the forest into a small clearing. Fifty feet away, on the opposite side, was the wood chopper. His back was toward her, his legs braced for the shock of each blow of his ax as it took decisive chunks out of the trunk of a tall maple tree. Standing on a stump to the side was seven-year-old Davey, his hands covering his ears. The edges of his blond hair swung over his ears as he flinched with each ringing chop of the ax.

A wagon to Naomi's right was the man's home. A cooking fire ringed with stones had been built nearby, and a dozen tree stumps filled the clearing floor. The felled trees lay stacked in the center, stripped of their branches. A pile of brush rose at the edge of the space, and a stack of firewood lined the woods near the wagon, testifying to the new neighbor's skill with a saw as well as the felling ax. There was no sign of a family, though, just as Daed had said. He must have come ahead to build a cabin before bringing the rest of the family along.

Just then a loud crack boomed through the evening air, and the tree swayed, twisted, and tilted — right in the direction of the stump where Davey was standing. Naomi's feet started moving toward her son with no thought beyond snatching him out of the path of the tree that rushed downward with increasing speed. But the stranger was faster and grabbed the boy off the stump, out of the path of disaster.

Man and boy rolled to a halt at Naomi's

feet, Davey's gleeful laugh showing that he had never realized the danger he had been in. The panic drained from her body, leaving her sore and irritated.

"Davey." Naomi balled her fists on her hips for emphasis. "Didn't you hear me calling? You know you're not to wander off in the woods without telling someone."

Her voice startled both of them, and two pairs of eyes looked at her. Davey's blue gaze met hers briefly, then lowered as he blushed, embarrassed that he had been caught misbehaving again. But the man's brown eyes changed from a startled flash to a crinkling smile. He rose from the ground, setting Davey on his feet. He retrieved his hat from where it had rolled and brushed it off with a practiced sweep of his hand.

"You must be Davey's mamm." As he settled his hat on his head, he shifted his gaze from her cast eye to her good one, and she felt her cheeks heat. "I'm Cap Stoltzfus, just arrived from Holmes County."

Naomi grasped Davey's hand and pulled him close. "I'm Naomi. I'm thankful you snatched my boy from the path of the falling tree."

She glanced at Cap again. His eyes weren't only brown. Reddish-brown flecks in the golden irises gave them an intriguing depth.

She looked away. His beard touched his chest, indicating his married status, and her face burned to think she had been looking at him so closely.

"I met your husband yesterday. He came by to welcome me, since we're close neighbors."

Naomi's face heated again. "You met my father, Eli Schrock. He told us about you at supper last night."

"Then I look forward to meeting more of your family tomorrow. Your daed told me where the Sabbath meeting is to be held." He reached out to brush some leaves and twigs from the back of Davey's shirt.

"Will we meet your family soon?" Naomi asked.

Cap took a step back, his face as closed as if he had slammed a shutter tight. "My family is . . . is lost."

Lost. Gone. He was alone. "I'm sorry."

He didn't meet her eyes, and Naomi was suddenly aware of the shadowed twilight under the surrounding trees. She hugged her elbows as the cooling air reminded her it was still early spring.

"Davey and I must be getting home. No one knows where we are."

"*Ja,* for sure." He took another step back, half turning from her.

Davey pulled his hand out of Naomi's grasp and tugged at Cap's sleeve. "Will we see you at meeting?"

He squatted on the ground, his face level with the boy's. "I'll be there."

Davey grinned and threw his arms around the man, giving him one of his impetuous hugs. Before Cap could respond, Davey was off, running toward the deer trail and home.

The man hadn't moved, even when Naomi looked back as she followed Davey into the woods. He still knelt on the ground, his head bowed.

The damp seeped through the knees of Cap's trousers, bringing him back to the present. The clearing full of stumps. His wagon home. His new life . . . without reminders of Martha at every turn.

He retrieved the felling ax from where he had dropped it when he had heard the sickening, twisting crack of the maple tree and realized Davey was in its path. His knees still trembled at the thought of how close disaster lurked on every side of this life in the wilderness.

Cap found a rag in his toolbox and wiped the head of the ax until it was clean and dry. Winding his way between the stumps, he spanned the short distance across the clearing to his wagon, stowed the toolbox on the shelf in front of the rear wheels, and hung the ax on the hooks he had installed inside the wagon bed.

Silence rose all around him as he brought the coals of his fire back to life and rummaged through his food box for something to fix for his supper. Some smoked beef and schnitz, the sack of dried apple slices his sister had sent with him, were all he had left of his supplies. Come Monday he would have to take some precious time to go fishing or hunting, unless he chose to starve to death here in the forest.

He set a pot near the fire with some water and the schnitz in it, wishing he had some ham. The smoked beef was food, but after almost three weeks of nothing else, he was getting hungry for something different. He wasn't one to complain, though. He was thankful for what he had. Sticking a bit of the beef in his mouth, he savored the smoky, salty flavor as he waited for the water to boil.

That Davey. A grin spread over his face in spite of himself. The boy was bright and lively, a curious lad. When he had emerged from the woods an hour or so after Cap's noon meal, he had changed everything. Not only did he keep the conversation going, he was never still. Cap had finally told him he had to stay on the stump, out of the way, while he worked to fell the maple tree.

And his persistent questions! Davey never stopped with his why-this and why-that until Cap was out of answers.

Staring into the flames, Cap chewed the beef, softening the tough fibers. He knew why he had been drawn to Davey. The boy was the same age as his son would be now. The son he had never known.

He put another stick on the fire, turning his thoughts in another direction, and Davey's mother came to mind. Naomi. She looked too young to be the mother of a seven-year-old, but some women looked young for their age. She hadn't mentioned a husband, beyond correcting his mistaken assumption that Eli was Davey's father, and Davey hadn't mentioned a father in his nonstop talking. Could it be that she was also widowed?

He might find out tomorrow, if he could follow the directions Eli gave him. The meeting was at one of the Yoder farms, one mile south and a half mile east. He was looking forward to meeting more of his new neighbors. After enduring his sister Ruth's nagging him to get married for years, a new beginning in a settlement where no one knew his past was a welcome idea. Perhaps he could hope that no one would be trying to set him up with one of their daughters or offering farmland in exchange for marrying their sister. He had had enough of that back in Ohio.

He didn't intend to marry again just because he was lonely or because he settled for some likely girl he could never love. When Martha had made him promise to marry again, on that horrible day when her life was draining from her, he had intended to keep that promise. But as the years passed, he hadn't met anyone who appealed to him. Now, nearly seven years after Martha's death, the sting of losing her had faded, but not the memory of the joy of being her husband. He didn't intend to settle for anything less if he married again.

Sunday morning dawned with the promise of rain. The sky above Cap's clearing was overcast with a cover of light gray clouds, and a chill breeze was blowing in from the northwest. Even the birds were subdued, their usual morning cacophony reduced to a few chirps from the surrounding trees. To the west, where the forest sloped toward the marshy ground along the Little Elkhart River, wisps of morning mist floated between the tree trunks. Not quite fog, but not rain, either.

After grabbing a handful of the dried apples to eat as he walked, he started for the trail that ran north and south along the edge of his property line. The rain held off until he reached the crossroads where Eli had said to turn east. The road there was crowded with families heading to the Sabbath Meeting. As he hurried to reach the meeting before the drizzle turned into heavy rain, he caught up to a young couple and exchanged nods with the husband as they reached the yard of a two-story house. The board siding was new, covering the bare logs of the original cabin. Cap took his place in the line of men and followed them into the house for worship. He found a seat on a bench near the back of the rows.

The room filled quickly with families, couples, and single men. Just like at home in Ohio, the young people filled the front benches, directly behind the ministers. Cap glanced at the benches on the other side of the room where the women and children sat, and sure enough, there was Davey sitting with Naomi and an older woman. Davey stood next to his mother, craning his neck to search through the rows of men until he spotted Cap and waved. Naomi shushed the boy, sitting him on the bench beside her, but not before she glanced his way and he saw a telltale blush creep into her cheeks.

As the crowded room grew quiet, Cap waited. He slid his glance to the face of the man beside him, an older man with a graying beard halfway down his chest. Bushy eyebrows knit in concentration as the man studied his clasped hands. A stray fly circling and then landing on the man's thumb didn't distract him from his meditation. Finally, one of the ministers started the first hymn. The long, low note gained strength and volume as other members of the congregation joined in. Copies of the *Ausbund* had been scattered among the congregation so that everyone was able to follow the words.

The familiar sense of unease tugged at Cap. He knew the hymn they were singing, understood the words of praise to the Lord, and he knew what to expect next as another one of the ministers called them to prayer. A kneeling prayer, long enough to make his knees ache in agony, followed by more singing, and then sermons until noon. A simple meal, fellowship with the community, and the long walk home to his empty clearing.

He let his gaze wander around the crowded room, finally stopping when he saw Naomi's face. Davey's mother held a copy of the *Ausbund,* sharing it with the women sitting near her. Her face was peaceful as she sang, as if she really was singing to God. As if God cared enough to listen.

Cap glanced up at the ceiling of painted boards and mentally shook off the thought. The Lord was in his place, and Cap was in his. That was the way it should be.

Naomi had been painfully aware of her new neighbor sitting to her left and slightly behind her all through the morning. She hadn't planned to look for him until the noon meal after the service, but when Davey had erupted with delight and she had looked to see what he wanted to show her, she had met his smiling gaze in spite of herself. For the rest of the morning, no matter how hard she tried to concentrate on the worship, all she saw were his golden brown eyes.

But now, with the service ended, she had tasks to do that would keep her mind off Cap Stoltzfus. While Davey ran off to play with the other children, Naomi threw herself into the final preparations for the noon meal. Annalise Yoder had set a huge kettle of bean soup to cook all night long, and the savory aroma had filled the house all through the morning worship. Naomi ladled the steaming stew into bowls and handed them to others, who set them on the long tables for the first sitting.

The ministers and older men ate first, and as soon as they were done, the bowls were washed and filled again. Naomi ladled soup until the kettle was nearly empty, and then it was finally her turn to sit at the table with the other young, unmarried women. Susan Gingerich took a seat on the bench beside her.

"Have you met the new man from Ohio?" Susan broke pieces of cornbread into her soup. "Isn't he the best-looking man you've ever seen? And so tall!"

Naomi shifted slightly. "I met him yesterday. His farm joins ours on the north side."

Susan's brow lifted. "Is that right? He came by to visit with your daed?"

"I went to his clearing to fetch Davey."

Susan's brow lifted even higher. The Gingerich family had come to Indiana from Wayne County, Ohio, at the end of the winter, and Naomi hadn't been able to get to know Susan very well yet. Her family had settled in the western part of the community, near Rock Creek, in Elkhart County. Naomi felt her cheeks heat as Susan prepared to ask the question that new folks always posed whenever Davey was mentioned.

"I've been wanting to ask you." Susan's voice dropped to a whisper. "What happened to Davey's father?"

Naomi covered her irritation with a spoonful of soup. As she ate that spoonful, and the next, she wondered what would happen if she told Susan something that would send gossiping tongues wagging. But she couldn't lie. Davey's story wasn't anything she was ashamed of.

"Davey's parents were killed in a storm when he was little. Our family took him in, and I became his mother."

As she blew on her next spoonful of the thick bean soup, she glanced at Susan's face. A frown passed quickly before the other girl recovered.

"That's a terrible thing for him. It must be hard for you, though, to have to care for such an active boy. Were you and his real mother close friends?"

Naomi ignored the slight. As far as she was concerned, her adoption of Davey made her his real mother, even if she hadn't given birth to him. "They were strangers to us. We found Davey hiding in his family's cabin after it had been destroyed by a fierce storm." Naomi's stomach wrenched as it always did when the memories of that day surfaced. How they had found Davey's parents and baby sister in the wrecked cabin, and Davey hiding in the fireplace. From the moment she had taken him into her arms and her heart, Davey had been her son. It was a feeling she had never been able to explain.

"How long have you and your family lived in Indiana?" Susan smiled at her, friendly now that Davey's background had passed inspection.

"We moved from Somerset County three years ago."

"Somerset County? In Pennsylvania? Most of the folks who live in our part of the district are from Ohio."

Naomi took a piece of cornbread from the plate that was being passed down the table. "And most of this part of the district was settled by families from Pennsylvania. Folks like to settle near their friends and family."

"I suppose so." Susan looked toward the barnyard where the men had gathered to talk. "I wonder why Cap Stoltzfus chose to buy land in this part of the district. After all, he's from Ohio too."

"Did you know him when you lived there?"

Susan shook her head. "He must be from Holmes County. There are some pretty tradition-minded folks down by Walnut Creek, and we never had much to do with them."

When Susan turned to say something to the woman sitting on the other side of her, Naomi stood, taking her empty soup bowl and Susan's to be washed. She didn't want to hear about the distance between the two parts of the Indiana church district. The folks in Holmes and Wayne Counties in Ohio were in different districts, but they were still Amish. Susan wasn't the first person she had heard who talked as if there was some kind of wall between the two Ohio counties. If they weren't careful, the same kind of division could happen here.

After the dishes were clean, Naomi found her sister, Mattie Yoder, and their friend, Hannah Bender. Hannah scooted over on their bench so Naomi could sit between them and threaded her arm through hers.

"We don't get to see each other as much as we did in the winter, since we've been so busy planting the gardens and all." Hannah squeezed Naomi's arm. "What have you been doing lately?"

"The same things you have been, for sure. Getting the garden ready, cleaning out the potato hole —"

"Now you sound like Jenny Smith." Mattie laughed as she said it. Jenny lived on the farm south of Mattie and Jacob. Her father had been one of the first pioneers in the area fifteen years before and was one of their few non-Amish neighbors. "She always calls their root cellar a potato hole."

Naomi laughed with her. "Jenny's way of talking is so funny, I find myself using her phrases instead of our own. Besides, when the only vegetables in the root cellar are potatoes, we might as well call it a potato hole."

Hannah turned to Mattie. "Did Jacob give you the carrot seeds I sent over? They will be a fine addition to our gardens this spring."

As Mattie and Hannah continued discussing their gardens, Naomi's attention was drawn to her mamm, sitting on a bench across the room with Annalise Yoder, Hannah's mother. Annalise was holding her granddaughter, Hannah's new baby, born just two months earlier. The baby lay in her grandmother's arms with her face turned slightly, fast asleep. Mamm held her four-month-old granddaughter, Isaac and Emma's Dorcas. The two grandmothers chatted quietly, content to let the babies sleep. Annalise kept one eye on the group of children playing in the yard, where her twelve-year-old daughter, Margli, and some of the other girls were supervising the little children. Annalise's three-year-old twins, Gideon and Rachael, were among them.

If Mattie felt left out when the young mothers of the community discussed diapers and feedings, she never showed it. She and Jacob had been married for more than two years now and hadn't been blessed with any little ones yet. Naomi felt the pain of her own empty arms as she grew older and no man considered her a good companion for marriage, or even friendship. Even with Davey to care for, she still couldn't completely resign herself to never giving him a father, or brothers and sisters, even though she knew it would probably never happen. If she felt this way, how must Mattie feel as the months and years passed by?

2

By Wednesday, Cap had felled another half-dozen trees. Trimmed and cut to a uniform length, the logs lay in the center of the clearing, waiting to be built into a cabin. But before starting on the walls, he needed to put the footings in place. He pounded a stick into the soft ground to mark the first corner and started pacing off the front wall.

"How is the cabin coming?"

He looked toward the road. Christian Yoder had hailed him, and with him was a man who Cap didn't remember seeing at the Sabbath meeting. Pulling off his work gloves, he headed toward the road to greet his visitors.

"Good day, Brother Christian. What brings you in my direction?"

"This is Shem Fischer, newly moved to our area. He wanted to meet the folks in our corner of the settlement."

Shem Fischer? Cap felt the blood drain

from his face as he looked at the other man. It had been nearly twenty years since he had last seen Shem, but yes, this man could be the same one.

Shem didn't seem to recognize him as Christian introduced them. He had a pleasant smile on his face as he acknowledged Cap with a nod. "This is your clearing?" Shem's close-set blue eyes darted from the logs to the stumps, and then to the wagon. "You live here alone?"

Cap's gut twisted. Shem must recognize him, or at least his name. Cap had been Shem's favorite target when they were boys in Ohio. He could still hear the bully's voice, singsonging his name, tattling to the teacher for the mischief Shem himself had caused. But the other man ignored him, as if he had no reason to think they had once been boyhood enemies. As if this wasn't the same Shem Fischer at all.

"Ja," Cap said, determined to play the same game. "I'm alone here."

"And yet you're building a house, for just one man."

The condescending tone, the eyes flicking, meeting his for just an instant, the shadow of that familiar grin passing over his face before it disappeared. This was the same boy, now grown into a man.

"There is nothing wrong with building a cabin for myself."

Christian looked from Shem to Cap, his brows knitted. "Shem has just moved to our settlement from Canada."

Shem smiled at Christian. "I heard this new community is growing and there was a need for more ministers."

"You're not a preacher." Cap meant for his words to be a question and flinched at the accusation he heard in his own statement. But the Shem he knew had been the farthest thing an Amish boy could be from a minister of the church.

Shem's smile grew wider. "I am a minister, Cap." He stressed the name and Cap heard echoes of the old schoolyard in Holmes County. "I was ordained nearly three years ago."

Cap met Shem's eyes and held them. A minute passed. Two.

Shem gave up the challenge and dropped his gaze. "Brother Christian, there are other families in this area?"

"The Schrocks are next."

Shem started down the road, but Christian held back. "Is there something between you and Preacher Shem?"

Cap found his head shaking in the negative. "I don't think so. We knew each other as boys, but that was a long time ago."

Christian looked past him to the pile of logs in the center of the clearing. "It looks like you're ready to start raising the walls. Jacob and I will be over to help you first thing tomorrow morning. Josef also. I'll pass the word along to the Schrocks."

Cap's tense muscles relaxed. "I appreciate the help. Everything will be ready."

"Ja, for sure." Christian patted his shoulder and then followed Shem down the road.

Cap watched them go. Shem Fischer a minister? He shook his head. There was no telling how that had happened. People changed. But something in the set of Shem's shoulders and the look in his eyes said Shem's change hadn't been for the better.

Resuming his work, Cap walked back to the stake and started pacing off the wall again. He counted twenty steps, then drove a second stake into the ground. He stepped off the remaining walls, ending up at his original mark. After stringing a line from stake to stake to mark the walls, he measured the corners with his framing square.

Stepping back from the outline he had made of his cabin, the corners looked true, but when he measured, the rectangle was off-kilter. Cap sighed and wiped his sleeve across his forehead. Daed had always told him not to trust his eye but the tools, and he had been right. To his own judgment, the cabin outline was perfect.

Cap looked down the road. Christian and Shem had disappeared around the bend. Could he trust his own judgment where Shem was concerned? Probably not. His view could be just as skewed as the cabin walls he had outlined.

"Cap!"

Davey's call came from the deer path through the woods on the other side of the clearing. Shem Fischer left his thoughts as he turned to greet the boy's headlong rush toward him.

"Good morning." Beyond the boy, a quiet figure made her way through the trees, and Cap felt the corners of his mouth twitch toward a smile.

"We brought you some dinner." Davey jumped over one stump, then perched on another one. "*Memmi* made a basket for you, since she said you would be working so hard that you wouldn't take time for a decent meal."

Cap looked past the boy, meeting Naomi's flustered gaze as she wound her way through the tree stumps toward them. She dropped her eyes, but not before her face turned pink in a pretty blush.

"Hush, Davey. I only said that if we shared our dinner, he wouldn't have to take time from his work to cook."

"Whatever the reason, I appreciate it." Cap reached for the basket Naomi carried. The scent of fresh bread wafted from under the cloth cover.

"You've made a lot of progress since I was here on Saturday."

"Do you think so? I feel like I'm working too slowly. I need to get a garden planted soon, and the wheat." Oats, too. And the root crops. The familiar knot of worry twisted in his chest. Work loomed over him everywhere he turned.

Naomi waved her hand toward the western edge of the clearing where Davey played the game of jumping from stump to stump. "For sure. The last time I was here, you were cutting that tree. Now you have gone at least ten feet farther west."

She was right. From her perspective, he could see the larger slice he had taken out of the forest wall. "I finally have enough good logs to start building the cabin."

Naomi stepped into the string rectangle. "You'll need help."

"Christian Yoder was just here, and he said he and Jacob would be here tomorrow morning."

Her smile lit the clearing as if the sun had come out from behind the clouds. "I'm sure my daed will come too, and Henry. They'll pass the word, and you'll have more help than you can handle. I'll tell Mamm, and we'll get the noon meal organized. Your house will be built by tomorrow night."

He studied her profile as she paced the length of his rectangle, measuring it. She looked so young. She and Davey's father must have married when she was barely old enough. A prick to his conscience reminded him to avoid gossip, but he couldn't help a rise of irritation. Had the father been someone who had wronged Naomi? But her family and the community seemed to accept both Naomi and Davey without reservation. Whatever the mystery was, the church had either forgiven the sin or overlooked it.

Then she glanced his way again, the smile still gracing her face. Her cast eye flickered toward him, and then away, but it was only a slight distraction to her beauty. Someday he would know her well enough to ask about Davey's father. Until then he would enjoy the promise of friendship that her smile held.

■ ■ ■ ■

The first of the men arrived just before sunrise, while the sky still held on to the pearly gray of early morning. Cap stepped around the piles of logs to greet them.

"You've started already," Christian said. He set his toolbox on the ground and shook Cap's hand.

"I only pulled out the biggest logs to use as sills. There is still the whole cabin to build."

Josef Bender and Jacob Yoder set their toolboxes on the ground near Christian's and walked over to the outline Cap had made in the center of the clearing.

"You've planned a good-sized place," Jacob said. "Not too large, but with plenty of room."

"Your family will be joining you?" Josef asked.

His question brought the familiar twinge. "I'm a widower." Cap turned away from the three men, toward the space where his cabin would soon stand. They were right. His cabin would be large enough for a family.

"I'm sorry," Josef said, laying a hand on Cap's shoulder. "I shouldn't have said anything."

"It's all right. I've been alone enough years that I should be used to it." But he wasn't. Nothing he had tried filled the empty space in his life. Cap shrugged and put a smile on his face. "It's light enough to work. Should we get started?"

"Eli and Henry Schrock are coming." Christian indicated the men coming through the woods. The deer trail between the two farms had already widened to an easy path after only a few days of Davey's daily use.

Eli and Henry carried a large coffeepot between them and set it near Cap's breakfast fire.

"Lydia sent coffee." Eli pulled a cup out of his toolbox and poured himself a cup. "She thought we'd need something to keep us going between now and dinner." He glanced at Cap with a grin. "We can look forward to that dinner too. The meat was roasting before we left the house this morning."

While the men drank their coffee, they planned the morning's work. By the time the sun was climbing to its zenith, the walls were seven logs high. They had just raised the last log when Shem Fisher showed up.

"I heard you fellows were working on Cap's cabin today." He approached the half-built cabin. "I think I would have stopped at six logs." He eyed the top of Cap's hat, just even with the seventh log.

Cap tried to ignore the seething in his gut.

"It's too bad you weren't here to give your opinion earlier," Josef said. He kept his expression solemn, but gave Cap a slow wink. "We could have used your help."

Jacob hid a grin as he joined his brother-in-law. "I was thinking that we should go eight logs high. After all, we don't want Cap to be hitting his head on the doorframe every time he enters the house."

All of the men looked at Cap's six-and-a-half-foot height, and chuckles broke out.

Just then Davey came running around the corner of the house, stopping short when he saw the men.

"Memmi is bringing dinner." He was panting from his run through the woods. "*Grossmutti* says they need help carrying the pot."

Cap happened to glance at Shem's face as Davey ran off down the trail again, followed by Jacob and Josef.

Shem rubbed his chin, watching the boy. "His mother isn't married, is she?"

Eli glanced at Christian before he answered. "*Ne,* my Naomi isn't married."

"Has she ever been married?"

Eli's face reddened as dark as Cap was

sure his own was. The Shem Fisher he knew was a troublemaker, and he sounded like he was fishing for something. Preacher or not, Cap didn't trust the man.

"Ne," Eli answered. "She has never been married."

Shem's eyebrows raised.

"She adopted the boy three years ago, after his parents died."

Christian and Eli went to the water barrel to wash before dinner, but Shem looked toward the trail where Davey had disappeared, tapping his pursed lips with a forefinger.

Cap stepped closer to him, keeping his voice low. "You don't believe Eli?"

Shem's eyes swiveled toward Cap. "Does it matter what I believe? What matters is that the church must be pure. If what Brother Eli says is true, then that is well and good. But if the family is covering up some unrepentant sin, then the church must step in."

He left Cap standing alone as Jacob and Josef came back, carrying a pot of soup and a platter with bread and ham on it. Lydia and Naomi followed them, each of them carrying two pies.

As soon as she entered the clearing, Naomi looked past the cabin and found

Cap. She gave him a smile that started a soft warmth spreading through his middle. Her smile was welcoming, friendly, and just for him. It had been a long time since a young woman had looked at him without the calculated look of a girl hoping to snag a husband. Cap felt his own smile answering before he thought to restrain it. But there was no reason to hold it in.

Davey trailed behind his mother, a loaf of bread in his arms. As soon as he set it down on the table where Naomi indicated, he ran to Cap.

"Your house is almost done. Can I live in it with you?"

The unexpected question clenched at Cap's heart. He dropped down on one knee to be level with the boy's face. "Don't you think your mamm wants you to stay with her?"

Davey's face screwed into a pouting frown. "She never lets me do what I want."

Cap almost succeeded in repressing a smile. "What is it you want to do?"

"Hunt and trap and fish. Canoe down the river like the Indians. Trade our furs at Fort Wayne like Jed Smith does, and wear buck-skin."

Straightening his smile, Cap looked into the boy's blue eyes. He remembered having dreams like Davey's when he was young.

"That sounds like an interesting way to live."

"Ja, for sure." Davey nodded. "No one to tell us what to do. That's what Jed says."

"But there's one problem."

Davey's eyes narrowed. "What?"

"Who would cook our dinners?"

"You would. You cook yours, don't you?"

Cap shook his head. "I'm not a very good cook. Your mamm, though . . ." He glanced at the tall, slim figure slicing bread at the makeshift table. "Your mamm and grossmutti cook fine meals. That isn't something to turn your back on, even for a life in the woods, like Jed."

Davey scuffed at the ground with one foot. "Ja. Even Jed has Jenny to cook for him."

Cap grinned at that. He hadn't met this Jed yet, but he sounded like an interesting character. "A man can get awfully hungry, out hunting and trapping all day long."

"I guess." Davey stopped scuffing.

Cap lifted the boy's chin until Davey looked at him. "That doesn't mean we can't go hunting together sometime, if your mamm says we can."

The delighted grin was back as quickly as it had disappeared. "Really? Can we?"

"I'll ask your mamm." Cap snagged Davey's arm as he turned to run toward Naomi. "Hold on, there. Not so fast." Davey stopped. "I'll ask your mamm when the time is right. She's busy right now."

Davey nodded, watching Naomi work. "Ja, you're right." He sighed.

"This isn't the time of year for good hunting, anyway. The autumn is better, when the nights are cool. We'll plan on it then, and that will give your mamm time to get used to the idea."

The boy launched toward Cap and flung his arms around his neck. Cap grabbed the small body in a hug so fierce it surprised him.

"*Denki,* Cap."

Cap's eyes pricked as Davey clung to him. This was what he had lost when Martha died. A boy's trusting love.

Shem Fisher took a tin cup from the table and poured himself some coffee from the pot at the edge of the campfire. He sipped at the hot, bitter liquid, watching Cap and the boy over the rim of the cup. Cap Stoltzfus. That was one name from his past that he never thought he'd hear again. Little Casper Stoltzfus. The snotty-nosed kid who always tattled on him in school. Two years younger, but somehow a grade ahead.

Shem took a swallow of the coffee, forgetting how hot it was. He spat it out and whooshed air in through his mouth, trying to cool his burned tongue.

Cap looked different, that was for sure. Instead of the skinny twelve-year-old who avoided him whenever he could, Cap was tall and self-assured. Taller than most men, slim and well-built. His dark hair and eyes were still the same, though. And that sideways look he had given Shem when Christian introduced them yesterday told him that Cap remembered too, even though so many years had gone by. Back then, Cap had always outshone Shem, whether it was the school spelling bee or foot races during recess. The canker of jealousy was still sore.

Shem took another sip of coffee, cautious now. The bitter liquid burned anyway.

Shem straightened and threw the rest of the coffee into the underbrush at the edge of the clearing. Enough observing. It was time to plan his next move.

The folks here had accepted his word that he was a minister, and if they thought to check up on him, Ontario was a long way from Indiana. When he was elected at last fall's council meeting, that should have been the end of it. But the church wouldn't listen to him, and the other ministers had asked him to leave.

Shem rubbed the cup along the edge of his leg, wiping the stray drops of coffee off the rim. He didn't mind leaving, especially when Priscilla had chosen to stay with her folks instead of following him to Indiana. She claimed she was too fragile to travel, and her parents supported her decision to stay. But riding away from his wife, he had seen the satisfied look on her pretty face and it gnawed at him. She had looked as pleased to be rid of him as he had been to leave her behind.

He shook his head, clearing that thought from his mind. He was a minister, and there would be no doubts or discussion. Once these people heard him preach, they wouldn't even think to question his right to lead them. And once he was established, he would send for Priscilla. By then she would be proud of the progress he had made even without her prodding him, and wouldn't make his life so miserable.

Another wagon drove into the clearing, and Shem watched Cap step forward to greet the newcomers, along with Christian Yoder.

"Good morning," called Christian. "Did the word about the house raising spread all the way to Clinton Township?"

So Christian hadn't sent the message about the house raising to the folks in the western part of the district. Shem filed the information away.

"Ja, for sure." The tall man lowered himself from the wagon while an assortment of half-grown boys jumped out of the back. A petite girl, blonde and strikingly pretty, followed more slowly. "My boy Peter was over this way yesterday and heard about the plan. We came as soon as chores were done this morning."

Christian saw Shem watching the conversation and motioned for him to join them. "This is Shem Fischer, just arrived from Ontario a couple days ago." He nodded toward the newcomer. "This is Tall Peter Gingerich."

Shem lifted his gaze to the top of Tall Peter's hat, a good foot above his own. "I can see where you got your name."

Tall Peter laughed. "Ja, for sure. I've had it since I was a boy and grew taller than my daed. He was Peter too. So folks called me Tall Peter, and I haven't been anything else since."

The girl walked by with her mother. "This is my wife, Mary, and my daughter, Susan."

Mary stopped next to her husband. Shem could see where her daughter's beauty came from. "It's good to meet a newcomer to the area. Will you be settling here, then?"

Christian spoke before Shem could answer. "We hope he will. Shem is a minister of the church in Ontario, and he'll be a blessed addition to our church here."

A well of satisfied pride rose in Shem's chest, but he kept his response down to a slight upward turn of his lips. "I only hope to bring the Word of God to the people of his church, wherever he may use me."

Mary smiled, pleased with his answer. "You will have to visit both ends of the district, then. Clinton Township has much to offer a man looking to settle."

She sniffed slightly, as if to say that Clinton Township was the only proper place to live in the Indiana district.

Shem smiled at her words and let his gaze drift to Susan, standing to her mother's right as she listened to the conversation. Her blue eyes captured his gaze and returned it with her own appraising stare before her mother tugged at her sleeve.

"Come, Susan. We must help the ladies serve dinner."

Susan walked away with an unconscious sway. Shem rubbed at his beard, shifting his gaze before one of the other men noticed.

Perhaps that sway hadn't been unconscious at all.

He joined the other men at their dinner. They ate quickly and went back to the work of shaping the attic portion of the house with progressively shorter logs that rose to a peak. Shem took his time eating. If they needed his help, they would ask.

The women took their seats at the makeshift table, ready to have their dinner while they watched the men work. Susan Gingerich sat across the table from him and passed the plate of cornbread.

"Do you want another piece of bread, Preacher Shem?" She kept her voice quiet, but those blue eyes were fixed on him with a bold stare.

"Ja, for sure." Shem chose the largest piece on the plate.

"Will your family be joining you soon?"

Shem broke off a corner of the bread and chewed it as he watched her face. "My wife wants to stay with her parents in Ontario as long as possible. She won't be joining me until later. Perhaps not until next year."

"That's a long time to be apart." Susan's words were sympathetic, but Shem received the message her smile gave him.

"Ja, well, I'm certain I will make new friends here, and the time will pass quickly."

He finished his bread and stood, brushing the crumbs off his lap. As pleasant as it would be to sit and visit with Susan, he needed to show his support for the house raising. He needed to become part of this community. He joined Christian Yoder, busy at the simple task of whittling pegs.

"How many more of these do we need?" Shem asked, taking a seat on a stump and pulling his knife from its sheath.

"At least a dozen. The men will be using these to fasten the roof at the eaves, so they need to be longer than the others."

Christian handed him a piece of oak branch, the bark already removed. Shem started cutting a circle around the stick, about the length of the pegs Christian had already made.

"How large is this settlement, Brother Christian?"

"We have about thirty families. It's hard to keep track with new people arriving nearly every month."

"Tall Peter and his family are from a different area?"

Christian threw another finished peg onto the pile. "Folks have settled here in Eden and Newbury Townships in LaGrange County, and also in Clinton Township, over in Elkhart County. The river and its marshes make a natural barrier between the ends of the settlement, so we're scattered between the two counties."

He worked at narrowing one end of the next peg into a point while Shem watched. Christian's pegs were appearing out of the stick like clockwork, while he was still working to get his first peg cut off the stick.

"All of the families I've met in this area over the last couple days seem to be related to each other."

"Ja, for sure." Christian blew a stray shaving off the end of his finished peg. "Several of us traveled here together from Pennsylvania a few years ago, and we settled close to each other, for the most part. Some of our children have married each other, and others coming from Pennsylvania later on settled near us, as well."

"And Clinton Township?"

"Many of the families there moved together from Wayne County, in Ohio." Christian shrugged. "Folks like to settle near their family and friends."

Shem concentrated on his whittling. The Amish in Wayne County were known for their change-minded bent, while the folks from Pennsylvania tended to be more conservative. Churches tended to have difficulties when there were things to disagree on.

He glanced at the men working on the roof of the new house. And difficulties meant that there could be an opportunity for someone like him. Someone to take control of the situation.

By the time the dinner dishes were washed, the men had started laying the shingles for the roof.

Naomi shaded her eyes with one hand as she watched Cap hammering shingles into the roof supports with the precious iron nails he had brought from Ohio. He joked with the other men on his side of the roof. Jacob Yoder and her brother Henry worked on either side of him, telling tall tales that had all three of them laughing so hard that Henry nearly slipped off the roof.

"Watch it there," Cap said, catching Henry's arm.

Henry grinned as he regained his balance, then waved to Naomi when he saw her watching. "I'm all right."

Naomi waved back and caught Cap watching her. The smile he sent her way before he went back to his work started a warm glow inside.

It was kind of him to notice her. She twisted her *kapp* string between her fingers. Someone as handsome as he was could have his pick of any girl. He probably had someone in mind right now, back in Ohio, and was getting his farm ready before going back to marry her. Suddenly aware that she was staring at him, Naomi shook herself and concentrated on the conversation between Mamm and Annalise Yoder.

"Did the apple saplings survive the winter?" Annalise asked.

"Ja," Mamm said. "Well, most of them. There are a few that haven't put out leaves yet, but the branches are still green. Eli says if they survive the summer, they'll leaf out next year."

"I'm looking forward to an orchard again." Annalise sighed and turned the knitting in her hand. She was making a small sweater for Gideon out of light brown yarn. "When we left Pennsylvania, I didn't think it would be so long before we would have apple trees again. I'm glad Christian and Eli decided to start the seeds last year."

"When those apples come, what will you make first? Pie? Apple crumble?"

"*Ach,* Lydia." Annalise frowned and looked at Mamm over her knitting. "You know better than to count your chickens before they're hatched. We have a couple more years to wait before we'll get any apples off of those trees."

Mamm chuckled. "You are right. Eli says I'm always jumping ahead of my plans."

Annalise glanced at Naomi. "What about your plans to buy some of Jacob's sheep? Are you still thinking about that? The lambs will be coming in another month or so."

"I thought the sheep might be a good way for me to help the family." Naomi quelled the familiar turn of the stomach she always felt when she thought of raising sheep on her own. "I want to start with a small flock, though. I'm only buying three of the lambs, and Jacob said I could keep them with his flock for a share of the wool."

Annalise nodded her approval. "That's a good idea. And do you plan to sell the wool?"

"Daed said he would build a loom for me, so I can weave fabric, like you do. Then I'll be able to make clothes, and sell whatever material is extra."

Annalise's knitting needles stilled as she smiled at Naomi. "That's why you wanted me to teach you how to weave last winter."

"I wanted to see if I liked it before Daed went to the expense of building a loom for me."

"And you did, didn't you?" Annalise's hands started knitting again as she turned to Mamm. "I've never seen anyone enjoy

50

weaving like Naomi does, unless it would be my own Margli."

"It's so . . ." Naomi searched for the word.

"Peaceful," Annalise finished for her. "It's almost like watching the wind in the tree-tops, isn't it?"

Naomi nodded. "The rhythm is soothing, but at the same time it's work. Useful work, and then we have something both beautiful and useful at the end." She laced her fingers over her knee. "So I'm anxious to have my own flock of sheep, but a little scared at the same time. What if I can't care for them properly?"

"By the time your flock is ready to leave Jacob's, Davey will be old enough to care for them," Mamm said. "And Jacob will teach him."

"Speaking of Davey, I need to see what he's getting into." Naomi looked around the clearing, but her son wasn't in sight.

"Ja, and I must be getting home." Annalise stuffed her knitting into a cloth bag. "Margli is watching the twins, but their nap will be over soon."

Mamm stood as her friend did. "It's time to start fixing supper. I'll walk home with you."

As the older women left, Naomi looked around the clearing. When she didn't see

Davey around the men working on the roof, she went to the road and looked up and down the stump-filled way. Sometimes Davey liked to play a game of hopping from stump to stump, but he wasn't there. She walked on a bit to see around the new house, where some of the men had been splitting shingles, but he wasn't there either. Turning around, she walked toward Cap's wagon. Just as she reached the corner of the wagon, she saw him at the edge of the woods, playing with Stephen Gingerich, Susan's eight-year-old brother. She leaned against the wagon, watching the boys as they used sticks as pretend axes and chopped at a huge sycamore tree.

"It sounds suspicious, if you ask me." Susan's voice carried to Naomi from the other side of the wagon. Who would she be talking to?

"Where did she say he came from?" The answering voice sounded like the new minister, Shem Fischer.

"She said the boy's parents were dead, and she adopted him. But I've never heard of such a thing, have you? A young single woman adopting a child like that?"

"So you don't believe her?"

"I'm not one to accuse a person of lying . . ." Susan's tone of voice implied that

52

she was doing exactly that.

"This is a serious situation," Preacher Shem answered. "If she gave birth to the boy out of wedlock and covered up the sin, then she should be under the *bann.*"

"What about her parents?" Susan's voice dropped as she spoke, so that Naomi had to strain to hear her words. "Wouldn't they have known? Do you think they're covering her sin too?"

"They must be."

Naomi felt the blood drain from her face as she stepped away from the wagon. Why did she ever stay to listen as long as she did? Rumors were cruel things, meant to hurt and cast suspicion. But what could she do if the people of the church believed them?

She hurried to pick up the last of the dishes to carry home, but before she started down the path through the woods, she turned to look at the new house. Cap straddled the ridge pole, hammering the last of the shingles onto the roof. He caught her eye and waved, his smile just for her.

Naomi returned his wave. But if he heard the rumors, would he be so quick to smile like that?

3

"Memmi, take this."

Annalise Yoder wrung water out of her cleaning rag and laid it next to the basin on the kitchen table. Saturday chores could wait. Finding out what three-year-old Gideon was offering her this time was more important. He stood with his feet planted on the threshold, a wilted dandelion in his hand.

"Dear one, *liebchen,* you brought a flower for me?" She lowered her work-weary body onto the bench next to the door and reached for the flower.

Gideon opened his hand, letting the yellow-and-green mess tumble into her palm. "What is it, Memmi? What is it?"

"It's a dandelion. A spring flower."

His face, pink from playing in the late April sunshine, frowned. "Do we eat it?"

Annalise brushed a bit of dried mud from his cheek. "Ja, for sure. Ask William to help you find more. You and Rachael can fill a milk pail full of them and we'll have them with our supper tonight."

As Gideon stared at the dandelion, Annalise could almost see him trying to understand.

"But it's dirty." He looked up into her eyes. "Do we eat the dirt too?"

She smiled into his earnest face. Cobalt eyes surrounded by blond curls tugged at her heart. Both he and his twin, Rachael, looked so much like Liesbet. Poor, lost Liesbet.

"Ne, little one, we don't eat the dirt. I will wash them before I cook them."

"I go find William."

The little boy was out the door and gone before his sentence was finished, but Annalise kept her seat on the bench. Ach, what a pleasure to sit for a few minutes!

But no longer than a few minutes. She laid the wilted dandelion on the dry sink and rinsed her hands in the wash water. Dandelion greens would taste good with supper tonight. Christian had been tired and grumpy the last few months. Perhaps the tonic would help him feel better.

As she took the basin of water to the garden, she paused in the sunshine, turning her face toward the sky with her eyes closed.

A beautiful day. Another beautiful day. Annalise threw the water over the garden in a sparkling arc, then shook the last drops over the row of green lettuce shoots at her feet.

A sound from the barn drew her attention. The thump was followed by a bang, and then a shout from Christian. She hurried to the barn door.

"Are you all right? What has happened?"

Christian glared at her from the horse's stall, his face shadowed in the dusky interior. The animals were all in the pastures and Christian had been cleaning out the old bedding.

"I banged my elbow on the side of the stall." His voice was harsh. Impatient. So unlike her husband, yet she had grown used to his moods over the winter.

"You should have Peter help you with this chore."

He rubbed at his elbow. "Peter is busy grubbing shoots in the upper field."

"Then William."

"William is too young. He'd just make a mess."

Annalise looked at the dirt floor, covered with clumps of soiled straw in Christian's path from the stall to the manure pile outside. She didn't see how William helping his daed would increase the mess but didn't say anything. Christian's temper was short these days.

"If you're sure you're all right, I'll go back to the house."

"Ja, I'm sure." Christian's voice was a growl as he turned his back on her and gathered another forkful of straw from the stall.

Annalise headed across the grassy yard. William and the twins had found a milk pail and were hunting for dandelion leaves among the scattered tree stumps. Rachael waved to her, a clump of greens in her hand, then stooped to gather more leaves. For sure those leaves would need much sorting before she cooked them, but the children were busy and happy, and she had an hour or so to spend at her loom.

Christian had built an additional room onto the simple log house last year before he had sided the cabin with boards, and she had finally been able to set her loom up again. The room matched the one she had left behind in Lancaster County, with windows on three sides. Christian had brought the glass all the way from Fort Wayne to surprise her last spring, after trading furs from the foxes and mink he had trapped over the winter. Annalise smiled at the memory. She had scolded him for buying such a luxury, but with the windows she could still have sunlight all winter long, watch the leaves open on the trees as summer approached, and keep an eye on the children in the yard while she worked.

Sitting at the loom, she stretched to send the shuttle on its way between the threads, picking up where she had stopped yesterday. When she paused to shift the weaving to the next length of threads, she glanced out the window. The children had abandoned the milk pail and were playing tag between the stumps. Their laughing faces made her eyes prick, remembering another time and other children. God had been so good to restore their family after so much loss.

A roaring shout from Christian stopped the children in their play. All three of them froze, staring toward the barn as Annalise ran to the door. Christian stood on the threshold of the big barn.

"William," he shouted, his face red. "Aren't you supposed to be working? Get back to the chore your mamm gave you."

Annalise glanced at William. The six-year-old's head hung down, his shoulders quivering, but Christian wasn't done.

"Gideon, you help him. Stop running

about like a bunch of chickens."

"Christian —" Annalise held a hand out toward him. This was wrong, and nothing like the Christian she knew.

"Don't interrupt, Annalise." He shouted the words, then rubbed at his forehead with one hand. "I know what I'm doing."

Annalise walked toward him, making sure her path kept her between Christian and the children.

"Something is wrong," she said, her voice low as she drew close to her husband. "Do you feel all right?"

Christian shook his head, pushing his hat up and rubbing his forehead again. "I'm fine. My head hurts, but I'm fine."

He jerked away as she reached for his arm.

"Maybe you should come in and lie down until your headache goes away. I'll brew some dandelion tea for you."

He leaned against the doorframe, his hand over his eyes and his shoulders slumped. He stood without moving for a long minute. Two minutes. Then he sighed. "I don't know why I shouted at the children." He looked at her. "I'm sorry, Annalise. I was angry with you too."

"Come in and rest."

"Who will finish the work, then?" Christian stood upright again and reached for the manure fork. "I have to clean out the barn."

"Are you sure?"

He smiled and ran a finger down her cheek. "Ja, dear one. I'm sure."

Christian turned to go back to the stall, but Annalise lingered, watching him. He wasn't all right. This was the third time his anger had flared so suddenly in the last few weeks, anger that Christian had never shown before. He had no fever, and the spells left him as quickly as they came. Something was wrong, but she had never run across anything like this in her experience.

She started back to the house. William and Gideon were on their knees, silently picking dandelion greens and filling the bucket. Rachael sat on a stump, crying. Annalise took Rachael in her arms, patting her back.

"Your father isn't feeling well."

William scowled at her. "He yelled at us."

She nodded. "Ja, he did, and he's sorry."

Gideon watched as William sat back on his heels. "We weren't doing anything wrong. We were just playing."

"Was the pail filled?"

William's face turned red. "Ne, but almost."

" 'Almost' means your chore wasn't done.

When the chores are done, then you can play."

"What if Daed yells at us again, even if the chores are done?"

Annalise sighed as she sat on the stump. Gideon climbed onto her lap along with Rachael and she circled both of them in her arms. William was right. Christian's moods had become unpredictable.

"I don't know what to tell you, William." Annalise smiled at her son to reassure him. "When Daed feels better again, he'll be back to his own self. Until then, perhaps you should play on the other side of the house."

"I'll help Peter when I'm done here."

Annalise nodded. "That's a good idea. I'm sure Peter will appreciate your help." She squeezed Gideon and Rachael. "I think you two are ready for a nap."

Rachael was already half asleep, her thumb in her mouth. Gideon had been leaning against her but pushed himself up at the mention of a nap.

"I want to help Peter too," he said.

Annalise put Gideon down and stood, holding Rachael. She took Gideon's hand. "Not right now. I saw you yawning. Let's go inside."

As she took the twins into the house,

Annalise looked toward the barn once more. Something was wrong with Christian, and with that worry she could feel the pulsing darkness at the edge of her consciousness. She pushed it back. A spring tonic was what he needed. The dandelion greens would help him get back to normal.

Cap eyed the sun peering through the tree branches on the west side of the clearing. Saturday afternoon was nearly over, but he still had enough time to finish chinking the last cabin wall before darkness descended.

He stuck the wooden slat in the pail of mud and clay, lifting it carefully to the opening between the two logs next to his knees. He had wedged some small stones and pieces of wood in the narrow opening before plastering it over with the clay. Eli Schrock had shown him how to mix moss and ground limestone into the clay to help make it stronger. The result should be a waterproof barrier that would make the cabin cozy in the winter months.

As he spread the chinking, his mind wandered in the direction that it had often taken this week. Thoughts of Naomi and Davey came up as he worked on finishing the cabin, or as he cooked his meals, or while he was fishing or planting the seeds for his garden among the stumps that littered the clearing. He found himself wondering if Naomi liked peas fresh or in a winter soup. Or if Davey would want to go fishing with him.

More times than he wanted to admit, Cap had needed to pull himself back to his work instead of staring blankly at the deer trail through the woods that led to the Schrocks' farm.

There was no reason he should be thinking of Naomi so much, except for that intriguing tilt of her head when she was listening to a conversation among the women, or when she was deep in thought. And the expression on her face whenever Davey came into view.

He swallowed down the lump that had risen in his throat and turned back to chinking the logs again. That expression reminded him of Martha.

Cap pushed a wad of mud and straw into the gap where a knot kept the logs from fitting together.

Too much about Naomi reminded him of Martha. That coincidence was enough to tell him that he shouldn't be more than friends with his neighbor, no matter how much he loved spending time with her son. He would like to find a new wife, but not just a replacement for his first love. That wouldn't be fair to Naomi. She deserved a husband who could love her for who she was.

"Cap!" Davey's shout came ringing down the deer trail and the boy burst out of the leafy underbrush. "Cap, are you here?"

"What is it?"

Davey halted beside him, but his attention was captured by the bucket of sticky mud and straw. He pulled at the stick Cap had used to stir the mess.

"Can I?" He looked into Cap's eyes, his face full of hope. "Can I help you? I can stir the mud."

Cap grinned and pulled at the blond hair sticking out from under Davey's hat. How could he refuse such an offer?

"For sure. The mud is stirred enough, but you can slap some right here, and I'll chink it into the logs. That would be a fine help."

They worked together until they finished the length of the wall, Davey silent for once, except for his grunts when he lifted the paddle loaded with the heavy mess up to the spots Cap indicated.

"That's fun," Davey said. "Can we do another one?"

Cap looked toward the setting sun. "I'm done for today. It's nearly suppertime.

Won't your mamm be looking for you?"

"She knows I'm here." Davey's voice was confident. "She sent me to —" He looked toward Cap, his eyes round. "I forgot. I was supposed to ask you to come to dinner tomorrow. Grossmutti is making rye'n'corn bread, and there's a ham baking in the oven. Say you will."

The next day was an off Sunday, when the church wouldn't meet for services but the Sabbath was still observed. Cap would not work tomorrow, and the thought of spending his time in the company of his neighbors made his answer easy.

"Ja, for sure I will." He stooped down to look at Davey's face. "Say 'denki' to your mamm and grossmutti. I would be glad to come."

Davey's grin burst onto his face and he took off running toward the deer trail. "See you tomorrow," he yelled.

"Tomorrow," Cap repeated, but Davey was too far away to hear.

The warmth that Davey brought with him stayed with Cap while he cleaned up from the day's work and ate a light supper of cold ham and bread. The food was the last of the leftovers from Thursday's house raising, and he chewed each bite with thankfulness. So far, the decision to move to Indiana had been a good one. The Amish settlement was all he had hoped it would be, and the neighbors had welcomed him with open arms. He had been here for just over a week, and he already had a house built with the help of the community and his first crops planted in the fertile ground around the stumps in the clearing.

And then there was Naomi. He couldn't deny that the thought of seeing her the next day had put a smile on his face that wouldn't go away. Was it so bad that she reminded him of Martha? As he learned to know her better, that feeling would fade. She was a lovely woman, and dedicated to Davey.

That thought brought a ribbon of regret with it. He should trust Eli's story of the boy's adoption, so why did this suspicion still linger? The story must be true. After all, Davey didn't look very much like his mother. In fact, Cap couldn't see any resemblance.

He rubbed at his beard as he leaned back against the wagon wheel and stuck his long legs toward the fire that had dwindled to coals. Darkness had descended while he ate his supper, and he should make his way into the house. He had made a bed for himself in one corner so he could sleep under a roof at night, but he still had a lot of details to finish before the house felt like home. Meanwhile, resting under the stars on a pleasant evening was something he would miss after weeks living out of his wagon. He laced his fingers behind his head and looked up at the sky.

Naomi pushed her way into his thoughts again, along with that unanswered question. What would he do if he found out that Naomi's son had been conceived in sin? Would that make a difference in how he felt about her? The stars blurred together. He wouldn't know until he faced that possibility head-on. He had to ask Naomi about Davey soon. Tomorrow, even.

If he could find a time to talk to her when Davey wasn't around.

Naomi hurried through her chores on Sunday morning, saving the flock of chickens for last. She spread their feed on the ground in front of the chicken coop door, then opened the hatch and waited for the chickens to make their way out. The rooster was first, flapping his way to the roof to crow over his domain before joining the hens for his portion of the cracked corn. His wives followed him down the cleated plank, but they ignored his crowing, pushing at each other for their share of the corn.

Soon she would add this chore to Davey's growing list. He was old enough now to take full responsibility for the chickens.

Naomi fastened the little hatch open, then went into the coop through the door on the end. The shadowed, dusty henhouse always made her sneeze, but it took only a few minutes to gather the eggs. She went along the row of nest boxes, reaching in for the smooth eggs, still warm from the hens' bodies. When she reached the last box, the hen was still on her nest.

"Ach, Biddie. You need to go out with the others." Naomi reached in to push the chicken out, but Biddie pecked at her. Trying a different tactic, Naomi set the egg basket at her feet. "Biddie bird, Biddie bird." She kept her voice soft, crooning. The hen cocked its head to the side. Naomi kept crooning to the bird as she slid her hand under the hen's body and grasped the egg.

Biddie squawked and launched herself out of the nest box, landing square on the front of Naomi's clean apron, then flapped to the ground and out the door. Naomi laid the egg in the basket with the others and brushed at her apron, only to feel the wet, soiled straw the hen had smeared on her clothes. And Cap was coming today.

She fastened the door behind her and

made her way to the house.

Mattie met her at the kitchen door. She and Jacob had come to spend Sunday with the family. "What happened to you?"

Naomi handed her the basket. "Biddie didn't like it when I tried to take her egg. I think she's getting broody."

"Biddie is always broody. Come on, I'll help you change."

Naomi led the way to her room, an addition to the log cabin Daed and Henry had built for her. The two bedrooms on either end of the house were for herself and her parents, while Henry and Davey shared the loft. Naomi closed the door behind her sister and reached to untie her soiled apron.

"I'll have to wear my old one today." Naomi held up the apron, neatly patched on one side where she had torn it last fall.

"That's all right." Mattie took a seat on her bed. "You'll look fine. Besides, it's only the family today, isn't it?"

Naomi's throat felt as dry as if she was eating stale cornbread.

"Isn't it?" Mattie asked again.

"Cap is coming for dinner."

Mattie started laughing and then clapped a hand over her mouth.

"It isn't funny." Naomi's hands shook as she tried to tie the apron strings. "He will be here sometime this morning, and he'll see me wearing my old apron."

Mattie stood behind her, untangling the ties from her clumsy fingers. "He won't even notice the patched place. Your stitches are so fine that no one will see them." Mattie tied the bow with a tug and turned her around. "Is he that important, this Cap?"

Naomi felt her face redden. Since Mattie married Jacob three years ago, it was as if she was the big sister and Naomi the younger one. She would feel the sting of being left out, except for the sadness that dominated Mattie's expression when she thought no one was looking. The sadness brought on by month after month with no sign of a baby joining their little family.

"Ja, I think he is that important." Naomi grasped Mattie's shoulders. "But don't tell anyone."

Mattie grinned and sat on the bed again, patting the spot next to her. "I will keep your secret, but you have to tell me all about him."

Naomi sat next to her sister. "We really should join the rest of the family."

"They can wait for a little bit. You tell me about Cap, and then I have something to tell you." Mattie's smile held a secret, and her eyes glowed.

Naomi grasped her hand. "You're expecting a little one."

"How did you know? I haven't told anyone except for Jacob."

Naomi wrapped her arms around Mattie. "I could see it in your face."

"I can't tell you how excited we are, after waiting for so long."

"You're sure?"

Mattie nodded. "Mamm will figure it out soon, but we still don't want to tell anyone else. We'll wait until the little stranger makes his appearance."

"As it should be." She hugged Mattie again.

Her sister returned the hug, and then pulled herself out of Naomi's arms. "Now tell me about Cap."

"What is there to tell?"

Mattie grinned. "What do you like the best about him?"

Naomi's face heated again. "I guess . . ." She closed her eyes and thought. "His eyes are very kind."

"Ja, but what else?"

"He has a nice smile."

Mattie groaned and Naomi squeezed her eyes tighter. In her thoughts, Cap straddled the peak of his cabin, hammering the ridge pole in place, and glanced at her. The look in his eyes . . .

"He is happy when he sees me, and he likes Davey."

She opened her eyes to see Mattie staring at her. "How can you tell he's happy to see you?"

"The look on his face. He . . ." Naomi searched for words to describe what she had seen at the house raising on Thursday. "His face relaxes. As if when I'm there, he's happier."

Mattie nodded. "I think I know what you mean. When Jacob has been working out in the fields and comes home for dinner, he looks like he's been missing something all morning, and when he sees me, he knows that he's found it."

It was Naomi's turn to stare at her sister. She had watched Jacob's love for Mattie grow from the time they met again as adults after being childhood friends. Could Cap be the one whose love for her would grow like that?

They sat in silence for a few minutes, both staring at their hands that were intertwined between them. Naomi's thoughts went to the coming babe. Childbirth could be a dangerous thing, even though the joy at the end was great. She had watched her sisters-in-law bear several children between them, and there was always that danger, that traveling through the "valley of the shadow of death," as Mamm said. But they had traveled that dangerous road, and her nieces and nephews were joys for the family. Mattie would be all right. Mattie would have to be all right.

Suddenly Mattie squeezed her hand. "It's the beginning of a new adventure for both of us, isn't it?"

Naomi grinned back at her. "A wonderful adventure."

4

"Cap, your plate is empty." Eli Schrock rose from his seat on the porch and reached for the plate. "Let me get you some more."

"Ne, denki." Cap held one hand up to ward off any more food. "I am set."

Eli took his plate. "You're ready for cake, then. I'll get a piece for you."

The older man had gone into the house before Cap could object.

"You'll never get him to stop offering you food until it's gone." Jacob Yoder laughed as he nudged Cap with his knee. "And since you're the guest today, you get the best of everything."

Henry leaned toward the bench at the edge of the porch where Jacob and Cap were sitting. "You're just glad you aren't a guest anymore, Jacob. I remember when you and Mattie were first married. Mamm and Daed wouldn't let you go home after a visit without loading you up with food."

"And we appreciated every bit of it." Jacob pointed his fork at Henry. "You will, too, when you set up housekeeping on your own."

Henry laughed, reaching for the piece of cake his daed had brought him. "I know I'll miss Mamm's cooking."

Cap took a bite of the cake Eli handed him as the older man returned to his chair. He didn't join in the conversation between Henry and Jacob, but he could agree with both of them. Lydia's cooking satisfied an empty place deep inside. Taking another bite, he had the fleeting thought that Naomi's cooking was probably just as tasty.

Jacob gestured toward the road. "Is that Shem Fischer?"

A figure walked toward them on the road from the west. It was. What was he up to?

Eli turned toward the road. "Ja, for sure. The minister coming to visit us." He stepped off the porch and met Shem halfway across the road.

"Hmm."

Cap glanced at Jacob. A frown covered his normally smiling face. "What's wrong?"

"There's something about that man that rubs me the wrong way." He scratched at his beard and looked at Cap. "Sorry. I tend to say what I think a little too often."

"That's all right. I've always felt that way about him."

Jacob's eyebrows raised. "You knew him before he moved here?"

Cap nodded. "We were boys together in Ohio before his family moved to Ontario. I was surprised to hear he was a minister, but people can change as they get older."

Eli and Shem reached the porch. "Henry, go get a piece of cake for Preacher Shem." He turned to the newcomer. "I hope you'll join us for the afternoon."

Shem took the cake as Henry handed it to him. "I had planned to see as many of the church members today as possible."

"The Christian Yoders will be coming later, after the children's naps." Eli gestured toward the chair he had vacated and Shem sat down. "On a beautiful day like this, there isn't any reason not to enjoy pleasant conversation together."

"As long as it is God-honoring." Shem's voice echoed, as if he was repeating words he had often heard and often said.

Cap's stomach recoiled. The words were hollow, void of meaning coming from Shem's mouth. He mentally shook himself. He must give Shem a chance to show what kind of man he was now, in spite of the memories of the bully he had been as a boy.

The conversation drifted from the families in LaGrange County, to spring planting, to the weather, but each time someone brought up any part of their daily lives, Shem was quick to bring the subject back to the church.

"Where is the meeting next Sunday?" Shem finished his third piece of cake and brushed the crumbs off his knees.

"At the Gingerich farm, in Clinton Township."

Eli laced his fingers around one knee and leaned against the wall of the house, grimacing a bit on the hard bench. Cap glanced at Shem, comfortably lounging in the older man's chair.

"A long distance to walk, isn't it?"

"It is nearly six miles from here to the Gingerich place."

"Has anyone been tempted to drive on the Sabbath when the distance is so great?"

The tone in Shem's voice set Cap on edge. That was the old Shem, goading with his words. Searching for a weak point.

"Of course not," Eli said. "We don't take the *Ordnung* so lightly here in LaGrange County."

Shem leaned forward. "You mean they do elsewhere? In Clinton Township, perhaps?"

Eli let the question hang in the air as a

group of the older children walked by, led by two boys. Davey was among them, and waved at Cap before trotting after the others.

Shem frowned as he watched them, then turned to Cap. "Your house is just a short walk through the woods, isn't it?"

"My property joins Eli's in the middle of the section."

"That's very convenient." Shem gave him a quick grin. "I'd like to see the progress you've made since Thursday. Can we walk over there?"

Walking anywhere with Shem didn't sound like something he'd like to do, but he couldn't refuse the request. Not when he could make sure Eli regained his comfortable chair at the same time.

Shem walked beside him as they passed between the chicken coop and the barn.

"How long have the Schrocks lived here?" Shem gazed at the white-washed barn with the high hay loft.

"They came three years ago, with the Yoders and a few other families. At least, that's what I heard."

"Eli is doing pretty well for himself, ja?"

Cap shot a glance at him. Shem was leading this conversation somewhere.

"God has blessed him. And he has worked

hard." Cap hadn't spoken with Eli concerning what kind of labor it had taken to build such a barn and house when they had so recently come to this settlement, but the fruits of his labor were obvious.

"Such a large barn is bordering on pride, don't you think?"

Pride? Cap shook his head. "It shows his good stewardship in taking care of his animals and crops."

Shem gave him that half smile that was so familiar. Cap's stomach clenched.

He stopped and confronted the other man. "What do you want, Shem?"

Shem's smile didn't change. "Want? I want for nothing, Cap, except to preserve the purity of the church."

Cap couldn't hold back a short laugh. "You? I can't think of anyone less likely to take on that task."

The other man's eyes narrowed. "You will work against me, then."

"To preserve the church, never. But to help you with whatever scheme you're thinking of, I will work against you if I need to."

"Be careful, Cap." Shem's voice was flat, the edge of his words sharp. "You don't know who you are dealing with."

"Don't I?"

Shem's eyes shifted and Cap turned to see what had caught his attention. Naomi came out of the house with the other women. She and Mattie Yoder spread a blanket under a small tree, and the women settled themselves on it.

When Shem spoke again, his voice was soft, with almost a dream-like quality to it. "Don't you wonder how Naomi is the mother of a seven-year-old boy? She would have been quite young when he was born." He turned hooded eyes toward Cap. "Is the boy a result of sin on Naomi's part or someone else's?"

"Eli said Naomi adopted Davey."

"Ja." Shem stroked his beard, his gaze on Naomi. "Eli says that."

Cap's clenched stomach soured, but he didn't have an answer.

"Have you asked her to tell you of the boy's origin?" Shem smiled again. "You haven't, have you?" He leaned closer to Cap, smelling of some scent that Cap couldn't place. Spicy and smoky at the same time. "Are you afraid of what her answer may be?"

Shem turned and walked toward the road, stopping to greet the group of women as he walked by. Cap took a deep breath and let it out, willing the cramped muscles in his hands to relax. Shem had always known where to aim to hit his weakest spots. He turned his back on the Schrock farm and made his way down the deer trail toward home.

Shem Fischer had interrupted the conversation Naomi and Mattie had been enjoying with Mamm, Miriam, and Emma. Their brothers' wives had joined them with the babies while their other little ones played nearby. Mamm had been telling about the time when she was newly married and lived in the same house as her parents back in Chester County when Shem walked up to them.

As he leaned down and helped himself to one of the cookies Mamm had brought for her grandchildren, he smiled at Naomi.

"I thank you for your hospitality, but I must be going on. There are a couple more families I want to visit before the afternoon is over."

"Where are you staying, Preacher Shem?" Miriam asked. "Have you purchased land for yourself?"

"For now, I'm camped near the lake at the edge of the Planks' land. During my visits, I'm looking for a parcel of land to buy."

"And will your wife be joining you then?"

Naomi was startled to see a frown flash across Shem's face before he resumed his usual pleasant smile.

"I hope she will be able to soon." Shem flicked some dust from his black Sunday coat. "She has been ill and needed to stay with her parents while I traveled out here to find a place for us."

"I'm glad you were able to join us," Mamm said. "Come back anytime."

"I will." Shem laid a hand on Naomi's shoulder. "I hope you all have a good Sabbath rest this afternoon, keeping your words and thoughts pure and centered on our Lord, as the Good Book says."

"Ja, for sure, Preacher Shem." Mamm smiled at the young man as he left.

Naomi refused to watch him walk toward the road like the others did, and when she turned her back, she saw Cap slip into the woods, heading toward his house. Why would he leave so early in the afternoon? She hadn't had an opportunity to speak with him at all. She rubbed at the mended spot on her apron. Something was wrong.

While Mamm, Mattie, and the others were still watching Shem, she rose from the blanket and followed Cap. Before she started down the deer trail, she turned back to see Mattie watching her and waved. She wouldn't be gone long.

She found Cap stirring the ashes of his fire. He looked up as she approached.

"I didn't get to say hello when you were at the house . . ." Her words faded at the sight of his stormy face.

"I didn't stay very long."

"Why not? Did Daed say something to scare you off?" She kept her words light, making a bit of a joke to draw him out, but his frown told her that it wouldn't work.

"Not your daed."

Someone else, then. She watched him push a few red coals together and lay some wood shavings on top of them. Once they caught, he added some larger pieces of wood, then sat on a nearby stump.

He gestured toward a nearby log. "You might as well sit down." He added another bit of wood to the growing fire. "Davey didn't come with you?"

"Ne. I wanted to . . . well, talk to you."

"About what?"

"Just get to know you a little better."

She glanced at his face, still set in a frown. He didn't look very happy to see her this afternoon. She must have imagined that he held some affection for her. Her face heated as she remembered Andrew Bontrager and how she had wanted him to love her. Had believed that he could love her, and all the time he was falling in love with Johanna. She had been so foolish, but she would not repeat the mistake.

"Ja. Sure. We can get to know each other." He threw another stick on the fire. The smoke curled into the still air.

She stood. "I shouldn't have come here. You want to be alone."

She started toward the deer trail, but Cap rose and grasped her arm.

"Don't go. I do want to get to know you." He led her back to her seat. "Shem Fischer always puts me in this kind of mood." He smiled, but his face showed no humor.

"You knew him before he came here, didn't you?"

Cap sat back down on his stump, more relaxed. "Ja, I did." He looked at her with his dark eyes. "I've never known him to be a kind person."

She shuddered a little and his eyebrows raised. "I haven't found anything about him to like, either."

Cap gave a short laugh as he leaned forward to lay a small log on the fire. The log was pine, and the pungent aroma filled the air.

Naomi scooted a little closer to him on

her log. "Where did you meet Preacher Shem?"

His eyebrows went down again. "Long before he was called a preacher. We were boys together in Ohio. His family moved to Canada before I was fourteen. I thought I'd never see him again." He picked up a wood chip from the ground and threw it on the fire. "I hoped I'd never see him again." He ran his hand over his beard and sighed. "You must think I'm an unforgiving man, to hold a grudge against him for twenty years."

Naomi's fingers grew cold at this confession. "Twenty years is a long time."

"He said something about you, something I don't want to believe."

Naomi's back stiffened. "How could he know anything about me? We've never met before he came here."

Cap leveled his gaze at her. "He was wondering who Davey's father is."

The overheard conversation between Shem and Susan came back to her. "He has been listening to rumors."

"What rumors?"

She bit her lip. How could she answer him?

Cap leaned closer to her. "What rumors, Naomi?"

"That Davey is illegitimate. That I sinned and he is the result."

Cap sat in silence.

"The rumors aren't true." Her voice sounded weak to her own ears. He would never believe her.

"Tell me the truth, then. Where did Davey come from?"

"His parents were killed in a storm, and he was the only survivor. I adopted him —"

His grunt interrupted her story. "Your daed told me the story, but how could a single woman like you adopt a young child? Where were your parents? How would they let you do this?"

Her thoughts skittered back to that far-away day when she had taken Davey into her arms and her heart had claimed him. "He needed so much care. He had been injured in the storm and had seen his family killed. He needed me."

"Why didn't someone else adopt him? One of your brothers' families, or your parents?"

Naomi was at a loss. He didn't believe her. "Because when he clung to me, I couldn't let him go. From that moment he was my son."

Cap was silent, staring at the fire. Naomi's eyes stung as they filled with tears. Another thing she remembered from that time three years ago was telling Mattie that she didn't care if adopting Davey meant that no man would ever want her. That Davey needed her and that was enough.

Ja, it was enough. Until now.

She rose from her seat and stumbled toward home. Her footing grew more sure and her pace quickened as Cap made no move to stop her.

5

Monday morning brought a cold, drizzling rain that dampened Cap's spirits as well as his campfire.

Tired of trying to get the tinder to light, Cap sat back on his heels and looked at the half-finished fireplace on his new house. He could complete it today, even in the rain, with a stick and daub chimney, now that the body of the fireplace was done. But that shortcut didn't sit well with him. He'd rather take the time and finish the stone chimney the right way. He could cook over the campfire for as long as it took.

He turned back to the pile of tinder just in time to see the little flame gutter and go out in a stream of gray smoke. Crouching down, he blew gently on the smoking embers, trying to coax a flame from them, but the cold, damp air won. Even as he gave up, a larger raindrop fell directly on the last ember, extinguishing it completely.

Cap stared at the gray-and-black ashes as if wishing could make the fire roar to life. As if wishing could make Naomi's story about Davey ring true.

Why couldn't he believe her?

The rain fell harder and Cap stood, hunched under his hat, and made his way to the house. At least he would be dry there. Cold and hungry, but dry.

He would give almost anything for a hot cup of coffee.

He leaned against the doorframe and watched the rain. The Schrocks would welcome him this morning. Lydia would offer him a cup of coffee from the pot she always had on the back of the stove, and Eli would be happy to sit and talk for an hour or so. Naomi would . . . what?

Cap shrugged his shoulders against his wet shirt and grabbed the blanket off his bed to wrap up in. The back door faced the deer trail, and as he watched a rabbit hop slowly across the path, the rain eased.

Naomi might welcome him, if he dropped in for a cup of coffee. Perhaps she would even join in the conversation as if yesterday afternoon had never happened.

He should never have let Shem's words worm their way into his mind. When Shem was a boy, he had sent his words flying like embers in a high wind, starting fires wherever they landed, and Shem as a man was no different.

If he had to make a choice between trusting Shem's words or Naomi's, he had to choose Naomi. He might not know her well, but he knew Shem.

Before he could think himself out of the decision, he tossed the blanket back on the bed and started across the clearing to the trail. He trotted along it through the trees, dodging the large drips that gathered on the young leaves before plummeting to the ground. The forest was silent after the brief rain, the sky a gray fleece batting covering the earth. As he reached the Schrock farm, the steady stream of smoke from the kitchen chimney prodded him onward.

Davey spotted him from the covered porch next to the kitchen door, where he was skimming cream from the milk pail.

"Cap!" He jumped off the porch and ran toward him. "Do you want to come fishing with us? Henry said he'd take me, but it would be wonderful-*gut* if you could come too."

Watching Davey's face put a grin on his own. Seeing the boy's excitement drove his gloomy thoughts out of his mind. "Fishing?

It's perfect weather. Where do you plan on going?"

"Henry said the river, down past Josef's farm. He says there's a bend there that's perfect for catfish."

Cap kept walking toward the house and Davey hopped along to keep in step with him.

"What did your mamm say? Will she let you go with Henry?"

Davey's face fell as if someone had slapped him with a wet rag. "Memmi said she would think about it." He kicked at the porch step before he followed Cap to the door. "That means she won't let me go."

"You have to obey your mamm."

"I know." Davey's voice dripped with disappointment. Then he hopped up onto the porch, the grin back on his face. "Maybe if you go, she'll let me. She said she wanted a grown-up to go along, and Henry said he was a grown-up, and Memmi said he was only seventeen, and too young to watch me by the river." He tilted his head back to look at Cap. "I thought Henry was a grown-up."

Cap fought to keep from smiling. "We'll see what your mamm says when she finds out I'll be going along."

Davey whooped and crashed through the kitchen door. "Memmi, Cap is here!"

As Cap stepped through the open door-way, Naomi grasped her son by his arm. "Davey Schrock, what has gotten into you? You know better than to run and yell in the house. We walk quietly when we're inside."

"But, Memmi," Davey wriggled from her grasp but tried his best to stand still as he spoke. "Cap is here, and he said he'll go fishing with Henry, and if it's okay with you I can go too. Is it, Memmi? Tell me. Is it?"

Naomi glanced toward Cap, her face turning a pretty shade of pink. "I don't know if he wants to do that."

"He said so. And he's a grown-up, isn't he? More grown up than Henry?"

Cap nodded and Naomi knelt on the floor to talk to her son. "If Cap will watch you, then you may go fishing." Davey started to leap into the air, but Naomi held him down with a hand on his shoulder. "Henry isn't going to go until after dinner, though, so you have plenty of time to finish your chores."

Davey ran out to the porch, slamming the back door as he went.

"I don't know what I'll do with that boy. He's never still for a moment."

Cap took his hat off and hung it on one of the hooks by the back door. "He's a boy. Boys aren't meant to be still."

"I suppose not." She gestured toward the table in the middle of the kitchen. "Would you like a cup of coffee?"

"For sure, I would." Cap sat in a chair while she poured a cup for him. "My fire went out and I just didn't have the patience to get it going again in the rain."

Naomi set his coffee in front of him and sat down with a cup for herself. "And you knew there was coffee here that we would share with you."

"I hoped there would be." He wrapped his cold fingers around the stoneware cup. He could hear Lydia in the loft. "I don't want to disturb your workday, though."

"I'm ready for a short rest, and Mamm will be too, after she finishes gathering Henry's and Davey's clothes. We're late getting wash day started, but Mamm is hoping the rain will clear up in time to hang the clothes out to dry."

He watched her delicate hand grasp the coffee cup as she brought it to her lips. "Before Lydia comes down, I want to tell you I'm sorry for yesterday."

Her cheeks turned pink and she set her cup on the table. "You don't need to do that."

"I know better than to listen to anything Shem Fischer tells me. I have no reason to believe what he says, and every reason to believe you."

His hand moved across the inches separating them and grasped hers. She turned her hand and intertwined her fingers in his, squeezing his hand slightly.

Cap smiled and took a drink of his coffee. He was forgiven.

After dinner, Cap walked with Henry out to the barn, Davey hopping and skipping ahead of them.

The short time spent with Naomi in the kitchen had warmed his spirits, and the rest of the morning helping Eli and Henry build a new farrowing pen in the barn warmed his muscles. He had been alone too long, living on his own in Ohio, and then here in Indiana too. Working with Eli took him back to the days when he had been Henry's age, working alongside his daed. The memories were good ones, up until he lost Martha.

"Maybe we'll catch a snapping turtle." Davey hopped on one foot as Henry sorted through the cane rods balanced on pegs along the barn wall. "Remember, Henry? You said if we caught one, Grossmutti could make turtle soup."

"I was making a joke with you." Henry grinned at his nephew. "If you catch a snapper, we'd be spending our time pulling you out of the river." He crouched down on the boy's level. "Snappers aren't something to fool with. If you catch one, you let go of your pole right away."

Davey's body stilled, his brow wrinkling as he thought this through. "Mose said his mamm would make him turtle soup if he caught one."

Henry handed the bundle of poles to Cap. "Mose would do better to catch a catfish. I can't imagine his mamm touching a snapping turtle. You remember how she turns up her nose when he brings her crayfish."

Davey laughed and started hopping again.

"Did you dig the worms like Henry said?" Cap asked as Henry handed him the third pole.

"For sure I did. They're in a bag on the porch."

"Get them, then," Henry said. "We're ready to go."

Cap laughed as Davey dashed back to the house. "He's some boy."

"For sure, he is. Into mischief all the time, just like I was at his age."

"I was too." They both watched as Davey grabbed the dirty cloth bag and ran back toward them. "Sometimes I think it would be fun to go back to being a boy."

Henry grinned. "It sure would."

The sky was still overcast, but the rain had stopped over the noon hour. Cap and Henry skirted the puddles in the road as they walked, while Davey ran from stump to stump, jumping off one just to run to the next.

"Do all the roads still have these stumps in them?"

"All through here they do." Henry kicked at the short stump in front of him, cut off just inches from the ground. "When the first settlers came twenty years ago, they followed the Indian trails from one settlement to the next. By the time we bought our land, some of the trails had been widened to roads so a man could drive a wagon through. But the stumps were left. No one wanted to take the time to clear them out, I suppose."

The stumps were short enough to drive over, and rot had set into the center of many of them. They would disappear with time.

"I was surprised to hear Jacob Yoder call this area Pleasant Prairie," Cap said. "I haven't seen any prairie since I got here. Only dense woods all around."

Henry laughed. "Ja, that's what Jacob and Mattie call it, and others have started, too, as more trees are cleared. There is prairie to the southwest of here, and a bit of it is on Jacob's land. Mattie always wanted to live on the prairie, so Jacob made sure he found open land for her." He swept the air in front of him with his arm. "Soon all these trees will be gone, just like in Ohio and Brothers Valley, where we came from. Can't you see it? Open farmland all around. A real prairie."

Cap could see it, and he was working as hard as anyone else to clear his land. Soon he would have a pasture for the horses, fields of grain growing, a garden for vegetables. He grinned at the thought of the work ahead of him. Useful work. Work that would build a home for . . . His grin disappeared. He might have a house and land, but it wasn't a home, yet.

"I see the river!" Davey's shout drifted back to them from around a bend in the road.

"Wait there for us," Henry called.

The water was high, flooding into the low stands of trees along the edge. Henry led the way along a small ridge of clay until they reached a wide spot where the river had made a cut in the bank and a tree had fallen across the stream years ago, making a cove of quiet water.

"There's a big trout that lives by that

stump." Davey whispered the information to Cap. "I'm gonna catch him someday."

"I'm certain you will," Cap answered. If Davey knew enough to keep still and quiet while fishing, he'd do well.

Henry chose a spot to the right along the bank, while Davey led Cap to a rock closer to the fallen log. They baited their hooks and dropped them into the water.

Davey sighed. "Now we wait."

"Fishing helps a man develop patience."

The boy leaned against Cap. "Patience is hard."

"It helps you be content while you wait for something you want."

Davey wiggled his feet. "I know something I want, but I don't think I am very content while I wait for it."

"Why not?"

"Because I pray for it, and I hope for it, and nothing ever happens."

Cap thought of all the things a boy might want — a dog, a knife, a pony. Any of those things could be possible for him to give to Davey, with his mother's permission.

"What is it that you want?"

Davey leaned his head back to look at Cap's face. "I want a daed, like Mose has, and Henry has."

A knot grew in Cap's stomach. "You have

your *grossdatti*."

Davey looked back at the fishing line in the water. "He's my grossdatti." His feet wiggled again, as if he couldn't keep them still even when he was sitting down. "I had my own daed once."

"Ja, everyone has a daed."

"Memmi said he died, and my other memmi too. And a baby sister."

"Do you remember them?"

Davey shook his head. "Did you ever have someone who died?"

Cap blinked back sudden tears. "Ja." He cleared his throat. "I had a wife once, and a baby boy."

"Do you remember them?"

When didn't he remember them? "Every day."

Davey's head leaned against him again, and Cap put his free arm around the boy, tucking him in under his shoulder. Together they watched the still water. A ring of ripples appeared where a fish struck at an insect on the surface, and the little waves ran to the sandy mud at their feet.

"Do you miss your boy?"

Cap cleared his throat again. "For sure, I do." He had never gotten to know his son, to know if he would have been anything like Davey. But that life was gone. Forever gone.

Davey pushed away from him and turned to look into his face. "You don't have a boy, and I don't have a daed."

Cap nodded. What was Davey trying to say?

"Could you be my daed?"

His throat tightened. "I think your mamm would have something to say about that."

"Not really my daed. We could pretend." Davey's grin was infectious and Cap found himself smiling.

"Maybe we could."

Davey threw his arms around Cap's neck. "I love you, Cap."

Cap's cane pole dropped as he wrapped his arms around the small body. "I love you too, Davey."

Naomi checked the damp clothes hanging from the clothesline on the back porch. The dresses and shirts were dry enough to bring inside to iron, but Daed's and Henry's trousers needed more time. As she took her dress off the line and rolled it into a bundle, her gaze went down the road toward the river where Davey had gone with Cap and Henry to fish. The thought of her active and careless boy along the banks of the spring-swollen river set her nerves on edge.

"There's no reason to be concerned," she

told herself, and bit her lower lip. Davey would be fine with Cap there, and Henry. The two of them together would keep her boy safe. She fought the urge to leave the laundry for later and walk down to the river to check on them.

"He'll be fine."

Naomi jumped at Mamm's words and reached for the next dress. "I know you think it's silly for me to be worrying about Davey, but I can't help it."

Mamm sighed as she pulled Daed's shirt off the line. "You get used to it. When your brother Isaac was young, I didn't want to let him out of my sight. But Noah and Annie kept me so busy, I couldn't keep my eye on him all the time."

"What did you do?"

"I had to trust your daed. By the time Isaac was five years old, Eli convinced me that it was time to let him spend his days working in the barn." Mamm smiled at her. "I soon learned that he could keep his son just as safe as I could, and that working with his daed was good for the boy. It was easier when Noah got bigger."

"And by the time Henry came along, you nearly pushed him out of the house to help Daed."

"You're right." Mamm gathered the bundles of shirts in her arms and started toward the kitchen door while Naomi followed. "As much as I would have liked to keep him with me, I knew it was better for him to be with his daed and older brothers."

Naomi paused on the threshold, her mind still with the fishermen. "Do you really think Davey will be all right with Henry and Cap?"

Mamm spread the first shirt on the table and lifted the iron from the stove top. "For sure, I do. Your brother loves Davey nearly as much as you do and will watch out for him. And Cap seems to be a man you can trust. Don't worry about him."

Don't worry? Naomi had worried about Davey from the first moment she had taken him in her arms. Mamm might as well tell her to stop breathing.

After the dresses and shirts were ironed, Naomi gathered the clothes that needed mending while Mamm went out to work in the garden. The empty house was quiet. Naomi sat in the rocking chair and kept it going with her foot while she sewed, just to have the company of the chair's comforting squeak. But with no one to talk to, she couldn't keep her mind off Cap's words from the morning. Shem Fischer seemed to be intent on spreading rumors about her, but there was no reason for him to do that.

Naomi finished mending Daed's torn shirt sleeve and reached for Davey's trousers.

Why was Preacher Shem so interested in Davey? And why didn't Cap like him?

For sure, she didn't like the man, either. She would never admit it to anyone else, but Shem gave her an unsettled feeling whenever he was around. She couldn't be the only one who felt that way, which made her wonder how he had been nominated for election as preacher in his home church.

But the rumors. First Susan Gingerich, and then Preacher Shem, and then Cap. Cap said he didn't believe them, but he had to doubt her story. He must, or he wouldn't have mentioned it.

"Lydia?"

Naomi thrust the mending in her sewing basket and met Annalise Yoder at the kitchen door. "Hallo, Annalise. Mamm is in the garden." She held the screen door open for her mamm's friend.

"That's all right," Annalise said. "I came to see you. I finished the cloth I have been weaving and I'm ready to thread the loom again. I thought you'd like to come over tomorrow morning to help me."

"I'm so glad you thought of that. I would love to help."

Annalise sat at the table and took the cup of tea that Naomi offered. "You haven't seen the entire weaving process yet, and there is nothing like doing the work to learn."

"Do you think I'll be able to learn to make fabric on my own? It is so complicated, isn't it?" Naomi sat at the table with her.

"I'm sure it seems that way when you're first starting out. But once you learn how the warp and woof work together —"

"Wait," Naomi said, stopping Annalise with a hand on her arm. "Wait until you can show me as well as tell me. I'm lost already."

"For sure, it can wait until tomorrow." Annalise sipped her tea while Naomi stirred a spoonful of honey in her cup. "It's very quiet here today. Where is that Davey of yours?"

"Off fishing with Henry and Cap."

"That's good. I hope they catch plenty of fish." Annalise finished her tea. "I must get home. Christian isn't feeling well, and the twins do vex him so at times."

Annalise fumbled with her shawl as she walked toward the door.

"I hope Christian feels better soon," Naomi said.

The other woman smiled, but it didn't extend to her eyes. "I'm sure he will." Annalise stepped onto the porch. "I'll see you tomorrow then, ja?"

"For sure."

Annalise was gone so quickly that Naomi doubted if she had heard. She took the tea cups to the sink to wash, but paused, the scene through the window capturing her attention. From here she could see the road leading to the river ford. Anytime now Henry and Cap would be returning with Davey. Catching her bottom lip between her teeth, Naomi forced her thoughts away from dark imaginings of Davey falling in the river and being swept away. Or Henry and Cap concentrating so much on their fishing that they don't notice Davey wandering off and getting lost. Or a fish hook catching itself —

Naomi shook herself and rinsed the cups.

Mamm had said she should trust Cap and Henry and stop worrying. If only she could.

6

After an afternoon of fishing, Henry had three good-sized fish on his string, while Cap had two. The rain had stopped and the clouds melted into puffs of light gray in the cobalt sky as the sun sank toward the treetops.

"I guess it's time to head back home," Henry said, pulling his line out of the water.

"I haven't caught a fish yet." Davey balanced on a log, turning his longing eyes first on Cap, then on Henry.

"We don't catch something every time we go fishing." Cap reached a hand out to the boy to help him over a muddy spot. "I'll share mine with you."

Davey stopped and pulled his hand out of Cap's. "I want to stay here until I catch one."

Cap glanced at the sun. "It's almost suppertime. Your mamm will be waiting for you."

The thought of a meal waiting got Davey's feet moving again, but his steps were slow, and he turned to look back at the river. "Can we come back tomorrow?"

"Too much work to do tomorrow." Henry's pace was faster than Davey's, and he was already several yards ahead of them on the road.

Davey tugged at Cap's sleeve. "Can you bring me?"

Davey looked into Cap's face, his lower lip pulled in and his eyes full of hope. Everything in Cap wanted to say he would take Davey fishing again tomorrow, but work came before pleasure. "I need to finish building my chimney tomorrow."

Davey hopped onto a stump. "Maybe I could help you do that."

Cap considered the idea. Building the chimney involved carrying heavy rocks up his makeshift ladder, cementing them in with a sand and lime mixture, then going back down the ladder to do it all over again. He'd never be able to keep his eye on an active boy.

"I'm sorry, Davey. It's a one-man job tomorrow. You can help me another day."

Davey stepped off the stump and trudged up the road ahead of him, his head hanging down.

"Maybe your grossdatti will have some work for you to do."

Davey ignored him.

Cap lifted his hand to reach out to the boy, but kept himself back. Learning to live with disappointment was a lesson best learned early. If a child had all of his wants satisfied, he would never learn to be content with what God had given him.

When they reached the Schrock farm, Henry headed to the barn with his fish. Naomi was waiting on the porch by the kitchen door, and Cap drank in the sight as Davey ran to her, gave her a quick hug, and then went into the house. He forgot about Davey's mood when Naomi smiled at him.

"Did you catch any fish? Davey said he didn't."

Cap held his string of two fish up as evidence. "Henry and I both got some. They'll make a good supper tonight."

"Did Davey behave himself?"

"Ja, for sure. He's a good fisherman." Davey's bad mood wasn't worth mentioning. Naomi could figure that out for herself. "I'd be happy to take him another day, if that's all right."

Naomi paused for just an instant, then nodded. "Ja. He would like that fine."

Cap took a step toward his clearing. "I

need to get ready for tomorrow's work, now that the rain has stopped."

"Denki."

Naomi went into the house. But with that one word, and the smile she gave him with it, Cap's mood shifted. Davey's pouting had affected him more than he had thought, but Naomi's smile had banished it.

The trail through the woods had become packed earth in places, the grass worn away by Davey's feet running along it between his home and Cap's clearing. Another sign that this was becoming home for him. Eli and Henry, the Yoders, the Benders, and the Planks were all becoming good friends. And the families in the Elkhart County end of the district would, too, as he got to know them better. When he had made his plans to move west, his sisters had all argued against it, saying that he needed to be part of a church, part of a community.

Cap paused to listen to an oriole singing from its treetop perch. Ruth and the others were right, he did need to be part of a church, and he had found it here. Someday soon he needed to write a letter, ease their worries.

As he drew near his clearing, he heard Blau's and Betza's nervous grunting. Through the trees, he could see them on their picket ropes, heads up and ears pointing toward the cabin. Near the road were two riders holding the reins of two other horses with empty saddles. He put the cabin between him and the riders and approached the back door. When he eased it open, two men were crouched on either side of his tool chest and had just opened the lid.

"Who are you?" Cap asked the question in Deitsch.

The younger of the two, a boy who couldn't be older than eighteen, answered. "Never mind who we are. Where do you keep your cash?"

The older man boxed the other one on the ears. "Stop talking that gibberish." The man's voice was rough, and he spoke in English. "You." He pointed at Cap. "Give us your money. Where is it?"

Cap kept his eye on the younger one. The one who had spoken Deitsch. What was a young Amish man doing with a gang of English ruffians?

The older man strode over and pushed Cap against the wall. "Look at me when I talk to you. Where is your money?"

Cap shook his head, glad he had thought to leave the money he had received from selling his Ohio farm with his brother-in-law in Holmes County. "I don't have any here."

The man, shorter than Cap, but double his weight, shoved him against the wall again. Cap felt the rough logs dig into his back through the fabric of his shirt. "Tell us before we take this place apart."

"All I have are my tools, and the horses."

The younger man had risen to stand behind his friend. He laid a hand on the other man's shoulder. "If he says there isn't any money, he's telling the truth."

"How do you know?"

The young man shrugged. "He's Amish. They don't lie."

"He's just trying to put us off."

"He wouldn't do that."

The man shoved Cap again, then turned to the other one. "All right then. Get the horses and we'll get out of here." He pushed past the young man on his way to the door. "Don't be all day about it. We've got to ride."

The young man didn't look at Cap as he followed his friend, but at the door he turned back. "I'm sorry." His words were Deitsch again. "I try to keep the gang away from the Amish community, but I didn't know you were one of them." His gaze flicked up to meet Cap's. "We have to take the horses, though." He closed the door behind him.

Cap leaned against the wall. He heard Blau's and Betza's nervous nickers as the young man pulled their picket pins. The thud of the big horses' hooves as he led them around the house. The other riders' voices as they set off down the road, leading his horses away. Blau, with his habit of nuzzling Cap's chest when he wanted more grain. And Betza, so gentle that his two-year-old niece could play around her feet in the meadow. Where would he find such horses again?

He sank down until he was sitting on the dirt floor of the cabin and wiped his hands over his face. Everything in him wanted to follow the men. He would take his gun from the hooks over the door and confront them before they got any farther away. He would demand that they give his horses back to him.

But the teaching of the church, the way he had been taught to live his life, was nonresistance. To give way, to give in, to love your enemy. This was Christ's example.

Cap's muscles ached from the effort of remaining still. Of holding himself back. He would obey the teachings of the church, even though his head pulsed with rage.

■ ■ ■ ■

The next morning, after chores and breakfast were done, Davey ran to the barn.

Henry was hitching the big horses to the
plow.

"Can I come, Henry? Can I?" Davey
stood behind Henry.

The horses' feet could be dangerous,
Mamm had said, so Davey stayed away from
them. But he watched the big black hooves
closely. They didn't look dangerous. They
looked like the pieces of flint arrowheads he
had found on the hill in back of Mose's and
Menno's house last fall. Did they feel as
cold and slick as those stones? Someday,
when no one was watching, he'd touch one
and find out.

Henry moved to the horse on the far side
and Davey followed.

"Can I, Henry? I can drive the horses."

"Ne. You'd only be in the way. You'll be
big enough to help in a year or two, but
until then, it's a man's job."

Davey watched him gather the long leather
reins in his hand. He balanced on one foot
while Henry drove the horses out of the
barn. Only big boys could stand on one foot
for so long. He thrust his arms out to keep

113

from tipping. If Henry could see how steady he was, he'd let him come and help plow. But when he looked up again, Henry was gone.

He stood in the center of the empty barn. The cow was in the meadow. Grossdatti had taken the second team of horses and the felling ax to the woods while Davey was finishing his breakfast mush.

Sunlight streamed in bars through the gaps between the pole slats of the corncrib outside the open door. Davey swished his hand through the motes floating in the beams and watched them swirl. Just like the water when a fish struck at an insect.

The fishing poles hung on the barn wall next to the door, right where Henry had put them away yesterday.

The barn was quiet. No one was around. No one could see him.

A creeping shiver ran up his spine. He didn't dare turn around. Someone could be watching him. A wolf, maybe, in the dark corner where Grossdatti piled the manure in the winter. Davey's breathing came in little gasps. Not a wolf. An Indian. Mose had told him how the Indians who used to live in the Haw Patch wanted to come home, and sometimes they did. He said one lived down the river a ways all winter long.

He took a step toward the door. All was silent behind him. He ran as fast as he could until he reached the porch. Then he turned around, breathless, and waited for whatever was in the barn to come out. The open door was empty. He could see the sunbeams lighting the floor, just as they had when he was standing there.

The danger was past. This time.

Footsteps rang on the kitchen floor. Grossmutti.

Davey opened the door and peeked in. Ja, it was Grossmutti, but Memmi was there too.

"Davey, are you ready to go?" Memmi smoothed her skirt and picked up a towel-wrapped loaf of bread.

"Where?"

Grossmutti tousled his hair as she passed him on the way to the dry sink. "Didn't you listen at breakfast? We're going to the Yoders' this morning. You can play with William and the twins."

She stacked the clean plates and put them in the cupboard.

"I want to go see Cap."

Memmi grasped his shoulder and turned him toward the door. "Cap is busy working today. Come along, Annalise will wonder where we are."

Davey ran ahead of the women until he got to the road. The stumps were farther apart between his house and the Yoders' farm, but there were still enough to play the game. The ground was sinking sand, and the stumps were the only safe place. Memmi and Grossmutti walked past him, talking to each other about sheep.

When Memmi got their sheep, he would take care of them. He stood on a stump, cradling a pretend lamb in his arms. Soon he would have his very own lamb. It would follow him just like Mose's and Menno's puppy did. And when it got big, it would never hurt him with his horns. They would be best friends, and he would always have someone to play with.

"Hurry up, Davey." Memmi's voice came from far ahead. "Don't fall behind."

He and his lamb ran fast through the sinking sand and it never grabbed his ankles and pulled him under. When he got to the Yoders' farm, he jumped on a tall stump next to the road. William waved to him.

"Davey, come on. We're playing Indians. You can build your house over there."

Davey built his Indian house out of branches William and Gideon had dragged out of the woods, while Rachael helped. They played until dinnertime, and then

Gideon and Rachael had to take a nap while William went to help his daed in the fields. Davey sat alone on the front porch. Through the window he could hear Memmi's voice, along with William's mamm and Grossmutti. He leaned against the post by the steps, but his eyes kept closing.

His head bobbed and he jerked awake. If Memmi caught him sleeping, she'd make him take a nap like Gideon and Rachael. He jumped up, ran to his Indian house, and crawled inside. Now that his house was finished, he should go hunting. Maybe he would find a deer and shoot it with his bow.

Davey looked around. He didn't have a bow, but he had a fishing pole. He would catch a fish instead of a deer. Both were good.

His fishing pole was hanging on the barn wall.

He ran home and into the barn. He stopped in the doorway, then walked on his toes, like an Indian, until he reached the horses' stalls. All was quiet. Henry and Grossdatti had taken their dinner pails with them to work. No one was around. No one would see him take his fishing pole to the river.

The silence of the barn loomed above and behind him. Davey looked straight into the dark corner, but no wolf or Indian was there. He was alone. The only sound in the quiet afternoon was the chopping of Grossdatti's ax far away in the woods.

He reached his hand toward the fishing rod. Nothing happened. No one stopped him. He grabbed the rod, balanced it over his shoulder, and ducked out of the barn.

The sunshine bore down on Davey's head as he walked toward the river. He moved to the edge of the road. The center was too open. The hand that held the fishing rod was wet, as if he had dunked it under water. He stopped and wiped his hand on his trousers, looking back toward the barn and the house. No one was around. No one could see him.

When he brought home a string of fish, then Memmi would be proud. Henry, too. He could bring home enough fish to feed everyone.

He started trotting toward the river.

Naomi fingered the indigo-dyed skein of yarn Annalise had given her and eyed the warping board while Mamm watched. Annalise had tied the end of the skein onto the yarn already threaded on the board, so Naomi was ready to continue the pattern her teacher had started. She reached for the top peg.

"Remember," Annalise said, her voice gentle behind Naomi's left shoulder, "this time you go over, under, over, and then back and forth on the pegs."

Naomi let the yarn slide between her fingers as she followed the path on the warping board. The board was a square frame, about four feet wide, with pegs at intervals on four sides. When she reached the bottom, she wove the yarn under, over, under, around, and then started the path back up. Over and over.

"How many threads did you say we needed?" Naomi grunted as she reached for the top peg again.

"Six hundred to make a full width of cloth." Annalise grasped Naomi's hand. "The tension isn't even. Remember to let the thread out from between your fingers at a steady pace, just like when we were spinning the thread, and keep your arm moving at a steady pace too. Each of the threads needs to be like the others."

Mamm stepped forward to run her fingers over the threads already wound on the board. "Uniform and consistent. The order gives the warping threads a beauty all their own."

"I think so too," Annalise answered as she

watched Naomi's endless motion. "Each conforms to the other."

Naomi kept winding. When she reached a tangle in the skein, Mamm took it from her and sorted out the knot while Naomi continued. When she reached the end of the yarn, Annalise took it and counted the threads on the board.

"How do you know how many threads you need?" Naomi asked, watching Annalise finger the threads in groups of ten.

Annalise stopped, her finger holding her place. "This cloth will be for dresses, so we'll set the loom up with about ten threads per inch. Six hundred threads will give us a width of about fifty-five inches when it's done."

As Annalise continued counting, whispering the numbers to herself, Naomi became aware of how quiet the house was.

"Mamm, do you know where Davey is?"

Mamm shrugged, her lips moving as she counted along with Annalise. Naomi stepped into the kitchen and listened again. No sounds of a boy playing. He must be outside.

Pushing away a rising panic, Naomi walked across the front yard to where the children had been playing before dinner. Davey probably fell asleep in the little house he and Rachael had made. She stepped softly when she reached it, not wanting to wake him. But when she peered in between the branches, the little hut was empty.

"Where could he be?"

Naomi shaded her eyes and looked around the clearing. No one was in sight. Even Christian was away, plowing the field on the other side of the hill, Annalise had said. She had sent William there with Christian's dinner in a pail. Could Davey have followed William?

She went back into the house.

"I'm glad you're back," Annalise said. She had a strip of soft cloth in her hand. "We're ready to tie the warp together so we can remove it from the board."

"I'll help in a moment." Naomi took a deep breath. "I can't find Davey. Do you think he might have followed William out to the fields?"

"I saw him sitting on the porch after dinner," Mamm said. "That was quite a while after William left."

"Did you check the barn?"

A knot in Naomi's stomach unwound. "I haven't. I'll go do that."

"And the henhouse too."

Naomi walked with long strides toward the henhouse. The chickens were drowsing in the afternoon sunlight. No seven-year-old boy had disturbed them. Her walk turned into a run across the grass toward the barn. Christian had replaced his log barn with a beam-and-board one last summer, with a lofty hay mow that enticed William and Davey to explore. Naomi stood in the middle of the barn floor, listening. No sound.

"Davey!"

He might be sleeping.

She climbed the tall ladder and peered over the edge of the loft. The pile of last year's hay had been reduced to a small mound in the center of the floor. Not enough for a boy to hide in. The knot in her stomach tightened again.

"Davey?"

Her knees were weak and watery and Naomi clung to the ladder. She always knew where Davey was, but now —

Naomi climbed down the ladder. Her fingers, cold and clammy, barely gripped the rungs. She stumbled out of the barn and scanned the Yoders' farm again. The stumps in the grass, the new apple trees in the orchard, the henhouse . . . There was no boy anywhere.

Cap. Davey had wanted to go to Cap's today. Would he have gone there alone?

Naomi ran to the house. "I can't find Davey anywhere. I'm going to see if he went to Cap's."

She spun in the doorway before Mamm or Annalise could answer, but she heard Mamm's voice floating behind her. "Wait, Naomi. Let us help you look."

She wouldn't need anyone's help to find her son. He was at Cap's. He had to be.

As she emerged from the woods, she scanned the small clearing. Cap stood at the top of his ladder, a hod full of mud in his hand and a line of round rocks on the roof at his elbow. Davey must be inside the house.

"Cap! Is Davey here?"

He settled a rock into the chimney. "I haven't seen him today."

As she bit her bottom lip to keep the tears at bay, Cap let the hod fall to the ground and slid down the ladder.

When he reached her side, he grasped her arms. "Steady there."

Gray clouds swirled as he helped her sit on a stump.

"Put your head down, and breathe."

She hiccuped, but lowered her forehead to her knees and wrapped her arms around her legs.

"I have to find Davey." Her skirt muffled

her voice.

"When did you see him last?"

She raised her head and her sight was clear. "After dinner. He was sitting on the porch at the Yoders'."

Naomi stood, but too quickly, and the ground tipped. Cap swung her into his arms and started down the trail toward home.

"Let me down." She struggled, but he kept walking. "I have to find Davey. Let me down."

He stopped and set her feet on the ground. "Are you all right?"

"Ja, ja, ja." She took a deep breath as the ground swayed a little. "I'm fine." The knot in her stomach rose to her throat. "I . . . I don't know where he is." The next breath came in a hiccuping sob. "What will I do? How will I find him?" Her voice rose as she spoke and she closed her mouth before the threatening scream made itself heard.

Cap took both of her arms in his hands and faced her toward him. "We'll find him." He shook her a little until she looked into his eyes. "We'll find him. I'm going to take you home, and then I'll get the Yoders and your family, and we'll look for him."

The tears spilled out as he crushed her to his chest.

"We'll find him, Naomi. We will."

■ ■ ■ ■

That evening, Naomi sat on the porch step. Mattie and Hannah sat on either side of her, holding her hands. Cap and the other men were still looking for Davey, but twilight crept toward the clearing from the overhanging branches of the forest. Her boy was in the woods, alone, in the dark.

Henry had discovered that a fishing pole was missing. He and Cap had run down to the river where they had been fishing yesterday. The pole was there, but no Davey.

Naomi shut away the voices clamoring that Davey had fallen in the river. He hadn't. He couldn't. He didn't know how to swim. She wouldn't believe it. Davey was lost in the woods. He would find his way home. He would be hungry —

"I need to make supper for him." She shrugged off the quilt Mamm had put around her shoulders and tried to stand.

Mattie grasped her hand tighter and pulled her back down. "Annalise has supper ready for those who want it."

"Where is Cap?"

Hannah put one arm around her shoulders as she replaced the quilt. "Cap went with the other men to search along the riverbanks. If he fell in the water —"

Blackness spun in front of Naomi's eyes. "He didn't fall in. He couldn't."

"He might have." Hannah's voice was strong. Reassuring. "If he fell in, the water would carry him downstream."

Naomi leaned her head on Hannah's shoulder. Davey didn't know how to swim. He was afraid of the water. She squeezed her eyes shut to block out the scene Hannah's words had created. Davey wasn't in the water. He wasn't. Instead, she made herself remember him as he was when she put him to bed last night. Little-boy hair falling over his pillow, his ruddy cheeks glowing in the candlelight. His long eyelashes resting on those cheeks as his eyes closed in sleep.

A sob escaped and Mattie squeezed her hand again.

She couldn't live if something happened to Davey. He was all she had.

"They're coming."

Mattie stood and pulled Naomi up with her. For sure, there were the men walking up the road in the twilight. Only the men. Naomi strained to see if any of them were carrying a boy, but they all walked as if they were weary, their arms hanging at their sides.

No one said a word as they came into the yard. Mattie met Jacob before he reached the house, and they went on to their own farm. Hannah and Josef did the same after Hannah gathered up her little ones. Mamm met Daed while he was yet near the barn. Naomi could see them talking, Daed supporting Mamm with one arm around her waist.

Only Cap walked all the way to the house, stopping when he reached her.

"You didn't find him?"

Cap shook his head. His face was etched in lines she had never seen before, his eyes dark hollows in the half-light. "We searched all along the riverbanks for a mile, until it started getting dark. We'll look again in the morning."

Rage shot through Naomi like hot lightning. She launched herself at Cap and her fists were pounding, pounding on his chest. "You left him in the woods? You left my boy in the woods? How . . ."

Her rage, gone as quickly as it had come, left her weak. Cap caught her as her legs collapsed and held her against him. Her fists still clenched between them.

"How could you leave my little boy alone in the woods?"

Her words sounded alien in her ears. A

keening wail.

"We'll look again in the morning." Cap held her closer as the sobbing gasps forced their way out. "I promise. I won't stop until I find him."

7

After the Schrock family had taken Naomi into the house, Cap started for home. He thrust his hands into the waistband of his trousers, hunched his shoulders against the chill wind that had risen, and put one foot in front of the other down the worn path between the Schrock farm and his clearing. The path worn smooth by Davey's feet running down it almost daily.

His feet stopped and a shudder ran through him. If he closed his eyes, the scene by the river that afternoon would haunt him. If he opened them, he saw Davey everywhere he looked. So instead, he stared straight up, into the sky blazing with white stars. He swallowed once. And then again.

He could never tell Naomi what he saw. The fishing pole on the bank of the river, half in and half out of the water. The small footprints on the sandy edge of the water, leading in . . . but none leading out. He had led the search along the riverbanks. He had yelled Davey's name over and over until he was hoarse. Jacob and Josef had pulled him away from the wooded banks when it became too dark to see, and he had only agreed to halt the search when they convinced him that if Davey had been able to climb out of the water, they would miss the signs.

Cap's body was as sore as if he had been carried down the rushing water himself, pummeled by the rocks under the surface, his lungs straining for a breath of air.

Where was Davey? He grabbed his hat and ran desperate fingers through his hair. Why hadn't they found him?

The answers to those questions were too obvious, but he couldn't face them. He couldn't admit the possibility that Davey might never come home.

He forced his feet to move once more, heading down the trail to his cabin. He needed food. Sleep, too, if he could. Step after step, he moved closer to his cabin and his bed. Finally, he reached the dark, cold house. No horses nickered their welcome, but he no longer cared. He made his way to the door of his cabin.

Cap must have slept, because when he opened his eyes again, the gray light that preceded the dawn glowed through the window opening in the log wall.

As quickly as he hurried to get down the trail to the Schrock farm, the yard between the house and the barn had already filled with people from the community. Lydia and Mattie passed out fried cakes and cups of hot coffee as Eli Schrock went from man to man, expressing his thanks for their willingness to help.

Naomi wasn't among the crowd, but Shem Fischer was. He circulated among the men much as Eli was doing. When he reached Cap, he smiled in the way ministers do at such occasions. But the smile didn't extend past his mouth. His eyes narrowed as he gauged Cap's mood.

"Your presence here is appreciated by the family." Shem's voice was quiet, but Cap's spine tingled.

"Who are you to speak for them, Shem Fischer?" He took a step closer to the man, speaking through his clenched jaws. "Why are you even here?"

Shem took a step back. "I'm only trying to help." He held a hand out to Cap. "The community needs all of us to help find the boy."

Cap eyed him. His words didn't match the smile on his face, but he wasn't about to turn down another pair of feet and another set of eyes. "You're right. We all need to help find Davey."

Mattie Yoder approached them with a plate of fried cakes.

"I'm glad you're here, Cap," she said as he took one of the cakes. "Daed intends to start the search as soon as there is light enough to see."

Shem took two of the cakes before Mattie went on to her brother, Henry, and Josef Bender. He took a huge bite of the first one, watching the scene around them.

"You don't think we'll find the boy too far away, do you? Someone said his fishing pole was found by the river, and you know what that means. We'll probably find his body caught in some reeds along the bank and be back here by noon."

Cap had taken the first bite of his fried cake when Shem spoke, but the other man's certainty turned the sweet pastry to sawdust in Cap's mouth. He swallowed. "There's no reason to believe the boy isn't lost somewhere downstream. We'll find him."

Shem shrugged. "You know as well as I do that Naomi's son is ripe for judgment. His mother's sin will be atoned for in the boy's death. It's probably best that it happened this way, before the sin could go any farther."

Cap stared at him. "What do you mean?"

"The boy. The result of his mother's sin." He spread his hands as if to show the written proof of his words. "The same as when David sinned with Bathsheba. The child of that unholy union had to die to atone for their sin."

"You have twisted the story. That isn't what the Good Book teaches." Cap took a deep breath. "And that isn't what our church teaches. Where did you get such an idea?"

Shem laughed, the sound plunging the somber mood of the morning into a well of icy water. The men around them looked in their direction. Cap's frown matched the expression on Josef Bender's face.

"I was just testing you, Caspie. You take things too seriously."

Cap bristled at the sound of the old nickname. Minister or not, Shem Fischer spread poison at every turn.

"It's time to go!" Eli called from near the barn.

Cap left Shem behind and walked quickly, passing neighbors and strangers in his hurry to reach the river first. He glanced once more toward the house and saw Naomi. She stood on the covered porch, in the spot where he had seen Davey only a few days ago. As she watched the crowd of searchers leave, she seemed to shrink. Small, vulnerable, and frightened in her pale gray shawl.

"They will find him." Mattie had come to stand next to her on the porch as the men left. She put her arm around Naomi's shoulders. "They will."

Naomi's eyes burned, dry and sandy after a sleepless night. Her Davey was still out there in the woods, and she could do nothing. Nothing but wait. She couldn't even hope. He was gone. Gone.

"Come sit down, liebchen," Mamm said, bringing a kitchen chair out to the porch. "There is nothing to do now but to wait and pray."

Hannah brought a cup of coffee, but Naomi turned away from it. The smell caused the knot in her stomach to shift.

The women sat, silently praying as they waited. Annalise and Magdalena Hertzler had taken the children to the Yoders' house for the day, and the farm was unnaturally still, as if death had already settled here.

Naomi couldn't pray. What would she say that she hadn't already said? To keep Davey safe. To bring him back to her. To protect him from the dangers of the forest. To lead him in the paths that would bring him home. Everything she had prayed for through the night.

"I'm glad so many men are searching." Naomi's voice sounded hollow in her own ears. "They will be able to cover more ground that way. They will find Davey."

"Do you trust in men?" The woman speaking was Nancy Troyer, Preacher Abraham's wife. They lived north of the Schrocks, near Shipshewana Lake in Newbury Township. "The Good Book tells us to trust in God alone."

Mamm reached out a hand to grasp Naomi's folded ones. "We trust in God, and we also trust in the ways he provides for his will to be done. More men means that they will be able to go farther in their search."

The morning passed. Naomi's head ached with the constant pain of a grinding millstone. The aroma of stew cooking in the kitchen drifted out the open door, but Naomi refused the plate Mattie brought to her at noon. The other women talked together, but the words of their murmured conversation made no sense to Naomi's aching head. She kept her gaze on the place past the barn where Cap had disappeared so long ago and waited. As the afternoon wore on, some of the gathered women went home to tend to their chores. Still Naomi waited.

The sun had set and the twilight was growing purple when the men returned, trudging up the road. Cap walked straight to Naomi just as he had the day before. Once again the searchers went home. Mamm went into the house with Henry, and Daed followed, stopping only to lay his hand on Naomi's head. His gentle touch brought dampness to her eyes, but she refused to cry. Crying meant giving in to the fear that she would never see her son again.

Cap stepped up onto the porch. He sat in Mamm's chair, next to her, and took her hands in his. "I'm not going to give up, Naomi."

"The rest are, though. I heard them talking."

He was silent for a long moment. He laced her fingers through his. "They have chores to do. It's planting time."

"You found nothing? No sign?"

He stroked the back of her hand with his thumb, but didn't answer her question. "He's out there somewhere." His voice was rough, strained. "He didn't just disappear."

The tears threatened again. "He can't be . . . gone. What will I do without him?"

Cap slipped his arm around her shoulders and pulled her to him. "What did you do before he came?"

Naomi sniffed. "I was so lonely. Mattie and Jacob . . . you don't know how hard it is to watch your younger sister fall in love. When Davey came, when he needed me so much, I knew he was a gift from God."

"Why would a beautiful woman like you be lonely?"

She shook her head. "I'm not beautiful."

He rubbed her hand with his thumb again. "Why would you say that?"

"You know I'm plain, and I'll always be plain." She lifted her free hand to her cast eye, then let it drop. "I'm more than plain."

Cap rested his chin on her head. "You'll always be beautiful to me. I've never known someone like you. Your eyes are lovely." He shrugged. "I know your cast eye is there, but I only see you. Naomi. A beautiful woman and a wonderful mother."

His words washed over her hurting heart like a soothing balm. She leaned into his strength, drawing warmth and comfort from him. A man like Cap thought she was beautiful? It was a notion that tempted her to accept it without question.

The balm turned cold as the memory of Davey's disappearance jolted her. She had forgotten. For a brief moment, she had forgotten Davey. A sob rose in her throat before she could stop it. Naomi pulled her hands away from his and rose from her seat. She clung to the railing at the edge of the porch and stared into the twilight woods all around them.

Cap stood behind her and laid a hand on her shoulder, but she shook him off.

"You don't understand. No one does. How can I be a mother when I let my boy wander off on his own?" Naomi let Cap turn her toward him, but she couldn't look up into his eyes. "I've failed him. God trusted Davey to me, and I've failed."

Gentle hands squeezed her shoulders. "It isn't your fault. Davey is a boy, and boys don't think about their actions sometimes."

"That doesn't make a difference. I'm responsible for him. Me."

Cap drew her toward him until she leaned into his chest. He was solid, strong, and confident. Without his presence, she would sink into the ground.

"Memmi!"

Davey?

Naomi looked toward the road where it sloped down toward the river. Two figures were walking, and one was a boy. She pushed past Cap and ran. Through the rough grass of the yard, onto the road. Davey ran to meet her and barreled into her arms. She held him against her until he struggled free, but she still couldn't keep from stroking his hair, straightening his shirt, caressing his cheek. Her son was home.

Cap was behind her, and the rest of the family gathered around, everyone talking at once, until Daed's voice broke through.

"Thank you."

Daed spoke in English to the man who had brought Davey home. Davey wiggled out of Naomi's caresses and went to the man, taking his hand. The Indian was old, his face dark and lined with wrinkles. He was dressed in ragged cloths wrapped around his waist and legs, but his chest was bare. His hair was gray and long, framing his face. Even though his age was apparent, he held himself straight and tall as he laid a hand on Davey's shoulder and looked at Daed.

"Smart boy. Good boy. He found the way home."

"We have stew for supper. Won't you join us?"

The old Indian shook his head. "A long trail waits for me. I must go."

Without another word, he turned and

walked away.

Mamm hugged Naomi. "It's a miracle. Davey is safe."

"Ja, a miracle." She watched Davey as Daed hugged him, then Henry. The boy's face glowed. He was muddy, and his shirt was torn in a few places, but he was home.

Cap joined the Schrock family as they crowded into the house for a late supper.

"We'll let Davey eat his stew, and then he can tell us what happened," Eli had said.

Cap stood against the wall behind Henry's chair and watched Davey shovel spoonful after spoonful of the savory chunks of venison and vegetables into his mouth as if he hadn't eaten in a week.

"Are you so hungry, Davey?" Naomi asked. She sat next to him on the bench on the opposite side of the table, her arm around him.

"It's been a long time since dinner, and we only had some roots that Crow Flies dug out of the ground."

"Roots!" Lydia said, shaking her head. "Roots and berries, that's all they eat."

Eli grinned at Davey. "Ja, Lydia. Roots, just like we eat. Carrots and potatoes!"

Cap joined in the laughter as Davey finally

put his spoon down and leaned against Naomi.

Henry leaned forward. "Tell us what happened. We've been looking all over for you. Where were you?"

"The boy needs his sleep," Naomi said. "He'll tell us in the morning."

Davey sat up. "I'm not so tired." He turned to Naomi. "Can I stay up? I want to tell you about Crow Flies."

Naomi relented as Eli said, "Go ahead."

"I wanted to go fishing —"

"You should never have done that," Naomi said. "What if you had fallen in?"

"Let him talk," Cap said, and Naomi looked at him. Her face was flushed. Her fear was turning to anger now that Davey was home and safe. "You can discuss the details with him later."

Naomi nodded, and Davey went on.

"I did fall in."

Naomi covered her mouth with her hand, but Davey kept talking.

"I almost drowned. The water was . . . was like a horse that keeps going one way when you want it to go another. It bumped me on the rocks." He pulled his shirt up and stood to show them a sickening purple-and-green bruise on his ribs. He sat again and continued his story. "I didn't know how far the river went, but I just kept going and going until there was a tree across the river. I got caught in the branches."

Naomi smoothed his hair away from the scratches on his face.

"I was almost asleep, so I don't remember much, but Crow Flies found me and took me to his camp." He turned to Naomi. "I threw up, Mamm. My chest hurt bad. But Crow Flies made me feel better."

"How did he do that?"

"He gave me some tea. It tasted bad, but I drank it. Then I slept for a long time. When I woke up, Crow Flies fed me and showed me how to hunt and do things in the woods. Then we went to sleep again, and then this morning Crow Flies said men were looking for me and I had to go home. And so we walked and walked and walked. It was getting dark, but then we came to the road and the place where we went fishing, and I knew how to get home from there."

Davey looked at Cap. "Were you really looking for me? Was Crow Flies right?"

"We looked for two days, Davey. All of us did." Cap swallowed. He couldn't say any more.

Eli leaned forward in his chair. "You know

what you did was wrong, don't you, Davey?"

Davey caught his lower lip between his teeth, then looked at Eli. "But no one told me not to go fishing alone."

No one spoke as Eli held Davey's gaze for a long minute. "But you knew it was wrong."

Davey nodded.

Cap looked from the boy's scratched and bruised face to a torn fingernail covered in dried blood. Would he learn from this episode, or would he still be as careless as ever?

Eli sighed. "We are thankful to our Father in heaven that you were returned to us safely, and I think your experience is punishment enough." He and Naomi exchanged glances and she nodded her agreement.

Davey yawned and Naomi stood. "This boy needs to get to bed."

Lydia kissed Davey's head as Naomi led him to the ladder, and Eli patted his shoulder as he walked by. Cap watched every step, every movement until Davey was up the ladder and in the loft. His eyes filled and he wiped the tears away. Davey's safe return was a miracle.

He slipped out the door as the Schrock family finished their meal. He paused on the porch. The trail home was dark, quiet, and lonely. In no hurry to leave the comfortable sound of the voices that carried out to him, he leaned against the porch rail.

The stars blazed above, just as they had the night before, but tonight they were glorious. Almost as if they were celebrating Davey's homecoming too. As if God was celebrating along with the Schrocks. Cap smiled. Henry had gone out to take the news to their neighbors as soon as Davey had gone up to his bed, so by now the whole neighborhood was celebrating and thanking God.

He chewed at his lip. Had God had a hand in this? In Davey's surviving the rushing river waters? The near drowning? He closed his eyes. He had prayed that God would lead him to Davey, to let him find the boy. But instead an old Indian had found him, cared for him, and brought him home.

Many times over the last couple days Martha's face had appeared in his thoughts. The hours he had spent praying for God to let her live, to give him the power to hold on to her life, had been wasted. Martha had died. His son had died. Nothing he had tried would save them.

Saving Davey, finding him alive, would have atoned for his failure so many years ago, but he hadn't been able to do that either. No matter how hard he tried, he wasn't good enough. He never accomplished what he set out to do. God — if there was a God — seemed to be working against him at every turn.

Soft footsteps behind him alerted him to Naomi's presence.

"Davey was asleep before he even laid down, I think."

"He was a tired boy."

Cap could see Naomi's face in the starlight. She should have been smiling, but instead a frown held sway over her features. She barely glanced at the stars above before she fixed her eyes on the dark forest that surrounded them.

"He came home." Cap picked a sliver of wood from the porch rail and twirled it between his fingers.

Naomi didn't answer, but sniffled a little.

"You should be celebrating. What is wrong?"

"I am glad he's home, and so thankful that God brought him back to me. But it shouldn't have happened in the first place. If I wasn't so wrapped up in learning how to set up Annalise's loom . . . if I had been watching him more closely . . . I could have kept him from —"

Cap threw the sliver into the yard and grabbed Naomi's hand. "Come with me."

He pulled her hand into the crook of his elbow and led her to the road. Turning toward the river, he guided her around the stumps and other rough spots in the road. The starlight was so bright that he could pick out his route between the shadows and the stumps glowing silver and gray.

"Where are we going?"

"I want you to see where Davey disappeared." He pulled closer. "I have to admit I had given up hope of finding him alive. I thought —" Cap's voice broke. Was that why he hadn't found Davey? He had been searching for a pale corpse instead of a living, vibrant boy. "Forgive me."

Naomi stopped and turned toward him. "Forgive you for giving up hope? How could any of us have held on to hope that we would find him alive?" She wrapped her free hand around his arm and hugged it. "You never gave up looking for him." She turned and started walking again. "I was afraid we would never find him. That he had disappeared without a sign of what had happened, no trail to follow." She shivered. "I don't know if I could have lived, not knowing."

Cap continued down the slope to the ford

through the river. The waxing moon, a silver sliver in the western sky, gave no light, but the spot where he and Henry had taken Davey fishing on Monday was as clear as the road had been in the starlight. The log where he and Davey had sat, the dark eddy where Henry had said the big fish lurked, and the spot where he had found Davey's footprints leading into the water yesterday afternoon.

"This is it. This is where Davey went into the river. If his disappearance is anyone's fault, it's mine. I'm the one who convinced you to let him go fishing. I'm the one who refused to take him again on Tuesday." Cap took a deep breath. "If I had gone fishing with him, he wouldn't have tried to go on his own. He wouldn't have been down here by himself."

Naomi stood in silence, watching the rushing water. The river splashed over the ford and rushed past them on its spring journey north to swell other rivers with its flood.

When she spoke, it was a whisper. "So either both of us are to blame, or neither of us."

Cap squeezed her hand as they stood by the spring-swelled flood.

Naomi shuddered. "He was in that?"

Cap nodded, his hand holding hers, still tucked in his elbow. He watched the churning water, dark and oily in the starlight, looking nearly as solid as the soil it carried with it. He could imagine the strength of the current pulling at Davey, rushing him from one rock to another.

"I don't know how he survived, but he did." Cap stroked the back of Naomi's hand.

"Thanks to Crow Flies."

Cap squeezed her hand. "Thanks to Crow Flies. We were lucky that old Indian happened to be close by."

"Some would say that God was watching over him."

"Maybe." Cap took a step back from the river, guiding Naomi to a drier spot to stand. "But if God had been watching out for the boy, he would never have come to the river alone."

God was so distant that there wasn't any way that he cared about a lost boy any more than he cared about a dying mother and her child.

8

Naomi let Davey sleep as long as he wanted the next day while she and Mamm caught up on the chores they had neglected while Davey was missing.

As she worked in the garden, planting lettuce in the row she had just hoed in the soft soil, her eyes strayed to the road, to the way Davey had gone down to the river. And the direction he had come from when he had been miraculously returned to her.

She wiped her eyes with the hem of her apron and went back to dropping the tiny seeds in the furrow, one by one.

It had been a miracle. How else could she explain how the old Indian had found Davey and cared for him? An old Indian man that she had never seen before and then had disappeared into the dark night?

Someone was looking after her boy. That was the only explanation.

Davey wandered out to the garden just as

Naomi dropped the last seed in the furrow and covered it.

"Good morning. You slept for a long time." Naomi gathered him close to her for a hug, then brushed his hair out of his eyes. He would need a haircut soon. "Did you have your breakfast?"

"Grossmutti made hoecakes for me, with maple syrup."

His favorite. Mamm was spoiling the boy, but Naomi would have done the same thing.

"Can I go to Cap's?"

Her stomach swirled. "Alone?"

"I won't be alone. Cap will be there."

Naomi glanced toward the trail leading to Cap's clearing. Davey had walked that trail many times, running through the woods along the shaded path, and had never gotten lost. But today, the thought of him slipping out of her sight made her fingers clutch at his shirt.

She took a deep breath. "I will go with you."

"Why? Do you want to see Cap too?"

Davey's question startled her. She had only intended to make sure Davey reached his destination safely, but to see Cap . . . Why did the thought of seeing him settle her turning stomach?

"Ja, I want to see Cap. Run and tell

Grossmutti where we're going while I put the hoe away."

Naomi had grown warm as she worked in the sunny garden, but the air was still cool in the shade of the trees in the woods. Davey ran ahead of her down the trail until she called to him.

"Not so far ahead. Stay where I can see you."

Davey stopped to wait for her. "Why? I want to get to Cap's before you and surprise him."

"I just don't want to let you out of my sight." She tousled his hair as she caught up to him and they continued down the path together. "I missed you . . ." Tears filled her eyes with a sudden flood that she dashed away before they could trickle down her cheeks. She swallowed. "While you were gone, I longed to see you so much. Now I don't want you to get too far away."

"All right." He walked next to her. "Did you really miss me?"

"Of course I did."

He grinned up at her. "I didn't have to do my chores."

"If you think you're going to get out of doing your chores by running off into the woods, you had better think again." Naomi forced herself to frown.

"Crow Flies gave me chores to do. He said everyone does chores, even Indians."

"What kind of chores did he have you do?"

"Gather wood, mostly." Davey hopped over a fallen log. "He let me watch him skin a squirrel, but he wouldn't let me do it. He said I had to learn how to use a knife first." He looked up at her. "When can I use a knife, Memmi? Mose has a knife, and William does. I'm old enough, aren't I?"

A knife in the hands of her active seven-year-old? What would he ask for next? "I think we'll wait a while before you start carrying a knife."

"What if I need one? Crow Flies said every man needs a knife."

"That's Crow Flies. He's a grown man, living in the woods." Naomi didn't let herself think about what his camp might look like, or how Davey lived when he was with him. He was home now, and safe. That was all that mattered.

"There's Cap. I can see him." His eyes pleaded as he looked at her. "Can I go ahead now? Can I?"

"Go ahead."

Davey ran toward the clearing. Cap was on his roof, setting stones into the top of his chimney. As Davey ran toward him, he climbed down the ladder to meet the boy on the ground. When they met, Davey threw his arms around his friend and Cap picked him up, swinging him in a circle.

Naomi paused, watching the two of them together. If she didn't know better, she would think they were father and son, the way Cap knelt down as he talked with Davey. And the way Davey clung to his hand as he told Cap whatever story he had to share with his friend. This was what Davey missed. He had men in his life, but not a father. That was something she could never give him.

Cap looked up as she walked toward the pair and his smile grew larger. He looked as if he was happy to see her. As he started toward her, Davey's hand firmly in his, a warmth spread through her and the raw nerves from the last few days melted away. Cap had a way of putting her at ease, as if he lifted a burden from her shoulders whenever he came near.

"It's good to see you smiling this morning," he said. "Davey tells me that you've been working in the garden already."

"Mamm wanted to plant the lettuce yesterday, but —" She stopped. Davey didn't need to know how his disappearance had turned her life into a maelstrom.

"Can I go in your house to see the fireplace?" Davey hopped, waiting for Cap's answer.

"For sure." Cap laughed as Davey took off at a run. "There isn't much in there to see."

"He'll want to look up the chimney," Naomi said. Cap's laugh had swept away the last of her anxiety. "He's curious about everything."

"Next he'll want to climb the ladder to look down the chimney from the top."

Naomi's hand grabbed his arm. Her panic returned with that one sentence. "Don't let him. Cap, make sure he stays on the ground."

Cap laid his hand over hers. It felt strong and sure. "Don't worry. I won't let him go up there alone. I'll watch him."

Naomi chewed her lip. "I don't want him on the ladder at all. What if he falls?"

"I won't let him fall." He glanced at her face and then turned her toward him, his hands gripping her shoulders. "You can't wrap him in a layer of fleece, trying to protect him from any danger. He's a boy. He's going to get into scrapes, but that's part of growing up."

Naomi couldn't look in his eyes. "Davey is so young. He'll get hurt, or . . . worse. I have to protect him. He's all I have."

"Look at me."

At the demanding tone of his voice, Naomi lifted her gaze to his warm brown eyes.

"Davey is not all you have. You have a loving family, a church family, and neighbors." His Adam's apple bobbed as he swallowed. "You have me. I love Davey as if he was my own son."

He ran his thumb along her jawline. His voice dropped to a whisper. "You can count on me. I'll do my best to keep him safe."

Annalise frowned as Christian took his place at the table for dinner. What was bothering her now? He glanced at her again. The frown was gone. Perhaps he had only imagined it.

He rubbed at the sharp pain just above his ear, right where his hat brim rested. Perhaps he could stretch the brim out a bit. Ease the pressure.

William and Peter ran into the kitchen, laughing and shaking wet hands at each other. His headache roared in response.

"How many times have I told you boys to use the towel on the wash bench?" He half stood, leaning over the table. "You've splashed water all over the floor. Go and dry off and come back in."

His head throbbed. The boys' sober looks struck him in the heart. Not sober. Scared. They were scared of their daed. He sank back into his chair.

Christian rubbed his face as Annalise took control. He leaned on his elbows, shading his eyes against the bright light of the open door. She was as capable and strong as she had ever been, but he felt so . . . old. Worn. His heart pounded in his ears.

"William, Peter, do as your daed says. Go finish drying your hands, and then come back to the table quietly. Save the noise for outside."

As they left, Margli and Annalise lifted the twins onto their stools.

She laid a hand on his shoulder. "Are you feeling all right?"

Ne. He didn't feel all right. But he had left the horses hitched to the plow in the upper field, tied in the shade with their noses in the feed bags. He had to eat his dinner and get back to work.

"Ja, I'm fine." He pushed away from the table. "Not . . ." He swayed as he rose from his chair and he grabbed the corner of the table to steady his balance. "I'm not hungry."

He gripped the table harder, but his fingers turned to jelly as the floor rushed toward him.

All was black. Small noises intruded, but as if they were filtered through a wool batting. Christian opened his eyes.

He was lying in bed. Midday sunlight shone around the edges of the window shutters.

Ja, for sure. He had fallen. But the horses . . . He had to get back to plowing the field. He tried to sit up, but his eyes still stared at the ceiling.

He hadn't moved.

"Christian?"

Annalise's voice was quiet. Strained. He tried to turn toward her, but his head didn't move. She slid into his field of vision.

"You're awake."

She smiled and he smiled back. He willed his hand to take hers, but his arm didn't move.

Her smile faded. "Your eyes are open. Can you hear me?"

He tried to answer, but only his chin moved. Or did it?

Annalise stroked the hair off his forehead. He could feel her warm, dry hand against his skin.

"Relax. Rest. I'll send Jacob for the doctor."

She was gone before he could ask. Why

the doctor? He had fainted. Had probably been working too hard. But the field needed to be plowed.

He tried to sit up again, but his body wouldn't cooperate. He tried to raise his left arm, but it stayed on the bed. He tried to lift his right hand and almost wept when he saw his hand come into his field of vision. Why couldn't he move the other one?

Someone came into the room. He tried to twist in the bed to see who it was, but nothing happened.

"Daed," Margli said, "I've brought you some water."

Her face loomed over him, thin and pale. Had Margli been ill? At dinner she had been fine, helping Rachael onto her stool.

Margli put a spoon against his lips. "Here, Daed. Swallow this."

Water trickled into his mouth and he swallowed.

"Mamm said to keep you company until the doctor comes." She spooned another trickle of water into his mouth.

He worked his mouth around the water. *Why?* But no words came out.

"Jacob finished plowing the upper field yesterday and is planting the corn today. Mamm said you would want to know."

Corn in the upper field? It hadn't been

plowed yesterday. He had just started it this morning, before dinner. He took another mouthful of water.

"That's enough for now. The doctor said three spoonfuls at a time."

The doctor had been here earlier? He tried to remember, but his thoughts were slow. Molasses slow. His eyes closed.

"Daed?" Margli's voice rose. Scared. Frightened.

He opened his eyes and tried to smile. *It's all right. I'm going to sleep now.*

The next time he opened his eyes, a strange man stood near his bed. He talked to Annalise as she sat near his knees on the bed. The words didn't make sense.

"Nonverbal . . . bed . . . sores . . . bathe . . . temporary."

An Englisch doctor.

And then a word that he understood. "Paralyzed."

Was the doctor talking about him? He closed his eyes again. Was he paralyzed? Of course. That was why his left hand wouldn't obey him, and why words didn't travel past his thoughts.

"Can you hear me, Christian?" the doctor asked.

He opened his eyes. The Englisch doctor leaned toward him. He tried to nod.

"If you understand what I'm saying, blink your eyes."

Christian closed, then opened his eyes. The doctor smiled and turned to Annalise.

"That's very good. You'll be able to talk to him and he can answer yes or no. Do you understand?"

Annalise nodded. Her eyes were shining with the tears that spilled down her cheeks. Christian reached his right hand toward her and plucked at her shawl.

The doctor smiled. "He's doing well, considering. The apoplexy he suffered has caused some damage, but the fact that he's alive now gives me hope that he may pull through this."

Apoplexy. The word rang through Christian's head.

"Will he . . ." Annalise choked back a sob. "Will he be bedridden for the rest of his life?"

Christian balled the edge of her shawl in his fist. It would be better if the seizure had killed him.

"We won't know for some time. I've seen patients in his condition recover so that they are able to function quite well. But there's always the possibility that this is as much progress as he ever makes."

Annalise stood as the doctor buckled his

satchel closed and put on his hat. She followed him to the door. Christian strained to hear her question, but her voice was hushed. The doctor's response was a slow shake of his head, and then he was gone.

When Annalise came back to the side of his bed, Christian tried to smile. Could Annalise see it?

Don't cry, he wanted to say, but Annalise cried anyway. Christian closed his eyes. Pieces of memory swirled through his mind, refusing to light on the tenuous surface. Tired. So tired. He groped with his good hand, searching for her arm. He pulled her down and pressed her head against his chest as his eyes closed. Her sobs faded as he drifted into sleep.

Cap stretched, extending his arms out from under the covers. No wind to cool his bare hands, no dew to dampen the blankets. The pulse of the glowing coals in the fireplace. He was finally home.

Sitting up, he rubbed his face to wakefulness. Maybe not home, but at least he lived in a house again. A comfortable house, made with his own hands and the help of his neighbors, on his own land. After he had finished the chimney on Saturday afternoon, he had built the first fire and cooked his supper of stew in his fireplace. He had even baked a corn cake to go with his celebration meal. A celebration of not only a house he could live in, but of Davey's safe return.

Today . . . fully awake, he remembered. Today was the Sabbath and the Sabbath meeting at the Gingerich farm in Clinton Township. He didn't know the way, so he had arranged to walk with the Schrocks and the other neighbors. He would need to hurry if he was to meet them in time.

As he washed, he thought about the events of the two weeks since the last Sabbath meeting. The loss of his horses paled in comparison to Davey's misadventure. But the news about Christian Yoder overshadowed everything else. Folks talked about him as if he was gone already rather than waiting for death's call. Naomi and Lydia had visited yesterday afternoon, and from what they said, Christian was awake but not able to get out of bed or speak.

"The doctor told Annalise that there is hope," Naomi had said the night before. "He said every day that Christian holds on, the more hope they could have that he would recover."

"Recover?" Cap had shaken his head. "Recover to spend the rest of his days in bed?"

162

"Whatever the Lord wills," Naomi had said.

Cap paused in his shaving, feeling for missed whiskers along his upper lip. He had seen what the Lord could will, and it seemed very random. Some people were struck and died instantly. Some lingered for a few days before succumbing. Once in a great while, a person would recover, somewhat. They might recover their speech or the ability to walk. But the effects of the apoplexy were still there, like a bone that had broken and mended crooked.

He liked Christian. He liked the Yoder family. Jacob would have to shoulder the bulk of his father's farm as well as his own, at least until Peter grew old enough to do the work. And of course, the neighbors would help.

Splashing water from his basin onto his face to wash away the soap, Cap caught himself. He was one of the Yoders' neighbors. It was his duty to help also.

He scrubbed himself dry with the rough towel. It fell to the church members to look out for one another, and hadn't Christian worked alongside everyone else when they built this cabin? Of course Cap would volunteer his time.

The sun had risen by the time Cap had

finished his few chores. Without the horses to care for, he only had water to haul from the river and his cabin to redd up.

He missed the horses, especially when he needed to move a tree he had just felled or plow the open space between the stumps to plant his oats. Eli had said he was welcome to borrow one of his teams, but he needed a team of his own. Even with as much work as he had to do before the end of the year, he would have to make time for the trip back to Ohio. He hadn't thought he would need the money from the sale of his farm so soon, but he had to have a team of horses to do his work.

He changed from his everyday clothes into his Sunday white shirt and black suit, carefully brushing off the dust that had accumulated during the house building over the last two weeks. He headed down the trail toward the Schrocks', taking one last look around the clearing. Everything was tidy, just as it should be on a Sabbath morning.

The six-mile walk to the Gingeriches' was pleasant in the company of Naomi and her family, if subdued. No one visited in the low tones normal for the Sabbath morning walk. Jacob and Mattie Yoder walked in the rear of the group. Jacob's face was strained and tired, and Mattie's matched his. Cap dropped back to walk beside them.

"How is Christian this morning?"

Jacob shrugged. "About the same. He eats the broth and gruel Mamm fixes for him, but I can see him wasting away, even after only a few days in bed."

Cap walked in silence while Mattie hurried to catch up with Naomi. Christian was a good church member. A leader in the settlement. He had lived his life the right way, following the Ordnung in all he did. And yet tragedy had struck his family more than once, from what Naomi had told him. But Jacob showed no bitterness, only concern and grief.

A shudder caught Cap and he stopped walking. If God could strike a man like Christian, what hope did he have? Christian had kept his part of the bargain, but God had still struck him down. And yet, he still believed. Jacob still believed. He shook his head. It didn't make sense. Cap knew what loss was. When God had destroyed his family, he had clung to the Ordnung. When his horses were stolen, he had followed the church teaching of nonresistance, even though the anger and worry remained. But he had been obedient to what he had been taught. If he followed the rules, then everything would be well, even in times of loss.

And then he had almost lost Davey . . .

Jacob waited for him and he jogged along the road to catch up.

Cap fell into step beside the other man. "What happened to your daed, don't you think it was a bit unfair?"

"Unfair?" Jacob glanced at him.

"Your family . . . your daed is a good man. He follows the Ordnung and is a good husband and father. So don't you think his illness is unfair?"

Jacob stared at the ground. "I would say it is, but I'm not God."

"I'm not sure God even cares about any of us."

"You question God's goodness?" Jacob's face held a slight smile.

Cap stopped and Jacob faced him in the middle of the road. "A man, sick and crippled, is lying in his bed, possibly dying, and you can say that is God's goodness?"

The other man nodded. "The Good Book teaches us that God uses everything that happens for good, even if we don't see it."

Cap stopped the question before it left his lips. The question of whether God even existed. Instead, he said, "In my experience, not everything that happens is good."

Jacob walked on down the road again and

Cap joined him. They were far behind the group now, but not out of sight.

"Just because something happens that seems bad for us, does that mean God isn't good?"

Cap stumbled over a tree root. Jacob wasn't making any sense. "When my wife died . . ." He stopped. He didn't want to talk about this. He never wanted to talk about Martha.

"When your wife died, that was a terrible thing."

He let the words tumble out. "Not only my wife, but our son also."

Jacob made a small noise, but let him continue.

"I knew that couldn't be from God, if there is a God." He shook his head, as confused as ever. "I don't know." He stopped again and waited for Jacob to look at him. "But I do know that if there is a God, I'm supposed to follow his law and obey his commandments. And I will do that the best I can. But when I see a man like Christian suffering, I wonder what hope there is for a man like me." He forced a half smile at the stricken look on Jacob's face. "I guess there isn't any, is there?" He shrugged. "But yet, I still follow the church and its teaching. I don't know what else to do."

"Cap —"

He turned his back on Jacob and continued down the road to the Sabbath meeting.

9

Shem smiled as he leaned into his bowl of bean soup after the worship service. News of Christian Yoder's seizure had rippled through the congregation before the services even started that morning, and now, as the men visited around the dinner table, it was the topic of conversation. He couldn't have planned things better.

"Who is plowing his fields and getting his crops in?" The question came from Elias Hertzler, a friend of Christian's, from what Shem could glean from the conversation so far.

"I'll be working Daed's land," Jacob said. The young man's face was pale, as if he hadn't slept well.

Shem scraped the last spoonful of soup from his bowl. "That puts quite a burden on you, doesn't it?"

Jacob shot a look in his direction. "I don't mind. I'll help wherever I'm needed."

"We all will," Eli Schrock put in. "We'll do Christian's work as well as our own. That's how we do things."

Tall Peter Gingerich cleared his throat. "Not that I don't want to help, but we're not close neighbors. The Yoder place is six miles from here."

"No one would expect the farmers in Clinton Township to help the same as Christian's close neighbors in LaGrange County." Shem kept his face neutral, with a slight frown to show his concern. "It would take an entire day for you to make the long journey there, put in a few hours' work, and then come home again in time to do your own chores." He looked around the circle of faces. "The eastern half of the community will need to be the ones to do the work."

Elias Hertzler frowned at his soup bowl but didn't say anything.

Tall Peter flushed, as if he was embarrassed, but Shem saw the relief on his face.

Cap's face was red as well, but his lowered brow showed his growing anger. Shem nodded to himself. Good. The seeds had been sown.

He rose from the table as Susan Gingerich took his empty bowl to be washed. She didn't look at him as she went on with her work, but her face was a pretty shade of pink. She knew he was watching her.

Following the other men out into the spring sunshine, he worked his way to Elias, Tall Peter, and another man Shem didn't recognize.

"I hardly know the man," Tall Peter was saying.

"But he's a member of our community." Elias pounded one hand with his fist to emphasize his point. "We help each other, don't we?"

"Of course we do," the stranger said. "I'm going to talk to Jacob about when he needs my help with Christian's farm."

"That's fine for you," Peter said. "You live closer to him than we do. But I'm still clearing my land, and I can't afford a day or more away from my work. It will mean my family won't have enough food next year."

"You must look after your farm," Shem said, nodding his approval at Tall Peter's words. "The Good Book says that we must be responsible for our own families."

The stranger stared at him.

"We haven't met yet, have we?" Shem put a hand out to shake the other man's. "I'm Preacher Shem Fischer, from Ontario."

"Yost Bontrager," the man said as he shook Shem's hand.

Yost's handshake was firm. Purposeful. That handshake told Shem this man could be a strong opposition. He'd have to get him on his side, and soon.

"You're a minister?"

Shem smiled his friendliest smile. "For sure."

"I have a cousin in Ontario. Daniel Troyer. Do you know him?"

Shem kept his smile. "Daniel was the man who told me about your settlement here, and your need for more ministers." He felt the blood draining from his face. Daniel had told him that his cousin had left the settlement and moved farther west, to Iowa.

Yost stroked his beard. "I told Daniel about the lack of ministers. But I also told him about the new settlers from Ohio and the minister that was coming with them. I never asked him to send anyone."

In spite of his best efforts, Shem's smile faded. "He didn't send me. I wanted to move my family west, so I came ahead to see how things were."

"How long have you been a minister, Preacher Shem?" Elias's question diverted Yost's scrutiny.

"Almost two years."

Yost's eyebrows raised. "And you are thinking of leaving your community already?

Don't they need you there?"

"I have already left Ontario, with their blessing. They felt I would find my calling in one of the new settlements in Illinois, or here in Indiana."

"You mentioned a family," Elias said. "Will they be joining you?"

"Once I find a place to settle and build a house." Shem paused. Priscilla had said she would never leave Ontario. "My wife is . . . sickly. She needs to stay with her parents for a time."

Shem moved on to the next group of men, along with Tall Peter.

"I hope you'll choose your land from the farms available here in Clinton Township," Peter said as they walked. "Two of the other ministers in our district live in Newbury Township, and only Preacher Elam lives here. We would feel more like a part of the community with an equal number of ministers living here among us."

"That is a fine idea." Shem had noticed that the Gingeriches' farm already looked prosperous even though they had moved to the area so recently. "I would be happy to look around this area."

"Where are you staying now?"

Shem had been offered a bed at Abraham Troyer's in Newbury Township when he first arrived but had preferred to be on his own. Being under the Troyers' roof would mean good food and a warm bed but put him in too close proximity to a man he didn't really like.

"I'm camping out, not really staying in one place very long."

Tall Peter swung around to face him. "Didn't anyone on that end of the district offer you a place in their home?"

Shem shrugged. Let Peter think what he would.

"You'll stay with us, then. We have room in the loft with the boys. You'll have your own bed, of course, and eat with the family." Tall Peter smiled. "It will be good to have a preacher under my roof."

He clapped Shem on the shoulder and led him to a group of Clinton Township men. As he joined them, Shem cast a glance around the Gingerich farm again. Susan was sitting with the other young women around a table in the yard. Her blonde hair shone in the sunlight where it peeked out from under her kapp. He would enjoy staying with the Gingeriches for a time.

Wednesday morning dawned cool and clear, with the promise of a fine day ahead. Cap had spent the previous two days planting corn in the cleared spaces between the tree stumps on his land with the help of Eli's horses, and now had time for another necessary job. He needed to replace the blanket covering the doorway with a real door. As soon as he finished breakfast, he set up the sawhorses and started picking through the logs left from building his cabin.

A straight log would be best, but most of those had been used for the cabin. He shifted the logs from the pile one at a time until he found one that suited him. A nice piece of maple, too narrow for the cabin walls, but it would do nicely for the door once he sawed it into planks.

He had just begun his first cut when Jacob hailed him from the path through the woods.

"You're getting an early start this morning." Jacob jogged over and steadied the log while Cap continued sawing.

"No better day to put up a door." Cap grunted the words as he sawed.

"For sure, better now than when a storm is blowing." Jacob's voice rose so Cap could hear him over the noise of the saw. "Jed Smith came by this morning. He says he wants to talk to all of the settlers in the area about a gang of bandits."

Cap stopped sawing. "Bandits?" The sight

of the two men opening his tool chest flashed in his memory.

"That's what Jed said. He's at Eli's now. Will you come?"

"Ja, for sure. I'll finish this board and then come with you."

Jacob held the log until Cap had sawed the first board off. He hung the saw in the wagon bed and followed Jacob through the woods to the Schrock farm. The men had gathered near the barn, standing with their hands clasped behind them and facing each other in a circle, listening to an Englisch man speak. Jacob and Cap joined the circle as the man continued.

"I know this gang, and I'm sorry that I do. Their leader is William Smith, my cousin. He's a bad one. Always been trouble."

"Why do you think they're going to cause problems for us? We're peaceful folk and have nothing worth stealing," Josef said. The other men in the circle nodded their heads in agreement.

"You have horses, don't you? Stores of grain? Cash money?" Jed turned and spat on the ground behind him before he looked from face to face around the circle. "The only way to keep the gang from attacking is to put up a strong defense. Arm ourselves.

Set a watch." He spat again.

Cap shifted from one foot to the other. "Jed is right about the gang. They've been to my farm."

"See? We need to be ready to fight." Jed stomped his foot in emphasis.

Jacob gripped Cap's shoulder. "They're the ones who took your horses?"

"Ja, Blau and Betza."

"But they didn't hurt you? Or threaten to?"

Cap felt the cabin wall digging into his back. "I don't think so, but I didn't resist them."

Should he mention that one of them had spoken Deitsch?

"Cap did well," said Eli Schrock, nodding in his direction. "We won't fight this gang. Nonresistance has been our way for two hundred years and more. We won't change that now."

Jed's face grew red as he stared at Eli. "You won't even defend your farms or your families?"

Eli looked at the ground, but with no hint of shame. "We will not disobey Christ's teaching."

Jed looked from man to man. Cap watched him with a steady gaze. Eli was right, they must do as the church taught, but a stab of worry and fear twisted his gut. He had been tested once and knew the rage that had threatened to take over. If the gang came again, looking for more to steal, would he respond as the church taught? Or would his fear and anger win out? His fists clenched and released.

The Englisch man raised one dirty finger, pointing it at Eli. "You would stand by as this gang attacked? You would let them run over you without fighting back?"

"We can only live as the Good Book teaches."

Jed threw his hat on the ground, revealing a bald head circled with a fringe of greasy black hair. "So you're leaving it up to me to defend the whole neighborhood?"

Eli's voice was quiet as he spoke for the group. "We are not asking you to defend us. We don't want you to take any action on our part. When we show that we aren't willing to fight, perhaps these men will leave us alone."

"Perhaps?" Jed's voice rose to a higher pitch. "You don't know these gangs. Outlaws strike at the weak, the vulnerable. They'll love it when you don't fight because that just makes it easier for them to take what they want."

"Then let them take it." Eli's gaze silenced

Jed's sputtering. "We will not fight. We rest in God's hands."

Jed picked up his worn felt hat and thrust it back on his head. "So be it." He turned and stalked toward the road and his home.

The group was silent. Cap studied the faces of his new neighbors. Some watched Jed as he left the road, following a trail through the woods to his land, some had bowed their heads in prayer. Solomon Plank rubbed at a spot on his thumb.

"Nonresistance is all well and good as far as it goes." Solomon kept his gaze fixed on his hands as he spoke. "But what if the bandits go farther than stealing from us? What if they turn to murder too?"

Eli sighed. "Our way is nonresistance. We cannot disobey Christ out of fear."

"You do as you wish." Solomon glanced around the group. "I'm going to keep my rifle within reach."

Josef ground his toe into the packed soil of the barnyard. "You would kill a man to protect your property?"

Solomon's voice was quiet as he spoke the words Cap wanted to say. "I would be willing to defend my family, if someone threatened to do them harm."

Eli's voice broke through the silence. "Think of this, Solomon, and any others who might be tempted to walk the same path: If you or your loved ones are right before God and are killed by one of these bandits, what is the result? Your soul is safe for eternity in glory. But if you kill the man who attacks you, what happens to his unrepentant soul? It means for him an eternity of woe without a chance to be redeemed. Which is better?" He looked into the faces of each of the men around the circle. Cap couldn't meet his gaze.

"We are to pray for our enemies," Eli said after a long moment. "I will pray for these bandits. I will pray that they will see the error of their ways and will live lives pleasing to God."

"And we can pray that if they don't change, something will stop them from carrying out their depredations against us," Solomon added.

Eli smiled. "Ja, I will pray for that, also."

The circle broke into smaller groups. Jacob and Josef joined Cap just as Henry stepped up beside him.

"What do you think?" Henry said, looking from one to the other of them. "You've encountered them, Cap. Do you think Daed is right?"

Cap nodded. "It is a difficult thing to do, but Eli stated what the church teaches. We must follow the Ordnung."

"I think Eli is right too." Jacob stroked his beard. "It's the same thing my daed would say if he was here."

Henry shook his head. "I think I'd rather fight, even if the church does teach differently."

Jacob sighed. "I know what you mean, but fighting doesn't gain anything for us or our families. Remember when the horse thieves were trailing us on our way here to Indiana? We tried to protect our horses, but in the end your daed and mine were right. We left the outcome in God's hands, and he protected us."

"It was not an easy road to follow, though." Josef clapped his hand on Jacob's shoulder. "It was a time most difficult. We may be facing a time just as hard now, or worse."

Cap studied Josef. His wiry build belied the strength Cap had witnessed as the man worked tirelessly the day of the cabin raising. Cap had also observed the man with his young children, correcting them with gentle words when they misbehaved and holding them with loving arms when they needed comfort. Henry had told Cap the story of how Josef had been a redemptioner, coming to Pennsylvania to escape the wars in Europe when he was only fourteen, traveling alone across the ocean.

Even though Josef was still a young man, he had proven his worth in the short time Cap had known him. If they were going to face this trial Jed had warned them about with continued attacks from this gang, he would be glad to face it next to a man like Josef.

On Friday morning Annalise set the children to do their chores, then slipped into the bedroom to check on Christian. His eyes were closed in sleep. She moved into the room with quiet steps, but at the slight rustle of her skirts, her husband's eyes opened.

"Good morning."

Christian's eyes blinked twice as Annalise straightened the quilt that lay over him. He had lost weight since the apoplexy and — she bit her lip as she realized — he was growing weaker. He didn't attempt to reach out to her as she moved around the bed, but only followed her with his eyes.

"Would you like a drink of water?"

Two blinks. Annalise raised his head and shoulders and put the cup to his lips. Water went in his mouth, and his Adam's apple bobbed as he swallowed, but even more water spilled out onto the bedding. When she laid him back down on the pillow, he closed his eyes again. Just taking a drink had exhausted him.

The doctor's treatments didn't appear to be helping at all. Annalise touched his sunken cheek with the back of her hand. Cool. Almost too cool. She choked back a sob. He was dying right here in the bed, bit by bit, and there was nothing she could do to stop it.

Margli stood in the doorway of the bedroom. "Mamm, Dr. Samples is here."

"How are we today, Mrs. Yoder?" the doctor said in his booming voice. He strode into the sickroom as if his patient wasn't lying at death's door.

Annalise rose to meet him. "I'm afraid he isn't doing very well. I can't get him to eat anything, and he will drink hardly any water at all."

"Hmm. Yes." The doctor puffed out his bushy mustache. "Let's have a look at him."

He felt Christian's papery skin and lifted his eyelids to peer into the depths behind them. He held Christian's wrist to count his pulse. Through it all, Christian lay on the bed, watching.

Dr. Samples puffed out his mustache again, and then smoothed it down with one hand. "All we can do is try bleeding him again."

Christian squinted his eyes shut once, then stared at Annalise.

"You've already bled him three times, doctor, and it hasn't helped."

"That's the standard procedure for apoplexy, Mrs. Yoder." The doctor opened his bag and removed the tubes he used for the treatment. "The seizure your husband experienced was caused by too much blood in his system. When the weak blood vessel burst under the strain, it nearly killed him. The only solution is to keep draining the excess blood out."

Christian stared at Annalise. She knew his answer.

"No, doctor. We will not do this procedure again."

Christian relaxed against his pillow.

"But you can't do nothing. He will die."

"He may die with the bloodletting." Annalise straightened her back. "But whether he lives or dies is in God's hands. We will not do the procedure again."

Dr. Samples put the tubes back into his black bag, snapped it closed, and stood. "If that is what you wish."

He leveled his gaze at Annalise and she nearly changed her mind at the disapproving look on his face. If Christian should die . . . His pale face against the pillow strengthened her resolve. The bloodletting treatments were doing no good.

"That is what we both wish."

"I can offer you more bottles of my tonic. That will certainly help him."

Annalise suppressed a shudder. The first bottle she had bought from the doctor at his urging smelled so strongly of turpentine that she couldn't force herself to give it to Christian.

"No, thank you. We have enough."

"Well then." The doctor gazed down at Christian, then moved toward the door. "Send someone for me if you need my services again."

"Thank you, Doctor." Annalise followed him out to the kitchen where she put a two-bit piece in the man's outstretched hand.

She closed the door behind him and leaned against it. She had just turned away the only help she knew of, except to pray. And yet her prayers had brought no changes other than Christian's gradual weakening. And when he died —

She stopped herself. She wouldn't think about death. Not yet. Not until Christian took his last breath.

10

On Sunday morning Mamm had her woven hamper on the table when Naomi came out to help prepare breakfast.

"You must be taking food to the Yoders today." Naomi laid plates on the opposite end of the long table for the family's meal.

"Annalise needs all of our help," Mamm said as she laid three loaves of the bread she had baked yesterday on top of the nearly full basket. "With her family to take care of and Christian —" She bit her lip as she sank onto the bench.

Naomi gave Mamm a hug. "Christian can still recover. We don't know what God has planned."

"Ja, ja, ja." Mamm nodded and wiped her eyes with her handkerchief. "But sometimes it is God's will that one of his faithful ones dies. It could be that Christian is facing his last days, and poor Annalise has already lost so much."

"We will be able to help her with anything she needs. She knows that."

Mamm cleared her throat and tucked a towel over the loaves of bread. "Ja, she knows, but it doesn't take away the fear and the worry." She paused, looking out the open door toward the barn. "I would be so lonely if something happened to your daed. I can't imagine . . . poor Annalise . . ." She sniffed again and tucked the last corner of the towel into the basket.

"When are we going to the Yoders'?"

"After breakfast. I talked to Annalise yesterday, and she said to come and spend the whole day. The children can play while we visit." Mamm set the heavy hamper on the floor near the door. "Jacob and Josef have set up a bed of sorts on the front porch so that Christian can join us. She asked if your daed could read some Scripture, and that we would sing a hymn or two together. Christian would like that."

"He'll feel like he's part of things instead of being shut away in a sick room. Does that mean he's feeling stronger?" Naomi laid a fork at each place.

"Perhaps. We can only hope."

Mamm opened the oven door and took out the big pan full of corn cake that she had put in last night to bake overnight in the slow oven, leaving the pan of chicken stew until they took it to their neighbors for the noon meal. Then she stood back, surveying the table.

"All we need to do is pour the coffee, and then breakfast will be ready. Go call the men."

Naomi grabbed her shawl from the hook by the door and ran out into the morning air. Chores took much less time on Sunday mornings, since only the necessary tasks were done. Davey had gathered the eggs and had put the basket into the root cellar to keep cool, and then had gone into the barn to watch Henry and Daed feed the horses. She stopped at the barn door when she saw Cap kneeling on the barn floor next to her son, his arm around the boy's shoulders and Davey's arm flung around his neck, their heads close together as they watched the horses. If she didn't know better, she would think that Cap and Davey were the ones who belonged together. A long-forgotten coolness seeped into her mind, as if a wall of ice had risen between her and the scene before her. She was on the outside looking in again.

Arresting that thought, Naomi shook herself. Cap and Davey could be friends without her. If she was married, her son and husband would have things that they did without her. Cap and Davey were no different.

Still, watching them, the jealous pang only grew stronger. Davey was spending too much time with his friend. Naomi bit her lip as she thought of what that could mean for Davey's future — hunting and fishing trips, Cap teaching Davey to hitch up a team, clearing the land. All sorts of dangerous things where a boy like Davey could get hurt, or worse. Folks died in farming accidents every year.

And what would happen when Cap married again? He wouldn't shut Davey out of his life just because he had a new family. He might even entice Davey to come live with him and his wife as their family grew.

Leaving her alone.

Just then, Davey turned and saw her.

"Memmi!" He left Cap kneeling on the dirt floor and ran to her. "Cap has been telling me all about the horse he had when he was a boy. It was little, and he could ride it."

Cap dusted the dirt off his knees and walked over to join them. His smile was infectious as he tousled the boy's hair.

"It was a pony." His eyes didn't leave her face, even when Davey grabbed his hand in both of his and swung it back and forth. "My daed thought a pony cart would be a good way to teach my sisters and me to drive while we were still young."

"Can we get a pony?" Davey didn't let go of Cap's hand, but grabbed Naomi's with his other one. "I'd take care of it, I would."

"Hush, Davey, don't beg." Naomi felt her cheeks heating under Cap's gaze. "Tell Grossdatti and Henry that breakfast is ready."

"A pony would be good for him," Cap said as he walked back toward the house with her. "I need to look for a new team, and I could find a pony for Davey at the same time, if you want me to."

Naomi thought of the few coins in her purse, but the cost wasn't the only impediment. A pony could be dangerous, and her boy could get hurt. "Davey doesn't need a pony, and I wish you wouldn't mention it to him again. He becomes discontented so easily, and I don't want there to be something else he wants but will never have."

Cap stopped walking and pulled her toward him with a hand cupping her elbow. "If it's the cost you're worried about, I will pay for it. I have money from the sale of my farm in Ohio, so it is no hardship. I can get the pony when I go back there to buy my new team."

"He doesn't know how to ride or take care of a horse. He's too young."

"Davey is seven years old. When I was his age, I was doing a full share of the chores, including taking care of the horses."

Naomi took a step toward the house, but Cap's hand was still holding her arm. "No one has time to teach him."

"I have time. I'll teach him."

His eyes narrowed as she faced him, and she felt her chin set. "He's my son, and I don't think he's ready to learn yet."

Cap took a step closer, towering over her. "You mean you don't want him to learn yet. He's a bright, active boy, but he is bored. You need to give him good, solid work to do or he'll continue to get into trouble like he did when he tried to go fishing by himself."

"You think it's my fault that he got lost?" A knot tightened in Naomi's stomach.

"As much as it was mine. In a way, we both had a part in it."

She pulled her arm out of his grasp and headed toward the house. Cap jogged to catch up with her.

"Don't walk away from me, Naomi. I want to talk about this."

She whirled to face him. "Why? He's my

son, not yours. Why do you care so much?"

Cap stepped back as if she had slapped him in the face. "I care because . . ." He paused, taking a deep breath. "My son would be his age now." He looked at her, his eyes wet. "I look at him and think of what I lost."

Naomi pushed at her stomach, willing the knot to loosen. "But he isn't your son." She kept her voice quiet, even. "He's my responsibility, and I need to take care of him myself."

"You won't let me help you?"

She straightened her shoulders. "Not when you want to go against my wishes."

His face grew red above his dark beard. "All right, then. He's your responsibility. But I hope you realize what you're doing to him with your coddling."

"Of course I know what I'm doing. And I'm not coddling him, I'm protecting him. Keeping him safe."

"No matter what you call it, the results are the same."

He walked past her toward the road and the Yoder farm as Naomi's heart pounded in her ears. She was right. She knew she was right. Cap just didn't know how frightening it was to raise a boy, and how easy it was to lose him.

■ ■ ■ ■

Christian tried to rest. Annalise had just taken care of his most private needs, bathing him and settling him back in his bed with fresh linens and nightclothes. He was tired. So tired.

He lifted his right hand. That was the only movement Annalise knew he was capable of. He hadn't shown her the progress he had seen in his left hand. Yesterday, when she finished bathing him, she had left that hand resting on his chest. Without even thinking, he had moved it back down to the bed. He had moved his right foot too, shifting it under the covers. There was progress toward his recovery, but he didn't want to get Annalise's hopes up. He should be getting stronger, and yet the weakness continued. He felt like a newborn kitten. Helpless.

Death didn't frighten him. He had faced it many times over the last two weeks. He could feel the presence of God in the bedroom with him, and the presence felt strongest when he was at his weakest points. More than once, he had tried to turn his head to catch a glimpse of the One who was there in spirit. Today the presence felt far away.

Voices sounded from the road outside. Visitors coming. Gathering for a Sunday visit, Annalise had said.

"Daed?"

Christian hadn't heard Jacob open the bedroom door. Two men walked into the room and into his line of sight. Jacob and Josef. He smiled, and blinked his eyes twice.

Josef leaned closer. "The Schrocks are here, and Mamm thought you might like to come sit on the porch. Do you feel strong enough?"

Ne, he didn't feel strong enough, but he wouldn't lose this opportunity for a Sunday visit. He blinked his eyes twice.

"We've set up a couch out there," Jacob said. "We'll take the blankets and pillows from here to make it comfortable for you."

Jacob lifted him in his arms as easily as he would a newborn calf, while Josef gathered the bedding into a roll. Jacob followed Josef out to the porch.

Christian closed his eyes against the bright sunshine and took a breath of the fresh air. Ach, how he had missed these simple things!

Even with his eyes closed, he could tell when Annalise pushed past Jacob to fuss with the bedding.

"Denki, Josef. Now fluff the pillows before you lay them out again. And save these two back to put under his head."

Christian smiled at the sound of her voice. He opened his eyes again as Jacob laid him on the makeshift bed. Annalise stuck a pillow behind his back.

He smiled at her. "Denki."

"Christian," Annalise said as she lowered herself to sit beside him. "You spoke."

One word. Christian moved his jaw, blinked his eyes, tried to push the word out again, but it wouldn't come.

She smiled and kissed his cheek. "Don't work so hard. One word is a miracle." She brushed his hair out of his eyes. "Rest now. We won't gather on the porch until dinnertime. The boys will do the chores first, and you can sleep."

Christian blinked twice and let his eyes fall closed. A breeze washed over his face, clearing his head of the worry and tension of the past weeks. The voices faded as he went to sleep.

The slow, soft singing of a hymn from the *Ausbund* woke him.

Gnadig bist du, o herr und gut . . .
Merciful are you, O Lord, and good,
We find your burden sweet.
Your will on earth is done,
Where you lead your children.

Christian knew the hymn well. As the next verse began, he joined the singing, his voice harsh from disuse. Annalise grasped his right hand as they sang together, tears spilling down her cheeks.

As the hymn drew to a close, Eli Schrock cleared his throat. "Brother Christian, it is good to hear you sing with us again. We have missed you."

Christian searched for the words to answer his friend, but they wouldn't come.

"You men keep on while Naomi and I finish getting dinner ready," Lydia said. She patted Christian's foot as she passed by his bed and smiled at him. "Singing is good for the soul, isn't it?"

Eli started the next song in the *Ausbund* and Christian sang without conscious thought of the words. By the time they finished, Lydia and Naomi were ready to pass plates full of food around to the folks gathered on the porch. But Christian's headache had returned and he blinked "ne" to the plate offered him. He relaxed back into his pillows and let his eyes close.

Singing was good. It seemed that his voice was coming back, little by little. Could he hope that the rest of his body might recover also?

He didn't open his eyes when Hannah

leaned across the bed to talk to Annalise, but his mind tried to piece together the meaning of her words.

"Shem Fischer is here, Mamm. We've all finished eating, but should we offer him a plate?"

"Ja, for sure." Annalise stood up, taking her warm hand from its place grasping Christian's fingers.

He opened his eyes and she leaned down. "I'll be back. I only want to be sure Shem gets some dinner."

Shem Fischer. Christian cast about in his mind. Ja, Shem Fischer. The new minister from Canada. Something played at the edge of his memory. He didn't like Shem, but why?

"Good afternoon," Shem said as he stepped onto the porch. The narrow space was crowded with the family and neighbors sitting where they could. "I see Brother Christian is still with us."

Christian looked toward the woods. Now he remembered. The man managed to rub him the wrong way every time he spoke.

"I thought you would spend the Sabbath in Clinton Township now that you're living there," Jacob said.

"The talk all week has been about Christian and his illness. I volunteered to visit today and report back to the Clinton Township people." Shem peered around Jacob's shoulders to get a look at the bed, as if Christian was on display for the curious.

Elias Hertzler stood next to Jacob, blocking Shem's view. "We're glad that Christian was able to join us today as we gather to enjoy Christian fellowship with our neighbors. You're welcome to join us."

Christian closed his eyes again. His head pounded.

"Do you folks gather together every non-church Sunday?" A chair creaked as Shem sat down.

Elias sat down in another chair. "When the weather permits."

"You folks all came from the same part of Pennsylvania?"

Christian's memory went back to the night, years ago, when Eli Schrock and Yost Bontrager visited their home in the Conestoga Valley. They had all been neighbors at one time, along with the Hertzlers. Shem was right — the four families had been together in Lancaster County long ago. They were as close as brothers.

"Ja, for sure," Elias said. "Christian's were neighbors with us along the Conestoga. Eli's and Yost's had moved on to Somerset County. We all traveled here together."

"So you three families remain close."

"Yost Bontrager's family also."

"But Yost settled in Clinton Township." Shem paused. "Was there a falling out between your families?"

Christian opened his eyes again, wanting to protest. Shem Fischer was driving a wedge of contention between the ends of the district as if he was splitting a log in two.

All the men had taken their seats and Christian had a clear view of Shem and Elias. His old friend's face was growing red as he faced the young man sitting opposite him.

"What makes you think that?"

Shem shrugged. "It's clear that Clinton Township is where the more change-minded of the district have settled. Yost settled there instead of here. There must be a reason."

"The reason was because that's where Yost found the land he wanted to buy. We are still in the same church district. We worship together, we work together. Not only Yost, but the rest of the settlers in Clinton Township."

Shem nodded. "That's what you say, but I've heard talk among the Amish men over there. They don't like the way things are done over here in LaGrange County."

Christian closed his eyes. Eli and Elias must see what this man was doing, sowing seeds of doubt with every word. He lifted his hand, opened his mouth, but no words came out. He grabbed Eli's sleeve and got his friend's attention.

"What is it, Christian? Do you want to say something?"

Christian's head blazed with pain as he searched for the words.

"Don't . . . listen . . ." He fell back on his pillows.

Eli patted his shoulder. "Christian is right. We won't listen to hearsay and gossip. If the folks in Clinton Township have concerns, they need to talk to us about them."

Shem smiled slightly. "I understand. I'll tell them what you said."

Christian clenched his good hand into a fist. Shem Fischer understood exactly what he was doing. The only question was why. What could anyone gain by driving the two ends of the church district apart?

Naomi listened to the men's conversation as she washed dishes in the kitchen with Hannah and Mattie. Shem's words had changed the day from a worshipful morning of hymn singing and fellowship to an afternoon of worry.

"Is there really a division between the two parts of the district, the way Shem says?" Mattie kept her voice low, to keep from being heard by the group on the porch.

"I know the folks from Ohio are a bit different than we are," Hannah said. "But not where it counts. We have unity in our church, in spite of what Preacher Shem says." She dried the last dish and gathered up the damp towels. "What do you think, Naomi?"

"The distance is a problem, and the marshy land between here and Elkhart County keeps folks from settling in between the two parts of the community. But until Johanna and Andrew moved to Iowa last summer, they were still as close to his folks as ever in spite of that."

Hannah nodded. "I still miss Johanna. I wonder if one of us would ever travel to Iowa for a visit?"

"You mean you wonder if Josef will ever want to travel that distance to take you to visit her." Mattie grinned at Naomi.

"Ach, we won't be traveling like that anytime soon." Hannah laid her hand on her stomach with a light gesture. "Not with little ones to care for."

Naomi exchanged looks with Mattie. Could Hannah be expecting again? But even so, Mattie could trust her sister to keep her own secret awhile longer.

Mattie took the damp towels to hang on the back porch while Hannah and Naomi went out to the front porch to join the others. The children had tired of their games and had come to join the group on the porch. Davey sat on the porch step next to Cap, his blond head leaning on Cap's arm.

Shem leaned his chair back on two legs, still dominating the conversation.

"I saw an interesting sight on the way here," he said. "I was passing by your place, Eli, and there was an old Indian there."

"Was it the same man who brought Davey back to us?"

"I don't know. It could be. They all look the same, don't they?"

"I'll go and see, Daed." Henry stepped off the porch and toward the road.

Davey sat up. "It has to be Crow Flies. Can I go with Henry?"

Before Naomi answered, Cap shook his head. "You don't need to go looking for trouble. If it is Crow Flies, Henry will bring him back here."

The men at the other end of the porch, near Christian's bed, started discussing their spring planting.

Lydia turned to Annalise. "How is your

garden doing?"

"Not too badly. Mattie planted the rest of the seeds with Margli's help. The boys are supposed to spend an hour every morning getting the weeds out, and even though they've missed a couple days to help with other chores, they're keeping ahead of them."

"I'll come by when the strawberries are ready to pick," Mamm said. "Naomi and I can both give you and Mattie a hand."

"Here comes Henry," Jacob said, his voice carrying over the other conversations on the porch. "It looks like Davey's old Indian coming with him."

Daed and Elias stepped off the porch as Henry and his companion approached. The man looked as old and ragged as he had when he brought Davey home. He walked with easy steps, his back straight.

"Good afternoon," Daed said in English. "We are glad to see you again."

"I come to see my friends," the Indian said. "My name is Edekwshkwe Pamsat."

Daed introduced himself and the others. The old man listened to the names and bowed to each man in turn.

"I came to see Davey. Your boy is well?"

"Crow Flies!" Davey pushed past Daed and ran to the old man. "Did you come for a visit? How long can you stay?"

Davey's appearance brought a smile to the man's face. "My young friend. You are well. I am pleased."

"Your name is Crow Flies?" Daed asked. "Then the other —"

"Edekwshkwe Pamsat is the name in my language. In English it means Crow Flies, and that is much easier for Davey to say and remember." His face grew serious again. "I come to bring you news. Bad news."

The rest of the group gathered closer. Naomi pulled Davey back into the group.

"Bad men are here." Crow Flies squatted on the ground and drew in the sandy dirt with his finger. A river appeared, and he drew a circle near it. "This is your farm." He glanced at Daed, then extended the river south in two branches, and then beyond that he drew another circle. "The bad men are here. You call this place The Knobs. They will come to the Haw Patch. They will come to your farms. I have seen this. Edekwshkwe Pamsat has seen this."

"Jedidiah Smith told us about them," Jacob said. "They're just horse thieves, aren't they?"

"A horse thief is a coyote. These men are wolves."

The Indian's words were low toned and even, but a prickle ran up Naomi's spine. She pulled Davey closer and he didn't protest. She glanced at Cap. The thieves had taken his horses, but he didn't volunteer to add anything to Crow Flies' warning.

Daed rubbed at his beard as Crow Flies stood again. "Is there anything we should do to keep them away?"

The Indian spread his hands in a shrugging gesture. "Fight."

"Our people don't fight." Shem pushed his way to the front of the crowd and faced Crow Flies. "Our people will give way to these men. They will take what they want and leave us alone. They will go away."

Crow Flies leveled his gaze at Shem until the murmurs in the group died away. "Your people will not survive. These men will take what they want. They will kill those who defy them. They will destroy your farms. They will send you back where you came from."

Shem straightened and pointed at the Indian. "That's what you want, isn't it? You want them to chase us off so you can have this land again."

The old man regarded Shem with a sad, pitying look.

"Shem." Daed's voice was sharp. "You will

show respect."

"Whether you stay or go means nothing to me," Crow Flies said. "My people no longer belong to this land. I only came to warn my friends, young Davey and his family, before I go home to my people again."

Shem looked from the old man to the group behind him. "If you aren't going to listen to reason about this Indian, I'm going. He is the danger, not this gang he says he is warning us about." He looked from face to face, but no one answered him. He backed away, toward the road, then turned and headed toward the west, back to Clinton Township.

As he left, Davey broke away from Naomi's grasp and ran to Crow Flies. "You can't leave. I wanted you to teach me how to fish like a Pottawatomie. I wanted you to show me how to make a bow and arrow."

Crow Flies laid a hand on the boy's shoulder. "Another time I will do this. Look for me next winter, when the geese have gone south." The Indian gestured toward the porch. "One of your men is sick?" He looked at Daed.

"Christian Yoder. He had a seizure, an apoplexy. He hasn't been able to walk or talk since then."

Crow Flies handed his walking stick to

Davey and followed Daed onto the porch. Annalise sat by Christian's side. Naomi stayed close to Davey as he stuck by his friend's side.

The old Indian felt Christian's wrist and looked into his eyes. "You speak?"

"One word, today," Annalise said. "And he sang hymns with us."

Crow Flies nodded. "He is very weak. The white doctor has been here."

"Dr. Samples."

Crow Flies snorted. "That man leaves dead men lying in his footsteps. He took blood?"

Annalise nodded.

"Blood is the strength of a man. Do not let the doctor do this again." Crow Flies lifted Christian's left arm, held it, then let it fall to the bed once more. "You may regain some of your strength back."

"He won't . . ." Annalise held a hand to her mouth. "He won't die?"

"You must give him hawthorn. Tea made from the flowers and berries of the tree." He looked toward the forest surrounding the farm. "There are haw trees. They are blooming. Take the flowers. Dry them. Make a tea. He must drink some of it every day."

"How will that help?"

"It strengthens the man. Relieves the headaches. He will soon feel better, but he must not stop drinking the tea every day."

Annalise dabbed at the tears on her cheeks. "Thank you, Crow Flies, thank you. You have given us hope."

"You have given me a friend." He took his walking stick from Davey and started toward the road, motioning for the boy to follow. Was he expecting that Davey would leave with him?

"Ne, Davey." Naomi ran after them. "Don't go."

"Davey's mother come too," Crow Flies said. "To the road with us, then bring the boy back."

Naomi glanced behind her and saw Cap watching them. He wouldn't let anything happen to her, even after their disagreement.

When they reached the road, Crow Flies felt in the pouch at his belt and brought out a stone with delicate marks on it like spider webs and as large as Davey's fist. Naomi had never seen one like it before. He squatted down in front of Davey.

"This was my great-grandfather's stone. It has many memories in it. Do you understand?"

Davey took the stone as Crow Flies

handed it to him and nodded.

"You are young, and very few memories live in your head." He touched his own gray hair. "Many memories live in my head. I have carried this stone since I was a boy. My father carried it before me. His grandfather brought this stone from his home, far to the north, on the shores of the big lake. It was a holder of memories for him."

He closed Davey's hand around the rock.

"Long years before the white man came, our people lived near the big lake. When my grandfather's father was a boy, other tribes drove our people west to the big forest. Then we came to the rivers and waters of Michigan. This stone holds those memories." Crow Flies faltered, and Naomi saw tears welling in his sunken eyes. "This stone is a pledge to you. I will remember you. If I am not able to come back to you, this stone will help you remember me. It holds the memories."

"You might not come back?"

"My young friend, I am an old man. I do not know how many steps are left in my life, and I will use many to go north to Michigan to see my people. My family. My heart lives here, and I want to come back in the autumn. But I cannot see the future."

He stood and walked away, not looking

back as Davey buried his face in Naomi's skirts, the stone clutched in his hand.

11

Nearly two weeks after Crow Flies left, Davey still talked about his friend. He had placed the strange stone on a ledge above his bed.

"If Crow Flies doesn't have his stone, how will he remember me?" Davey asked on Friday morning while he helped Naomi wash the breakfast dishes. "I remember him every time I look at it, but he doesn't have anything of mine."

"I don't think he'll have any trouble remembering you." Naomi smiled as she dried her hands.

Davey dried the last plate while Naomi brushed off the table. "Jacob said our lambs will be born soon. Can we go over there today and see the sheep?"

She straightened her back. With so many chores to do, keeping tabs on Davey was wearing her out. Another trip to Jacob and Mattie's to look at the pregnant sheep was one thing she didn't have time for today.

"We'll go tomorrow, or perhaps on Sunday afternoon. The sheep will be able to have their lambs without your help."

"But I want to choose my own lamb as soon as they're born." Davey's eyes grew wide. "How will he know I'm his shepherd if he doesn't see me first thing?"

"How will you know which one will be ours?"

"I'll know." Davey put the dishes in the cupboard. "Can I go see the sheep by myself? I won't get lost."

The sharp, clawing grasp at Naomi's breath had become too familiar. Every time Davey wanted to go somewhere by himself, the fears clambered for her attention. The bandits, wild animals, a seven-year-old's careless curiosity . . .

"Ne, Davey. Not by yourself. Let me finish my morning chores, and then I'll see if I have time to go."

"Someone else could go with me. I could ask Cap. I haven't seen him since church at the Planks' on Sunday."

"He's busy with his work."

Naomi hadn't seen Cap since Sunday, either. And even then he had been cold and distant, almost as if he didn't care if she was there or not. He had greeted Davey, but his eyes hadn't sought hers. He hadn't found any excuse to talk to her. He had made it clear that he didn't approve of the way she was raising Davey, but his opinion didn't matter. He wasn't her husband and didn't have the burden of responsibility that she felt every second.

"Have you skimmed the cream yet?"

Davey's lowered head was her answer.

"When you're finished, you can help me in the garden."

Mamm came in the door as Davey ran out. She held her apron by the corners. "The lettuce is coming along so well that we're going to have to eat it quickly."

"Does that mean you're going to make wilted lettuce to have with our dinner?"

Mamm raised her eyebrows. "For sure. What else?"

"I'll fry the bacon after I finish sweeping." Naomi poured fresh water into the wash basin so that Mamm could clean the lettuce.

"Where was Davey going in such a hurry?"

"To do his chores. I think he's trying to finish them quickly so I'll take him over to Jacob's to see the sheep again."

"He could go on his own." Mamm swished the green leaves in the water.

Naomi bit her lip. She didn't want to

argue about Davey with Mamm too. "I don't want him to go that far by himself."

"It isn't that far. Just down the road a piece."

"Jed Smith and Crow Flies both warned us about the bandits in the area."

"On a quiet morning like this? Bandits won't bother our small homes. They'll be more interested in the big farms in Noble County."

Naomi gathered the damp dish towels to take out to the clothesline. "And I'm sure he would stop by the Christian Yoders' and play with William."

"There's nothing wrong with that. They'll send him home in time for dinner."

Naomi picked at a loose thread in one of the towel's hems. Mamm left the lettuce swirling slowly in the water, wiping her hands on her apron, and stood in front of Naomi.

"You're afraid he's going to get lost again, aren't you?"

Mamm's tender voice brought tears to Naomi's eyes. "I can't help it. I don't want to let him out of my sight, even here at home."

"Is that why you haven't let him visit Cap for the past week or so?"

Naomi couldn't answer. She could let Da-

vey run through the woods to visit their —
his friend. She hadn't spoken to Cap since
their disagreement about the pony, but she
hadn't tried to mend the torn place either.

Mamm sat at the table, pulling Naomi's
hand down so that she would sit with her.

"When Davey was lost, I was as frightened
for him as you were."

Naomi wiped at her eyes.

"But he came home, safe and sound. God
was watching over him." She took both of
Naomi's hands in her own. "There comes a
point in every mother's life when she learns
she has to trust God for her child. You can't
be with him every minute, and you can't
keep him from every danger."

Mamm paused until Naomi looked at her.

"He needs to learn how to take care of
himself in his day-to-day life so that when
something more dangerous comes along,
he'll know how to respond to it. He needs
to learn from his adventures, but he can't if
you don't let him take chances."

"But what if —"

Mamm squeezed her hands. "There will
always be the possibility that something will
happen. But you need to trust God."

Naomi's stomach turned. She couldn't
trust someone she couldn't see. She
couldn't shift her responsibility to some

unknown being in the heavens, could she? Davey was hers.

She rose from her seat and went out to the porch where her son was skimming the cream. Watching him work, she suddenly realized that he had grown. When had that happened? This morning he had still been her little boy, but now he reminded her of Henry. Mamm was right. She needed to start letting Davey grow up, and that started with trusting him to obey her, even when he wasn't with her.

She clasped her hands together to keep them from trembling and stepped closer to him.

"When you have finished taking care of the milk, I would like for you to go to Jacob's to check on the sheep."

Davey looked up with a delighted grin. "Really? Truly? May I?"

Naomi smiled at his excitement. "Ja, for sure. But finish with the milk first, and be home in time for the noon meal. Even if Mattie invites you to stay and eat with them, I want you to come home."

"I will. I promise." He attacked the remaining cream with his skimmer.

"Davey, not so hard. You don't want to mix the cream back into the milk."

"Sorry." He ran the skimmer over the

surface of the milk pail and looked at her. "Denki, Memmi. I'll tell you all about the sheep when I get back."

Naomi tousled his straight, blond hair and swallowed the cautions she wanted to give him. "Have fun."

"I will."

His grin was so wide that she couldn't help smiling herself. She hadn't seen Davey this happy in a long time. Perhaps Cap had been right all along.

Cap lifted his rifle and took aim on the movement that flashed in the corner of his eye, but the squirrel darted around the tree trunk before he could set his sights on it. Dinner had been sparse and supper would be even less if he didn't find some meat for his stew. A man could exist on beans for only so long. At least there were plenty of greens around. They had added a welcome change to his diet.

The wetland between the forks of the Little Elkhart River was a perfect place to hunt. No farmers had settled in the area because of the work needed to drain the swampy ground, so the area provided plenty of opportunities to find what game was available.

A movement to his left brought his rifle

up again, but there was no squirrel this time. Instead, Jed Smith appeared from between some bushes. His leather clothing stood out against the light green leaves surrounding him.

"Mornin'." Jed punctuated the word by spitting off to the side. He gestured toward Cap's rifle. "Found anything?"

"Not yet." Cap struggled to find the right words in English. "The squirrels, they are quick this morning."

Jed laughed as he walked toward Cap. "You've got that right. Them squirrels got to be faster than anything if they're going to survive." He looked closer at Cap, peering at his face. "You're one of those Ay-mish fellows, aren't you?"

Cap smiled at the strange pronunciation of the word. "Ja, I'm from the Amish settlement. My name is Cap Stoltzfus."

"I thought so. You're the feller what got his horses stole."

Cap didn't answer this. He hated to think about that day.

Jed ran his fingers through his beard, his shotgun resting in the crook of his arm. "Yeah, you Ay-mish fellows are all right, even though we differ on how human varmints should be treated." He nosed the wind like an unconscious habit. "When those Yoders first bought the land north of mine a few years back, I wasn't so sure about them. But they've been good neighbors. They let a man be, you know?"

"The Yoders are good people." Cap motioned toward Jed's gun. "Any luck hunting today?"

Jed hefted the game pouch tied to his belt. "A couple squirrels is all. Enough for stew tonight."

Jed settled himself on the trunk of a fallen tree and pulled out a chunk of tobacco. Cap squatted on the ground near him, but refused the offer of the tobacco.

"Yep," Jed said, "time was you couldn't walk anywhere through this swamp without scaring up game. Deer, moose, anything. Even a bear or catamount once in a while." He nodded in Cap's direction. "Yes, sir, hunting was child's play back then."

"Where did the game go?"

Jed spit over his shoulder. "Too many people, I guess."

Cap made himself more comfortable. "How long have you lived here?"

"I ended up here twenty . . . no, twenty-five years ago. Was on my way west when I came upon this Indian town." He gestured vaguely toward the north. "They were a friendly people back then, the Miami and the Pottawatomie. Winter was coming on and the chief invited me to stay."

"The West. Did you ever go?"

Jed chuckled and bit off another chunk of tobacco. "No. Never did make it. The chief's daughter . . ." Jed stared off into the trees. "She was a pretty one, she was." He looked at Cap. "You ever been in love, boy?"

Cap nodded, the pain of losing Martha fresh once more with Jed's words, but just as quickly the memory of Naomi's smile eased the hurt.

"Then you know why I never went any farther than these woods. I married the girl. The chief and that Catholic priest living in the town insisted on that. But I was never sorry." Jed shuffled one foot in the leaf litter. "My Jenny's ma was lovely. So lovely. But she's gone now. Died one hard winter when Jenny was still a little girl."

Lost in his own memories, Cap didn't respond. The only sound was the constant spring birdsong.

Finally, Jed sighed. "My wife's tribe wasn't sent west with the rest of the Indians back in thirty-eight. Her uncle comes around here sometimes, just to spend some time along the river, visiting his old haunts." The old man stood up and Cap rose too. "He's supposed to stay on the reservation the government gave them, but every winter he shows up around here. He told me he found one of your boys a couple weeks back, floating down the river."

"Ja, he saved our Davey. We owe him much."

"Well, he's got some people spooked."

"Spooked?"

"Yeah. People who lived through Black Hawk's War don't want to see it happen again. When they see an Indian, all they think is that there's going to be trouble." He looked sideways at Cap. "They wouldn't be happy to know about Crow Flies being here, so if anyone asks, you've never seen him. Just to keep the peace, you understand."

Cap rubbed at the stock of his rifle with his thumb. He might not understand English as well as he could, but he understood when someone was asking him to lie.

"Crow Flies, is he in danger?"

Jed's narrow gaze bored into him. "He's always in danger. Those bandits I told you fellas about wouldn't think twice of taking his scalp, just because he's an Indian. I don't want to see the old man hurt or killed."

Cap nodded. "I will do what I can."

Jed nodded in return. "Good hunting."

221

He walked back through the bushes and Cap was alone again. But he had lost his taste for hunting after the news Jed had told him. The thought that anyone would kill another turned his stomach, and that it could happen to that kindly old man who had saved Davey was something he didn't want to think about.

But could he lie, even if it would save Crow Flies's life? Lying would mean breaking the Ordnung. The Good Book didn't permit Christians to lie. There was no getting around it.

As he picked his way through the wetlands toward home, all he could think about was what he would say if a stranger asked him about the old Indian. He had promised Jed he would do what he could, but what could he do? He could say that Crow Flies had been in the area. That he had seen him. That he wasn't here any longer.

And then they would ask where the old man had gone. He knew. Davey had told everyone that day when Crow Flies left that he had gone to Michigan. If he said he didn't know, he would be lying. If he said that Crow Flies never told him . . . that might work.

That wouldn't be lying. At least, not too much.

By the time he left the bogs and reached higher ground, he gave up. He couldn't talk himself into believing that hiding the information he knew wouldn't be lying. It wasn't what he did that counted, it was what was in his heart. In this case, his heart knew he would be lying. God would know. There was no getting around it. He had to obey the Ordnung to keep on God's good side, and if he lied, he would be going against everything the church taught. If anyone came looking for Crow Flies, he would have to tell them what he knew.

As he approached his clearing, a familiar sound reached his ears. A horse's comfortable grunt, the sound Blau made when he gave him a handful of grain after a long day's work. Cap broke into a trot, then stopped when he caught sight of his horses standing in front of the cabin. He walked up to them slowly. If they were loose, he didn't want to risk spooking them. But as he got closer, he saw that the young Amish man from the gang was holding their lead ropes.

"Hallo." Cap spoke softly, in Deitsch. He stroked Betza's sleek neck.

"I brought your horses back." The young man, more of a boy, didn't look at him.

"Denki." Cap cupped Betza's cheek as she

nuzzled his neck with her whiskery nose. "What's your name?"

"Johnny . . ." The boy's voice trailed off. "I didn't want to take your horses, but Bill was there. I don't dare cross him."

"But you brought them back."

"Ja. I'm supposed to take them to Fort Wayne to sell them, but I felt bad. These are good horses, and I knew you would miss them."

Cap patted Betza's neck. "They are good horses. What will Bill do if you go back without the money you would have gotten when you sold them?"

Johnny shrugged. "I've got money. I'll give him that."

"Would you like something to eat? I'm about ready to make my supper." He held up the one squirrel he had shot. "Stew."

The boy handed the lead ropes to Cap. "I can't. I have to get back to the camp. I've been gone long enough already." He glanced at Cap's face, then away again. "It took me a while to decide to bring these two back. I didn't know what you'd say."

"Why?"

He shrugged again. "My daed, he would have taken me to the sheriff. Or beaten me."

Cap frowned. "That doesn't sound like the way an Amish man would treat his son, or even a stranger."

Johnny lifted his hat and ran dirty fingers through his hair. "Ja, well, not all Amish are like you." He scanned the clearing. "I need to get on my way."

"You don't have to go back to the gang. You can stay here."

Johnny shifted his eyes up, and then to the ground. "Ne. I can't. I can't come back."

"Are you worried about the gang?"

The boy shook his head. "I turned my back on the church. There's no going home for me."

He set off down the road, toward the wetlands and the wilderness.

Annalise leaned her forearms on the loom, resting for a minute after rolling the woven inches onto the cloth beam so that she could reach the unwoven warp threads. The windows in the weaving room brought the world into her lap as she spent her afternoons at her loom. From here she could gaze across the yard where dishcloths swung on the clothesline to the pasture where the cow grazed in the soft grass. Stumps from the trees Christian had cleared still remained there, but he had spent long summers removing them from the fields beyond the river that he now plowed every spring.

Before she started on the weaving again, she went to the kitchen to make Christian's tea. When Crow Flies had told her to give it to Christian, she thought that it couldn't be any worse than Dr. Samples's patent medicine, but as the days passed, it appeared that it was helping.

As she walked into the bedroom with the tea in a cup, Christian smiled at her. A true smile, and not lopsided, the way it had been after his seizure.

"I brought your tea." She set the cup on the side table and helped Christian scoot to a sitting position.

"Denki." He took the cup in his right hand, finally strong enough to hold it without help.

"How are you feeling this afternoon?"

He looked at her over the rim of his cup.

"That's right, I just asked you that at dinner." Annalise leaned over and kissed his cheek. "You seem to be getting better."

He lifted his left arm. "Not this hand."

The words slurred together, but she could understand him.

"But you look so much better. Your coloring is almost normal, and you act like you have more strength."

"No headache."

"That's good."

Christian gave her the empty cup, then grasped her wrist, looking into her eyes. Willing her to understand. "Peace."

Annalise took his hand as tears welled in her eyes. Peace had been missing from their home for months before Christian's seizure, but his illness had crept up on them so quietly that she hadn't noticed the tension until now, when it had slipped away again. Christian's face was peaceful. Whatever had been eating at him before was gone now.

"Peace is good." She squeezed his hand. "I am so glad you feel better."

He leaned back against the pillows. "Still tired."

"I'll let you sleep. Lydia brought some rich chicken broth for your supper."

His eyes closed. "Good. Good."

Annalise ran her fingers through his hair, pushing it back from his forehead, and let her hand trail down his cheek. Crow Flies had said Christian should drink some of the haw tree tea every day. She would need to send someone out to gather more flowers before they all disappeared. She could dry them so that she could make the tea all through the year until the trees bloomed again next year.

On her way back to the weaving room, she paused at the bottom of the stairway to listen for any noise from the bedrooms above. She had moved Gideon and Rachael to the bedrooms upstairs when Christian was so ill after his seizure, and they had taken to the move as if they had been ready to make that step toward growing up all along. After three years, it appeared that they would be her last babies. She was only forty-one, and her mamm had her last child when she was nearly fifty. But the years passed so quickly, and no new baby had made itself known.

Clasping her arms around her middle, Annalise leaned against the post at the bottom of the stairs. She could never think of her little ones growing older without remembering the ones who would never grow old. Losing Hansli, Fanny, and Catherine thirteen years earlier had been a bitter time, followed by years of dark grief. And then when they lost Liesbet . . . such a sad end to her Liesbetli's life. She let her head rest against the post. What would this house be like if all of those children had survived?

No matter how much time passed, she would never forget her sweet children.

She sat at her bench again, picked up the shuttle, and started the rhythm once more. She swayed from side to side with each pass of the shuttle, pulling the beater to tighten the threads after each pass. Then she switched the foot levers and passed the shuttle through the threads again.

With each pass of the shuttle, Annalise scolded herself.

"You should be happy that Christian is getting better," she said, shoving the shuttle through the threads to her left hand. The thump of the beater and the clatter of the reeds changing as she pressed the foot peddle. "But you act like you're afraid he's going to melt away." Thump, clatter. "He does seem to be getting better." Thump, clatter. "But what if . . ."

The loom was still as Annalise looked over the fields to the green woods beyond. "What if he never gets better?"

That was the question she must face.

She sent the shuttle through again. Swish. Thump. Clatter. Swish, thump, clatter. Swish, thump, clatter.

Catching the shuttle in her right hand, she straightened two threads that had twisted. Just like their lives had gotten twisted. Christian was confined to his bed. She cared for his every need, ran the household, and cared for the children. Jacob, Josef, and the neighbors took care of the farm work, but how long could they keep neglecting their own farms to help out? If

Christian survived, but was crippled . . . lying in his bed day after day . . .

Annalise straightened and sent the shuttle through again. She had cried enough tears. This life . . . this was the life God had given them. The Lord giveth and the Lord taketh away . . . The tears rolled down her cheeks unchecked.

"Blessed . . ." She clenched her fists. She must believe, even in this dark hour. "Blessed be the name of the Lord."

12

Davey ran to the chicken house and hid behind it. He stood with his back pressed against the wall for a long minute, his breaths coming in gasps. No call from Memmi or Grossmutti, so they hadn't seen him. He peered around the corner of the coop. No one was in sight.

He leaned against the chicken house again, letting his breathing settle to normal. Indians were silent and skillful in the woods. If he was going to learn to be an Indian, he needed to be quiet.

Davey scanned the yard between the house and the barn again. Unless Memmi happened to look out the kitchen door, he was safe. He could head through the woods to Cap's house, and no one would know.

His stomach turned with a sick feeling. That would be wrong. Memmi worried so when she didn't know where he was, and he had gotten into a lot of trouble the last time he went someplace without her knowing.

He kicked at a dandelion with his toe. He should tell Memmi that he wanted to visit Cap. She had let him go to Jacob's every day this week, but Cap was different. Memmi didn't want to visit Cap like she used to. Davey had to know why, and Cap would tell him.

Heavy footsteps crossed the porch and Davey risked looking to see who had come out of the house. Uncle Henry, on his way to the barn.

When he got close to the chicken coop, Davey tossed a stone so that it bounced in front of him. Henry stopped like Davey knew he would.

"Uncle Henry, I need to ask you something."

Henry glanced back at the house, and then at the barn, and came to Davey's hiding place. "What are you doing back here?"

Henry was tall but not as old as Memmi and Grossdatti. He understood what Davey meant. Sometimes.

"I want to go see Cap, but Memmi doesn't want me to go anywhere without telling her."

"So why don't you tell her?" Henry crouched down to Davey's height, sitting on his heels.

"She won't let me go."

"Then you shouldn't go."

"But I want to. If I tell you, then I've told somebody, and Memmi will be happy."

Henry picked a tall stem of grass and chewed on the soft, sweet end. "If you know your mamm doesn't want you to go to Cap's, you need to obey her."

Davey kicked at the dandelion again. Henry was acting like a grown-up. "I want to talk to him." His eyes prickled like he was going to cry. He couldn't cry in front of Henry. He blinked fast. "I know he wants to see me too."

Henry watched him for a minute, chewing on the grass stem. "All right, I'll tell your mamm. But don't go anywhere else, and come home by dinnertime."

Davey grinned. "I promise."

Henry stood up, tousling Davey's hair. "You better keep that promise. Don't forget."

Davey ran toward the woods before Henry could change his mind. "I won't."

The trail was smooth and cool under his feet. He hopped over the roots that showed through the dark, dusty surface of the dirt path before he remembered. He stopped. Indians were silent. He took a step, resting on the ball of his foot the way Crow Flies taught him. No sound. He took another, and another, always landing on the ball of his foot. Halfway to Cap's clearing, the trail took a jog around a big oak tree. Davey's steps slowed. Silent and skillful. When an Indian couldn't see the trail ahead, he went forward with caution.

Around the tree, standing in the middle of the trail, looking straight at him, was a deer. Davey froze. The deer stared. Davey lifted his hand as if he carried a bow and drew the arrow back. He let it fly as the deer bounded off into the bushes under the trees. If he had a real bow and arrow, he could have brought the deer to Cap and they would have eaten it for dinner.

Cap. Davey forgot about being an Indian and ran the rest of the way to the clearing.

His friend was digging a hole as Davey ran up to him.

"Hallo." Davey remembered to step back as Cap lifted a shovelful of dirt. The hole was narrow, and so was the shovel.

Cap straightened and pulled a handkerchief out of his waistband. "Hey, Davey." He wiped the cloth over his face and tucked it away again, looking beyond Davey to the woods. "Does your mamm know you're here?"

"Ja, for sure." Davey grinned. "I told

Henry, and he told Memmi."

"That's good."

Cap thrust the shovel into the hole with a grunt and lifted another bit of dirt.

"What are you doing?"

"Digging a hole for a fence post."

Cap gestured toward the line of fence posts behind him. They looked like funny stumps along the edge of the clearing.

"What are you building a fence for?"

"To make a pasture for the horses." Cap grunted again. It was a funny sound.

"So they don't run away?"

Cap leaned on his shovel and wiped his face again. "So they don't run away." He frowned at Davey.

"I didn't run away. I got lost."

Then he smiled. "Maybe we should build a fence to keep you in."

"I could climb over it."

"Not if we built it high enough." Cap dug out some more dirt, then stuck the shovel in the ground at the side with another grunt. He picked up a fence post and dropped it into the hole. He looked at Davey again. "Do you want to help me?"

Help Cap? For sure! "What do I need to do?"

"Hold the post just like this while I put dirt in the hole around it."

Cap didn't grunt as much as he shoveled the loose dirt back into the hole.

"If you hadn't made the hole so big, then you wouldn't have to work so hard to put the dirt back in."

"You think so?"

"So why didn't you make it smaller?"

Cap finished tamping the loose dirt around the pole with the end of the shovel, then sat on a stump, wiping his face again. "When you dig a hole, you have to make it a little bit bigger."

"Why?"

Cap looked at him, then at the fence pole, and then back at him. "I don't know why. That's just the way you do it."

"That's what Memmi says. Whenever I ask why I can't wear leather clothes like Jed Smith, or why we have to walk to church, or why Grossdatti talks so long during the kneeling prayers after we eat, Memmi says that it's because it's the way we do things."

"Ja, for sure. The Ordnung."

Davey had heard that word before. "What is the Ordnung?"

"It's a list of rules . . ." Cap stopped and wiped his face again. "Ne, not rules. More like a way to live. We do things certain ways because the church decided long ago that when we did things this way, we wouldn't be distracted from seeking God."

"Why?"

Cap didn't answer for a long time. He went to a bucket by the house and got a dipper of water. He drank it, letting some of the water drip down his front, and then splashed some on the back of his neck. Finally, he came back and sat down on a big stump. Davey squeezed onto the stump next to him.

"If I didn't build this fence and let my horses go wherever they wanted, what would happen?"

"They might get lost." At Cap's nod, Davey went on. "They might eat something that is bad for them. Or someone might steal them again."

"All those things are true. And people are a lot like horses. When we don't have a fence holding us in, we're likely to get lost. Make the wrong decisions. We might hurt ourselves or others."

"We don't live inside a fence." Davey looked to see if Cap was joking, but his face was serious.

"The Ordnung is a kind of fence. It tells us where the boundaries are and helps us make the right decisions." Cap patted Davey's knee. "Just like the rules your mamm makes for you. She wants you to obey them for a reason. They are there to protect you."

"But what does God have to do with it? Following the rules is just . . ." He shrugged. "Just following the rules. What does God have to do with that?"

Cap didn't answer, but only looked into the woods. Davey pushed at the edge of the tree stump. He could get a piece of the bark loose and show Memmi.

"Why doesn't Memmi come to visit you anymore?"

"We're both busy."

"You were busy before, when we brought your dinner. Memmi said we help our friends when they're busy."

Cap shrugged. "We disagreed about something, and until we sort it out, it's best that we keep busy with our own work."

"It was about my pony, wasn't it?"

"What makes you think that?"

"I saw you talking to her that day. Your face was red, and Memmi looked like she had been crying when she came back to the house."

Cap put his arm around Davey's shoulders. His warm, firm grip felt good. Like he was strong, and wasn't afraid of anything. "Adults have disagreements sometimes, but it isn't anything you need to worry about."

"It is if it means you and Memmi aren't

friends anymore."

"I'll do what I can to fix it." Cap squeezed his shoulder again. "You had better be getting home. It's almost dinnertime."

Davey stood up. "I'd rather stay here."

Cap smiled, but his eyes didn't. "You need to get home. Disobeying your memmi won't make her like me."

He could help Cap and Memmi be friends? "I'll do anything to make her like you."

This time his eyes did smile. "You don't need to worry about it. I'll work on being friends with her again. You just concentrate on being a good son."

Davey returned his grin and took off for the trail through the woods. If Cap wanted to be friends with Memmi, then it would happen.

After Davey left, Cap started digging the next post hole. With each shovelful, Davey's question rang in his ears.

"Just following the rules. What does God have to do with that?"

Cap put one foot on the edge of the shovel and leaned his weight in.

What did God have to do with following the rules? Cap scanned his memory, searching for the conversations he had had with the ministers before he had been baptized.

He threw the circle of sod he had just dug up to the side and inserted the shovel again.

Obedience. Humility. Love of your family and church community. That's what the Ordnung was. Obedience. But does a man obey the Ordnung or God?

Another shovelful of dirt.

He could hear the Holmes County preacher's words echoing in his mind. "Obedience to God is first and foremost."

Of course. But the Ordnung was filled with rules and guidelines made by men, not God. And yet, if a man disobeyed the Ordnung, he was in danger of being placed under the bann. He leaned on his shovel. It was still a puzzle.

After a quick dinner of leftover stew, Cap took his ax and started walking to Christian Yoder's farm. He had pledged to split firewood for their family this week, and it was already Wednesday afternoon.

Christian Yoder sat on the porch, his legs covered with a blanket in spite of the heat of the late spring afternoon. He waved as Cap approached the house.

"Hallo, Christian." Cap climbed onto the porch and sat in a chair that had been placed near Christian's seat.

"Good afternoon." The older man smiled

as he shook Cap's hand. "So glad you came."

"I stopped by to split some firewood." Cap lifted his ax.

"Denki, denki. Annalise, she will be pleased."

"You are looking much better than the last time I saw you."

"I feel better." Christian smiled. Where only one corner of his mouth had lifted when he smiled a couple weeks ago, now his entire face lit up. "I think the tea is helping me. Annalise makes the tea Crow Flies told her about."

Cap stared at the older man. His speech was slower than normal, but for a man that most people had given up for dead a few weeks ago, he was recovering well.

Christian grinned. "You are surprised?"

"Ja, for sure. The last time I saw you, you couldn't sit in a chair, and you could only speak a word or two at a time."

Christian looked at his hands, folded in his lap on top of the blanket. "That was a dark time. I was weak. Very weak. Now I have hope, and I am filled with gratitude."

"You look well enough to go to the Sabbath meeting at the Bontragers' on Sunday."

"I hope so." Christian rubbed his thumb over the back of his hand. "It is the spring council meeting. I would not want to miss it."

"Will the ministers make an exception for you to use a wagon for the trip?"

"They already have. Abraham Troyer came by on Monday to see me. He said they had already discussed it."

Cap rested the head of his ax on the porch floor and leaned on the butt of the handle. "So there is a way around the Ordnung?"

Christian's right eyebrow raised. "Of course, when there is a need. The Ordnung isn't the same as God's Word."

"Some treat it as such."

"Ja, well, that can happen. We place so much store in our own rules and ideas that we forget what the Good Book really says."

"And what is that?"

Christian glanced at him. "Our sin requires his redemption. It is as simple as that."

Cap rubbed at his nose. "And as hard as that."

Christian nodded. "Of course the Good Book tells us more."

"How we're to live, for example?"

"And how we're to worship God."

"That's why we have the Ordnung." Cap rubbed at a rough spot on the end of the ax handle. "So, what does God have to do with whether we follow the Ordnung or not, if obedience to it isn't the same as obedience to him?"

"Submission. Humility. Doing unto others as we would have them do unto us." Christian slurred his last words together as he laid back in his chair, and Cap stood to go. But the older man leaned forward and grasped his arm. "Don't make the mistake of thinking that by following the Ordnung you have made everything right between you and God. He wants you. Your heart. That is more important than obedience to man-made rules."

Cap laid his hand on top of Christian's, surprised at the strength in his fingers. As he relaxed in his chair again, Cap went on his way to the back of the house where a pile of cut firewood waited to be split.

As Cap balanced the first length of wood on the chopping block, he let Christian's words fill his mind. God wanted his heart? He raised the ax, and adding his strength to the momentum of the heavy ax head, let it fall into the center of the log. The seasoned wood split in two with a crack. If only it was as easy to open his heart to a God he wasn't sure he could trust.

On Thursday morning, Naomi worked in

the garden with Mamm. The early crops of peas and lettuce had come in and been harvested, so Naomi hoed the empty rows while Mamm planted the beans and corn. The late May sunshine had done its work to warm the soil, and with the rain that had come every few days, the seeds should sprout easily.

Davey came wandering from the chicken coop and stooped to pick up some worms Naomi had unearthed. "Can I keep these for fishing?"

Naomi smoothed the soil she had just loosened and pulled the corner of the hoe through the soft dirt in a V-shaped line for Mamm's seeds. "When are you going fishing?"

Davey shrugged. "Henry is too busy to go."

"Then leave these worms here in the garden. You can always dig more when you need them."

Davey opened one dirty hand and watched the worm wiggle on it. He turned his hand and the worm dropped to the soft dirt. "Can I go to Jacob's and check on the sheep?"

Mamm caught up to Naomi's hoed earth. "You've been there every day this week."

"Except yesterday when I went to Cap's."

Naomi bit her lip. When Henry had told her where Davey had gone, she had almost gone after him to bring him back. But even if she didn't want to see Cap and risk another argument, she didn't need to keep Davey from seeing him.

Mamm smiled. "That's good. How is he doing? We haven't seen much of him lately."

Davey balanced on one foot, and then picked up a fat, white grub. "He's building a fence for his horses." He stared at the grub. "They don't wiggle like the worms do."

"Ugh." Naomi took his shoulders and turned him toward the grass by the barn where the chickens were hunting and pecking. "Take that thing and feed it to the chickens. I'd like to check on the sheep with you, since Jacob said the lambs should be coming this week. We'll go when I finish the hoeing."

Once Davey was out of earshot, Mamm stepped closer to Naomi. "It makes me wonder."

"What?" Naomi glanced at Mamm, but the older woman's face didn't give any clue of what she was thinking.

"Why did Davey go to Cap's when all he's thought of for the last week or so are those sheep?"

"He and Cap are friends." Naomi pushed down the bothersome twinge in her stomach. Whenever Cap's name was mentioned, she felt that heavy, turning feeling, as if a giant butterfly was trying to unfold its wings under her apron. "They have become quite close since Cap moved here."

"They have, haven't they? Davey treats Cap like a favorite uncle, or . . ." Mamm shot a look at Naomi.

"Or what?"

Mamm dug into her sack and pulled out more seeds to plant. "Never mind. I'm probably just imagining things."

Naomi continued hoeing, staying ahead of Mamm's seeds by a few feet. She knew what Mamm had been about to say, that Davey and Cap acted more like father and son than friends. Ever since the two of them met, they had been close. But that didn't mean Cap had any say in how she raised her boy.

She reached the end of the row and rested on her hoe. She still regretted every word she had said to him that day. But angry words, once sown, can sprout quickly into ugly weeds. "I'm going to take Davey over to Jacob's before dinner, if that's all right. I'm anxious to see if the lambs have started coming, too."

Naomi put the hoe away in the barn and called for Davey.

"I'm here, Memmi."

His voice trailed down to her from the hay mow and she climbed the ladder.

"Look what I found!"

Davey sat on the floor next to a litter of kittens. Naomi joined him.

"So this is where Sheba has been." She picked up one of the kittens. It was striped orange and white, and its eyes were still shut tight. It opened its mouth in a silent mew and reached out with tiny transparent claws as she set it back down with the other four in the nest Sheba had made for them.

"Can I have this one, Memmi? Can I?" Davey was cradling a black kitten in his lap. The little thing was sound asleep.

"I think you can. I know Grossdatti wants to keep one or two out of Sheba's litter to help keep the mice down. It will have to sleep in the barn, though." She took the sleeping kitten and put him with the others. "It needs to stay with its memmi for now. Let it eat and sleep for another week or so. When it's bigger and stronger you can play with it." She went back to the ladder. "Are you ready to go over to Jacob's?"

Davey sprang up to follow her. "Do you think the lambs have come yet? Is my own lamb born yet?"

Naomi laughed as he hopped next to her out of the barn and toward the road. "I don't know any more than you do."

"My lamb is going to be a boy. Jacob said we would need a ram for our flock, and that one would be mine."

Naomi squeezed the hand that he had slipped into hers. "We have a lot to learn about sheep. We'll have to listen closely when Jacob teaches us how to take care of them."

"I already know a lot." Davey let go of her hand and hopped up on one of the stumps in the road. "They eat grass and always need a quiet place to drink their water. And they lamb in May, and they get sheared in the summer." He stopped and stared at her, his eyebrows drawn together. "What does that mean? Does it hurt them?"

"It only means that they get a haircut. The shepherd cuts the wool off, and that's what we use to make yarn and fabric."

Jacob and Mattie's place was just over the rise past Christian and Annalise's farm. Davey ran ahead of her when they drew close. Jacob was in the sheepfold next to their log barn, standing in a sea of woolly bodies.

"Two were born last night," Jacob was saying when she caught up with Davey at the fence.

"Were they boys? Is one my own lamb?"

Jacob shook some grain into a feeding trough for the sheep. "Both of them are ewe-lambs." He looked past Davey and gave Naomi a grin. "Two lambs for your flock."

Naomi smiled over her nerves. Planning to raise her own sheep was one thing, but now that her plans were becoming a reality, she felt like she was stepping out on shifting sand.

"I can use your help, along with Davey and Mattie. I need to sort the ewes who are ready to drop their lambs from the others." Jacob lifted Davey up and over the fence as he spoke. "Go on in the house and get Mattie. She'll be pleased to see you."

Naomi walked up the short slope to their house. Jacob had built it into the side of the hill with a cellar facing south, away from the road. The main house sat on top of a hill and had a Dutch door that opened onto the slope leading to the barn. The top half of Mattie's door stood open to the fresh spring air, while the lower half was closed to keep the chickens from wandering into her kitchen.

Naomi leaned over the door, but the comfortable kitchen was empty. "Mattie?"

Mattie's answer came from inside the house. "Come in. I'll be right there."

Naomi let herself in and went to Mattie's kitchen window. Jacob had built their house around this window, Mattie said. From this spot, perched on top of the hill in the center of their land, Pleasant Prairie stretched away to the southwest. Jacob had cleared some of the acres that had been wooded three years ago, opening up the view even farther. Every day Mattie looked out this window and drank her fill of the rolling prairies that she loved. Every day Mattie was reminded of how her husband's love had put a frame around her dreams.

The sound of bleating sheep came through the open door behind her and Naomi leaned her hands on the counter below the window. A warm feeling rose as she thought about the future she had planned. She would raise her sheep, spin her wool, weave her cloth, and support herself and Davey. She would remain forever in her parents' house, taking care of them as they aged and then died. And then she would live with Henry and his family. The warm feeling disappeared.

The maiden aunt with the cast eye.

Or perhaps she would live with Davey when he married. She sighed, thinking of grandchildren and a future daughter-in-law.

So much could happen before then, but the future was starting now, with those two little ewe-lambs that were the first of her flock.

But in all that future that lay spread out before her, there was no man who would love her enough to put a frame around her dreams.

13

Naomi tied on her long black apron. Today was a church Sunday. She both dreaded it and looked forward to it.

When she sat in church with the rest of the community, surrounded by Mamm, Mattie, and the others, she could lose herself in the worship and the sermons. What was it that Paul said? There is no slave or free, no man or woman . . . they were all equal in the sight of God. Even Naomi, with her cast eye. During the Sabbath worship, she could forget about her appearance. No one paid attention to her and she could pretend she was Mary, sitting at the feet of Jesus.

"I can't find my Sunday shirt." Henry clattered down the ladder from the loft.

"It's hanging on the hook right next to Davey's," Naomi said. She shook her head as her brother ran up the ladder again. She may be a Mary at church, but she was a

Martha everywhere else. Between now and that moment of peace she craved was a mire of chores to get through, followed by the long walk to the Bontragers' farm.

Davey climbed down the ladder just as Mamm came out of the bedroom, both dressed in their Sabbath clothes.

"Are we ready to go?" Mamm smoothed a crease in her apron.

"I am." Davey hopped on one foot until Naomi laid a hand on his shoulder to keep him still. "Can I wait outside?"

"Ja, for sure." Naomi cringed as he leaped off the back porch into the yard. "I don't know how he's going to make it all the way to the Bontragers' without getting mussed."

Mamm smiled. "Don't worry. He can't get too dirty on the walk."

Henry climbed down the ladder. "There's a spring wagon coming down the road."

Cap was in the yard with Davey when they came out of the house.

"It's the Yoders' wagon," Mamm said. "Annalise said Christian might come to church today if they could use the wagon to bring him."

"Is he so much better, then?"

"Annalise said he's talking more every day, and the headaches are rare now."

Naomi walked toward the road as her

parents and Henry fell into line behind Christian's wagon. Hannah and Josef followed them, carrying their little ones, and then Mattie and Jacob. Again, the pang of jealousy. Ne, not jealousy, but something. Mattie and Jacob looked so happy together, with Jacob taking her hand as they walked over a rough place in the road. Mattie and Hannah had someone to share their days with, while Naomi walked along the road behind them, still alone.

"May I walk with you?" Cap said, falling in beside her. Davey walked by his side for a few steps before running ahead to walk with William.

"Do you want to?"

"Would I ask if I didn't?"

Naomi glanced behind her on the road. The other families from LaGrange County were coming along, their voices subdued in the early morning air.

Cap matched his steps to hers. "We haven't talked for quite a while."

Ever since their discussion about how she was raising Davey. Naomi pulled her bottom lip between her teeth. She didn't want to have another talk like that on a Sabbath morning.

"Davey said you've let him go to Jacob's to check on the sheep."

From the corner of her eye, Naomi saw him glance at her.

"By himself," he added.

Her face heated. Her cheeks must be bright pink. "I let Davey go to Jacob and Mattie's alone. Several times."

"And everything went well."

"Everything went well."

"He came home safely."

Naomi stopped in the road until he turned to face her. "I know what you're trying to say. You were right. Davey needs to have some independence." She turned and walked on.

"You don't need to get angry with me about it," Cap said as he caught up with her. "I'm glad to see you took my advice."

"I don't need your advice." Naomi muttered the words to herself, but Cap heard them.

"I think you do."

He took her arm and pulled her to the side of the road as families walked past them. Her brother Isaac's wife, Emma, stared at her as they walked by, but went on when Naomi reassured her with a smile. Once the group had passed them, Cap guided her back onto the road.

"Even though you have your parents to help you, you take too much of the responsibility of raising Davey onto yourself. You can't raise a boy alone. It's too hard."

He was right. Naomi stalked down the road in spite of Cap following with a hand holding her by the elbow. No matter how she tried, Davey didn't obey her like he should. He was wayward and noisy at times. He should respect her parents and Cap, but instead he begged and whined until he got what he wanted. And on top of everything else, when she took her eyes off of him for one minute, he got lost.

She blinked back the tears that threatened to fall.

"You're right." She turned to face him, sniffing. "I'm not a good mother for him. He should have a real family. A mother and father. Sisters and brothers. I will never be able to give him that."

Cap stared at her until she turned and walked down the road. He caught up with her and pulled her aside while the Plank family passed them.

"That is not what I said."

He loomed over her, his face red.

"But it's what you meant." She shook her head, willing the tears to stop. "I can't raise Davey. That's what you said."

Cap grasped her shoulders. "I said that it's too hard for a woman to raise a boy on her own. Don't be afraid to ask for help."

"Who would help me? I'll never get married, so a father for Davey is out of the question. And Mamm and Daed have already raised their family. I can't expect them to raise Davey too."

"Why do you say you'll never get married?"

She looked down at her dusty shoes. Cap had said before that he didn't see her ugly flaw, her cast eye. But how could he not? She had seen the way people stared at her all her life. As if they didn't know which eye to look at when they talked to her. Some people even looked past her, or anywhere else to keep from seeing her wayward eye.

Cap cupped her chin in his hand and lifted it until she looked into his face.

"Any man would be blessed to have you for a wife." He passed his thumb over her cheek with a light stroke. "You're a beautiful woman, and a good mother to Davey."

Naomi's brother Noah and his family walked past them. Cap took her hand and fell into step a few yards behind them. He squeezed her hand once, and she looked at him. His smile drew her to him, and she answered with a smile of her own.

"Friends again?" His eyebrows raised as he waited for her answer.

She swallowed against the rising of butter-fly wings in her stomach. "Friends again."

Shem concentrated on keeping his feet still. The minister droned on and on about humility, of course, since today was a council meeting. After a quick dinner, Shem intended to propose that they accept him as a minister in the church. The district was certainly large enough to support more than three ministers.

Elam Schwartzendruber was a good minister. Not too pushy, kept to himself. But at twenty-one years old, Sep Troyer was the youngest minister Shem had ever known of, and full of pride about it. The only reason Shem could find for him having the position is that his father was also a minister. Somehow they must have influenced the lot when Sep was elected.

He didn't make his pride too obvious, though. Shem could commend him for that. But he saw it in the way Preacher Sep pushed his way forward into conversations with the older men in the district, and in the proud way he looked at his pretty wife and their two little boys. He acted as if his position in the church was his by right, and maybe he thought it was.

Scanning the row of men sitting in front

of him, he found Preacher Abraham Troyer, Sep's father. The old man watched his son's face, nodding from time to time. Another prideful one there. This entire district was full of sinners.

Shem rubbed one thumb along the seam of his trousers. He risked a glance toward the women's side of the room. Susan Gingerich sat next to her mamm at the end of her row, right on the aisle between the two sides of the room. Sitting one row behind her and on the aisle opposite her, Shem could reach forward and touch her shoulder if he dared. Living in the same house as her family was more pleasant as time went on and he became better acquainted with Susan. Her parents trusted him, of course, and didn't mind when he accompanied her on the long walks she liked to take in the evening. Walks down shadowed lanes where the trees were thick and travelers were few. He looked down at his feet. He needed to keep his gaze anywhere but on that lovely curve of her cheek.

One of these evenings, he would kiss her. The temptation was too great not to. And the last letter from Priscilla sounded like his wife would never join him here in Indiana. It was burdensome having a wife so far away when Susan was so close. Just an arm's length away. Perhaps Priscilla would die from one of the many illnesses she claimed to have. He let the images of a grieving Shem being comforted by Susan and the other women in the district pass through his mind until Sep's voice ended and the benches creaked as the congregation turned to kneel on the floor for the final prayer.

After dinner, the adults of the community took their seats on the benches once more while the older girls took the little ones outside to play. Preacher Abraham opened the meeting with prayer.

Before Abraham brought up the first item on his agenda, Shem stood.

"Brother Shem?"

Preacher Abraham looked a bit annoyed as he sat down to let Shem speak.

"Brothers and sisters," he began. He smiled at the faces turned toward him. "I haven't been in this district long, only two months. But I have talked with most of you, and you have learned to know me. I am an ordained minister from the Elm Grove district in Ontario, and I came here because I had heard that you were in need of another minister. When I arrived, I saw that this is true." He ignored the frown on Sep Troyer's face and turned toward the women's side. "This district is large, and growing bigger with every family that moves into the area. There is a need for another minister, and I'm here to fill that need. I ask that you give me your approval to take my turn at preaching and to shepherd the congregation."

He sat down. His speech had come off better than he could have hoped. He glanced around the room to gauge the reactions of the congregation and met Cap's eyes. The other man's face held a frown, but Shem wasn't worried. Cap was too new here to have his opinion carry much weight.

Preacher Abraham stood again. "We have heard Brother Shem's request. Do any of you have anything to say, either in favor of or against accepting Shem Fischer as a minister of this congregation?"

Shem smiled as Tall Peter stood to speak. The man was as close of a friend as anyone in the room.

"I agree with Brother Shem that we need another minister. We are spread out over two counties, and the distance to visit the families is too far for the ministers we have. And since two of the ministers live in Newbury Township and only one in Clinton Township" — he paused to nod toward Preacher Elam — "I think we should accept Preacher Shem's suggestion, as long as he settles in Clinton Township."

After Tall Peter, two other men from Clinton stood to talk, both of them agreeing with what he had said.

Then Eli Schrock stood. "I think we can all agree that a fourth minister is needed in our district. But I propose that we hold an election for the position. Then if it is God's will that the new minister will be Shem Fischer, we are all agreed. But if it is his will that someone else should fill that role, then we need to be open to that possibility and allow God to move among us in his selection." He took his seat again.

Shem worked to keep the frown off his face as Eli's comment drew nods and murmurs from around the room. He couldn't take the chance that he wouldn't be taken by the lot to fulfill the role. It had been pure luck the first time he had been selected. He wiped the beads of sweat from his upper lip. All of his plans would come to nothing if he didn't hold on to his position.

He stood and held his hand out as if in a benediction until the congregation was looking at him. "Would you put God to the test? He spoke when I was selected to be a minister of the gospel in Ontario. By holding another election, wouldn't we be risking his displeasure?"

When Yost Bontrager rose to speak, Shem

flexed his fists. Yost and Eli were as thick as thieves, and Christian Yoder was right there with them. He glanced at the sick man who sat in an arm chair at the edge of the group. Christian's eyes were on Yost, bright and interested.

"I agree with Eli. Not that we doubt or question your calling" — he paused to nod in Shem's direction — "but it is important for us to select the minister that God wills our church to ordain. We need to be certain that God's call on Shem includes a calling to serve our community."

Shem breathed deeply. He must control his temper, in spite of the foolishness of these men. The path ahead was clear to him, but he must use the gifts of persuasion that God gave him to make things happen his way.

"Then we will accept nominations at our next Sabbath meeting." Shem looked around the room, giving a smile to each pair of eyes that met his. Too few. But he would have two weeks to influence the undecided to put his name forward in the nominations.

"That isn't the way we do things, is it?" Cap stayed seated as he spoke. "The tradition is to take nominations at the council meeting. If not today, then we should wait until the fall meeting, shouldn't we?"

Elam Schwartzendruber shifted his seat so that he was next to Abraham and Sep. As the three ministers conferred among themselves, Shem clenched his fists again. He would not give up. Not without a fight. As long as he stayed standing, they couldn't ignore him.

Abraham Troyer stood and waited until the congregation was silent. He motioned for Shem to sit. Shem looked to the others for support, but they were all waiting to hear what the ministers had decided. Shem dropped to his seat.

"Brother Cap has made a good point. The only thing we have neglected that we would normally do before accepting nominations is to remind the congregation of the qualifications for a minister of the church. As long as no one objects, we will do that now. Afterward, there will be a time of silent prayer, and then we will take your nominations for minister. Also, please remember that as you pray about the man you will nominate, there should be no consideration of which end of the district he resides. Submit yourselves to our Lord's leading."

The congregation agreed, so Preacher Abraham rose and started listing the qualifications from Scripture. Shem rubbed at his knuckles, waiting for him to finish. When

Abraham reached the end of the Scripture passages from 1 Timothy and Acts, he opened a copy of the Dordrecht Confession.

"In addition, remember this from our forefathers: We must all 'assist in word and doctrine; so that each one may serve the other from love, with the gift he has received from the Lord.' " Preacher Abraham laid the book down and laced his hands together, his head bowed. "We must consider all of these things as we pray for the Lord's guidance in the selection of a minister for our congregation. Be diligent in seeking God's will. Now let us pray."

Shem knelt at his seat as the congregation around him shifted to their own positions for the silent prayer, some sitting with head bowed, some kneeling.

He centered his thoughts on his desire. *Let no other name other than my own be put forward in the nominations. None other.*

Cap willed his thoughts to settle as he sat with his head bowed, his hands clasped between his knees. He had seen the expression on Shem's face. It was one of greed, not love. Selfishness, not service. He breathed deeply, calming his racing thoughts.

They said this was God's will, this way of selecting a minister. It was the Ordnung. It was the way they had used to select their leaders for hundreds of years. He couldn't doubt that this was the right way to do things. But Shem could not be the one who would come out as their new minister at the end of the day.

Cap sighed. He had to control his thoughts. He glanced toward the women's side of the room, where Naomi knelt next to the bench, her eyes closed. Every inch of her body betrayed her attitude of prayer. Her submission to God's will.

He closed his eyes again. If God directed all things . . . He steered his mind away from the image of Martha lying on her death bed. *Think of now. Think of Shem wanting to be the new minister.*

Naomi seemed to believe without question, while all he wanted to do was obey the Ordnung so that things would go well for him.

But if God was sovereign . . .

Martha's last words came to him, as if he was sitting by her death bed once more. "Don't turn your back on God. Believe on the Lord Jesus Christ, and you will be saved."

She had whispered the words as she lay

on the bed. His mind tried to turn from the scene, but he wrenched it back. In her last minutes of life, weak from childbirth and blood loss, her plea had been for him. And he had ignored it. He had turned his back on God, just like she had been afraid he would. Somewhere in those numb hours and days after she and their son had died, after he had thrown the final clods of dirt on their grave, he had turned his back on the God who had caused his pain.

No loving God could cause so much pain.

Cap clamped down a sob that nearly escaped. The fists pressed against his eyes were wet.

I'm sorry. Please forgive me.

His thoughts were of Martha when he said the words, but like a door creaking open, a light glimmered from far away.

He rested, still in prayer, still buried deep within his thoughts. Minutes passed. All around him the community was laboring in prayer. As if from far away, he heard sighs and even a sobbing, whispered cry or two. But he paid no attention. Had he been right to blame God for Martha's death? He let his thoughts probe the memories of those awful days. He had never felt so lonely as he had then, and the loneliness had continued through the long years. Even his move to this new community hadn't repaired the damage.

The door creaked a little farther, the light grew stronger.

Whether God had caused his pain or not, he was also the only one who could relieve the agony. The only one who could heal his wounded soul. The only one who could open his heart and give him peace.

Oh, how he longed for that peace!

Like a wave lapping onto the sand, the light washed over him. Peace infused his whole being. He nearly gasped from the relief as his grief . . . his pain . . . fell from him like a burden released.

He remained still, his head bowed, letting his thoughts rest in the light like a leaf in a gentle breeze.

Then, like a bell, came a name. *Christian Yoder.*

He had never felt so sure about a nomination for a minister in his life. He knew the name that God wanted him to put forth.

After the community quieted, each member silent and still, Preacher Abraham stood and called them back to the world. "If all are ready, we will begin the nominations."

The three ministers filed into the bedroom in the back of the house. One by one, the members of the congregation went up to the door and whispered the name of the man they wished to nominate into the narrow opening of the cracked door. After Cap had gone up and whispered Christian's name, he took his seat again.

Shem watched each person, his face set in a pleasant smile that wasn't reflected in his eyes.

The final person was Christian. Preacher Elam came to his chair and listened to the whispered name, then disappeared into the bedroom.

After only a few minutes, the ministers emerged. Preacher Elam held four copies of the Ausbund in his hand. He laid them on the table at the front of the room one by one. Only a single slip of paper rested between the pages of one of those books and no one, not even the ministers, knew which book held the lot.

Preacher Sep looked at the sheet where the names of the nominees had been written. Each man whose name had been whispered at the door by at least three people were the ones to stand for election.

"This is as far as humans can act. From here, we leave the matter up to the Lord. When I call your name, please take your place here behind the table." Sep cleared his throat. "Shem Fischer."

Shem's grin was genuine as he walked to the front of the room.

"Isaac Schrock."

No one moved. Emma, Isaac's wife, broke out into a sobbing cry. Finally, from a bench behind Cap, Isaac rose and walked to the front of the room. His steps were slow, his head bowed. Cap nodded with approval. Isaac understood the grave responsibility the minister shouldered if he was chosen by God to fulfill this role. Isaac's life would be forever changed if he was selected.

In the pause, Cap felt a sudden clench of fear. If his name were chosen . . . But ne, he wouldn't be nominated. He was new in the district. No one knew him well enough to put his name forward.

Preacher Sep lifted the paper again. "Peter Gingerich. Tall Peter."

Tall Peter rose from his seat and took his place next to Shem. He eyed the books set before them on the table.

"Christian Yoder."

The name brought a flurry of exclamations, but Cap watched the older man closely. Christian put his right hand over his eyes, his head bowed. Several men helped to move the table close to Christian's chair. Shem stood back and watched the proceedings with a scowl.

Cap prayed as he watched each of the nominees pick up a book. Isaac leafed through the pages quickly, then set the book down with a whooshed-out breath of relief. Tall Peter skimmed through the pages more slowly. After he had gone through the entire book, he set his book down next to Isaac's.

Shem flipped through the pages, then held the book upside down and shook it, frowning. He flipped through the pages again, and then looked at Christian.

Christian Yoder let his book fall open in his lap and stared at it. Between the pages was a light blue slip of paper.

The lot had been cast.

14

The evening had turned to blue dusk by the time the Eden Township group reached home. Naomi walked with Cap, Davey's hand in hers, but they didn't speak. After the lot had been cast, Christian and Annalise had started for home in the spring wagon, and the group that followed on foot was too tired to comment on the day's events.

Naomi's own thoughts were jumbled. She had whispered Christian's name into that narrow opening where the ministers had been waiting for the nominations, but she had no reason to, other than she had often wished she could confide in him as she would a minister. No one else in the community could fill the office as well as he would. But after the lot had been drawn, the doubts crowded in. Could Christian fulfill his duties as frail as he was?

When they reached the ford across the

Little Elkhart River, Davey tugged at Naomi's hand.

"Can I go see if there are any crayfish?"

"Not now. This is still the Sabbath."

Cap reached for the boy's shoulder and squeezed it. "Tomorrow morning, before I begin my work, I'll take you crayfish hunting if it's all right with your mamm. I could do with some crayfish stew for dinner."

"Could we?" Davey turned to her, his eyes bright.

The familiar turn of her stomach almost brought her automatic "ne." But when she looked at Cap's eyes, every bit as expectant as Davey's, she had to laugh. "All right. But only with Cap. Not by yourself."

Davey grinned at his friend, but Naomi eyed the dark, flowing water. He would be safe with Cap. She repeated the thought to convince herself.

As they came into sight of home, with the whitewashed barn showing through trees, Davey ran to catch up with Henry. Chore time meant he could change out of his Sunday clothes and into work clothes. Naomi followed him toward the house, Cap still beside her. At the chicken coop, where his path toward home headed toward the woods, Cap grasped her hand in a quick squeeze.

"I'll come for Davey in the morning, right after chores."

"You could have breakfast here." Naomi felt her face flush. She wouldn't have suggested that yesterday, but after their talk this morning, she could step on the tenuous bridge between them.

Cap smiled, and Naomi answered with her own smile. She couldn't resist.

"That would be fine. Denki."

"I wanted to ask you, now that we're alone . . ." Naomi paused.

He stepped closer to her, waiting for her to continue.

"About the election. What do you think of the lot falling to Christian?"

"I think he will make a fine minister." Cap's gaze went past her shoulder, toward the road where the rest of the group was making their way home, and his eyes took on a faraway look. He focused back on her and a soft smile crept across his face. "I was one of those who nominated him."

Naomi rubbed the edge of one finger. "So was I, but then I wondered if I was right in doing that. He's been so ill. Have we asked too much of him?"

Cap caught her elbow and ran his warm hand up her arm. "We aren't the ones who put this burden on him. God is the one who called him to this task."

The enormity of what Cap said made her catch her breath. "God? I know we say that God chooses through the lot, but it's just . . . chance, isn't it?"

His hand gripped her shoulder, then released. Cap blew out a long breath. "That's what I believed too, until today."

The dusk had grown deeper. Stars shone in the sky, and in the west, a crescent moon glowed through scattered clouds that were gathered above the trees. Cap's face, still with that gentle smile lifting the corners of his mouth, was serious.

"You mean you believe that God decided the outcome of the lot."

"I know he did."

Naomi let his words sink in. "But God doesn't — I mean, he isn't interested in everything we do."

"Why wouldn't he be?"

She laughed. "Even what I have for breakfast?"

Cap's eyes crinkled as he smiled at her. "I don't know why, but I think God is even concerned with what we eat."

Naomi looked toward the house. Davey had just disappeared through the door.

Cap lifted her hand in his. "Doesn't Davey occupy your thoughts all day long?"

She nodded, biting her lip.

"You think about what he's doing, if he's safe, if he's happy, if he's behaving himself."

"Of course I do. I'm his mother."

"And God is our Father."

Her thoughts swirled, none of them clear.

"I'll see you in the morning."

Cap squeezed her hand once more and then walked away, down the trail toward his clearing. Naomi covered the warm place where his hand had been with her own. Without his presence, she teetered alone at the edge of a cliff. Below her lay a vast, unknown space. Cap believed that God had actually chosen Christian. That he was present in their lives all the time.

If that was true —

She shook herself, clearing her thoughts. Church was church. Stories from the Good Book were stories. Events like that didn't happen today. Of course she believed in God. Everyone she knew believed in God. She would never think of believing in anything else. But —

The trail leading to Cap's clearing was empty and dark. Daed's voice singing hymns in the barn as he did chores floated toward her through the evening air. Chickens clucked and murmured to themselves as they gathered around the chicken coop, ready to be put to bed for the night. She nudged the last ones into the coop and shut the door. Then she closed the gate of their yard and looked toward the house.

Mamm had lit the lamps in the kitchen and light poured through the doorway onto the porch, making a path across the yard. A path beckoning her home.

A niggling thought pulled at her mind, and she glanced toward Cap's trail again. If he was right, that meant that everything she had been taught, everything she believed was more than a story. More than a way to live.

What if it was true?

Cap's chores took only a few minutes the next morning. Since he finished too early to go to the Schrocks' farm, he worked on putting rails between the fence posts he had set in place last week.

Over the noise of his hammer and the early birdsong, a rhythmic drumming intruded. Quiet at first, when it grew loud enough to catch his attention, he stopped hammering and listened. Hoofbeats. So loud that they must come from a group of horses. He stretched to his full height and looked toward the narrow trail that ran past his clearing. Only hoofbeats, without the accompanying jingle of harness.

Only the gang of outlaws would ride their horses hard like that so early in the morning. He stepped back into the uncleared edge of the forest next to his fence and waited.

The horses and riders galloped by at a pace most riders never attempted on a rough road like this one. As they filed past, Cap saw them clearly. Hats pulled down to their eyes and collars standing up around their ears, it was impossible to identify any of them. Sweat stained the flanks of the horses, and a couple stumbled as they passed the clearing. They had been ridden far and hard, probably all night. Trailing toward the back, strung out along a lead rope, a half-dozen riderless horses trotted with brisk steps.

Then, almost at the end of the line, one of the riders looked at him. Johnny. Still riding with the Smith gang.

When they had disappeared down the road, Cap stepped out of the underbrush. He stared after the riders until the last hoofbeat faded away and the final cloud of dust settled. They had passed by without stopping. Without even looking toward his clearing and the horses picketed between the cabin and the woods. But that didn't mean they wouldn't be back.

Cap swallowed, his throat suddenly dry. He glanced at the sun. The Schrocks would be waiting breakfast on him if he didn't get going.

Davey ran to meet him as soon as he emerged from the woods. "Cap! Guess what?"

The boy bounced beside him as he walked toward the house.

"What?"

"It's my birthday today!" Davey laughed and turned a cartwheel. "I'm eight years old now. I'm as big as Menno."

Cap laughed along with him, the worry about the Smith gang fading. "Who told you it was your birthday?"

"Memmi did, just this morning. And we're going to get my box out after breakfast like we do every year." Davey stopped. "Can we wait to go crayfish hunting? Memmi said we'd look at my things after breakfast, but it won't take very long."

Cap gave up trying to make sense of Davey's words. "The crayfish hunt can wait until you're ready. But I need to get home before dinnertime, so don't take too long."

Davey ran back to the house. As Cap watched him run up the steps to the door, Naomi stepped out onto the porch to halt his headlong flight. She leaned her head down to his to speak to him, and from the slump of his shoulders, Cap could guess that she was reprimanding him. She rubbed his back gently as she spoke, and when she was done, Davey gave her a hug. The boy was careless and never still, that was for sure, but Cap couldn't find any fault in Naomi's mothering of him, except being a bit overprotective.

Cap sighed as he started toward the house again. With a boy as headstrong and lively as Davey, he would probably be just as worried about the scrapes he could get into.

"Good morning." Naomi waved from the porch. "You're just in time."

Cap stepped up next to her. "I hear it is Davey's birthday."

"We're having a special breakfast for him. Mamm made all of his favorite foods."

She tipped her face up toward his, and it was all he could do to not lean down and brush a kiss against her blushing cheek.

"Davey said something about looking at a box before we go down to the river. Will that take long?"

"It depends. Last year he spent all day looking at the things in the box, but other years he hasn't done any more than glance at it."

"What makes it so special?"

Cap followed Naomi into the kitchen. The table was already set, waiting for the men to come in from the barn. Lydia waved a good morning to him from the stove where she was cooking potato pancakes. Cap breathed in the delectable aroma and stepped around the table to the sitting area. Davey sat on the floor, tracing the ornate painting on the top of a small chest with his finger.

"This is the only thing Davey has left from his first family," Naomi said, stepping next to him. "It's his parents' marriage chest. It has some of their things in it, along with papers like their marriage certificate and Davey's birth record. After breakfast, we'll open it."

"You can see everything in it." Davey smoothed his hand over the chest. "It's mine, but I want you to see it."

Once breakfast was over, Davey pulled Cap back to the chest. "We have to wait for Memmi to wash the dishes. Can you read what these words say?"

Cap traced the ornate letters with his own finger. "Muller. And there's a date. 17 July, 1837."

Davey's finger followed Cap's. "That's when they got married. And then I was born, and then my baby sister." The boy's voice was hushed, reverent.

The words echoed in the empty chambers of Cap's heart. "I'm glad you have this box." He put his arm around Davey's shoulders. "It's good to remember what you can about them."

"I don't remember anything."

"But you have this box to help you learn to know them."

Davey nodded and leaned against Cap.

Naomi came in from the kitchen, followed by Lydia. Eli and Henry had gone back to the barn as soon as they had finished the kneeling prayer after the meal.

"Are you ready, Davey?" She dried her hands on her apron.

Davey nodded and reached for the clasp. He twisted it and raised the lid. Inside, on top of everything else, was a white lace shawl, knitted out of fine wool. Davey ran his hand over it, then lifted it out and laid it to the side. Beneath it was a tiny blue gown with lace on the hem.

"We think this was probably Davey's when he was a baby." Naomi held the gown up. Tiny sleeves extended on either side, and the skirt was so long that it spilled onto her lap. She folded it again and smoothed over a wrinkle with a gentle touch.

Next was a china plate with delicate roses

painted around the edge, some more pieces of linens, and then some papers.

"There aren't any toys." Davey brushed his hand over the papers. "But these tell what my name was when I was a baby, don't they, Memmi?"

Cap lifted the top sheet. It was a certificate of baptism from a church in Philadelphia. The baby that had been baptized was named David Charles Muller, born June 1, 1838. The next paper was the marriage certificate for Edwina Schlachter and Charles Muller. Below them were other papers. One was the deed to a parcel of land in Steuben County, Indiana, dated 1840. Below were baptism certificates for Edwina and Charles.

Cap put the papers back in the chest. Naomi handed the other things to Davey one by one and he laid them on top of the papers, closed the lid, and fastened it. Cap glanced at Naomi. With those papers, she could find Davey's relatives, if she wanted to. Or perhaps Davey might want to when he was grown.

He watched Davey trace over the painted letters on the lid once more as he tried to ignore the clenching feeling in his stomach. If Davey wished, he could leave them one day. He could go off into the world to find his relatives and never come back.

After Cap and Davey went to the river, Naomi helped Mamm set the washtubs up on the grassy space near the clothesline.

"We have a beautiful morning to wash, don't we?" Mamm poured a bucket of water into the first tub, and then lifted her face up to the sunny sky. "There is nothing so lovely as a June morning. God has blessed us."

Naomi added a paddle full of soft soap to the water and swished it around as Mamm went back to the house for more hot water. She had heard Mamm talk about God's blessings all of her life, but since Cap had said he believed God was actually present and active in their lives, the words took on new meaning. She glanced up at the sky. Puffy white clouds drifted toward the east, looking as solid as the pillow on her bed. If God was as real as Cap said, he could be peeping over the edge of one of those clouds, watching her stir the wash water.

She shook her head and chuckled as Mamm brought another bucket of hot water to pour into the tub.

"What are you laughing about?" Mamm tested the temperature of the soapy water with one finger.

Naomi shrugged. "I was just wondering if God was watching me work this morning."

"Of course he is." Mamm picked up the first white shirt from the basket on the ground, shook it, and tossed it into the tub. "He sees everything we do."

Naomi glanced at Mamm's face. No, she wasn't teasing. "Everything?"

Mamm tossed an apron into the tub and looked at her. "God knows our hearts, our thoughts, and our actions. Nothing can be hidden from him."

Biting her lip, Naomi stirred the hot, soapy water, pushing the clothes around until they were all under the suds. Thinking that God was watching made her want to hide somewhere. Mamm was still looking at her.

"How do we know he's interested, though? Why would he even care whether I wash the clothes or cut Davey's hair? He has better things to do, doesn't he?"

"What can be better than taking an interest in the activities of his loved ones?" Mamm started sorting the rest of the clothes into piles. "Knowing that he does makes it easier to be parted from Annie and her family. I still miss them, but knowing God is watching out for them keeps me from worrying about them."

"But you were so sad when we had to leave them behind in Brothers Valley."

"Ja, I was. I still am. But I can rest in the knowledge that God loves them even more than I do, and he will take care of them."

While Mamm went back to the house for more hot water for the rinsing tub, Naomi stirred the clothes again, making sure every inch of fabric would be exposed to the wash water. Of course God would watch over Annie. She was sweet and beautiful, and a good wife and mother. But there was nothing special in her own life. Nothing to make him take a special interest in her.

She let the washing paddle fall to the side of the tub and reached in the water for a shirt. It was Davey's Sunday shirt, with a stain on one sleeve. She propped the washboard up against the tub and rubbed the sleeve against it. She swished the shirt in the wash water, then scrubbed again. And again. What had that boy gotten into? Slowly the stain lightened as she scrubbed it. She swirled it in the wash water again, then held it up to inspect it.

"Can't you get it out?" Mamm grunted as she poured steaming water into the rinse tub.

"Davey got something on his shirt. I got most of it out, but the shadow of the stain is still there."

"We'll have to let the sun bleach it. If it doesn't come out, Davey can still wear the shirt. You've gotten most of it out."

Naomi rubbed the dark stain between her fingers. "It might be too set in for even the sun to get it out."

"Then he'll have to wear it for an everyday shirt." Mamm reached into the wash water and pulled out Daed's white shirt. "He won't be able to wear it on Sundays with that stain." She twisted the shirt in her hands, wringing out the soapy water.

"But it's a new shirt. He only wore it one time."

Mamm inspected the stain, rubbing it between her fingers. "It's too bad, but it can't be helped."

Naomi dipped the sleeve in the wash water again and scrubbed at the stain. When Mamm laid quiet fingers over her frantic hands, Naomi stopped her scrubbing.

"Let it soak while we take care of the rest of the whites, then try again."

Pushing the shirt back into the water, Naomi sorted out an apron from the swirling clothes and swished it in the water before pulling it out and inspecting it for stains.

"That stain on Davey's shirt reminds me

of something." Mamm swished Daed's shirt in the rinse water. "We have stains on our consciences all the time. Stains from our sins."

"You don't sin." Naomi swished the apron in the water once more.

"We all sin. The Good Book tells us that not one of us is righteous. The only man that never sinned was Jesus Christ."

Naomi pulled the apron out of the water and watched the soapsuds run back into the tub.

Mamm went on. "The only way we can be clean is to take our sins to God, repent of them, and let Christ's blood wash us clean."

Naomi almost let the words wash over her without hearing them, the way she had every time she had heard them, but something caught at her. If God was real and his words were true, then what Mamm was saying was true too.

She wrung the wash water out of the apron, twisting it tightly in her hands. When the apron was rinsed clean, and then hung in the sun to dry, it would be as clean and white as a fresh snowfall.

Like an itch she couldn't reach, an uncomfortable thought came to her. If all people sinned, then she must sin too. Sins that couldn't be washed away by taking a bath on Saturday night.

She pushed away the thought as she wrung out the apron and tossed it in the rinsing tub. She found Davey's shirt again and searched for the stain. Had the soaking helped? She turned the sleeve over and saw it. Nothing she could do would get rid of that stain.

15

Shem broke the twig he had been worrying in his hand into two pieces and threw them into the underbrush. Life wasn't fair.

Here he was, ready to start a new life for himself as a minister in a new, growing church district, and they voted him down.

He slumped against the tree trunk.

And on top of that, he had spent the last four days sitting here in these woods because Tall Peter thought he was looking for land to buy. He'd sooner buy land in Hades than in this swamp-ridden, mosquito-infested hole.

He gritted his teeth as he scratched at a patch of poison ivy on his wrist. It was all Cap Stoltzfus's fault. All of it. If he hadn't suggested that they go ahead with the election on Sunday, Shem could have drummed up more support. He would have gotten so many nominations that they would have had to give him the position. But as luck would have it, the paper had been in Christian Yoder's book.

That was another thing that set him off. Christian Yoder was a cripple. A dying man. How could anyone think he could be a minister?

So a cripple, half a man, was going to have the position that should be his.

Shem stood and paced in front of his log.

And instead of shepherding the flock and making something of this community, he was stuck. No power. No influence. No one looking to him for leadership.

The only thing for him to do was to leave. Move on.

Unless —

Shem stopped short. The crowding trees faded away as the idea took shape in his mind.

This Indiana church was already fractured. The two halves of the district were already separated by the swampy lands between them and the distance. And then there were the differences between the change-minded people who had come from Ohio and the old-timers from Pennsylvania. It wouldn't take much to turn that fracture into a split. A word here, an argument there.

Shem sat on the log again. With the district divided in two, the Elkhart County people would need another minister.

He took his hat off and ran stiff fingers through his sweaty hair. Tossing the hat aside, he ran both hands over his hair, letting the slight breeze cool his head. He needed to plan his moves carefully.

He rose to his feet with a rush, grabbing his hat. The first task to do was to buy the farm he was supposed to be looking for. There was a likely looking spot just a half mile west of the Gingerich farm. He had looked at it once, but then dismissed it because the man selling it had already cleared much of the eighty acres and had built a house. He was asking much more than a man would expect to pay for eighty acres of untouched land.

Shem picked his way through the woods to the road. A nicely built frame house already stood on the property. He smiled. No living in some backwoods cabin for him.

That evening, Shem returned to the Gingerich farm just in time for supper.

"Any progress today, Preacher Shem?" Tall Peter's Mary poured a cup of coffee for him, smiling at him.

Shem reached for the pitcher of cream. "I bought my farm today." He grinned at the response around the table and then dared to meet Susan's eyes. She would be a welcome visitor once he moved into his new house.

Tall Peter reached for the cream when Shem was finished. "Where is it?"

"I bought the Taylor place, just down the road here."

"Richard Taylor is selling?"

Shem stirred a spoonful of white sugar into his coffee. Mary knew he liked the fine sugar and kept it on hand for him. "He said he was going back home to Tennessee. The winters are too much for him, and since his wife died . . ." He shrugged and took a sip of the hot liquid. "He said there is nothing left for him here. She was the one who wanted to live here. I guess her folks live nearby."

"You'll be close enough to visit often," Mary said. She laid a platter of sliced ham in front of him. "I hope you'll feel welcome to drop by for meals whenever you wish."

Tall Peter's half-grown sons set in to eating as soon as Shem passed the platter their way.

"Will your wife be joining you soon?" Tall Peter shoveled a spoonful of mashed potatoes into his mouth, then spoke around them. "The Taylor house is a fine one, and she should be pleased."

Priscilla. Shem put a somber look on his

293

face and shook his head. "I haven't gotten any letters from my wife since I came here. When I left Ontario, she was feeling rather ill, and no one expected her to recover for several months." Shem pushed at the delicious ham with his fork. "I'm not certain that she'll survive this illness."

He had to struggle to keep from smiling as Mary and Susan both uttered sounds of dismay. Priscilla could die. She might have already. Then he would be free to seek a wife who was both pretty and pliable. He forced himself to keep his eyes on his plate and not glance at Susan. He had to be patient.

Tall Peter put his fork down. "Should you return to Ontario to see her?"

Shem shook his head. "She is in good hands with her parents. And I need to be here. My work is here."

"Even though you aren't officially a minister of our church?"

Shem waved the words away as if they were unimportant. "The ministers aren't the only men needed to lead in a church. As far-flung as this congregation is, every member is needed to minister to the rest." He took a bite of ham and chewed it slowly, as if he was considering his own words. "In fact, there might even be an advantage in dividing the district into two parts. It is nearly large enough, as far as the number of families goes, and it is certainly large enough in distance."

"I would welcome a division like that." Tall Peter scraped the last of his potatoes from his plate with the edge of his fork. "The folks in LaGrange County dig their heels in whenever one of us makes a suggestion that they think is too progressive." He waved his fork in Shem's direction. "But change will happen, and must happen, if we are to survive."

"You're talking about meetinghouses?"

"I'm talking about farming. Now that we have nearly forty acres cleared for farming, I could use one of those new inventions. The McCormick Reaper." Tall Peter helped himself to another scoop of mashed potatoes from the bowl in front of him. "Now if we had a machine like that, our harvesting time would be more efficient. The boys and I could raise enough grain to sell at the market in Fort Wayne."

Shem allowed himself to smile. With Tall Peter's enthusiasm for change and technology, he was just the man Shem needed to carry out his plans.

"So you consider the reaper to be a tool to increase efficiency. A prudent use of our resources."

Tall Peter slapped his hand on the table. "Exactly."

"We could also institute other changes — just for efficiency."

"Such as?"

Shem shrugged, as if he was thinking about the question. "Such as a meeting-house. One building where we could meet for worship as well as community gatherings. A focus for the congregation."

Tall Peter met his eyes. "And we wouldn't have to haul the church benches from one end of the district to the other every two weeks."

Shem picked up his coffee cup and Mary refilled it with fresh coffee. "Perhaps you could mention the idea to others in this end of the district."

"The LaGrange County folks wouldn't like the idea."

Shem nodded his thanks to Mary. "They wouldn't need to like the idea if they were in a different district."

Tall Peter met his eyes again with a grin. "You're right. Maybe it's time for a change."

Cap leaned on the top rail of his new pasture fence. The horses cropped the rich blades of grass that had grown in thick clumps since he had cleared out the trees. It was a beginning. He turned his back on the horses to look over the rest of the clearing. Everywhere he looked, work loomed. He needed to keep clearing the forest to make more open land for crops. The garden he had planted with a few vegetables, corn, and oats needed to be weeded constantly. And before winter, he needed a barn to shelter the horses.

Hard work, but good work.

Leaving the horses to their grazing, Cap fetched his ax from the lean-to he had built next to the back door of the cabin and started through the woods. He had looked forward to this morning all week. Friday was his day to help with the heavy chores at Christian's farm. Both times that he had been there in previous weeks, Christian had been happy to welcome him to sit and visit for a while. Today he anticipated talking with the older man about the events of Sunday.

As he emerged from the woods at the edge of the Schrock farm, Davey ran from the house to meet him. He was carrying a small black kitten.

"Did you come for a visit? Can we go fishing?"

Cap pulled Davey's hat off and tousled

his hair before wrapping an arm around him in a hug. "Hallo to you, too. I'm on my way to Christian Yoder's to chop some wood."

"Memmi said to invite you in." Davey pulled out of Cap's grasp. "She's making a cake."

"Cake?" Cap folded his arms and frowned, pretending to think. "I don't know. Is cake good to eat? Do kittens like it?" He reached out a finger to scratch the little thing underneath its chin.

Davey hopped around him. "Kittens don't eat cake." He tugged at Cap's arm. "You will like this kind. Memmi used cinnamon."

Cap grinned. "I'd be glad to have a piece of cake and a cup of coffee too."

"Ja, ja, ja. That's just what Memmi said."

By the time they reached the porch, Naomi had the door open, waiting for him.

"So Davey talked you into coming in for a visit." Her smile lit her face with a glowing beauty.

"He told me I was invited."

"Ja, for sure you are." She turned and he followed her into the house where the aroma of cinnamon filled the air. "The coffee is ready, and the cake has just come out of the oven."

"Should I tell the others?" Davey hadn't come in the house but leaned in the door, the kitten still in his arms.

"Ja, go tell the others it's time. And leave the kitten in the barn with the rest of the litter." Naomi set the steaming cake on the table as Davey disappeared. "Ever since I put this in the oven to bake, Davey has been beside himself. He couldn't wait to have some."

She pointed to a chair and Cap sat down while she poured a cup of coffee for him.

"Were you coming over for a visit?"

Cap breathed in the rich coffee smell. "I'm on my way to Christian's."

"That's right. You took Friday's chores, didn't you?"

She sat down across from him and leaned over her own cup of steaming coffee, breathing in. "Davey wants to see our sheep before dinner and I've been wanting to pay Mattie a visit. I haven't seen her since Sunday."

"Then you could walk part of the way with me."

She looked into his eyes and smiled. "You'll have to walk pretty fast to keep up. Davey runs all the way there."

Cap looked into the cup of dark liquid between his hands. "So he gets there before you?"

Naomi laughed. "I run with him."

"Why don't you just have him walk if you

don't want him to go ahead?"

Naomi's smile disappeared. "Have you ever tried to get that boy to walk when he wanted to run?"

The comfortable kitchen faded away as Cap faced her. He took a deep breath and let it out. He didn't want to have this conversation with her now, but it was here. "I always make him walk beside me whenever we go anywhere. It's important that he learns to rein in his own desires and submit to his elders."

"You sound like you heard that from the Ordnung." She didn't look at him.

Cap shrugged, trying to relieve the tension in his shoulders. "It's what I know."

"There is more to raising children than following the Ordnung."

"From what I've seen, you give him too much freedom. He has no discipline in his life."

Naomi blinked rapidly, her hands wrapped around her coffee cup. "He's happy."

"There are more important things in life than being happy."

Her face was flushed. He should be quiet or he would make her angry with him. But the words wouldn't stay inside his mouth. "A boy needs to learn responsibility and humility."

Her gaze flashed at him across the table. "And you would teach this to him? How? With a whip?"

"Only when necessary. He needs a better foundation to his life than a mother who worships him."

Naomi stood so quickly she knocked her chair over. "I don't worship him." Her voice was shaky. "He's just a little boy who needs —" Her voice caught in her throat.

Cap stood and took his hat from the hook next to the door. "He's a little boy who needs to grow to be a man."

"He'll grow up to be a man who can live by grace instead of rules."

Cap shoved his hat on his head. "Grace without rules spoils a child."

"And following rules for their own sake is . . . ," tears spilled down her cheeks, ". . . is cruel. That's what the Ordnung can be, and the men who follow it blindly."

She ran into the back of the house. He heard a door slam.

That was it. He had told her what he thought and she grew angry. More than angry.

He ran his hand down his face.

Ja, ja, ja. He was angry too.

He left the house just as the rest of the Schrocks reached the back steps.

"Is anything wrong?" Eli asked, catching Cap's arm as he tried to shove past.

"Everything is fine." Cap forced a smile.

Lydia's expression was troubled.

"Naomi and I had a bit of a disagreement, but we'll patch it up. Don't worry about it."

Lydia took Davey into the house. Henry followed them, but Eli waited until they were inside.

"If you and Naomi disagree about something, you shouldn't let it fester. You need to talk it out."

Cap looked toward the house, shifting his weight from one foot to the other. "I think she needs to have some time alone first."

Eli chuckled. "Madder than a wet hen?"

Cap nodded.

"Lydia can get that way too. But she gets over it." He reached up to grasp Cap's shoulder and shook it slightly. "Grace is what women need. Grace and understanding."

Eli went into the house while Cap headed for the road. If Eli was right, he wasn't sure Naomi would get over this one. He didn't understand her at all.

"Do you think Jethro will remember me, Memmi? Will he?"

Davey bounced as he walked, shaking the

hand he held with every step.

"I'm sure he'll remember you. He did when you saw him on Monday, didn't he?"

"But he's such a little lamb. And little ones forget easily. That's what Grossmutti says."

Naomi's head hurt, and the jerks on her arm were making it worse. She was tempted to let go of his hand and let him run ahead, but that would mean that Cap was right. He could discipline him and she couldn't.

"Davey, can you walk instead of bounce?"

His answer was another bounce, a bit gentler than the last one.

"How do you walk with Cap?"

"You mean like this?"

He let go of her hand and matched her steps. The bounce was gone. Her head throbbed.

"I see Jacob." Davey turned his sweet face up to look into hers. "Can I run ahead now? May I?"

Naomi nodded and he took off. How could she refuse his request when he looked at her that way?

And there was the problem. Cap was right. She couldn't discipline him. He was becoming spoiled, and she would have to deal with it soon.

Was Cap right about the other? That she

worshiped Davey?

Her steps slowed as she watched Davey run up to Jacob. The boy jumped up and down, pestering Jacob until he stopped his work and let the boy into the barn where their new baby ram was kept. Naomi bit her lip. If Henry had acted like that when he was Davey's age, Daed would have taken the switch to him.

But Henry would never have acted like that. Davey was different.

Her feet were planted in the ground as she faced this thought. Was Davey different because he was born that way, or was he different because of how she had raised him?

She turned toward Mattie's house. Mamm had sent a loaf of bread and Naomi needed to deliver it before she went to the barn to see the lambs.

The door was closed. That was unusual for such a pleasant day. Mattie loved to leave the top half of her Dutch door open to let the breezes into the house. Naomi opened it part way.

"Mattie?" She took a step into the kitchen and set the bread on the table. "Mattie?"

"I'm here."

Mattie's voice came from the back bedroom. Naomi pushed at the half-closed door. The shutters were closed and the room was dim. Mattie was on the bed, lying on top of the covers in her everyday dress.

"Mattie?"

A sob answered her and Naomi sat on the edge of the bed.

"What's wrong?"

Her sister sniffed. "It's gone. The baby."

Mattie's voice held a painful edge that Naomi had never heard before. She laid a hand on Mattie's shoulder. "What can I do?"

Her sister's hands gripped the bed cover. "Nothing." She cried harder, with wracking sobs. "There's nothing . . . anyone can do."

Naomi sat, helpless. Mattie's cries brought her own tears to the surface. The baby that Mattie had waited so long for . . . dead? This precious tiny life . . . gone?

"Mattie, talk to me." Naomi pushed Mattie's loose hair away from her face. "Don't shut yourself in like this."

"I just want it to go away. I want it to be a bad dream, but it isn't."

"Do you want me to get Jacob?"

Mattie shook her head. "Jacob has been so patient. He says there is nothing we could have done to save her."

"When did this happen?"

"Monday night."

Naomi rubbed Mattie's shoulder. Four

days ago.

"Why didn't you tell anyone? Why didn't you send Jacob to get help?"

Mattie sat up and clung to Naomi. "I didn't want anyone with me except Jacob. It was awful. Terrible." She took a deep, shuddering breath. "The baby was born, but she —" Mattie buried her face in Naomi's shoulder. "She was so, so small. So little. So perfect. She died before she could even live."

Naomi held Mattie close and let her cry. In the face of such suffering, what else could she do?

Mattie wiped at her eyes. "Jacob dug a grave for her at the edge of the woods." She blew her nose on a handkerchief. "I never thought we would bury one of our family so soon." She blew her nose again and sniffed. "We buried her where she could look over the prairie . . ."

She turned the handkerchief over in her hands, searching for a dry spot. Naomi got a clean one for her from the linen chest at the foot of her bed. She handed the scrap of cloth to Mattie. There must be something she could do to help her feel better.

"Can I open the window for you? It's a beautiful day outside."

Mattie wiped her eyes with the dry handkerchief. She shook her head at Naomi's suggestion. "Nothing is beautiful today."

"Can I make dinner for Jacob? Mamm sent some bread."

Mattie grasped her hand. "Don't tell Mamm . . . about this. She didn't know we were expecting . . ." Another sob escaped and Mattie pressed the handkerchief to her mouth.

"But Mamm would know what to do. She would know how to help you."

Mattie shook her head. "I d-don't want anyone to know. They already think there is something wrong with me because I haven't had a baby . . . and now . . ."

"But you need someone to share your sorrow."

"You don't understand. I lost my baby. I should be able to carry a baby, to protect it. But I couldn't do that." Mattie blew her nose again. "I failed to do the one thing a woman is supposed to do."

"It isn't your fault. It can't be your fault."

"I should have done something to save her." Mattie stared at the handkerchief in her hand, twisting it into knots.

Naomi put her arms around Mattie again and held her. After Mattie's breathing grew soft and deep, Naomi helped her lie on the bed again. She stood to open the shutter to let some fresh air into the stuffy bedroom.

Through the window she could see a little mound of fresh earth on the hillside at the edge of the woods. Naomi caught her lower lip between her teeth.

When she turned back to the bed, Mattie's eyes were open, staring into a distant place.

"You should sleep." Naomi sat next to her on the bed again.

"All I've done is sleep." Mattie didn't look at her. "I need to make dinner for Jacob. I've neglected him so much." She drew a deep breath that shuddered at the end. "I'm letting him down. He deserves better."

Naomi squeezed her sister's shoulder. "He needs a wife who is well and whole. You need to rest a few more days and get your strength back."

Mattie looked at her then, her eyes dark. "I've never felt so empty, Naomi. Even before, when month after month went by with no child, I never felt as hollow as I do now."

"You'll have another child." Naomi grasped at the only straw of hope she could think of. "Soon there will be a new baby, don't you think?"

Mattie turned her face into the pillow and brought her knees up. Her arms were crossed over her stomach, protecting the baby that was no longer there. "But we will never have this child." Her voice was as empty as her womb. "This baby is gone. No other child will take her place. Even if we have another baby someday, it won't be this baby." Mattie looked up at Naomi again. "Think of what it would be like if Davey was gone. Remember when he was lost, and you thought he might never be found?"

Naomi nodded, her throat tight as she remembered those long hours.

"Would another little boy ever take his place? Would you want him to?"

Naomi shook her head. "I wasn't thinking when I said that. I'm sorry."

Mattie gave her a thin smile and Naomi stood up.

"You're exhausted, and you need a good meal. Let me fix dinner for you and Jacob."

Her sister nodded. "That sounds good. Denki."

When Naomi looked back as she reached the bedroom door, Mattie's face was turned toward the window, as if she could see the little grave from her pillow.

Going into the kitchen, Naomi dabbed at her eyes with the hem of her apron. She would do anything to help Mattie feel better, but there was nothing she could do.

In the kitchen, she found eggs in a bowl

on the counter. She built up the fire and found a frying pan under the kitchen shelf. Ham and eggs would make a quick, simple meal. As she worked, she wondered what Mamm would say to Mattie. Would she say that God was in control?

Naomi broke an egg on the side of her mixing bowl with such force that the egg broke in two and both the bowl and the shelf were covered in egg shell and whites, with the yolk bleeding onto everything.

If God was in control, babies wouldn't die. Old men wouldn't get sick. Little boys wouldn't get lost.

She cleaned up the broken egg and threw it into the slop pail.

If she could, she'd tell God a thing or two about how he controlled his world.

16

Christian hadn't been on the porch when Cap arrived, so he had gone out back to the woodpile to begin splitting more firewood. After he had an armload done, he gathered up the pieces to take into the house.

"Annalise?" He peered in the open door. No one was around, so he placed the split wood in the wood box by the stove as quietly as he could. He glanced toward the bedroom off the kitchen. The door was open.

"Cap? Is that you?" Christian's voice came from the bedroom.

Cap crossed the kitchen to the open door. Christian sat on the edge of his bed, one boot on and unfastened. He held the other one in his hand.

"Good morning," Cap said.

Christian smiled, the sparkle in his eyes was back. "I told Annalise I could put my own boots on, so she took the children berry picking." He lifted the boot in his hand. "But this task is still beyond me, I'm afraid."

"Let me help you." Cap knelt in front of his friend and eased the second boot on his stockinged foot. He snugged the laces tight and tied them off.

Christian leaned forward until his weight was on his feet and stood. Cap extended a hand to balance him, but Christian didn't need it.

"Every day gets easier." Christian took a slow step, then another, making his way toward the door. "Except for the shoes, I handled everything myself this morning."

Cap followed him to the kitchen. "You're getting along better than we could have hoped a few weeks ago."

Christian eased himself into a chair at the table. He pointed toward the shelf next to the sink. "Annalise left my tea there for me. Would you bring it over? And there's a pot of coffee on the back of the stove, if you'd like a cup."

Cap set the teacup in front of Christian, then poured his cup of coffee and set the pot back on the stove. He stared into the dark liquid. He had forgotten about the coffee Naomi had poured for him this morning. He had left it sitting on the table in the Schrocks' kitchen.

"Is anything wrong?"

Cap gave himself a mental shake and turned toward Christian with a smile. "Nothing a cup of coffee won't take care of."

He took a seat across the table from the older man.

"But there is something wrong." Christian stared at him under bushy brows.

"I had a disagreement with Naomi this morning." Cap wanted to shrug it away, but the argument weighed on him.

"Um hm." Christian took a swallow of his tea.

"I told her she should change how she's raising Davey."

The bushy eyebrows went up.

"I know. I shouldn't have said anything."

"How did she take it?"

Cap squirmed in his chair. "She ran off to her room and slammed the door."

"Um hm."

"She's spoiling the boy." Cap leaned his elbows on the table. "Don't you think so?"

Christian settled back in his chair, fingering the handle of his mug. "It isn't my place to say."

Cap dug the side of his thumb in a space between two planks on the table. "It wasn't my place to say, either, was it?"

"Oh, I don't know. I've watched you and Naomi together. And Davey has a special place in your heart. You're the father he hasn't had since his parents died."

"Davey and I have talked about that. I told him he could think of me as his daed."

"And he's the son you've never had."

Cap glanced at Christian, but the older man wasn't looking at him.

"I had a son, but he died at birth. I lost my wife the same day."

"Then we have something in common. I have also lost a son and three daughters." Christian sighed. "The ache is like no other."

A wrenching pain went through Cap's heart as he looked at Christian's face. The grief still showed, but like Cap's, time had softened the memories. They sat in silence while Cap finished his coffee.

"Do you plan to marry again?"

"Ja, for sure. When I find the right woman."

"How long has it been?"

Cap dug his thumb into the plank again. "Seven years."

"Could it be that you don't want to find the right woman?"

Cap eyed Christian. When God had selected him as a minister, he had chosen the right man. Christian's questions picked at his old wounds like a boy picked at his scabby knees. "I don't want to settle for just anyone."

"It seems that maybe you aren't willing to see the woman who is right in front of your eyes."

Tall and slender, Naomi filled his vision. She wasn't just anyone. "After our disagreement this morning, I doubt if she'll even want to talk to me again."

Christian waved Cap's words away with his hand. "She needs you. All you have to do is make her see that."

Cap stood and took the two empty cups to the kitchen shelf. "I don't think anyone can make Naomi do anything she doesn't want to do."

"You're probably right. But I have a feeling she's waiting for you to show her that you're the man she's been waiting for."

Cap let the words sink in as he picked up his hat from the table where he had dropped it. He ran his finger along the edge of the brim. He had been intent on his own needs, but had never considered Naomi's needs.

"I have more firewood to split." Cap paused at the door. "Do you really think Naomi has been waiting for a husband?"

Christian smiled. "I think Naomi has been

waiting for you."

When he reached the woodpile, Cap pulled his ax out of the chopping block and set a length of log on it. He swung the ax down, splitting the seasoned wood in two. As he leaned down to put one of the halves back on the chopping block, Naomi's face flashed through his mind again.

Marry her? He swung the ax. Of course he'd marry her, if she'd have him. Another log, another swing of the ax.

He had never known a more independent woman, though. Christian could be wrong. She seemed to think that Davey was enough of a family for her.

He split another log, then leaned on the ax handle.

That would be a burden for the boy to have his mother depend on him like that. She needed a husband, if only so that she would put Davey in his proper place instead of the center of her life.

Cap wiped his face on his sleeve. He had been right when he told Naomi that she worshiped the boy, but how could he make her see that her priorities were upside down? He glanced at the sky. He wasn't used to praying when he wasn't at the dinner table or in church, but the God who had sought him out was the only one who could show Naomi what she needed to see.

Naomi walked home slowly while Davey chattered next to her. Jethro was getting bigger. He ran faster than the other lambs. How long would it take before he had horns? Her head throbbed.

"Davey, why don't you run ahead home. You can tell Henry all about the lamb."

"Can I? Can I run all the way?"

Naomi nodded and Davey wrapped his arms around her waist in a tight hug. Once he was out of sight, she sank down onto a tree stump at the side of the road and buried her head in her hands. What a terrible, terrible day. Her argument with Cap had spoiled the morning, and then Mattie's news placed a burden on her that she couldn't bear. She wrapped her arms around her waist and rocked. If only she could talk to someone, but Mattie had been adamant. She and Jacob would bear their tragedy alone. But they had each other. Who could Naomi share her grief with?

She caught sight of movement up the road and wiped the tears from her cheeks. Cap strode down the road from Christian's farm, carrying his ax. When he spotted Naomi, he ran to her and set the ax on the ground.

"What is it? Are you all right?"

He took her hands in his, as if they had never had an argument this morning. His concern brought tears once more. He wrapped his arms around her and held her close while she cried. Once the tears slowed, he sat back on his heels and lifted her chin.

"Are you hurt?"

Naomi shook her head.

"Is it Davey?"

She shook her head again.

"Tell me what is wrong, then."

"I can't tell you."

Cap let go of her hands and stood, pacing across the road and back. "I'm sorry that we argued this morning. I said things that I shouldn't have."

She shook her head once more. "I'm not crying about that." She stared at the toes of his work shoes. "Although that was an awful way to start my day."

He knelt in front of her again. "I'm sorry."

She sniffed and looked down the road. He waited.

"I'm sorry too." She sniffed again. "Maybe some of the things you said were right. Davey is . . . a little spoiled."

He picked up his ax again and reached for her hand. "I'll walk you home."

Naomi shook her head. "I can't go home like this. Mamm will see that I've been crying, and she'll ask about it, and then I'll have to tell her."

"Then walk the long way around with me. We'll go to my farm, and then through the woods. By the time we reach your house, you will have forgotten all about your troubles."

"Walking with you will help," Naomi said as she took his hand and stood. "But I don't think anything will help me forget my problem."

"Tell me about it. When you talk about it, you'll feel better."

Naomi longed to share this burden with him. His shoulders were stronger than hers. "It isn't my problem, it's someone else's. And I promised I wouldn't tell anyone."

Cap guided her north at the crossroads and they followed the trail toward his farm. "Keeping this secret is making you miserable, but I understand. If you made a promise, you made a promise." He shifted her hand to the crook of his elbow. "But I can still help you. Just lean on me, and I'll help you carry your secret, even if I don't know what it is."

Naomi stopped and Cap turned toward her. "I've never known anyone like you."

Cap shrugged. "I'm not anyone special."

"But you are. You are kind and patient.

Any other man would have demanded to know why I was crying by the side of the road."

"That's because we always want to fix what is wrong." Cap brushed one knuckle against her cheek, then started walking again, her hand still in his elbow.

"You're nothing like my brothers." Naomi bit her lip. What made her say such a thing?

Cap chuckled. "I hope not. Your brothers shouldn't have the feelings for you that I do."

A warm glow started in Naomi's stomach and spread, forcing her to smile. "What kinds of feelings are those?"

He glanced down at her and shook his head. "I don't think I'm ready to tell you yet."

Cap pulled her closer as they walked. The sun was beginning to dip toward the west. The afternoon was wearing on.

"Would you like —" Cap stopped.

"What?"

He shrugged, not looking at her. "I thought maybe on Sunday, you and I could go for a picnic."

"Just the two of us?"

"Davey too, of course."

Naomi felt a little stab of disappointment that had nothing to do with Davey. Of course he would come on the picnic, but this walk with just the two of them was special. She wanted nothing more right now than to spend more time with Cap. Alone with him. She felt her face heating with a blush of embarrassment. "Of course Davey should come."

"If you pack a lunch for us, I'll plan where to go."

"I'm looking forward to it."

Cap stopped and turned her toward him. They had reached his farm, and her home was just through the woods. He looked into her eyes and ran his thumb along her cheek.

"So am I." He smiled, then reached down and kissed her, soft and warm, on the cheek that was already burning from his touch. "So am I."

Davey startled awake. The loft was dark, the house quiet. Only Henry's heavy breathing told him he wasn't alone.

No fire. No crashing logs. No screams.

He wiped at his wet cheeks with the edge of his blanket. The dream made him cry. He still felt like crying. He wiped his cheeks again.

In his sleep he had heard Pa yelling. Shoving at him.

"Hide, Davey. In the fireplace. Hide!"

Pa spoke in English, like Crow Flies. Davey reached up to the shelf above his bed and took the stone in his hand. Crow Flies had been right. When he held the stone, he remembered his friend.

A flicker of the dream came back. The glowing coals in the fireplace that had hurt his arm. And then Ma and Pa were gone. And baby Pru. The walls fell and covered them and Davey was left alone.

Davey rubbed at the stone, feeling the tiny raised ridges. He remembered Crow Flies, his wrinkled brown face, the crinkles around his dark brown eyes when he smiled.

Putting the stone back on the shelf, Davey sat up. A glow of starlight came in the windows at the ends of the loft. Davey went to the chest. His chest. After Memmi closed it again on his birthday, he asked if he could keep it in the loft.

He opened it and took out the shawl. He scooted across the floor to the window, where the starlight made the shawl glow with soft whiteness. He held it to his cheek, then buried his nose in the knitted wool and took a deep breath. The familiar scents washed over him. A song. A gentle voice.

Ma.

Davey kept his face buried in the shawl, and as he breathed more memories came.

Blue eyes, and a smile as loving as Memmi's. Baby Pru pushing her tongue out and waving her hands toward him as she lay in her cradle.

The shawl had drawn him when he opened the chest on his birthday, but Memmi's worried frown kept him from speaking about it. When he was alone, though, he could breathe in Ma's scent, and the memories came. It was like the memory stone Crow Flies had given him. He breathed in again.

He woke again when he heard Grossdatti's footsteps on the kitchen floor. The starlight had faded while he slept, curled on the planks beside his bed, his head pillowed on the shawl.

"*Gut Morgen,* boys." Grossdatti's call came up the loft ladder. "Time to get up."

Davey scrambled to the chest and shut the shawl in before Henry sat up in bed, rubbing his eyes.

"Get going, Davey," Henry said. He stood and pulled his pants on, then ran his fingers through his hair the way he did every morning. "Time for chores."

As Davey fed the chickens, gathered eggs, and pumped water into the troughs for the animals, he thought about his dream.

Pushing the pump handle down made his

arms ache. He rolled up his sleeve and looked at the scar. Pink flesh in the shape of a pig. He rubbed it with a finger. Smooth and tight. Memmi had told him it was from the burn on his arm when he was little.

Memmi came out on the porch to ring the bell for breakfast and Davey started pumping again. The trough had to be filled before he went in. Animals before people, Grossdatti always said. The animals were helpless and couldn't pump their own water. They relied on Davey to give them their water. He pumped harder.

If he talked to Memmi about his dream, it would make her sad. When they opened his chest on his birthday, he had seen the tired look in her eyes.

He finished pumping and followed Henry into the house. Could he talk to Henry? Davey watched the tall back and long legs of his uncle. Henry would say he was too busy.

Crow Flies would understand. He would listen to Davey the same way he listened to the birdsongs in the morning. He would listen, and nod his head. And then he would tell Davey what he needed to know. He would tell him where Ma and Pa had gone. He would tell him how to find them. But Crow Flies wasn't here, either.

Eggs, bacon, and oatmeal for breakfast.

Davey poured cream over his cereal and sweetened it with honey. He stirred until the cream and honey disappeared and then took the first bite.

"Are you feeling all right, Davey?" Memmi frowned at him.

Davey nodded, his mouth full.

"You're never this quiet at the table."

"Leave him be." Grossmutti put another slice of bacon on his plate. "Growing boys need to eat."

Grossdatti started the prayer before Davey was done chewing his bacon, but he knelt beside his chair and closed his eyes. The prayer went on. Davey chewed, then swallowed. The bacon was salty and smoky. Maybe he could have another piece after the prayer.

After the prayer he would skim the cream from the milk, and then he was done with chores. He could go see Jethro. Could he tell Jacob about his dream?

Ne. When he was there yesterday, Jacob looked sad. He didn't want to talk.

Cap. He would go to Cap's.

He waited for Grossdatti's "Amen." When it came, he peeked at the bacon platter. One piece left. He grabbed it and ran out the door.

When he had put the milk and cream in

the kitchen, Memmi was in the garden, pulling weeds. If he asked her if he could go see Cap, she would make him help her weed the garden instead. Davey chewed his lip. If he didn't ask her, he would get in trouble.

He looked around the barnyard. No one else was around. If Memmi didn't see him, he could run through the woods —

Davey shook his head. Cap said that good boys ask. He ran to the edge of the garden, and Memmi looked up from the weeds.

"Are you done with the milk already?" She had been crying.

"Ja. All done." He scuffed his toe in the dirt at the edge of the garden. "Can I go see Cap?"

Memmi sat back on her heels and smiled, even though her eyes were still wet with tears. "You like Cap, don't you?"

Davey grinned. "For sure. He knows everything, and he lets me help him work."

"Go ahead, but be home for dinner." He turned and ran toward the trail through the woods, but Memmi called after him. "Tell Cap to come for dinner too."

The trail was shaded and cool. Davey ran, his feet pounded on the packed dirt. When he got to the clearing, he ran to the garden where Cap was working, just like Memmi had been doing in theirs.

"Hey." He dropped down on a stump, breathing hard. He had run so fast he had gotten a stitch in his side.

Cap looked up with a smile. "Hey, yourself."

"Can I help you?"

"For sure." Cap pointed to the row of beans next to his. "You know how to weed beans, don't you?"

Davey took the stick and scratched at the weeds growing among the bean plants.

"What brings you over here this morning? Don't you have weeds in your garden?"

"I want to ask you something."

"Go ahead."

Cap kept on weeding, but Davey stopped and watched Cap's face. "Where did my ma and pa go?"

Cap stopped digging at the weeds and straightened up. "You mean your first ma and pa?"

Davey nodded. "They are gone. Memmi says they died. But where are they?"

Cap stepped across the young plants to a stump at the edge of the garden and sat down. "Why do you want to know?"

Davey sat on the grass next to Cap's foot. He pulled at a long grass shoot and stuck the soft end in his mouth to taste the sweet flavor.

"I want to see them." Davey blinked at the tears filling his eyes. "I miss them, and I want to see them."

"I thought you didn't remember them."

"I had a dream. Ma's shawl smells like her, and then I had a dream about her." Cap nodded, just like Crow Flies would, and Davey leaned close to his knee. "It smells like Ma. When I smell it, I can see her, and Pa, and baby Pru. And I remember them."

Cap ran a hand over his beard and looked toward the cabin. "You can't go see them, Davey. Not yet."

"Why not?"

"Because when someone dies, we can't see them again. They're someplace else." Cap's Adam's apple bounced up and down as he swallowed. "If they know God, and believe in Jesus, then they are in the Blessed Land."

"How do I get there?"

"You don't go there until you die."

Chickens died when you cut their heads off. And cows died when Grossdatti butchered them. People died when they got old. "Do chickens go to the Blessed Land?"

Cap smiled. "I'm not sure, but I know people do."

Davey stood up and went back to the

weeds. "I'll wait until I'm old then." He pulled up a clump of grass, roots and all. "I still miss them, though."

"Ja." Cap joined him and dug with his stick. "That's part of living. We miss people when they die."

"Did your little boy die?"

Cap nodded. "And my wife."

"So little boys and memmies die?"

"Sometimes. But we don't have to worry about that. God knows who will die and when, and he takes care of us."

Davey felt the truth of that. He didn't have to worry about dying. He pulled out another weed. "Why are there weeds?"

Cap squatted down next to him. "That is the question of a lifetime, and I don't have an answer for you. Weeds are just part of life."

Davey pulled at a dandelion. "I wish there weren't so many of them."

Cap reached out and tousled his hair. "For sure."

17

"Memmi, come on." Davey pulled at Naomi's hand. "Cap said he would be here after chores."

"He won't go anywhere without us and the food." Naomi turned Davey toward the door. "Why don't you run down the trail and meet him?"

Davey was out the door and gone before Naomi finished the sentence. She turned back to the picnic dinner she was preparing. She put a package of cold fried chicken into the basket next to a bottle of water, fresh and cold from the well. Vegetables from the garden followed, along with some boiled eggs and a paper packet of salt. On top of everything else, she put in a loaf of bread from yesterday's baking, but the pie wouldn't fit anywhere.

Mamm smiled as she watched the process. "You'll have to wrap the pie in a towel and carry it separate."

"That's the only way, I guess." Naomi took a clean kitchen towel and wrapped it loosely over the pie.

"Where are you going for this picnic?"

"I have no idea. Cap said he had a place in mind."

Mamm poured a cup of coffee and sat down at the table. "You enjoy spending time with Cap."

It wasn't a question. "Ja, I do. He's good with Davey, and the two of them get along well."

Mamm tapped the table across from her and pointed to the seat. Naomi sat.

"But what about you? He's a nice man, ja? A good man. He would make a good husband for you."

Naomi laughed. "I don't think he's looking for a wife."

Mamm raised her eyebrows and took a sip of her coffee.

"He's still suffering the heartache of losing his first wife." Naomi shook her head. "He isn't looking for another. And certainly not here."

"Why not?"

Naomi glanced out the door, hoping Cap's appearance would rescue her from this discussion, but the yard was empty. "You're right. He is a nice man, and he's becoming a good friend. But I've faced the truth. No man will want me for a wife, not with Davey along too."

Mamm leaned closer. "You can't use Davey as an excuse. You've done that long enough."

Naomi felt her face redden.

"Why wouldn't any man want you for a wife?"

"You know more than anyone."

Mamm grasped her hand. "Your cast eye doesn't make you any less loving or capable. It doesn't make you any less of a woman." She tugged at Naomi's hand until Naomi looked at her. "Has Cap ever said anything about it? Does he treat you any less because of it?"

Naomi shook her head. Cap had never been anything but kind. "He says he doesn't notice it, but I know the truth. What people say and what they really think are two different things."

"That's only in your mind. You are a beautiful, loving woman."

A movement in the yard caught Naomi's attention. Cap and Davey were walking toward the house together, deep in conversation. The sight of the two of them squeezed her heart. "But does Cap think so?"

Mamm nodded. "Who did he ask to go on a picnic?"

Davey's footsteps rang on the back porch and he burst in the door. "Memmi, Cap is here. Is the picnic ready? He says we have to walk and walk and walk."

Naomi smiled her thanks to Mamm and took the pie in one hand and the basket in the other.

"I'll carry that." Cap stood in the door, reaching for the basket. He nodded toward Mamm. "How are you today, Lydia?"

"Very well, denki. Enjoy your picnic."

Davey ran toward the road as Naomi fell in step beside Cap. With only the pie to carry, her burden was light. Cap was the one carrying the heavy basket.

"I hope we don't have too far to go. I'm afraid I packed the basket too full."

Cap grinned at her. "Far enough. It's a surprise for Davey, and a place I think you'll like too. I found it when I was hunting one day."

After nearly an hour's walk along a trail that followed the river, Naomi heard a soft roar, like the sound of wind through a stand of pines.

"I know this place!" Davey said. He had run ahead and come back. "This is where

Crow Flies camped. I remember the waterfall."

Naomi's feet halted on the trail. She had been following behind Cap, and he didn't notice. She glanced at the calm stream next to the trail. Davey had come this far, carried by the flooded river that day?

She hurried to catch up to Cap. "Did you search this far for him, when he was lost?"

Cap shook his head. "This is farther than any of us thought he might have been carried by the river. If Crow Flies hadn't been by the stream and happened to see him —" His voice was rough. "God was watching out for him that day."

Naomi pressed her lips together, but couldn't keep still. "If God had been watching out for him, he wouldn't have gotten lost to begin with."

Cap stopped and grasped her hand. "We don't know the full extent of God's plans. Davey is all right, and we have God and Crow Flies to thank."

She nodded. It wouldn't do to argue with Cap, not when things were going so well between them, and especially on a Sunday.

The waterfall was low and melodious as the river flowed down the gentle drop. Rocks split the water's surface and made a picturesque scene. Cap carried the basket

334

to an open meadow of long grass and set it down.

"Look, Davey." He pointed to an area where the grass was pressed down against the earth. "Here's where some deer slept last night. Can you find any hoofprints?"

While Davey and Cap followed the deer trail, Naomi spread the quilt she had brought on the soft grass and sat down, glad to rest her feet. She had the picnic unwrapped and waiting when Davey ran up to her.

"I found Crow Flies' camp, but he isn't there."

Cap sat on the edge of the blanket, opposite Naomi. "You know Crow Flies said he was going home for the summer, and he will come back in the autumn."

Davey's shoulders slumped. "This is his home. He is supposed to be here."

Naomi heard the threatening tears in his voice and reached for him. "You must have misunderstood. He went to Michigan to be with the rest of his family."

"He's gone." Davey jerked away from her hand, his face red. "He went away and he's never coming back. Just like —" Davey stopped, biting his lower lip.

Naomi glanced at Cap. "Just like who, Davey?"

Her son's blue eyes brimmed with tears under his lowered eyebrows. He shook his head, hard and fast.

Cap moved around the blanket to sit next to her and pulled Davey close. Her son resisted at first, but then let Cap hold him tightly on his lap. Davey buried his face in Cap's shoulder.

Cap stroked Davey's hair. "I think I know. You mean your ma and pa, right?"

Davey nodded and Naomi's heart turned. She never thought Davey remembered his parents who had died.

Cap laid his cheek on top of Davey's blond head. "Crow Flies only went to spend the summer with his family. He plans to come back, and you'll see him again. He didn't die."

Davey lifted his head. "But he left, just like Ma and Pa. When people leave, they don't come back."

Naomi reached for his hand. "They do if they can. Sometimes things happen so that we can't do what we want to do."

"Why not?"

Cap laid his hand over Naomi's, grasping both of their clasped hands in his. "Because even though we make our plans, sometimes God has something different in mind for us." He squeezed Naomi's hand and she looked into his brown eyes. "Something just as good, or better than what we thought we wanted."

Davey twisted his head to look up at Cap. "Like my new family? Memmi and everyone?"

Cap didn't stop looking at Naomi, but tears pooled in his eyes. "Ja, like a new family." He smiled at Naomi. "God's plans are always best."

Shem spread a spoonful of rich butter on the bread Peter's Mary had sent over with one of their boys, sighing with contentment. He sat back in his chair, his feet propped on his kitchen table, and brought the thick slice to his nose to savor the aroma. Fresh baked and still warm.

And his plans for the new Clinton church district were falling into place.

He smiled and took a large bite out of the bread, letting the sweet butter melt against his tongue as he chewed. Peter's Mary was the best baker he had ever known. He took another bite. And Susan was walking in her footsteps. Her cakes were as light as a cloud.

Shem dusted the crumbs off his fingers and contemplated the remaining half of the loaf. He should save the rest to have with his supper. He was reaching for the knife to cut one more slice when he heard footsteps on his front porch.

"Preacher Shem?" A timid knock followed the sweet voice.

Shem brushed the crumbs from his shirt front as he passed from the kitchen into the front room where Susan's lovely profile showed through the glass window. Opening the door, Shem leaned one hand against the doorframe and took a deep breath. She always smelled like vanilla and flowers.

"It isn't time for our evening walk yet."

Susan blushed. "I thought you might need some cleaning done, or your laundry."

Shem stepped back as an invitation for her to enter the house. "Do you think I'm in need of a woman's touch around here?"

"I know you are." Susan closed the door behind her, smiling. "And you know it just as well as I do."

She stepped into his arms and he nuzzled his beard into the sweet-smelling skin under her ear. She was so soft and willing, he ached from the restraint of keeping his affections in check. He hadn't done more than kiss her tender lips, and he wouldn't until they were married. He caught her mouth with his and lost himself in the overwhelming joy of her surrender to him.

The jangling of a harness brought him to

his senses, and he stepped back, holding her at arm's length. Her lips were swollen where he had claimed them, and her smile was seductive.

He took another step back from the temptation. "Someone is coming."

She closed the distance he had put between them and threw her arms around his neck. "It's only a wagon passing on the road."

She lifted her face for another kiss, but footsteps on the porch sent a rush of adrenaline through him. He pushed her away, holding both of her arms at the elbow. At the knock on the door, her eyes went wide.

"Go through the kitchen, and don't let anyone see you." Shem tried to whisper, but dread made his voice rise. If they were caught, he would never be a preacher in this district.

As Susan passed into the kitchen, the visitor knocked on the door again. Shem straightened his clothes and ran a hand down his beard. He could throttle whoever thought a Thursday afternoon was a good time to visit. He pasted a smile on his face and pulled the door open.

Priscilla.

His knees turned to water.

She glanced at him, then turned to the

driver of the wagon. "Bring my trunks in here, please."

Priscilla stepped aside for the man who brought two trunks into the front room and dropped them on the plank floor. From her shawl to her black skirt, she was covered in dust from traveling, and the corners of her mouth were pointed down in the expression Shem knew so well. Priscilla was displeased.

He dropped to the horsehair sofa that dominated the room, unable to stand any longer. All he could hope was that Susan was safely gone.

Priscilla counted out some money and handed it to the silent driver. He nodded and left. She walked to the door with measured steps and closed it behind him. Then she turned her back to the door and held Shem with her gaze.

"Hallo, Priscilla." Shem tried to smile. "I wasn't expecting you."

"I could tell. She is gone, isn't she?"

He swallowed, his throat dry. "Who?"

"That little girl I saw in your arms when I looked in the window. You sent her out the back door, didn't you?"

Shem nodded. The horsehair itched his thighs through the fabric of his trousers.

"And she won't be back."

Shem shook his head. Ne, Susan wouldn't

be back. Not as long as Priscilla was here.

Priscilla walked around the room, surveying the space. "Is this the house you expect me to live in?"

Shem stood, his hands spread out. "It's the finest house in the area." He followed her into the kitchen. "I knew you wouldn't want to live in a log cabin like the other settlers here."

"Hmm." She opened the oven door on the cast iron stove. Her nose wrinkled.

Shem sidled along the kitchen wall to the loaf of bread he had left out and wrapped it in its towel. "Why . . . I mean, what brings you here?"

"Once I got your letter telling how you were having trouble finding a place to live and settling in here as a preacher, I knew you needed my help."

He felt his face heating. She always assumed he needed her help. "You were wrong. Things are going very well here."

She caught him with the look of a cat holding a mouse under its paw. "Are you installed as a preacher yet?"

"Not exactly."

"Do you have the confidence of the families in this district?"

"It's complicated."

"I am not happy."

"I can tell." Shem tried a smile. "You look like you're feeling better than you were when I left Canada, though."

She sniffed. "For now." She walked back into the front room and peered up the stairs. "I assume there is more than one bedroom?"

The bread was a stone in his stomach. "Three bedrooms. Two upstairs, and a nice one with a fine bed in here."

He scuttled ahead of her and opened the door to the bedroom. A large oak bedstead and chest of drawers dominated the space, along with his clothes and bedding piled on the mattress.

Priscilla opened one of the drawers. "This will do. You will have to move your things. And I want the bedding washed."

"Move my things?"

Her look pierced him through and he squirmed. "You said there were two bedrooms upstairs, didn't you?"

He moved past her and started picking up his clothes from the bed and floor where he had tossed them over the last week, then slid toward the door.

Priscilla caught his elbow with an iron grip as he passed by her. "Shem, dear, I'm so happy to be here with you."

Her smile turned his stomach to a fiery

mass. "Ja, for sure. I've missed you."

She released his arm, but he refrained from rubbing his aching elbow. "Bring my trunks in here. And draw a bath. I need to lie down, but I won't until I'm clean."

"Ja, Priscilla. For sure. Right away."

He walked into the living room. His head hurt, his stomach burned, and his temper sizzled like it hadn't since he had left Ontario. Of all the people to show up on his doorstep. He looked from the trunks to the stairs. Should he take her trunks in first, or take his things upstairs? And where in the world would he find a bathtub for her?

Because she was going to have a bath or she would make his life miserable. He gritted his teeth and started up the stairs.

Saturday morning started out warm and sunny, but in spite of the weather, Naomi couldn't look forward to her trip to visit Mattie.

Since the picnic with Cap on Sunday, her mind had taken her places she had never dared to consider before. The feeling of his hand holding both Davey's and hers in his grip tugged at her thoughts, compelling her to open the door to the hope of a family, a husband, a future for the three of them.

But as she and Davey reached the lane

leading to Jacob and Mattie's farm, the apprehension of seeing Mattie again overshadowed all of her other thoughts. How was she feeling? It had been almost a month since she lost the baby.

"Come with me to see Jethro," Davey said, tugging at her hand. "If you go talk to Mattie, you won't come to the barn before we leave."

Naomi glanced at the cozy house on the top of the ridge, but she didn't see her sister anywhere. "All right, but only for a minute. I need to talk with Mattie."

She let Davey lead her through the barn to the sheep pen on the other side. Most of the ewes and lambs had gone out to the large pasture beyond the trees, but one sheep and her little brown lamb were in the pen by the barn. Jacob joined them as they walked through the barn, leaving his task of greasing the wagon wheels. He wiped the grease off his hands with a rag.

"You've come to see the little ram again, I see."

"Davey said I had to look at him before I go in to see Mattie."

Jacob's expression darkened slightly, but he smiled at her. "She will appreciate your visit."

Naomi's heart wrenched. Jacob tried not

to let his grief show, but she could see how much he was hurting.

Davey hung over the top board of the fence, waving at the lamb. "Jethro. Come here, Jethro." He wiggled his fingers, but the lamb hid behind his mother.

"Why aren't they out with the other sheep?" Naomi joined Davey at the fence, captivated by the little ram.

"Since he is going to be your ram, I thought you'd like to raise him at your place. I talked to your daed, and he said there is room in the barn for him."

Naomi frowned as Davey turned toward her, his eyes shining with excitement. "I don't know. Aren't rams a lot of bother?"

Jacob shrugged. "They can get into mischief, just like any boy." He tousled Davey's hair. "But he'll be a better ram if he isn't raised with the other lambs, especially the wethers."

"What are wethers?" Davey asked.

"They're the sheep we'll butcher for mutton in the fall. They're like the steers we butcher for beef." Jacob turned to Naomi. "You'll need to make a sturdy pen for him."

"How soon can we take him?" Naomi's thoughts whirled with the idea of caring for her own sheep.

"Not for another month. He'll be weaned

by then, and that gives me enough time to teach Davey how to take good care of him."

"Davey?"

"Ja, for sure. He's plenty old enough, and he needs to learn."

"Can I, Memmi? I want to take care of Jethro." Davey wrapped his arms around her waist.

Since when had he gotten so big? Naomi hugged him, but her mind was on Cap's advice. Davey needed this responsibility.

She tilted his chin up. "You'll need to listen carefully to everything Jacob teaches you. You'll be Jethro's shepherd, and that is a big task."

Davey couldn't keep still. He ran into the barn and back, jumping as he went. "My own lamb!" He stopped at the fence, leaning over it as close to the lamb as he could get. "We'll be best friends, Jethro. I'm going to take good care of you."

"We'll start as soon as I finish with the wagon." Jacob glanced at Naomi with a smile. "I'll teach him everything he needs to know, so don't worry."

Naomi pushed down her lingering doubts. Davey loved the lamb already and would work hard to take care of him. "I had better go see Mattie. She'll be wondering where I am."

Jacob's smile grew tight. "She's been looking forward to your visit." He looked down at his feet, and then back at her. "She needs a woman to talk to."

Naomi tried to give Jacob a reassuring smile, then left the barn and went to the house. The top of the Dutch door was open, and dish towels waved on the clothesline. She knocked on the door and then opened it.

"Mattie?"

Her sister came out of the spare room. "I'm so glad you're here." She gave Naomi a tight hug.

"How are you doing?" Naomi looked closely at Mattie's face. She was looking better, even though her eyes still held the shadow of her grief.

"I'm looking forward." Mattie smoothed her apron, then turned to the stove. "Can I get anything for you? A cup of tea?"

Naomi shook her head. "I don't need anything. Davey is with Jacob, learning how to take care of the lamb."

"Then come with me. I'm sorting out some pieces for a quilt, and you can help me."

Mattie led the way back to the spare room where scraps of fabric covered the floor.

Naomi picked up a length of dark blue.

"Is this from the dress you wore for your wedding?"

"Ja. The sleeves wore out, so I saved the rest of the dress to make over into . . . into . . ." Mattie hiccuped.

Holding up the fabric, Naomi finished Mattie's thought. "You were going to make a gown for the baby."

Her sister nodded, her eyes pooling. "I'm all right most of the time, but then something happens to remind me."

"I noticed that you avoided Hannah and the others at church on Sunday." Naomi put the blue cloth down and sat on a low stool near Mattie's chair.

The tears flowed down Mattie's cheeks and she rubbed them off with the heel of her hand. "I just couldn't listen to them talk about their babies." She squeezed Naomi's hand. "It's not that I don't love them, I do. I want to see their little ones grow and be healthy, but it makes me —" Mattie sighed with a deep, shuddering breath. "It makes me so sad." She wiped at her tears with the hem of her apron. "But I'm not going to let the sadness linger. I've cried enough tears, and I want to look forward to something else now."

"So you're starting a quilt." Naomi raised her eyebrows and Mattie laughed, still dabbing at her eyes.

"I know, I know. I hate to sew and I always have. But I need a new project. Something to keep my hands busy and something that will keep me from thinking about myself and my problems." Mattie looked at the piles of scraps around the room. "Besides, I have to do something with this mess, don't I?"

Naomi grinned as she hugged her sister. "That's the Mattie I know. You're going to be fine."

Mattie fingered the navy cloth. "Do you remember Betsy Zook, back in Brothers Valley?" She picked up a green scrap and laid it next to the blue. "She wove a coverlet one winter."

"I remember. It was such an intricate design that it must have taken hours of weaving."

Mattie nodded. "She told me one time that it was for remembrance. Her husband had died that autumn, and they had been married for nearly sixty years. She said that every time she couldn't sleep, she would weave and pray. Every pass of the shuttle was accompanied by a prayer for one of her family or for someone in the church."

Naomi sorted out three dusky rose–shaded scraps of fabric. "So your quilt will be for remembrance?"

"By the time I finish, I should be past my grief, don't you think?"

Naomi matched her sister's tremulous smile. "Ja, I think so."

18

Cap grunted as he pulled at the stump. Still no movement at all. He jumped back into the hole and swung his pick in the narrow space, loosening some more dirt. He dropped his pick at the edge of the hole and picked up the spade. Working between the roots, he managed to dig out a few more shovelfuls of soil.

He climbed out of the hole and flopped on his back in the long grass, sweat soaking his shirt and hat. The end of June had come with a series of hot days and no relief at night. But the garden was thriving, his oats were growing tall, and the grass in the pasture was rich and green. He couldn't ask for better growing weather.

Getting to his feet, Cap went to the well and drew a bucket of water. He raised the dipper and took a drink, letting the cold water run down his throat, and then splashed the remainder over his face. The well had been a big task, but Eli and Henry had helped. They had finished it in one long day of digging and the water was ice cold and tasty. He filled the dipper again and took it to a bench he had placed on the shady side of the house next to the stone chimney. He rested and sipped the water.

The farm wasn't the only thing he had on his mind, though.

Naomi.

He closed his eyes and leaned back against the cool stones of the chimney. When he had thought of looking for a wife, he never thought he would meet someone as perfect as she was. Beautiful, a wonderful mother to Davey, conscientious in her work, and faithful in her worship. He smiled. He hadn't gone a day without seeing her since their picnic a little more than a week ago. Even if they had no more than a few minutes for a quick conversation in the late twilight of the summer evenings, he cherished the time he spent with her. Someday soon he would ask her to marry him. They could have the wedding at the end of the summer, and she and Davey could move into his cabin.

With that thought, he sat up and drained his dipper. Davey would need a loft to sleep in. Once he finished pulling this one stump out of the way of the barn he planned to build in the fall, he would start felling trees to get the lumber for the loft. He'd have it done before the wedding, that's for sure.

By the time evening came, Cap had severed the taproot of the stump. Tomorrow he could hitch the horses to the chain and pull the stubborn thing out of the ground.

He glanced at the sun as he cleaned up in the cold water from the well. Nearly sunset, and he had missed his supper. He had just enough time to see Naomi before full dark came on and she went to bed.

When Cap emerged from the woods between his farm and the Schrocks', he saw Naomi waiting for him on the back porch like usual, but tonight Davey was with her. They were sitting side by side on the porch step. As he came closer, Davey's words drifted across the yard toward him.

"But, Memmi, I know someone opened it."

"Was anything missing?"

Davey shook his head as Cap reached them.

"Is anything wrong?"

"Davey thinks someone got into his chest, but I can't believe that anyone in our family would do that."

Cap lowered himself to the step next to

Davey. "What makes you think something like that happened?"

Davey rested his chin in his hands, his elbows propped on his knees. "When I opened it, Ma's shawl was pushed aside. I always leave it on the top."

"Maybe you forgot the last time you looked at it."

Davey shook his head. "That was Ma's and I'm always careful with it. I lay it on top of everything else and smooth it with my hand." He demonstrated with a gentle motion, then leaned closer to Cap. "It's like I'm saying good night to her."

Cap nodded. He understood. He had done the same with Martha's dresses during the first year after her passing. "Was anything else disturbed?"

Davey shrugged. "The papers were messy, but I might have done that."

"Is everything all right now, though?"

The boy nodded. "Do you want to catch lightning bugs with me?"

"You go ahead. I want to talk to your mamm."

Davey jumped off the porch step. "That's all you two ever do. Talk and talk and talk some more." He grinned at Cap. "I'm never going to be a grown-up."

Cap grinned back at him. "Go catch your

lightning bugs."

Once Davey was off and running after the yellow lights that were thick in the dark shadows under the trees, Cap took Naomi's hand.

"Do you mind if all we ever do is talk?"

Her smile warmed his heart. "Not at all."

"Davey seemed pretty upset that someone had gotten into his trunk."

Naomi brushed her shoulder against his, but he resisted putting his arm around her, conscious of Lydia and Eli sitting at the kitchen table only a few yards behind them, deep in their own conversation.

"He says someone did, but couldn't he have just been careless the last time he opened it?"

Cap shook his head. "I don't think so. When he needs to be, he can be very careful. And that shawl means a lot to him."

"But who would disturb his things, and why?"

"Was someone home all day?"

Naomi leaned her chin in the heel of her hand. "I think so. Davey was up at Jacob's most of the day while I was at Annalise Yoder's. Mamm and Daed were home, though."

A footstep sounded behind them. Cap turned to see Lydia in the doorway. "I ran

355

an errand after dinner, up to the Hertzlers'. And your daed and Henry were busy plowing the east field all day."

"So the house was empty in the afternoon." Cap frowned.

"Do you think a stranger was here, in our house?" Eli had joined Lydia in the doorway.

"Was anything else disturbed?"

Naomi shrugged while Eli and Lydia exchanged glances.

"I didn't notice anything," Lydia said. "I suppose someone could have been here, but why would someone break in without stealing anything?"

Cap looked at Naomi. "Was anything missing from Davey's chest?"

"He didn't say so, but perhaps we should look."

Naomi went into the house and took the lamp from the kitchen. Cap followed her up the ladder to the loft. Davey's chest was along the left-hand wall, next to his bed. Cap took the lamp from Naomi as she knelt down to open it.

"Do you remember everything that was in there?"

"I think so." Naomi lifted the shawl from its place and set it on Davey's bed. One by one she put the other things on the floor until she reached the bundle of papers. "The papers are out of order."

"Are you certain?" Cap leaned over for a closer look.

She picked up the bundle and shuffled through them. "When we put them away on Davey's birthday, the deed to the land was on top. Remember? We wondered if Davey owns that land now. But look, Davey's baptism certificate is on the top, and then his parents', and then the deed to the land."

Cap handed her the lamp and took the papers. He looked through them one by one.

"You're right, and Davey's right. Someone has gone through his chest." He sat back on his heels. "But why?"

Naomi shook her head. "What use are papers like that to anyone?"

Friday morning dawned bright and hot, but Shem didn't notice. He hunched his shoulders as he sat on the wagon seat driving toward Fort Wayne and the only shop in the area where he could buy glass windows.

Who knew how much they would cost? But Priscilla had insisted on glass windows for the new addition to the house, and she had given him money. So he was driving to Fort Wayne whether he wanted to or not. It was just one of the many things he did now, whether he wanted to or not.

He shrugged. Priscilla had the money, and he had to admit she enjoyed fine things as much as he did. Not fancy enough to raise eyebrows among the members of the church, but nice things. Store-bought fabric for their clothes, soft linen sheets for the beds, white sugar for their coffee.

She curtailed his freedom, that was for sure, but since she came to Indiana, his purpose in life had already benefited from her ambition. Over the last week he had visited each of the eighteen families in the Clinton half of the district, and all but one had been in favor of splitting the existing district in half. That one, Yost Bontrager, was a stubborn farmer steeped in the traditional ways, in league with the Yoders and Schrocks in LaGrange County. Eventually Bontrager would either sell his farm and move east with the rest of the conservatives, or he'd just have to come around.

Priscilla had also been the one to urge him to seek revenge for Cap's interference in his plans. He patted the secret breast pocket sewn into the lining of his jacket and felt the satisfying crinkle. Even if he hadn't been able to prove that Davey was Naomi's illegitimate son, he had the names of the boy's real parents and other relatives from the baptism certificates. And the interesting twist that Davey's father had owned land in Steuben County. In some way that information would prove useful. He was sure of it. Cap Stoltzfus cared for Naomi Schrock, and the best way to hurt Cap was to make Naomi miserable. He patted the paper again.

Shem was about a mile past the little town of Ligonier in the late afternoon when a group of horsemen caught up to him. The leader slowed his horse to keep pace with Shem while the rest of the riders hung back, following the wagon.

"Good afternoon." The man's lowered hat made it hard to see the man's expression, whether friendly or not, but the voice was pleasant enough.

"Good afternoon." Shem glanced at the men behind him. There were at least eight in the group.

"You're out traveling late for one of them Ay-mish."

"I'm going to stop for the night along the way." Shem smiled, trying to put himself at ease. This was the area where the Smith gang was known to frequent, and he had no intention of falling on the wrong side of a bunch of thieves.

The horseman leaned toward him.

"There's a fine tavern up here, just where Stone's Trace meets this road. You'll want to stop there for the night."

"I thought I'd go a bit farther this afternoon." Shem worked to keep from glancing at the horsemen behind him. "I want to get to Fort Wayne early tomorrow and finish my business so I can start for home."

The man shook his head. "There's a dangerous band of criminals around here. You wouldn't want to be caught on the open road at night. Best stay at the tavern."

Shem weighed his options. Had the man just threatened him? Or was it only a friendly warning? He turned in his seat to study the rest of the riders. Priscilla's coins for the glass windows dangled in a bag from his neck. The heavy sack bumped against his chest where his heart beat so loudly they had to hear it.

He licked his lips. "How do I know you're not those same criminals?"

The entire group laughed at that. Shem licked his lips again as the leader pulled off a pair of leather cavalry riding gloves.

"At least you've asked a reasonable question." The man pulled a paper from his coat pocket and handed it to Shem. "We're some of the volunteers who watch this stretch of road, trying to keep travelers like you from

360

finding yourself at the wrong end of the gang's activities."

Shem glanced at the paper. It looked official enough, from what he could read of the English writing. "So you think I should stay at the tavern?"

The leader took his paper back and folded it with careful motions. "You should. It would be the safest course to take." He pulled his gloves back on and pointed down the road. "A half mile down there, just where this road goes southeast and Stone's Trace continues south. You can't miss it."

Shem nodded his thanks as the riders formed into a double line and continued down the road at a trot.

He hadn't planned to stop in a tavern, but at least he had brought some money of his own to spend on it. He could have a hot meal and a warm bed, and Priscilla would still get her window panes.

The tavern wasn't crowded when he arrived, but he wasn't the only guest. A wagon full of immigrants had pulled in from the eastern road just as he drove up, and the family was spilling out of the back of the covered wagon. A boy with light blond hair jumped down and Shem leaned forward. It wasn't Davey Schrock, but the boy looked enough like him to be his brother. Shem watched the rest of the family as the mother gathered them together while the father drove the wagon on to the barn.

"We're all here, then?" she said in German. The language was close enough to Shem's own Deitsch that he could understand her words.

"Ja, *Mutti,*" the oldest girl answered.

Shem counted the rest of the blond heads. Eight children? No, nine. The oldest boy and the father were walking back from the barn. The youngest was the boy he had seen first, and he seemed to be about nine years old. The oldest boy was at least twenty.

"Well, Mutti," said the father, "we stay in luxury tonight."

The mother frowned. "Costly luxury. If it wasn't for the danger from those thieves, we could save our money and camp along the trail."

"I'll not risk your life for a few dollars. It is better to be safe as we start on our journey to Oregon."

The family walked into the tavern together as Shem drove his team on toward the barn. He fingered the crinkling papers as an idea formed in his mind.

The tavern served supper in the common room. A long trestle table filled the space along one wall, and the innkeeper's family bustled from the kitchen to the table, setting bowls of steaming potatoes and bread pudding down among platters of roasted chicken, pork, and beef. Shem rubbed his hands together in anticipation. This meal would be well worth the price of the room.

He didn't take his seat until the German family filed in and sat at one end of the long table, as far from a group of teamsters as they could get. Their obvious distaste for the rough language and unwashed bodies of the other group would work in his favor. Shem smiled. His plans were coming together nicely.

He took a seat next to the oldest boy.

"Good evening," Shem said in German. "My name is Shem Fischer. You have quite a wonderful family."

The young man blushed. "*Vielen dank.* Thank you very much." He grinned. "Franz Hinklemann. There are many of us, isn't that right?"

Shem nodded, his mouth full of tender chicken.

Franz cut his beef. "You travel alone?"

"Ja, for sure. I live north of here. I'm on my way to do some trading in Fort Wayne."

"Ach, ja. Fort Wayne. We have just come from there this day."

Shem smiled. "You are heading west then.

How far are you going?"

Franz beamed. "To Oregon we go. Father learned of this place from a man in Philadelphia. Good country, he says, and a new home for us."

Shem glanced at Franz's parents. They sat at the corner of the table, heads together as they discussed something.

"Is your father worried about something?"

Franz glanced toward his parents. "Ja." He kept his voice low. "Very worried. We have already used much of our money, and Father is afraid we will not have enough to take us all the way to Oregon. It is already much farther than he was told."

"I might be able to help." Shem cut another bite of chicken with his knife. "After supper, ask your father to meet me on the front porch of the tavern."

Franz nodded. "Ja. I will. *Danke. Danke.*"

Shem finished eating before the Hinklemann family and wandered out to the front porch with a mug of coffee. He fingered the pouch under his shirt. Priscilla's windows would have to wait, but she wouldn't mind when she heard how he had worked things out. He grinned to himself. She would enjoy watching his plans unfold, just as he would. Now, if only the Hinklemanns would agree.

■ ■ ■ ■

Wilhelm Hinklemann paused by the large fireplace in the taproom of the tavern and took a twisted paper spill from the crock on the mantelpiece. He tamped the tobacco down in the bowl of his pipe, then lit the spill in the fireplace and held it to the leathery, pungent leaves. Drawing in air by puffs, he waited for the pipe to catch, but all the while he peered through the open door to the porch beyond. He hadn't missed Franz's conversation with the stranger at dinner, and when his son told him the man had an idea to help their family, he had grown suspicious. But it wouldn't hurt to see what the proposal might be.

Once the pipe was lit, Wilhelm strode out to the porch, as if wanting to take the night air.

"Herr Hinklemann." The little man appeared at his elbow before he was even away from the light that poured onto the plank flooring through the doorway.

"Ja, that is I."

"Let us go to the end of the porch over here and have a seat." He led the way to a table sitting in the lamplight that filtered through a window.

Wilhelm settled into his chair with a grunting sigh. The chair was well-built and felt good after a day on the hard wagon seat. "My son said you had a proposition for me."

The other man shifted forward in his seat and placed his fingers together in a steeple. "My name is Shem Fischer. I'm a minister in the Amish church."

Wilhelm nodded. "Ach, ja. I have heard of these Amish." He frowned. "No one seems to like these Amish people, and yet, here you are."

Shem Fischer paled, but went on. "I think you have a problem, and I think I have a solution."

"Ja?" Wilhelm settled back in his chair. He did have a problem. Money was jumping out of his pocket faster than he could stop it. "How can you help?"

Herr Fischer leaned toward him. "In our community, if there is one in need, someone will step in to help him out. Even if that one is a stranger to us."

Wilhelm raised his eyebrows, waiting for the man to get to his point.

"A few years ago, one of our members came upon an orphaned child. His family had been killed in a storm, and only this little boy survived. She took him in and has been raising him ever since."

Wilhelm nodded. "Go on. What has this child to do with me?"

Herr Fischer lifted his hands in a shrug. "The child is unhappy with us. He needs a family of his own kind."

Eyes narrowed, Wilhelm leaned forward. "You think we need another child to raise?"

"You must let me finish." Herr Fischer leaned back in his chair. "This boy, eight years old, inherited his family's property when they were killed. He is the owner of one hundred sixty acres of land in Steuben County."

Herr Fischer stared at him while Wilhelm took in this information. One hundred sixty acres of land? The child was as rich as Croesus.

"In addition, I am willing to pay ten dollars, in gold, for his care and any incidental expenses you might encounter."

Wilhelm tapped his pipe on the arm of his chair. Ten dollars would help him get his family farther west, but it wouldn't solve his problem completely. "You say the boy is unhappy?"

Herr Fischer nodded, his face solemn. "He misses his family, his real parents."

"Why do you think he would go with us?"

A grin settled over the other man's face. "We will tell him that you are his uncle. His

367

own mother's family. You have been looking for him, and now you are overjoyed to have found him." Herr Fischer leaned forward again. "The boy looks just like your family. In fact, when I saw your youngest son climb out of your wagon this afternoon, I thought he was our Davey."

Another son. Wilhelm knew he had crossed a threshold, but smiled anyway. This boy would fit in with their brood easily enough.

"Eight years old, you say?"

Herr Fischer drew some papers out of his jacket and turned them to catch the lamplight filtering through the window. "David Muller, born June 1, 1838. Parents Charles and Edwina Muller." The man peered at Wilhelm. "You'll have to say your wife is the sister of the boy's mother. That will solve any problems with names."

Wilhelm nodded. "And the land? It is nearby?"

"Ja, for sure. You can take the deed when you get the boy. It shouldn't be hard to sell the property." Herr Fischer grew very still. "That is my one condition. You must sell the land and take the boy away. Don't live here. And don't tell the Amish people where you plan to settle."

"Why not?"

Herr Fischer's smile seemed forced. "We don't want the boy torn between you, his real family, and the Amish woman who is caring for him now. We don't want him to be confused."

Wilhelm nodded. He could understand that. In these circumstances, the lies he would need to tell were nothing. The money in his pocket was what counted. "And if the boy doesn't do well?"

Herr Fischer shrugged. "There are orphanages in Chicago. If you don't like him, you can drop him off when you get there." He leaned forward, smiling a true smile. "Perhaps there he will find his real family."

Wilhelm tapped his pipe on the edge of the table. One hundred sixty acres. "I will need to discuss this with my wife. I can give you my answer in the morning?"

Herr Fischer stood and Wilhelm rose with him. "In the morning will be fine."

Wilhelm smiled as he shook the other man's hand. "I think I will be able to give a positive answer. But in twenty years of marriage, I have learned to always consult my wife before making a deal." He raised his finger. "She is the one with the head for business, but I think she will agree to this." Wilhelm imagined the smile on Greta's face when he told her the news. "Ja, I think she will."

19

Saturday morning dawned as bright and clear as the last five days had been. Cap pumped water into his washbasin, then cupped his hand to catch enough for a drink. He sucked in his breath at the icy coolness, then laughed. He felt like he could build a whole barn by himself today.

Naomi. Cap couldn't stop thinking about her. He saw her face in the reflection in his washbasin and heard her voice in the June breeze playing in the treetops. He grinned at the very notion. He was acting like a young man who had just discovered his first love.

His grin gentled into a smile as he washed his face. Not his first love. He had discovered what a blessing it was to fall in love for the second time, with the knowledge of how precious and fleeting life could be. He knew how important it was to make every moment count.

Done with his washing and shaving, he threw the soapy water in an arc over his garden and hung the worn tin basin from its nail in the lean-to. He went inside the house and pulled his Dutch oven out of the fireplace coals, then lifted the lid with the poker. The cornbread was baked to perfection. He cut out a chunk and sat at his rough table. After a silent prayer of thanks, he covered the steaming cake with honey and took a bite, savoring it as he looked around the cabin.

Building the loft would have to wait until he could take the logs he had cut to the new sawmill over in Goshen, and that wouldn't happen for another few weeks. Meanwhile, if he wanted Naomi to move into this cabin and make it a home for the three of them, he had more work to do. The rough table he had built for himself needed to be planed and sanded, and the sticks he had been using for legs needed to be replaced with something sturdier. Perhaps trestle legs would be good.

He took another bite of cornbread as he thought of what he would be asking Naomi to give up. Eli and Lydia had built a beautiful, functional home, but all he had to offer was this cabin. With time and work, it would become more comfortable. Davey could help, and any future children he and Naomi might have.

The cornbread stuck in his throat at that thought. He would never forget Martha and their son, but God truly did redeem the lost years. Like Job, he could hope to have all of God's blessings restored to him.

One evening last week, Naomi had spoken of Annalise's loom, and how she was learning to weave. Her dream was to help support herself and Davey by weaving and selling wool cloth with the wool from their own flock of sheep.

Cap shoved the last corner of the wedge of cornbread into his mouth and rose from the table. The sheep would need a place to graze, shelter, and water. He could have all of that ready for Naomi when he proposed to her. He wrapped the leftover bread in a towel and took the Dutch oven outside to scrub it clean. Jacob would help him plan what he needed to build for the flock and give him some pointers in how to care for the sheep. Naomi was determined to have her own wool business, and he wanted to do everything he could to help her.

Before the sun had climbed halfway to its zenith, he was walking into Jacob Yoder's farmyard. He saw his friend working in the pens next to the barn, and so headed that way. As he got closer, his steps faltered. Jacob seemed to be working at pounding a stake into the ground, but his movements were erratic. On the last swing, his hammer missed the stake, and Jacob sunk to the ground.

"Jacob!" Cap ran to the fence. "Are you all right?"

Jacob knelt on the ground in the middle of a herd of bleating sheep. His face had been buried in his arm, but when he heard Cap, he wiped his arm across his face.

"Ja." His voice was hoarse. He cleared his throat and tried again. "Ja, I'm fine." He didn't look at Cap.

He was crying. Strong, capable Jacob was crying.

"Something is wrong. Is it Mattie?" Cap glanced toward the house. "Is she all right?"

Jacob nodded and waded through the sheep to the fence. He climbed over it and joined Cap. "Mattie is fine. We've just . . . well, we've had a rough time."

Cap tried not to watch as Jacob wiped his face with a handkerchief and composed himself. Everything had seemed all right with them last Sunday at church, but now that he thought about it, Mattie had seemed pale and withdrawn. "Do you want to talk about it?"

Jacob leaned against the fence and Cap joined him, looking into the trees, watching the breeze turn the new green leaves this way and that as he waited for Jacob to speak.

"My mamm used to quote a verse from Job," Jacob said. He brushed some dried mud off his trouser leg. "The Lord giveth and the Lord taketh away. Blessed be the name of the Lord." His voice choked at the end, but he swallowed and went on as Cap's stomach sank. "I never really knew what she meant until now." He turned toward Cap. "I don't know how much you know of our family's story, but we've experienced death." He sighed and ran a hand over his face and through his beard. "Too many times." He shook his head. "But this . . . I don't know if I can handle this."

"Jacob, tell me what happened."

"We were expecting a little one, but she . . . she never made it far enough to be born. She never even had a chance at life."

"But Mattie is all right?"

Jacob nodded. "She is sad, and I try to make her feel better. I even stopped talking about . . . it, because it made her cry."

"Are you all right?"

"Me?" Jacob gave a short bark of a laugh. "Of course I'm all right. I didn't suffer the way —" He drew a deep breath that caught at the end. "I didn't suffer like Mattie did. I'm fine."

Cap looked for a place to sit and saw a bench in the shade of the barn wall. He grabbed at Jacob's sleeve and pulled him to it and sat him down, then he straddled the bench facing his friend.

"I know something of what you're going through."

Jacob glanced at him, and then down again. "I remember now, you said you lost your family."

Cap nodded. "My wife and son both died in childbirth. In one horrible day I went from being the happiest, most content man to the depths of despair."

The man next to him stared at his boots. When he spoke, it was as soft as a whisper. "How did you get through that? I mean, I lost my daughter, but I still have Mattie. I can't imagine losing her too."

Leaning his elbows on his knees, Cap let silence settle between him while he went back into his memories. How had he survived losing Martha and the baby? Perhaps he hadn't.

"I lost part of myself that day too. A piece of me died and was buried with them." He looked up at Jacob. "You'll never forget that baby. Even if you have a dozen children, you'll never forget the one you lost."

Jacob sniffed and wiped his eyes with his handkerchief again.

"Meanwhile, you need to show Mattie that you grieve as much as she does. You need to let this grief bring you together, not push you apart."

The other man sat back, nodding. "Ja, for sure. I remember how our family was when we lost our Hansli and the girls." He shook his head. "I can't even tell you how broken our family was during that time."

Cap nodded. The Yoder family had seen their share of grief.

Jacob went on. "It happened years ago, but you're right. My memories of my little brother are as fresh as if I had eaten breakfast with him this morning." Jacob smiled. "The pain fades, ja?"

Cap nodded again. "The pain fades, but the memories don't."

Jacob wiped his eyes again. "I didn't ask you why you came over. I'm sure it wasn't to have me tell you my woes."

"There's nothing wrong with that." Cap stood. "I came over to see if you would help me get my place ready for Naomi's sheep, but we can talk about that later."

Jacob raised his eyebrows. "Naomi's

sheep? Is there something you want to tell me?"

Cap lifted a finger to his lips. "Not yet. This is a secret. Naomi doesn't even know I'm planning this."

"She won't hear it from me." Jacob sighed and looked toward the house. "I'll come by your place on Monday. Right now, I need to talk to my wife."

Reaching down, Cap helped Jacob up. "I'll see you tomorrow at your folks', then. Remember, don't tell anyone what we're planning."

Jacob grasped his hand and grinned. "Not until you tell me I can."

"Look, Memmi, look!"

Naomi shaded her eyes to see what Davey was pointing toward. A turkey vulture's unmistakable outline soared in a wide circle above the road where they were walking.

"Will it get one of our lambs?"

Davey slipped his hand into hers as he asked the question, and Naomi looked down at his fingers curled around hers. When did his hands get so big? And his head was nearly even with her elbow. Long gone were the days when she could pick him up and snuggle him in her arms.

"Ne, the vultures don't hunt. Our lambs

are safe from them."

"What do they eat?" He turned in circles as he tried to keep the bird in view.

"They eat animals that have died, but they don't kill them."

As Davey turned to face the road again, he dropped Naomi's hand. "There's Cap!"

Her boy ran to meet his friend. Cap was walking out of Jacob and Mattie's lane and met Davey's headlong rush with open arms. He caught him and swung him in a circle, Davey laughing the whole way around.

Then Cap looked up and their gazes locked. He gave her a smile, then turned back to Davey. They spoke for a minute, and then Davey ran toward Jacob's barn while Cap continued on his way toward her.

"You're a fine sight to see this morning."

Even though Naomi was beginning to be accustomed to Cap's compliments, his words still brought a flush of heat to her cheeks.

"Hello yourself," she said as they met in the middle of the road.

"Are you on your way to visit Mattie?" Cap bent his head toward hers and she found herself leaning into his strength.

"Ja, for sure. And the lambs." Naomi was going to say something about how often they visited the lambs each week, but the look on Cap's face stopped her. "Is something wrong?"

Cap looked toward the barn, and then took her arm and started leading her toward home. "Jacob just went to talk to Mattie, so I don't think they want visitors just now."

Naomi twisted back. "What about Davey?"

"I told him to only visit the lambs and then come home. I told him not to bother Jacob."

"Jacob told you what happened?"

Cap nodded, his face solemn. "And Mattie told you?"

Naomi nodded and pulled her arm out of his grasp. Before he could react, she had slipped her hand into the crook of his elbow. He pulled his elbow close to his body and matched his footsteps to hers.

"I hate that Mattie has to go through this."

Cap made an agreeing sound under his breath. "Jacob, too. It's very hard for both of them."

"It isn't fair." Naomi felt a weight lift off her heart. At last she had someone she could talk to about Mattie's secret.

"What isn't?"

"Mattie and Jacob waited so long to have a child, and once they were finally expecting, this happened."

"We don't know why things like this happen, but God does."

"You think God cares about Mattie and Jacob, and what happens to them?" She gestured toward the sky where she had been told God lived. That God out there.

Cap's smile was crooked, as if heartache and joy were fighting a battle. "I know God cares about them. Nothing happens to us that he doesn't sift through his fingers first, and he knows every detail. He will help them get through this grief."

Naomi bit back the words she wanted to say. How could Cap believe such a thing? "If God knows everything, then why doesn't he just stop these bad things from happening?"

Cap shrugged. "I don't know the answer to that. But I do know he doesn't make us suffer alone. And he turns our sorrow into joy." He smiled again and took her hand. "He turns our mourning into dancing, as the psalmist said. What we think is the end of the story is only the beginning in his eyes."

Cap's mild words sent a lightning stab of fury through Naomi. She dropped his arm and faced him. "If God is so powerful, he could have saved Mattie's baby." His mouth dropped open, but she went on. "I think I can do a better job of running this world than a God who lets babies die and lets tornadoes take little boys' families away and sends rain when we don't need it and no rain when we do." Naomi took a deep breath. "There's so much wrong in this world that I wonder if there is a God who is sovereign and loves us the way the preachers say."

"Naomi, I thought —"

She blinked to keep tears from falling. "You thought what?"

"I thought you were . . . I mean, when we're worshiping, you look as though you're praying, and singing, and worshiping just like the rest of us."

A cold pit started opening in Naomi's stomach. "Of course I am. What does that have to do with Mattie and Jacob?"

Cap ran a hand over his face and rubbed at his beard. "When we worship, whom do we worship?"

The pit spun. "We . . . we worship . . ." Naomi had never considered the question before. "We worship God, of course."

"What God?" His words were quiet, gentle. "Is it a god that you've invented and decided you like? One who doesn't let our loved ones be hurt? Or do you worship the

God who is revealed to us in the Good Book?"

The pit swirled. Naomi walked to a stump at the side of the road and sat on it. Cap watched her as she thought about his words, then he squatted down in front of her and took her hand in his.

"Naomi, listen."

She shook her head and turned away from him. His words confused her, and that open pit in her soul threatened to draw her in. Why couldn't he just be quiet and let things be the way they had always been? She and Davey were happy. She didn't need God, or even Cap, to make her content.

"You don't know what or why I worship." Her voice came as a whisper. "But it doesn't matter, does it? I'm a good Amish woman. I follow the Ordnung, I take my son to church, I teach him about God . . ." She faltered. When was the last time she had spoken to Davey about God?

"I said it before, and I'm afraid it might be true." Cap paused until she looked at him. When he continued, his voice was gentle, but his words felt like stones thrown at her one by one, pushing her into the swirling darkness. "You've put Davey and your love for him in the place where God belongs."

"He's my son." She wanted her words to hit him like a rock, but they came out as a weak cry. "Shouldn't he be important to me?"

Cap stood up, looking down at her with pity in his gaze. "Until you put Davey in his proper place, I'm afraid you'll never understand what it is to put God in his proper place, as the only one worthy of your worship."

He turned and started toward his home, leaving her sitting on the tree stump. He looked back once, but he didn't pause. He kept walking away with relentless steps.

Cap found it easy to avoid Naomi the next afternoon at the off Sunday gathering in Christian Yoder's shady yard, since she seemed to be working just as hard to avoid him. But Davey noticed him sitting on the edge of the porch before dinner was ready and came running over.

"Memmi said she didn't want to talk to you today." Davey leaned against Cap's knees and looked into his eyes. "She said you said enough yesterday."

Cap glanced over at Naomi. She had her back turned toward him as she stood in the circle with the other women. The sound of their bright chatter and laughter floated toward him in the heat of the July afternoon.

"Ja, she probably thinks so." An uneasy feeling weighed him down today. Yesterday's disagreement with Naomi bothered him enough that he didn't sleep last night. How could he have been so wrong about her?

Davey leaned closer until he was nose to nose with him. "Aren't you and Memmi friends anymore?"

Cap sighed as he stood and took Davey's hand. "Let's go for a walk."

Davey fell in step with him as Cap headed toward Jacob's farm, directly across the road from Christian's. His first thought was to take Davey to see the sheep at Jacob's farm, but that thought made the unease buckle and swell. Yesterday he had planned to build a place for Naomi's sheep on his farm, but today . . . today those plans were dead.

"I'll show you Jethro." Davey bounced a little when he saw which direction they were headed. "He's my very own lamb. Have you seen him?"

Cap shook his head. "I don't think I have."

"He's the best ram lamb ever, Jacob says. And he'll be the *datti* of all of our flock. Memmi —" He stopped and looked up at Cap. "Can I talk about Memmi?"

"Why wouldn't you?"

"You frown when I talk about her."

Cap rubbed at the creases on his forehead. "I didn't know I did. It's nothing."

Davey let go of his hand and ran to the sheep pen by the barn. "There he is. There's Jethro."

By the time Cap caught up to him, the boy was in the pen, trying to wrap his arms around the lamb. Jethro butted him and pranced around, as if he recognized Davey and was happy to see him.

"He does look like he thinks you're someone special."

Davey grinned, his legs wobbling as the lamb rubbed against them. "He's mine. My very own lamb."

"For sure, he is." Cap leaned on the upper rail of the fence and Davey joined him as Jethro went to his mother and butted at her until she let him feed.

"I've never had something of my very own. Not like him."

"You have your memmi, and the rest of your family."

"It isn't the same. Jethro likes me, but he doesn't have to."

Cap tousled his hair. "I like you and I don't have to."

"Ja, but you're a person. An animal is different."

Too late, Cap remembered the pony he

had planned to get for Davey. Naomi wouldn't welcome the gift now. When he and Naomi disagreed yesterday, a rift had opened between them and he didn't see a possibility of it closing. This was what the Good Book meant when it said that the followers of Christ must leave all behind. If Naomi wasn't a true believer in Christ, then he must leave her behind, along with his dreams of their future together.

Davey jiggled his elbow. "Are you and Memmi going to get married?"

"What makes you ask that?"

"Mose and Menno said that their memmi said that you should get married."

Mose and Menno. Naomi's ten- and eight-year-old nephews were too smart for their own good. "Getting married isn't as simple as that."

"But if you married Memmi, then you would be my daed. My real daed, not just pretend."

Cap swallowed down the lump in his throat. What he wouldn't give to have Davey for his son. "Like I said, it isn't that easy."

Davey stared at him, his face solemn. "Once William and I had a fight. He wanted to look for tadpoles in the spring ponds in the woods, but I wanted to look for crayfish chimneys. He yelled at me and I went home. We didn't talk to each other for three whole days."

"I saw you playing with him today."

The boy nodded. "That's what I mean. We had a fight, but we made up, and we're friends again. That's what you need to do with Memmi."

Cap couldn't face Davey's hopeful gaze. "It isn't that easy."

"You keep saying that. But if you don't, you'll never be my daed."

A glance told Cap that Davey was about to cry. Tears welled up in his eyes, and his face was mottled pink. "It is important to you, isn't it?"

Davey blinked fast and hard to keep the tears from spilling down his cheeks, but one escaped and ran down to cling to the end of his nose. "It's all I've ever wanted. Ever since . . ." He swallowed and wiped his sleeve across his face. "Ever since Pa told me to hide in the fireplace."

Cap could imagine Davey's pa, knowing that the storm was bearing down and desperate to save his family, shoving his little son into the only safe place he could find. Had he hoped that Davey's mother and the baby would join him? He must not have had time to save them before the tornado hit and destroyed the cabin, leaving only the chimney intact . . . with Davey crouched in the fireplace. What had gone through Davey's head during the hour or so before the Amish families had found the cabin and rescued him?

Davey took his hand and tugged. "I want my family back. I want Ma and Pa. But I know they aren't coming back. If you and Memmi get married, then we could be a new family, couldn't we?" Cap looked away again. "Couldn't we?"

Cap put his arm around the boy's shoulders and drew him close. "I wish I could promise that, but I can't."

20

After the noon dinner of roasted chicken, mashed potatoes, and fresh green beans from the various gardens in the neighborhood, Cap rested on the shady porch with Christian, Eli, and the rest of the men. Jacob sat a little apart, but if Cap hadn't known his sorrow, he would not have guessed anything was amiss other than the usual Sunday afternoon rest.

Mose Schrock ran up to his father, Isaac. "Yost Bontrager is coming up the road. And he's in an awful hurry."

His brother, Menno, on his brother's heels as usual, echoed the end of the sentence. "He's in an awful hurry."

The porchful of men turned their faces toward the road as the boys, joined by Davey and the others, ran to meet Yost. Christian struggled to his feet, using a cane to steady his balance.

"What could bring Yost all the way over

here on a non-church Sunday, and without his family?"

Eli joined him at the edge of the porch. "We'll soon know."

Cap stood, too, and watched Yost's progress. The tall man was all angles and swinging hair as he strode up to the porch from the road. With the Bontragers living in Clinton Township, Cap hadn't spent much time with Yost, but knew he had been in the same party with the Schrocks and Yoders when they came from Pennsylvania.

"Good afternoon, Yost," Christian said.

Yost stopped in front of the group of men, breathing hard. "Good . . . afternoon."

Annalise brought him a glass of water and he made his way onto the porch, sitting in the chair Cap had vacated. Yost took a large handkerchief out of his coat and wiped his face. He took another drink and sat back as the group of men gathered around him. The women at the other end of the porch stopped their conversation and looked his way.

"Is anything wrong?" Christian eased into a chair next to his friend.

"I'll say." Yost drained his glass and Annalise filled it again. "You won't believe what happened in Clinton Township this morning." He shook his head. "They didn't give any warning at all. They just did it."

"Did what?" Eli pressed closer.

"Voted to form their own church district, that's what."

"How?" Christian leaned toward Yost. "Why? Did they say?"

Cap shook his head. It couldn't be true. Yost must have misunderstood.

"Since today is a non-church Sunday, we were having a quiet time together, just our family."

The men gathered around nodded. They had all started their Sunday mornings in the same way.

"But then at midmorning, Peter Gingerich, the boy, came by and said the community was meeting in his father's barn, and we were to come along. By the time we got there, they had already voted to form their own district. They said they were waiting for our votes to make it official, but I could tell which way the wind blew."

Stunned silence filled the porch.

"Was Shem Fischer there?" Cap knew the self-proclaimed preacher must be at the bottom of this.

Yost shook his head. "I thought that was strange. He's always in the middle of things. But his wife was there, and said she spoke for him."

Cap rubbed at the back of his neck. He had seen Priscilla Fischer at church last Sunday. She certainly seemed to be willing to speak for Shem, although the man had never had any problem making his own views heard.

Jonas Plank, Solomon Plank's twenty-four-year-old son, looked from Christian's face to Preacher Abraham's. "Can they do that? Vote to form their own district like that?"

Isaac Schrock's face was red. "We can't let them. We must stay together."

"What can we do to stop them? They've been working to destroy the church, and they have. I say we let them go their own way." Elias Hertzler crossed his arms and turned away from the group.

Then Josef Bender stood, his fists clenched. "I say we go talk to them. They are trying to make a mark of division where there should never be one."

Solomon Plank shook his head. "Let them go. If they don't want us, then we don't want them either. Let them go their own way and leave us be."

"Brothers. Friends." Christian looked tired. "It is the Sabbath, but ill will is working its insidious way into our hearts. This is a time to mourn, not fight."

Preacher Abraham nodded his agreement. "It is a sad day. We are torn in two."

Christian looked from face to face as the tension eased, and then back at Yost. "Did they say why they would take a step like this?"

"They said they live too far from La-Grange County, and that, well . . . ," Yost looked at the group gathered around him, "they said you were all stuck in the old ways. 'Afraid of progress' is how Tall Peter said it."

Christian tapped his cane on the floor in an absent motion, and Preacher Abraham stroked his beard just as absently, both deep in thought. The rest of the group waited for their response.

Finally, Abraham spoke. "If they want to remove themselves from our fellowship, there isn't much we can do or say to stop them."

Christian turned toward him. "But if there is a way to repair the breach, we must look for it and do what we can."

"I agree." Abraham settled back in his chair. "I will go to talk to the leaders, to Tall Peter and Preacher Elam. Will you go with me, Preacher Christian?"

"I will. But I ask that we pray for guidance and direction."

Preacher Abraham went to his knees, and all of the group who were able followed him. Cap dared to glance at Naomi, but she knelt in prayer with the rest of them just as she always had. Perhaps, he prayed, he had been mistaken. Perhaps her faith was as strong as his. Perhaps there was a way to span this rift between them and between the two halves of the church district.

The discussion about the threatened church split continued through the rest of the noon meal. Cap listened as he gathered plates from the men and took them to the shady table that had been set up for the women to do dishes. Naomi was helping, scraping the plates and stacking them, ready to be washed. She kept her gaze on her work, even when he set his pile of dishes at her elbow.

"I'd like to talk to you."

He kept his voice soft, hoping to avoid the notice of the other women, but the conversation around them slowed. Every ear waited for Naomi's answer.

Magdalena Hertzler took the spatula from Naomi's hand and shooed her away. "Go on, Naomi. Don't worry about the dishes."

Naomi still didn't look at him as she surrendered her job to Magdalena and followed Cap away from the crowd. He led her to the other side of Annalise's garden where the trees of the woods on the west side of the clearing cast afternoon shade in the still air.

"What did you want to talk about?" Naomi plucked a leaf from a sassafras branch and tore one of the three lobes from it with a careful motion.

"I hoped we could . . ." His voice faltered at her icy demeanor. He glanced across the big clearing to the group of boys playing near the barn. He could face her for Davey's sake. He started again. "I hoped we could go back to being friends. I spoke without thinking yesterday, and I'm sorry."

Naomi tore another strip off the leaf. "I know that would make Davey happy."

Cap suppressed a sigh. She would mend their friendship for Davey, but not for him. And not because it would please God, not because it was the right thing to do.

"He thinks we're having a fight, like he had with William. He wants us to make up." Cap plucked his own fragrant leaf from the shrub and twirled the woody stem between his fingers.

"We didn't fight, did we?"

Cap shrugged. "That's how he sees it." He dared to look at her. "There's more." He waited for her to meet his eyes before he continued. "He longs for a family."

She threw the shredded leaf to the ground. "He has a family."

"He wants a mamm and daed. He wants what his friends and cousins have." Naomi bit her bottom lip, but Cap went on. "Now that he remembers his first family, his ma and pa, he longs to have that life again." He stepped closer to Naomi and grasped her shoulders. They were hard and tight with tension. "And he thinks if we get married, he'll have that."

She looked at him then, both eyes focused on his. "Married? What gave him that idea?"

Cap tried to smile as he felt the tension drain from her arms. "It isn't such a bad thought, is it?"

Her face grew pink and she turned away from him, out of his grasp. The children's laughter drifted toward them in the sultry air. Her back was straight, and her skirt hung in gentle curves that moved as her body shook. He reached one hand toward her shoulder, but thought better of it. He had made her cry, just by suggesting they might marry.

"Naomi, don't cry." He waited for the shaking to stop, but she sunk to the ground, sobbing . . . or was she laughing?

He grasped both of her shoulders again

and turned her toward him. She was laughing, with tears streaming down her face.

"I've never —" She gasped and wiped her eyes with the hem of her apron. "I've never seen such a look on a man's face." She knelt in the grass, trying to catch her breath, but burst out laughing again.

He should be insulted, the way she was giggling at him, but instead, he found himself smiling, and then laughing with her. He sat in the grass beside her.

"I'm not really that funny."

She looked at him and snorted with laughter all over again. "You . . . you looked like you were afraid I would think you were serious." She got her laughter under control. "You looked like a startled deer, afraid you had been caught by the hunter."

Cap pulled a grass stem and stuck the soft end between his teeth. He chewed it slowly while her giggles faded. "I meant what I said." He threw the grass away and took her hand. "We could get married."

Her smile faded. "Yesterday . . ."

"Yesterday I was worried about Jacob and Mattie. I was worried about your casual attitude toward God." He looked at their hands entwined together. "Later, I realized that if I ever have to go through something like Jacob is going through again, I'd want you to be there with me." He looked into her eyes. "You are part of my life, Naomi. I want you to think about marrying me. Just think about it. We can talk about what it will mean for us, and for Davey."

Naomi gave a slow nod. "I'll think about it."

A shout went up from the house. A covered wagon was coming along the narrow road, dust in its wake. As it stopped by the house, folks poured off of the porch, and Cap and Naomi went to join them.

Shem Fischer jumped off the wagon seat and faced the group. His gaze swept the crowd and stopped when he met Cap's eyes. He smiled the smile Cap had dreaded as a boy. Shem was planning something.

"Is Davey Schrock —" Shem stopped himself and grinned. "Is Davey *Muller* here?"

Davey was pulled and pushed through the group until he faced Shem. Naomi threaded through the crowd until she stood behind him and Cap followed.

Cap's teeth ground together. He kept his voice low so that it wouldn't carry. "What are you doing, Shem?"

Shem ignored him and stepped aside as two strangers jumped down from the wagon seat, a man and a woman. Then a tumble of children spilled out of the back of the covered wagon, each of them as blond and blue-eyed as Davey. They stood in a silent line and stared at Davey. The woman wiped her eyes with a handkerchief.

"This is Wilhelm and Greta Hinklemann. I met them and their family when I was on my way to Fort Wayne to get supplies. They said they were looking for their lost nephew —"

Naomi gasped and Cap gripped her shoulder.

Shem grinned, looking from the strangers to Davey. "They said his name was Davey Muller. So I told them they should come and see if our Davey was the same boy they have been searching for."

Davey took a step forward, staring at the couple. "You have been looking for me?"

The man dropped to one knee in front of the boy, searching his face. "Ja, for months now. Ever since we reached the Muller place in Steuben County and found the grave markers, and saw that yours was missing." The man gestured toward his wife. "Your mama was my wife's sister, rest her soul."

Shem beckoned to the smallest child in the family, a boy about Davey's age, and stood him next to Davey. The man shook his head in disbelief. "Would you look at that. They could be twins."

Shem turned the boys to face Naomi and the community grouped behind her. Cap's jaw ached from clenching it. The boys looked as alike as if they were brothers.

Naomi's shock had turned to anger as quickly as it took for Daed to invite the strangers to camp at their farm. As if that woman could really be Davey's aunt . . . but there was no denying the resemblance between the boys.

Cap's hand rested on her shoulder and she leaned into it as Daed gave the strange man — Hinklemann — directions to their farm. "I'll be coming along behind you and show you where you can set up your camp."

Mattie found her way to Naomi's side and clasped her hand. "Are you all right?"

Ne, she wasn't. She would never be all right again. But she nodded, even though her head felt like it was wrapped in wool batting.

"I never thought that Davey might have relatives," Mattie said. "Do you think they only want to get to know him, or —"

"Don't." Naomi forced the word out through clenched jaws. "Don't say it. They will stay for a day and then leave, and we'll never have to worry about them again."

Cap's hand on her shoulder tightened. Beyond Mattie was Davey, climbing onto the wagon seat with the Hinklemann family.

"Davey, ne." She reached out to him, but he only turned and waved.

"I'm going to show them where to camp. I'll see you there."

As the wagon left, Naomi saw the other woman's arm around her boy's shoulders. The other woman's cheek resting on her boy's head. And then they were out of sight, blocked by the wagon as it rumbled down the road.

Cap turned her toward himself and embraced her. She buried her face in his shirt for a moment, and then straightened, pulling away from him.

"I need to follow them. I need to watch out for Davey. They might —" What? Keep driving with him? Take him away from her?

Steal his love.

Cap's jaw clenched and unclenched. He was as upset as she was. "I'll go with you. I know you want to stay close to Davey."

Mattie gave her a quick hug and Naomi clung to her, holding back her tears.

"It will be all right," Mattie said. "He knows you are his real mother. You are the one who loves him." Mattie gave a last hard squeeze, and then let her go.

Naomi hurried down the road to their farm. The whitewashed house surrounded by the green grass and gardens looked foreign with the strange wagon in the yard. Daed had led them to a spot between the chicken coop and the house. She and Cap stopped, watching Davey running and playing with the Hinklemann children.

Her knees shook and she leaned into Cap. "He's lost to us. He'll never want to come back to me."

Cap's grip around her shoulders was firm. "You don't know that."

"Look at him," Naomi said, barely able to speak. Cap leaned close to catch her whisper. "Have you ever seen him so happy?"

Mamm walked past them. "Naomi, come help me. We'll slice bread, cheese, and sausage for a cold supper tonight. I'm sure the Hinklemanns are hungry after traveling all day."

Naomi turned to Cap. "I can't just leave him."

"I'll stay here and watch him. I'll take care of him."

Supper was anything but the peaceful meal Naomi was used to on Sunday evenings. The Hinklemanns spoke German, and while Naomi could understand the language that was so similar to her own

Deitsch, they spoke so quickly that she couldn't always follow their conversation.

"You say you met Shem Fischer in Fort Wayne?" Daed asked, raising his voice above the shouts of the children. Davey's voice was just as loud as the others', but Wilhelm and Greta ignored them, as if their children's behavior was normal.

"A day's drive from Fort Wayne, near Ligonier. We stayed in the same tavern there." Wilhelm tore at his bread with his teeth. "We were warned that a gang of bandits lurked in the area and would steal from folks camping along the road." He stuck a slice of cold sausage in his mouth with the bread. "We were glad to meet him when he told us about Davey."

Greta stared at her plate, eating small bites. The children ran to the table.

"I want bread, Mama." The youngest one, the one who looked like Davey, pushed his way to the table between his parents.

"Hush now, Karl." Greta scooted over on the bench and helped the boy into a seat. "There is no call to act like a wild animal. Sit and eat your supper."

Davey climbed on the bench next to Naomi, across from Karl. "Memmi, Karl is nine years old, and his birthday is in June too. So he is one year older than I am."

"Ja, liebchen." Greta leaned toward Davey. "Just the right age to be Karl's younger brother."

The bread turned sour in Naomi's mouth and she gave Davey the rest of her supper. The other woman's eyes were shadowed in spite of the smile she gave Davey, as if she was worried about something.

Naomi glanced down the table toward Cap. He held a piece of bread in his hand, but wasn't eating it. He listened to the conversation between Wilhelm and Daed, but he watched Davey. When he caught her gaze, he gave a tight smile and a nod. He shared her fears.

Supper was cleaned up and Naomi took Davey inside the house with her after evening prayers. Daed had included their guests in the bedtime ritual and the other family had sat silently, listening.

"Why can't I sleep outside with Karl? He said I could."

"You'll see him in the morning." Naomi scrubbed at the dirt on Davey's chin with a wet cloth. "I don't think they plan to leave tomorrow, so Karl can help you with your chores."

"Can I take him to Jacob's? I want to show him the sheep, and Jethro."

"We'll see what the morning brings." She

turned him toward the ladder and his bed in the loft.

"Memmi, are they really my aunt and uncle and cousins?" His blue eyes, so like the other children's, tugged at her heart.

"They say they are. We'll talk about it more tomorrow." She chewed on her lower lip. "Do you want them to be?"

His grin said it all. "If they are, then they're my real family. All my own." He climbed the ladder, leaving her behind.

Naomi went into her room under the loft and closed the door. She didn't need a light to change into her sleeping clothes or brush her hair. She eased open the shutters and sat on her bed, watching the Hinklemanns' camp as she ran the brush through her hair, over and over. Wilhelm had erected a lean-to against the wagon using a canvas sheet. The younger children had taken their blankets under the shelter and soon settled into sleep. Franz, the oldest boy, sat with his parents for a while, then took his own blanket and crawled under the wagon.

Greta and Wilhelm remained, sitting at the table Daed had set up for their supper. Their voices were low, too low for Naomi to make out any part of their conversation, but they seemed to be arguing.

The rope of entwined fear and anger that

had been writhing inside her since the Hinklemanns had interrupted her pleasant Sunday afternoon tightened into a strangling knot, forcing hot tears that trickled down her cheeks. How dare they come here to steal her son! But how could she stop them? She turned possibilities over in her mind.

Perhaps she could take Davey and hide. They could go to the spot along the river where Crow Flies stayed, deep in the woods. No one would find them there.

That other woman, Greta, seemed to love her children. Maybe if Naomi insisted that she couldn't take Davey unless she left one of her own . . . but ne. That wouldn't do.

Only something tragic would stop them from pursuing this idea of taking Davey from her, from his real family. Her mind traveled a trail that led to a knife from the kitchen and a slaying in the dark wagon.

Naomi shook herself awake, the rope twisting inside her like a snake, reaching toward that dark place where temptation had led her. She shuddered, wiping her palms on her nightdress to rid herself of the bloody stains that didn't exist. She hadn't done it. She hadn't.

Covering her face with her hands, Naomi tried to banish the thought, the . . . dream, but it wouldn't leave her. She hadn't killed the Hinklemann family, but she could — that was the horror. She could because Davey was at risk. She was a mother. A mother protecting her boy. Nothing else mattered.

Cap's words penetrated her swirling thoughts, but she pushed them away. He was wrong. She hadn't put Davey in the place reserved for God. That would make him an idol, and that would never happen. She would never put Davey above her obedience to the church, to the Ordnung. To God.

She peered through the half-open shutter to the starry sky above the black outline of the barn roof. God. Cap believed that God knew what happened to them, cared about them, and even caused things to happen to bring them closer to him. But to her, God had always been like the stars. Pure. Untouchable. Distant.

Now, though, facing something she could never get through on her own . . .

Sinking to her knees beside the bed, Naomi closed her eyes and looked inward to the blackness. Nothing. Nothing was there. There was no one to pray to, no one to ask for help. She was alone, at the mercy of the God out there. She had loved her boy too much, had set him on the throne and worshiped him. And now God in heaven was going to punish her. She had broken the commandments. She had sinned and now she would lose her boy. And there was nothing she could do.

21

Cap woke with a start on Monday morning. He hadn't thought he would sleep at all during the night, but at some point he had drifted off, leaning against the cabin wall as he sat on his bed. Early as it was, Cap roused himself to complete wakefulness by splashing cold water over his head. He would feed the horses, then head over to the Schrocks'. He had work to do, but with Davey's future hanging in the balance, he had no desire to be anywhere else.

Even before he was halfway through the woods between his farm and the Schrocks', he heard the noise of children shouting in play. He paused as he reached the edge of the trees and watched Davey with the Hinklemann children. Davey was the youngest of the group, but Karl and his older brothers let him keep pace with them in their game of tag. The younger girls joined in and their shrieks added to the noise.

The game drifted in Cap's direction and Davey saw him.

"Cap!" he yelled, his voice hoarse from playing. "Come play with us!" He ran full tilt toward the woods, skirting a girl's outstretched hand and coming to a full stop two feet away, panting with his hands on his knees.

Looking around the farmyard, Cap didn't see any of the Schrock family. "Are your folks up?"

Davey nodded, still breathing hard. "Grossdatti and Henry are choring in the barn. Memmi and Grossmutti are fixing breakfast."

Wilhelm Hinklemann sat at the table where they had eaten supper the night before, puffing on a pipe. Greta was folding blankets and a large canvas sheet with the help of the two oldest daughters.

"Have you done your chores?"

Davey's breath puffed as he straightened up. "Karl was going to help me, but he wanted to play tag first."

Cap grasped the boy's shoulder. "So the chickens go hungry while you play?"

A glance toward the henhouse told Cap that his hunch had been right.

"Is this the way we work? Do we fill ourselves with our own pleasures before we see to our responsibilities?"

Davey kicked at a clump of grass. "Uncle Wilhelm said we could play. He said we're only children once."

Cap felt his jaw clench. "You have your chores to do. You can play after they are done."

The boy looked over his shoulder at the game that continued without him. "I'd rather play."

Squatting down so that he was eye to eye with Davey, Cap grasped his shoulders. "You need to do your chores first. You will have plenty of time to play with Karl this afternoon. I don't think they plan to leave until tomorrow."

"All right." Davey kicked the grass once more, then shuffled toward the chicken coop.

"Davey," Karl called. "Where are you going?"

Davey walked backward as he called back, "Doing my chores. Do you want to help?"

"Nein." Karl jumped aside as his sister ran toward him, her hand stretched out. "I'm going to play."

Cap saw the struggle within Davey as he watched the game, then glanced at the henhouse. He sent Cap a pleading look, but

Cap only nodded toward the waiting chickens.

Once Davey had gone in to feed his charges, Cap continued on his way to the house. He nodded a good morning to the Hinklemanns, and then stepped onto the porch. Through the open door he could see Lydia and Naomi bustling between the stove, kitchen shelf, and table, fixing a meal that would feed an entire church.

He stopped in the open doorway. "Is there anything I can do to help?"

Lydia gave him a smile of thanks. "Could you make sure the outside table is clean, and that there are enough seats for everyone?"

"For sure."

Naomi glanced at him, her eyes red-rimmed in her pale face. She looked like she hadn't slept at all.

Cap grabbed the broom from where it leaned against the porch wall and made his way to the long table Eli and Henry had constructed yesterday out of boards from the barn and sawhorses. When he started sweeping the table's surface with the broom to remove the twigs, leaves, and other litter that had fallen onto it overnight, Wilhelm knocked the ashes out of his pipe. Pocketing it, he reached for the broom.

"I can help with that."

"Denki." Cap turned his attention to the makeshift benches. He turned each board over to a dry surface and replaced it on the two lengths of logs that held it off the ground along the table.

"Is breakfast almost ready?" Wilhelm patted his stomach. "Such a small meal last night. My stomach is growling this morning."

Cap squelched his rising irritation. This family wasn't Amish, so would have expected a full, cooked supper on a Sunday night instead of the cold meal of meat, cheese, and bread they had enjoyed. "Lydia and Naomi are working on it. It will be ready when the men are done with the chores."

"Ja, ja, ja." Wilhelm looked toward the barnyard where his team of six horses munched on the hay that had been thrown out for them. "Eli and Henry were already working hard when we woke this morning." He finished sweeping off the table and handed the broom back to Cap. "These Schrocks, they are a good family?"

Cap nodded. "The best. Eli is a good man."

"They have taken good care of our Davey, then?"

The words hit hard in an unexpected blow. *Our Davey.*

"They are Davey's family, and this is his home."

Wilhelm nodded, stroking his short beard as he took in the sights of the freshly whitewashed fences, the large barn, and the comfortable house. "We will provide for him just as well when we reach our new home in Wisconsin."

Cap suppressed his shaking hands. "You plan to take him with you? Away from his family?"

Wilhelm smiled at him. "Ja, ja, ja. We are his family. Of course he will come with us."

Cap's stomach roiled. No wonder Naomi hadn't slept last night. "Have you asked Davey if this is what he wants?"

"We will discuss it at breakfast this morning." Wilhelm's smile faded when he saw Cap's frown. "We want what is best for the boy, and it is best that he lives with his own family. It is what his parents would have wanted."

Cap bit back his arguments. This was Eli's, Naomi's, and Lydia's decision to make, not his. Beyond Wilhelm's shoulder, Eli and Henry emerged from the barn.

"Chores are done. I will help bring the breakfast out to the table."

He turned to walk toward the house, welcoming the respite from Wilhelm's assumptions. He set the broom back in its place with careful motions. A black pit gaped in his mind, pulling him in. He couldn't let this family take Davey away. He couldn't lose Davey too.

Leaning one arm against the doorframe, Cap took a deep breath. He whooshed it out, and then took another. For the last few weeks, he had enjoyed seeing God's blessings all around him, in every task he put his hand to, the growing crops, and in his relationship with Naomi. But this —

He shook his head. Had he been so wrong? Could God have a purpose in tearing Davey away from them? Or was it just bad luck that had brought the Hinklemanns to their neighborhood?

Naomi's and Lydia's voices floated out the door. This would devastate Naomi. He knew the terrible emptiness of losing a son . . . if only there was some way he could protect her.

Naomi took a sip of her coffee and moved the eggs around on her plate with her fork. Davey had taken a seat at the other end of the table from her, between Karl and the youngest girl, Lauraine. He laughed at

Karl's jokes and poked Lauraine until she giggled. He was enjoying himself.

Cap sat across the table from her, watching her face with a worried frown. She took another sip of coffee and tried to give him a reassuring smile, but her face was made of wood, just like her stiff arms, and her legs, and her heart. She felt nothing. Nothing.

"We are thankful for your hospitality," Wilhelm was saying. "We will be leaving at noon today."

"Where are you planning to settle?" Daed asked.

"Wisconsin. My cousin lives in Milwaukee and I will work with him there."

Mamm dropped her fork. "In a town?"

"Ja," Greta said, smiling. "A growing city like Milwaukee provides many opportunities for our children."

Wilhelm blew on his coffee, even though it was nearly cold. He took a large swallow, then set the cup down on the table. He kept his eyes on it as he said, "We will take our nephew with us."

Naomi's stomach lurched, and she was glad she hadn't eaten anything. This was what she had feared, what she knew was their intention, but the words still fell like rocks into a pond. The ripples were felt all the way down the table to the children. Davey looked at her, then at Wilhelm.

"You want to take me with you to Wisconsin?"

Wilhelm beckoned to him. "Come here."

Davey moved around the table until he stood between Wilhelm and Greta, with Wilhelm's arm around him.

"You are our nephew, and already part of our family. We would like to make you our son. Karl's brother."

Davey's eyes grew round.

Greta pulled him close to her. "Would you like that, Davey? You will be with your own family again."

"My own family." Davey's eyes shone with tears as he threw his arms around Greta. "My own family."

Naomi couldn't move. Couldn't speak. She was his mother. He had a family. Why was this happening?

Wilhelm cleared his throat and turned back to Daed. "Does Davey have any, um, papers? Or anything else that he would want to bring with him?"

"I have my chest," Davey said. "It has papers in it."

Daed nodded. "Henry, go get Davey's chest."

As Henry left, Naomi found her voice. "Davey." She reached one hand toward him, but he ignored it. "Are you sure you want to do this?"

Davey looked at her, his clear blue eyes as wide as his smile. "This is what I've prayed for. My own family. They came to find me."

"They aren't your ma and pa."

Her son smiled at Greta, still enfolding him in her arms. "Ne, not Ma and Pa. But almost."

Naomi's wooden heart clenched, then melted into a hot puddle that burned in the pit of her stomach. She rose, grabbing the plates within her reach. Cap stood and picked up more plates from the end of the table. He followed her into the house and put his pile of dishes on the shelf just in time to catch hers as her strength left her. He set her plates down and pulled her toward him. She buried her face in his solid chest and let the hot tears flow. Cap's arms held her close. He bent his head to hers and let her cry.

Cap led her out of the kitchen and into the sitting room at the other end of the house, away from the open kitchen door and the events unfolding in the yard. Henry came down the ladder with Davey's chest and glanced at her, but continued out the door.

"Why, Cap? Why are they doing this?"

Cap kissed the top of her head. "I don't know. But if you had lost Davey and suddenly found him, wouldn't you want to take him from whoever had been caring for him?"

"I haven't . . . just been caring for him." Naomi took a deep, ragged breath. "He's my son. I've raised him and loved him for the last three years. They have no reason to take him from me."

"Unless they are his family. His birth family."

Naomi buried her face in his chest again, as if she could escape his words. "He doesn't know them. They don't know him. How can he think he wants to go with them?"

Cap rubbed a gentle circle on her back. "Davey has told me how he longs for a family. For his ma and pa. I can understand why he wants to be with the Hinklemanns, but that doesn't make his rejection of us any easier to take."

Another sob escaped Naomi's throat and Cap rubbed her back again. "He's only a little boy. How can he make a decision like this on his own? Shouldn't we talk to him, try to make him stay?"

"Naomi, it isn't his decision to make. If the Hinklemanns are his family, he belongs to them. There is nothing we can do to keep them from taking Davey with them, even if he didn't want to be with them." He lifted her chin with one finger until she looked into his face. "Isn't it easier to let him go knowing that it is what he wants?"

She shook her head and stepped away from him. "Nothing about this is easy." Her hands fisted as if she could fight for her son. "Yesterday he was my son, happy and growing. We . . . I had a future." The realization of her own words hit her and she sank onto a chair. "Without Davey, what do I have?"

Cap knelt in front of her, holding her cold hands in his strong ones. "You have me. I will never leave you."

"You want me to give him up."

He bowed his head. "With all my heart, I want him to stay here. But this thing is beyond our control. We must submit —"

"Submit to God? His will?"

When Cap looked at her, she saw her pain mirrored in his face. He was suffering as much as she was.

"Remember Mary."

"The mother of Jesus?"

He nodded. "From the very beginning, she knew her son wasn't hers, but she treasured everything about him in her heart. When the time came, she let him go, even though she knew where his steps would lead him."

"Davey probably won't be facing death."

He smiled a little at her words. "Ne. He's facing a future with a loving family, with brothers and sisters. A life in a new place, with an aunt and uncle who will educate him and help him get started in life."

"A life in the world, not as an Amish man." She gripped his hands, even though he was holding her tight. "I'm not only thinking of my own loss, but of his. He'll never know a life like ours again, living for others, living for God."

Tears ran down Cap's cheeks. "That is in God's hands. Perhaps one day, when he is older, he will come back to us."

Naomi sighed, resigned. She spoke the words she needed to say, even though she hated each syllable. "I will surrender to God's will, and to the law of the land. May our Lord keep Davey ever close to his heart."

Cap lifted her hands and kissed them. "He will. He will."

When Lydia came inside the house with another load of dishes, Cap went back out to the yard. Wilhelm was sitting at the table, sorting through the papers from Davey's box. Cap had intended to go to the barn for a talk with Eli, but the expression on Wilhelm's face stopped him. The other man wasn't casually scanning the documents, he was reading them, holding each one close to his face as he read the fine print. Davey's treasures, his mother's shawl and the other items, were flung onto the table as if Wilhelm couldn't bother with them. Cap took a seat on the bench with Davey's chest between them.

"You must be finding some interesting information." Cap picked up the lacy shawl and folded it carefully.

"Hmm?" Wilhelm looked at him over a pair of spectacles. "Ja, of course. The papers are very detailed, with the names of Davey's parents and grandparents, along with other information he will need when he grows older."

As he shuffled the papers, one left his grasp. Cap caught it before it fell to the ground. A land deed. Wilhelm snatched it from him before he could read any further.

"When you showed up at the Yoders' yesterday, you said you had met Shem Fischer near Fort Wayne."

Wilhelm's grin seemed genuine, but the man wouldn't meet his eyes. "Ja, ja, ja. We met Herr Fischer just outside of Ligonier."

"What made you think he knew your nephew?"

The man ran a fat finger between his throat and the collar of his shirt. "I . . . I'm not sure how it came about." Wilhelm stuffed the papers back into the chest. "Now I remember. He commented that our Karl looked exactly like a boy he knew."

"And that is when you thought he might know your nephew?"

"Nein, not then." A drop of sweat trickled down his cheek. "It was not until later, after supper."

Cap leaned forward, trying to put the chain of events together. "So Shem approached you? Or did you come to him after he made that comment?"

"He . . . he saw that we were interested, and then arranged to talk to me." Wilhelm reached into the chest to straighten the pile of papers. "Why does this concern you?"

"Davey is —" Cap shrugged. He had no claim on Davey, or Naomi. "Davey is a fine boy, and we've become good friends. I only want to make certain that he isn't hurt."

"He won't be." Wilhelm grinned again, his glance darting toward the wagon where Greta was busy washing laundry in a tub. "Greta and I decided to make him part of our family as soon as we learned of him . . .

of his circumstances."

"How long have you been looking for Davey?"

"Not long. We arrived in New Jersey only two months ago. Our plans were to visit my wife's sister on the way to Milwaukee." Wilhelm rubbed at his sandy-colored mustache.

"Your wife's sister? Davey's mother?"

"Ja, ja, ja. Greta had letters from her sister, telling where they lived and about the boy."

Wilhelm pulled a note from his pocket and handed it to Cap. The letter was short, from a sister asking the family to stop by their farm on their journey west and giving some general directions. He strained to read the signature, but it was smeared.

Plucking the note from Cap's grasp, Wilhelm stuffed it into his pocket again. He had only looked at Cap's face once, when he spoke of the family arriving in New Jersey. A growing suspicion that the man might be lying rose. Cap tapped one finger on the edge of the table while Wilhelm gathered the rest of Davey's things and put them in the chest.

"I'm trying to remember what Davey's mother's name was. She was your sister-in-law, ja?"

"Ja, but I only met her when she was a young girl. Just married. Before they left

Germany." Wilhelm's Adam's apple bounced as he swallowed. "When we reached their farm, that's when we found that the boy was missing."

Cap had tried to picture the farm in his mind from Naomi's descriptions. "What did you find?"

Wilhelm shrugged. "A barn. A cabin. Both in ruins. We also found the graves of Davey's mother and father, but no grave for the boy."

Sitting back, Cap ran his fingers through his beard. From what Naomi had told him, both the cabin and barn had been destroyed by the storm that had killed Davey's family. That part of his story rang true. But what did Shem have to do with all of this?

Wilhelm's gaze darted to the chest he had just closed. "We need to pack the wagons and be off. We want to make as much progress as we can this afternoon."

Cap stood as Wilhelm did. "On your way to Wisconsin."

"Ja." Wilhelm nodded. "Ja, on the way to Wisconsin."

As Wilhelm took the chest to his wagon, Cap went to Davey. He and the other boys were sitting on the grass in the shade of an elm tree, talking about the Hinklemanns' journey.

"Everybody on the ship got sick," Karl was saying, "except me. I didn't get sick once."

"You were as sick as a dog," one of the older brothers said.

"That was before we left England. I didn't get sick after that."

"I wish I had been there," Davey said. "I wouldn't have been sick."

"You might have died." That was the fourteen-year-old boy, Frederick. His voice was changing and it warbled up and down. "One of the Dutch girls died. They sewed her into a piece of canvas and dropped her in the water."

Davey's eyes grew wide. "Why?"

Frederick grinned. "So the sharks could eat her, *dummkopf.*"

Cap's knees trembled. This was the family Davey would grow up with. He would become as coarse and as worldly as Naomi had feared. "Davey, come with me."

"I want to play with the boys."

"You need to spend some time with your memmi before you leave."

The other brother, Johan, cupped his hands around his mouth. "Yoo hoo, Davey. Memmi wants you!"

All three of the younger Hinklemann boys collapsed with laughter, but Franz, the oldest, stopped them. "Let Davey go and stop teasing him. He needs to say goodbye to these people."

Cap nodded his thanks to Franz as he grasped Davey's hand.

As they started toward the house, Davey skipped next to Cap. "Is Memmi glad I'm leaving?"

"Why would you think that?"

"Karl said that since I didn't really belong to her, that she will be happy to see me go."

Cap took Davey to the far side of the house, out of the sight of the Hinklemann boys. He knelt and took Davey's hands in his own. "Your memmi has never, ever thought that you didn't belong to her. You are her son, and she loves you. She doesn't want you to go, but right now she doesn't have a choice."

Davey's eyes grew wet. "Can she come with us? And you? Can you come with us? I'll miss both of you."

"I know you will, but we can't come. We have to stay home." Cap reached up one hand and smoothed a tangle in Davey's straight blond hair. He took a deep breath. "I will miss you more than you will ever know."

Davey threw his arms around Cap's neck and Cap returned the hug with his own for a long minute. Then he set Davey away from him. He looked into the boy's eyes, memorizing the bright blue depths.

"You need to go in and see your memmi."

"I'll never forget you, Cap."

Cap smiled, though his heart was turning to stone in his chest. "I'll never forget you, either, Davey. You're a wonderful boy."

Davey stepped back, then turned and ran to the house. Cap let his tears flow.

Naomi watched the group of boys and girls from the loft window next to Davey's bed. They seemed to get along well, even though she caught sight of one of the middle brothers punching the other one in the arm. The oldest boy, Franz, was old enough to be a man, but he spent his time with his younger brothers and sisters. Perhaps he was watching over them to make sure they didn't cause trouble.

This rowdy group would be her Davey's brothers and sisters. Before Cap had taken Davey around the house, her son had looked and acted like one of them. It was as if he was a different boy than the Davey she loved and had watched grow up.

"Memmi?"

Naomi's heart flipped as Davey called. She dashed away the tears that were running down her cheeks. "I'm in the loft."

The ladder swayed as he ran up the rungs, just like he did every day. She made sure he would see her smiling when he saw her. She sat on his bed and patted the spot next to her as an invitation to join her.

"I saw you playing with the Hinklemann children. They seem to like you."

"I like them too. Karl is funny. He tells jokes all the time." His ruddy cheeks stood out like apples and his eyes were shining. "The other boys can be mean, but Karl says that they won't pick on two of us."

"Maybe you can teach them to treat each other with kindness."

Davey rubbed his finger along the stitching of his quilt. "Maybe." He looked at her. "Cap said I should talk to you before we go."

Naomi's nose prickled. She didn't want Davey to remember her tears. "I would like that."

"He said you don't want me to go with the Hinklemanns."

She couldn't stop the tears that trickled down her cheeks at his words. She combed her fingers through his hair, then cupped his chin. "What I want is for you to be happy."

His brow puckered. "Do you think I'll be

happy with them?"

Naomi put her arm around his shoulders and pulled him close. "You can choose to be happy. You will have a new life, but I hope you don't forget your old one."

He leaned against her and she held him closer, as if she could keep him with her always. As if he could always be her little boy. If Cap was right, and he did come back to find them one day, he might be a grown man. She would never hold him like this again.

"Cap said that Karl was wrong."

"What did Karl say?"

Davey pulled away far enough that he could look into her face. "He said that you aren't my real memmi, and that you will be glad to see me go so you won't have to take care of me anymore."

Naomi forced a smile as she straightened his shirt collar. "Do you think that could be true when I love you so much? Have I ever made you think you were a bother?"

He shook his head and leaned against her again. "You love me?"

She took a deep breath to squelch the sob that rose in her throat. She wouldn't cry, not until he was gone. "I have always loved you and I always will."

He looked toward the window. "Do you

think Aunt Greta will love me?"

"How could she not love you?"

"I want her to love me like Ma loved me. Like you love me."

Naomi laid her cheek on his head. "It might take some time. She has to learn to know you. But if you are helpful and kind, she will find out what a wonderful boy you are."

Davey sat up, pointing at the shelf above his bed. "There's my memory stone. I want to take that with me."

"Of course. I have a bag here to put your things in. We'll put your extra clothes in first."

As Naomi folded his new Sunday shirt, trousers, and jacket, Davey picked up the stone. "When Crow Flies comes back, I won't be here."

"We'll tell him where you are. You know he won't forget you."

"I don't have anything to remember you." Davey turned to her, his brow puckered once more. "I have Ma's lacy shawl, and I have Crow Flies' memory stone, but what can I take to remember you?"

She pulled him close and kissed his cheek. "You have my love for a memory."

"I know, but . . ." He turned the stone over in his hand. "If I had something to hold, that would be better."

Naomi held his hands in hers, the stone still cupped in his grasp. "If you had something to hold, then you might make that into an idol. And that thing would never be me."

"Then how will I remember you?"

"When you say your prayers, always remember to pray for me. I will always be praying for you."

"Will God hear me pray, even when I'm in Wisconsin?"

A door opened in Naomi's mind, and beyond was a future with Davey always a part of her life through her prayers for him. "Ja, for sure. God always hears our prayers."

Why hadn't she seen that before? She hadn't seen God's presence because it had always been a constant in her life, just like her love for Davey had always been such a constant in his life that he doubted its existence.

She gave his hands a squeeze. "He will hear your prayers whether you say them aloud or only in your head, and he will hear them whether you are here with us or in Milwaukee with the Hinklemanns."

New noises came drifting into the house from the yard below. The sound of horses being harnessed. Davey ran to the window to watch while Naomi put the last of his things in the bag. She wouldn't think past this moment. Thoughts of the future, even as close as this afternoon, were too painful to bear.

Davey ran to the ladder and started down it.

"Where are you going?"

"I need to help with the wagon. They're counting on me."

And that quickly, he was gone.

22

Every day that week, Cap woke with his head in a fog. Every morning he had to face the loss of Davey again. And again. Each morning his heart broke anew.

On Sunday, he sat at the edge of his bed, rubbing the sleep from his gritty eyes. He knew this loss was different from what Mattie and Jacob were experiencing. He felt their loss echo in his memories. But this . . . knowing Davey was somewhere, but beyond reach . . . This loss was an agony of uncertainty.

He stood at his washbasin and splashed his face with the tepid water. The cabin hadn't cooled down overnight, and today promised to be another hot, sultry day. Church was to be at Jonas Plank's. Would the Clinton Township group follow through with their threat to split the church between the two counties? He rubbed the towel over his face and hair. If they did, the worship today would be doubly solemn.

Naomi. His toweling slowed, and then stopped. A week ago he had asked her to marry him. Had she even thought about the idea since then? All through the last week he had wanted her near, to share their misery together and comfort each other. Neither of them had to travel this road alone, and yet she refused to talk to him. She had closed herself in the house and refused to speak to anyone, Lydia had told him. She would go to church today, though. He would talk to her then.

Pulling his suspenders over his bare shoulders, he went out to take care of the horses. With only the team to care for, chores didn't take long. He hauled buckets of water from the well and poured the cold, sweet liquid into the trough. The horses had been waiting for him at the edge of the fence, and when they smelled the fresh water, they shouldered each other aside to make room for both of them to get a drink.

Cap dangled the empty bucket from his fingers as he crossed his arms on a fence post, watching them. Someday, if Naomi agreed to marry him, they would have sheep, and chickens. Ducks, too, and geese. A milk cow and her steer calves for meat. A barn built into the bank where the ground sloped a bit just beyond the horse's meadow. A garden. Fields for crops and a hay meadow.

With Naomi by his side.

He glanced at the sun. It was still early. If he hurried, he could get to the Schrocks' farm before they left, and then walk to services with Naomi.

Later, he emerged from the woods just as the Schrocks were leaving. He jogged across the yard and fell in step next to Naomi. Lydia smiled at him and went ahead to join Eli, leaving Cap and Naomi alone behind the rest of the family.

"Good morning," Cap said. Naomi hadn't looked at him.

"Good morning," he said again.

This time she glanced at him. Her face was pale, and her cast eye darted toward him and away again.

"You haven't talked to me for a week."

She made a small sound, her knuckle pressed against her lips. Finally, she said, "We don't have anything to talk about."

"Ja, we do."

Her only answer was to keep walking, one step after the other. If he had stopped or turned around, she would have kept walking without him. He grabbed her elbow and turned her toward him, but she still wouldn't look at him.

"We both lost Davey last week. I miss him, and I know you miss him even more. We need each other."

She pressed her lips together, but didn't answer him.

"I need you. I love you. I want you to marry me."

Naomi looked at him then. "Why? Davey doesn't need a mother and father anymore. We don't have to get married for him."

They were alone on the road. Naomi's folks had gone over the rise toward the east. Their voices drifted back as they greeted the Yoders. At the next corner they would turn north. If he didn't hurry, he and Naomi would be late to the Sabbath meeting, but right now he had something more important to do.

He stroked Naomi's cheek with his thumb, and then pulled her close to him.

"I didn't ask you to marry me for Davey's sake. I asked you to marry me. To be my wife. To be the mother of our children, as well as Davey's mother."

She started to protest, but he stopped her with a finger to her lips.

"No matter where Davey is, you'll always be his mother. He knows that." He rubbed at the frown lines on her forehead. "We might not have Davey in our future, but we do have a future. God has put us together, and I want to see what he has for us in the years to come. But I don't want to do it alone. I want you beside me every step of the way."

Naomi pulled out of his arms, her head shaking back and forth. "I don't know what I want, except that I want to go back . . . as if the last week never happened."

"Naomi —"

She took another step back. "You need to leave me alone, Cap. Forget about me. Nothing can bring Davey back, and nothing can fix this —" she grasped at the bodice of her dress — "this empty hole in my heart. Without Davey, I have nothing." Her eyes were hollow and her face pale as death. "Just leave me alone." She left him and ran to catch up with the rest of her family.

Cap slumped onto a stump by the side of the road, his face buried in his hands. "You have me. And you have God." But she was too far away to hear his voice.

Shem tied his horse along the river near the Schrocks' farm. He pulled his watch out of the inside pocket in the waistband of his trousers, opened the lid to read the face, then snapped it shut and returned it to its place. Just past noon. The LaGrange County folks would be finishing their morning service, and the absence of the Clinton Township group would be the subject uppermost in their minds.

Priscilla was a genius at timing. The results of this morning's Sabbath meeting in Clinton Township were perfect, with seventeen of the families attending the newly formed congregation. Only Yost Bontrager had made the early morning journey to the meeting at Josiah Plank's, and the remaining families had been in joyful agreement about the division in the church.

His wife had been right. The split happening at the same time as the Hinklemanns taking Davey west would throw the tradition-minded half of the district into confusion, and they would never be able to reverse the change that had taken place. And on top of everything else, Cap Stoltzfus would be sure to be so miserable that Shem would finally be the one on top. He would never need to see the man's self-satisfied smile again. Not that Priscilla cared about Cap, but it was icing on the cake for Shem.

Shem started the walk toward Josiah Plank's, glad that Priscilla had suggested taking the horse to ride most of the distance.

It wouldn't do to show up at the meeting on top of a horse on the Sabbath, but riding as far as the river crossing prevented sore feet. When he arrived at the Planks' farm, the congregation was gathered around tables scattered between the stumps in a newly cleared field near the house. The tone was sober. Even the children refrained from their usual play. Things were working out perfectly.

The conversation died down as he drew closer, and people turned to watch his progress toward the table where Eli Schrock, Christian Yoder, and Cap sat along with Solomon and Josiah Plank and the Troyers, Abraham and his son, Sep. Yost Bontrager was the only one of the group who didn't turn to face him.

"Good afternoon." Shem greeted the men with a smile. His smile grew broader when Cap ignored him.

Eli moved over on his bench. "Sit down, Shem, right here between Christian and me. Have you had dinner yet?"

Shem smiled his thanks to the woman who set a plate of cold meat, cheese, and bread in front of him. "Denki, Brother Eli." He tore the coarse rye bread in two. "I must say, I hadn't expected such a warm welcome today."

Christian leaned forward, his arms folded on the table in front of him. "I'm sorry you arrived so late, Brother Shem. You have missed the worship service."

Shem took a bite of the bread and chewed it slowly. "I had other things to do this morning."

"Such as attending another meeting?" Yost's words shook with pent-up rage.

"Ja, I attended meeting this morning."

Next to him, Eli wagged his head. "So sad that it has come to this. We are one congregation, one family. We should worship together."

"Not anymore." Shem dabbed at some bread crumbs with his finger. "We are two congregations now."

Cap snorted. "Why are you here, Shem?"

Shem met Cap's gaze. That face that had always brought out the worst in him was gone. Instead, Cap looked exhausted. Beaten. Ready to give up. Shem smiled.

"I only came to see how things are going in this district, and to make sure there are no hard feelings."

"Hard feelings?" Yost rose halfway off his bench, but Abraham Troyer restrained him with a hand on his shoulder.

"We are disappointed," Abraham said, "and confused. As Eli said, we are sad that the Clinton Township group has decided to withdraw from our fellowship. We would like to meet with the leaders of the dissenting part of the congregation, Preacher Elam and anyone else who would like to. Surely we can repair this breach."

Shem shrugged. "As far as I am concerned, there is nothing to discuss. We parted amiably enough. From now on we'll be neighboring districts. That is the way a community grows."

Cap left the table. As Shem watched him stalk off toward the edge of the clearing, he couldn't keep back a grin. The confident, proud, can't-do-anything-wrong Cap was gone, and in his place was a shell of a man. Shem had finally gotten his revenge after years of waiting. He stuck the last bite of cheese in his mouth as Cap walked out of sight, down the road.

"Well, brothers, I must be going. My work here is done."

Abraham stood as Shem rose from the table. "Tell Elam that Christian and I will call on him this week. We do want to discuss this with him."

Shem brushed crumbs off the front of his coat. "I will give him the message, but like I said, there really isn't anything to talk about." He smiled at the grim faces around the table. "Have a good Sabbath, brothers."

The shady road was a welcome change from the heat of the sunny yard. Shem removed his jacket and unfastened his shirt at the neck. The day was hot and still, with the promise of an afternoon thunderstorm. As he rounded a bend where the road turned to go down the hill past the Yoders' farm, a figure stepped out of the underbrush at the side of the road. One of the Smith gang? They were known to waylay lone travelers. Shem almost laughed with relief when he recognized Cap.

"I thought you had gone home to pout."

Cap only stood in the middle of the road until Shem came up to him. "What are you doing here, Shem?"

"I told you." Shem grinned. He had imagined how this would feel, to be on the winning end of an encounter with Cap Stoltzfus, but the satisfaction was greater than he had ever thought. "I came to make sure there are no hard feelings between the two districts."

"That isn't what I mean. Why are you here, in Indiana?"

Cap seemed to grow taller as he spoke. Shem licked his lips. "I don't know what you mean."

"You are a wolf, a false shepherd. You have

no interest in being a preacher. You only want to have control, hovering in the background, spreading rumors and breeding dissent. You may have the folks in Clinton Township fooled, but I know you. You're the same now as when we were boys. A bully."

Shem laughed off his words. Cap was all bluster. He had found the other man's weak spot and hit it hard. Cap had nothing left.

"You don't know what you're talking about. What is it that you are accusing me of doing?" Shem held up a hand to stop Cap from speaking. "Not half-truths and ambiguous accusations. Tell me, exactly, what you think I've done?"

Cap's gaze flickered up and beyond Shem's shoulder. He turned to see Eli, Yost, and Christian coming up the road, along with Jacob Yoder and Josef Bender. All of Cap's new friends.

Shem raised his voice so that his words would carry across the short distance. "You are just in time, brothers. Cap here is in the process of laying false accusations at my feet." He turned back to Cap. "Go ahead." He kept his voice low, for Cap's ears only. "Go ahead. Make your accusations. But you are beaten. Done. Your precious Naomi will never recover from that boy leaving with the

Hinklemanns. You are left with less than nothing."

Cap's eyes narrowed. "How did you know that Davey left with the Hinklemanns? We haven't talked about that outside of the family."

Shem took a step back as the pieces fell into place in Cap's mind.

"You were the one who told the Hinklemanns where to find Davey." He moved closer to Shem as the other men drew close enough to hear. "But they aren't his relatives at all, are they? You brought them here, told them what to say, who to look for."

Shem tried to step away, but he was surrounded.

"Go on, Cap." Christian said. He leaned on his cane, but his eyes were bright. "What are you accusing this man of doing?"

"Ever since Shem arrived in our area, trying to pass himself off as a preacher, he's tried to undermine me." Cap looked from face to face in the circle. "Shem and I were in school together back in Ohio. He was a bully then, and he is a bully now. I think he wanted to drive me away from this community so that he wouldn't have any opposition to his plans."

Shem tried to laugh, but the sound that

came out of his mouth was more of a squeak. "That is ridiculous. He makes me sound like some political conspirator." He cleared his throat. "You're letting our past differences color your judgment, Cap. We're adults now. We've moved beyond our boyish disagreements."

"Is this true?" Eli looked from Cap to Shem, and then back again. "You can't think that this man, an ordained minister, would have such evil intent against you?"

"Haven't you noticed that he has been in the middle of every step of this division in our district? He whispers lies into men's ears, and sometimes those lies find a willing audience."

Movement up the road caught Cap's attention. More people were coming to see what was happening. Naomi and Mattie were at the front of the group.

Cap took a deep breath. "But I know he was instrumental in getting the Hinkle-manns to claim to be Davey's relatives." Naomi raised her hand to her mouth and he turned to Shem. "Did you bribe them? Offer them money? Do you know where they've taken Davey?"

Shem tried to shrug off the accusations, but he only met hard stares. "The Hinkle-manns said they were Davey's relatives.

Shouldn't he be with his family? I only orchestrated their meeting."

Eli stepped forward. "You did this thing? You took our Davey away and sent him off with strangers?"

Shem spread his hands out in denial. "Why would I do that? What would I have to gain? All I did was bring a broken family together." He looked around the circle of faces, avoiding Cap's stare. "Everything I've done has been for the good of others. I long for the purity of the church, and her continued growth. Even the division of the two districts allows each group to grow stronger."

"You've said some harsh words about a brother, Cap." Sep Troyer had joined the other men in the circle. "Do you have any proof that he did these things maliciously?"

Cap shook his head. "I can't prove anything." He turned his gaze from face to face, then looked back at Shem's smug smile. That was all the evidence he needed, but it wasn't enough to convince the others.

"I'll be on my way, then, if you are done spreading lies and rumors about me." Shem's smile stretched into a grin. He lifted his gaze to the men surrounding them. "Any of you are welcome to join us in the Clinton District. We're having a meeting on Wednesday to decide the future of our community. Any of you who are interested in progressing toward prosperous days ahead should be there."

No one spoke as Shem walked away, down the road past Jacob Yoder's farm, then around the bend and out of sight.

Cap clenched his jaw tight to keep his words in check. He could accuse Shem of many things, but Eli was right. Without any evidence, it was his word against Shem's.

The rest of the group turned to go back to the Planks' farm and their interrupted Sunday afternoon, but Naomi stepped up beside Cap and slipped her hand into his.

"I believe you. I think more people do too, but they aren't willing to confront Shem without proof that he's done anything to hurt us."

Cap squeezed her hand. "What I'm afraid of is that Shem has done more damage than we know of. He looked too satisfied with himself." He looked up and down the road, but the two of them were alone.

Naomi's face was troubled and sad, just as it had been since Davey left nearly a week ago. Hearing his suspicions that the Hinklemanns weren't really Davey's relatives would only strengthen her worries.

"It has been a long day. Do you want me

to walk you home?"

The look Naomi gave him was one of relief, and he pulled her hand into the crook of his elbow. As they walked, Naomi rested her head on his shoulder and he shifted his arm, pulling her close to him. The road was shaded and cool with only a few birdsongs to break the silence. Every branch was green and the undergrowth in the forest was thick and lush. The height of summer.

As they followed the bend and came in sight of the Schrock farm, a figure stood in the road, holding a riding horse by the reins. The sunshine was bright as they emerged into the clearing around the barnyard and Cap shaded his eyes, trying to see the man.

"Shem."

His voice startled Naomi. "Where?"

"Ahead of us. He looks like he's waiting for us."

Naomi withdrew from his embrace. "I don't want to talk to him. I don't think I could control my words."

Cap left Naomi behind as he strode toward Shem. "Are you looking for me?"

A smile spread across Shem's face. "I wanted to see your face when you realized the truth."

"The truth about what?" A cold lump

shifted in Cap's chest. What else had Shem done?

"You're finished." He took a step forward and jabbed a finger in Cap's direction. "I've dealt you a blow you'll never recover from, and you don't even know it."

A sound caught Cap's attention. Naomi was coming closer to listen to the conversation.

The smile spread further across Shem's face. "You'll never get that boy back. He's gone, and you'll never find him."

The cold lump grew larger as Shem confirmed his suspicions. "The Hinklemanns aren't his relatives.

"When I saw the deed to the land up in Steuben County, I knew someone would take the boy to get that farm. All I had to do was find a likely looking family, and the Hinklemanns were perfect."

Naomi came closer, in spite of Cap signaling her to stay away, where she wouldn't hear the truth. "The papers in Davey's chest," she said. "You're the one who looked through them, aren't you?"

Shem grinned at the panic in Naomi's voice. "It's too late. They've sold the land and have gone by now. You'll never get that boy back." Shem took a step closer and poked Cap's chest with his finger. "I've finally won, Cap. I've won. The district is divided and the Clinton folks have welcomed me in with open arms. Meanwhile, you've lost everything. How does it feel to be on the bottom for once?"

"You'll never be able to stay in this area once people know what you've done."

Shem barked out a laugh. "They will never believe you. It's your word against mine. You heard them." His voice dropped. "You don't have any proof."

The only sound was a quick sob from Naomi as Shem mounted his horse and started down the road toward Elkhart County.

As soon as he was out of sight, Cap encircled Naomi's rigid body with his arms and held her close. Finally, the stiffness eased as she started crying. The tears were hot, soaking his shirt.

"Go ahead and cry." He held her closer as sobs racked her body. When her knees collapsed under her, he picked her up in his arms and carried her to the house. By the time he reached it, she had fallen quiet.

When he reached the porch steps, she struggled in his arms. "I can walk."

Cap strengthened his grasp. "I know you can, but you don't need to."

He opened the door with one hand and

carried her through the house to her bedroom. He laid her on the bed and sat beside her. Cupping her soft cheek in his hand, he wiped the drying tears away with his thumb. "I will find him. I won't give up until I bring him home."

Naomi's red eyes were still wet. "You heard Shem. Those people lied to us about being Davey's relatives, and they probably lied when they said they were going to Milwaukee. Who knows where they've taken him? How will you know where to look?"

Cap took her hands in his and rubbed her cold fingers. "I'll start in Steuben County. I think I can find Davey's farm, and then I'll find a trail from there."

"When will you leave?"

"They have a week's head start, so the trail is already cold." Cap's eyes itched as they filled with tears. Finding Davey couldn't be as hopeless as it sounded. Once the Hinklemanns sold the farm, which direction would they take? "I'll take a few days to harvest my oats and get my farm ready to leave. I should be able to finish everything and be ready to go by Thursday."

"How long will you be gone?"

"I have no idea." Cap cupped her cheek in his hand again and looked into her eyes.

"But I'll do everything I can to find him. I'll bring him home to you."

23

Tuesday morning dawned with the same chores waiting for Naomi's attention that every Tuesday held. The housework and the garden demanded her attention, even though her body was aching and sore.

Yesterday had marked a week since Davey left with the Hinklemanns, and she hadn't slept well since that time. And with Sunday's news that her boy could be anywhere, she felt like her heart had been wrenched in two by a team of oxen. The only comfort was Cap.

Naomi paused in her task of washing the breakfast dishes and looked toward the trail through the woods. Cap's presence was like a gentle hand giving her support and strength. He knew the pain of losing Davey and shared it with her. As they grieved together, the pain eased some. Now she knew what Mattie meant. Grief was a heavy burden, but sharing it helped.

They had only two more days together before Cap left to find Davey. Two days that would fly past, and then she would be left alone. She rubbed at her aching forehead as she thought of all that Shem Fischer had taken from her.

Mamm came in from the side yard where she had been picking berries. She paused and looked into Naomi's face. "Are you all right?"

Naomi shook her head, biting her lip to hold back the tears. "The news that Davey isn't safe, like I thought he was —" She drew a shuddering sigh. "And then Cap is going away to find him. I don't think I can take any more, and all of this has happened because of Shem."

Mamm gathered Naomi into her arms. "I know. Ever since you told us what he confessed to you and Cap, all I can think about is that poor man, thinking he can gain approval from men."

"You feel sorry for Shem?" Naomi pushed away, the tears forgotten. "He purposely set out to harm Cap and used Davey to do it. I don't feel sorry for him at all."

Mamm was silent as she helped Naomi dry the dishes and put them away. When they were done, she turned to Naomi. "I do feel sorry for Shem. He is following a path that will lead to his destruction."

"It's the path he chose. He will reap what he sows and I don't feel sorry for him at all."

"Think about what you're saying. You are happy that one of our own brothers may spend eternity in hell because of his choices here on earth?"

Naomi caught her lower lip between her teeth. She had never thought about the reality of hell. It had always been something she didn't have to worry about. Only outsiders needed to do that. But with Mamm's words, she caught the vision of Shem suffering eternal torment.

"Ne. I wouldn't want anyone to perish like that."

Mamm laid her hand on Naomi's arm. "And you don't want to go through it yourself, either."

"Why would I need to worry about it?"

"The Good Book tells us to forgive as we have been forgiven. Have you forgiven Shem? Or the Hinklemanns for their part in this?" Her hand grasped tighter. "Have you forgiven Davey?"

"Forgiven Davey?"

"Didn't he hurt you badly when he was so anxious to go with the Hinklemanns, without a thought about how it would affect you?"

Ach, ja. His rejection was like a hot knife sliding into her heart. "For sure, I forgive Davey. He's a boy, hardly knowing right from wrong. He was so excited to go with his new family that he didn't know how much his leaving would hurt us. He wasn't cruel, he was only thoughtless."

"Thoughtless." Mamm nodded. "But even thoughtless actions leave stains that can't be erased so easily. Come over here. I want to show you something."

Naomi followed Mamm to the chair she often sat in to do the family's mending. Mamm reached into her mending basket and pulled out Davey's shirt. The one that had been new until Davey had done something to stain the sleeve, and Naomi had despaired of ever getting the stains out. Now Mamm held up the shirt. Naomi caught the sleeve in her hand. The stains were gone.

"How did you make it clean again?"

Mamm sat in her chair and smoothed the shirt on her lap. "Sometimes dirt washes out easily. We wash it once and the dirt is gone. That is like when Davey rejected you. It wasn't a little thing, but it was easily forgiven because you understand how young he is, and that he didn't mean to hurt you."

Naomi knelt on the floor next to her. "But

this shirt was so stained, I thought it was ruined."

"The stains on the sleeve wouldn't come out, even though we scrubbed and scrubbed. They were embedded in the fabric. There was nothing we could do." Mamm looked into Naomi's face. "That is like your feelings about Shem, and the Hinklemanns."

"What do you mean?"

"You haven't forgiven them, have you?"

Naomi started to say she had, but held back. She knew the anger she kept tucked away. She knew the thoughts she had of doing anything to prevent the Hinklemanns from taking her boy. She knew the depths of her own wickedness. She hadn't forgiven them, and she didn't think she ever would.

"How can I forgive them when they were so cruel?"

"That unwillingness to forgive, your refusal to forgive, is a stain on your heart that nothing will erase."

"But I haven't done anything wrong, they have."

"What counts is what God sees when he looks at our hearts. Is your heart good and pure, filled with the light of Christ? Or is it stained with the wickedness of an unforgiving spirit?"

Naomi turned the sleeve of Davey's shirt over.

"My dear daughter, the only way to remove the stain on your heart is to let God give you a new one. A heart turned toward him."

"Is that what you did to Davey's shirt?"

Mamm nodded. "I cut off the old sleeve and put a new one in its place. I couldn't erase the stains, so I had to replace the sleeve."

All that Naomi had heard in church and in Daed's reading from the Good Book through the years had remained a mystery until Mamm's words sunk into her heart. Phrases filled her mind, words of God's forgiveness of sinners, of being covered with Christ's righteousness . . . of his blood being shed for her salvation. As the remembered words fell into place, connecting to each other in an unrelenting progression, she recognized the truth. Blindly following the ways of the church wasn't what God was asking of her. He didn't want her prayers or her attendance at meeting. He wanted her. She felt the gentle tug on her heart to submit to God and his way.

"I need to forgive Shem and the Hinklemanns, I know that. But I don't want to."

Mamm sighed. "What we want and what

we should do are rarely the same. But I will pray for our Lord to strengthen you."

Fingering the sleeve again, Naomi waited for that strength to come. It would. In time. Until then, she still needed to forgive as much as she could on her own.

Mamm bent to kiss her head. "When you truly forgive them, the root of bitterness in your heart will be gone. You will feel healed and free. Free to love Cap the way he deserves to be loved."

Naomi sat back on her heels. "How did you know?"

"That he loves you?" Mamm smiled. "Mothers have eyes, you know. I've watched the two of you together, and I've prayed for your love to grow. He needs you, and you need him."

Uncle Wilhelm pulled the horses to a stop. "Davey, come here."

Davey ran to his uncle from the back of the wagon. The grass next to the sandy road was dusty, long, and dark green. It felt soft and cool on his hot bare feet.

His uncle's mustache twitched as he pointed with the whip he used to flick flies off of the horses. "Is that it?"

A pile of logs lay ten yards or so from the road, overgrown by weeds. Every day, two or three times a day, Uncle Wilhelm asked him the same question. He would stop along the road and point into the woods.

He shrugged.

"Your farm, boy. Is that your farm?" Uncle Wilhelm climbed down from the wagon seat, red-faced and sweating.

Davey looked at the pile of logs again and shrugged. "I don't know. I don't remember it."

Uncle Wilhelm took that folded paper he always carried out of his vest pocket. He looked at it, muttering to himself. "It's one hundred sixty acres in Steuben County, in York Township." He peered over the paper at the pile of logs. "This has to be it."

"Can we go exploring?" Karl had caught up to them. "Can we?"

"Ja, ja, ja," Uncle Wilhelm said. "Just don't go too far away. We'll camp here tonight."

Franz looked over his father's shoulder at the paper. "Is this Davey's land?"

Uncle Wilhelm frowned at him. "I think so, but we have to make sure." He smiled at Davey. "You can go play too. Just don't get lost."

Davey wandered toward the log pile, letting Karl and the others run ahead through the woods. What did Franz mean? Was this his farm? He didn't have a farm. His steps slowed when he reached his goal. The heap in front of him wasn't just a pile of logs. It was a cabin, wrecked and broken. A chimney rose at the far end, and in front of him was a doorway. He walked up to it and stepped on the threshold with one bare foot.

A voice sounded in his mind: *"Davey, stay inside. A storm is coming."* It was Ma's voice.

He looked around. No one was there. No one was watching.

He bent down to peer through the logs that lay stacked on top of each other. The stone fireplace filled the far wall. Weeds grew in the space where the fire would be. He swallowed.

"Hide, Davey. In the fireplace. Hide."

The wind had roared and the sunlight had disappeared.

Davey blinked and looked up at the leafy tree branches in the blue sky. He backed away from the tumbled-down cabin. Across the way was another pile of logs. The barn. The cow lived there, and Pa's horses. The boards covering the well halfway between the barn and the cabin had been broken. He never went near the well. Pa taught him to stay away.

He turned back to the cabin. Ma was in there, with baby Pru. The memories swirled through his mind. But they were gone.

Memmi said the storm killed them.

Memmi. She wasn't gone. She was at home.

"Father!" Franz stood beside some honey-suckle bushes. "Look what I found!"

Davey went to see. There wasn't anything there except two long dips in the ground, longer than him, with violets growing in the depressions.

Uncle Wilhelm looked at the violets. "Ja, ja, ja. Two graves. Just like Shem Fischer thought we might find. This is it." He looked at Davey. "I thought you were play-ing with your cousins. Go on, now."

Turning around, Davey ran past the well and behind the barn, but he wasn't going to find Karl. This was Pa's farm. This was what Uncle Wilhelm had been looking for. What was he going to do?

Davey crept around the stone foundation of the barn, walking like Crow Flies had taught him. He stopped when he saw a patch of poison ivy and stepped aside to avoid it. He reached the east end of the barn, the only wall still standing, and sidestepped along with his back to the warm logs until he reached the front corner. He peeked around it and saw Uncle Wilhelm, Aunt Greta, and Franz standing together by the well.

"Why don't we just settle here?" Franz said. "We have the deed, and it's a fine farm."

"Nein, nein," Uncle Wilhelm said. "Herr Fischer said we need to sell this land and head for Oregon again, and he was right. If we stay here, who knows what might happen when Davey gets older?"

"What?" Aunt Greta snorted as she laughed. "Are you afraid of a little boy?"

Uncle Wilhelm shoved the paper toward her. "His father put the boy's name on the deed, as his heir. If we don't sell the land now, while Davey's still young, he could decide to take it away from us when he is old enough." He folded the paper again and put it back in his pocket. "You and Franz stay here with the children and set up our camp for the night. I'll ride one of the horses back to Angola, to the land office there."

"Do you need to take Davey with you?"

"Nein. I don't need him. I'm his guardian, and I have the papers Shem Fischer gave us, making it all legal. I'll get the land sold, then we'll head west again tomorrow morning. Don't worry so, Greta." He pinched her cheek. "This is our lucky day. With this money we'll be able to travel to Oregon without any problems."

Davey leaned back against the barn wall. Uncle Wilhelm was going to sell Pa's farm, but what could he do to stop him? He leaned around the corner again. Uncle Wilhelm was driving the team and wagon up the little lane from the road to the cabin. Pa's cabin. His uncle unhitched the horses and climbed on the back of one of them.

"I'll be back this evening, unless I get to town too late. Then I'll have to wait until morning when the office opens again." He pulled his pocket watch out and looked at it. "See you then."

Ula, the oldest girl, climbed out of the wagon and waved after him. She didn't like Davey, and didn't like traveling. She looked happy to be staying here.

"Get the canvas out to set up the lean-to," Aunt Greta said. She sounded tired and grumpy.

Henrietta, the other big girl, pushed the folded canvas out onto the ground and jumped out of the wagon. "If Papa is going to sell Davey's land, do we need to keep the boy with us?"

Franz helped Ula unfold the canvas. "What else would we do with him?"

Henrietta put an arm around Aunt Greta's shoulders. "Didn't Papa say we could leave him in a city somewhere? In an orphanage?"

"Leave him behind?" Aunt Greta smiled. "That's something to think about. We already have enough mouths to feed on our journey west. He's so young that he won't be able to work for his living for quite some time."

Davey slid his back down the log wall of the barn until he sat on the ground. Aunt Greta didn't want him? She had said she wanted another little boy since Karl was getting so big. She had hugged him and petted him, and given him candy. He liked candy. But she had been telling tales. Even Franz didn't want him. When Henrietta said they should leave him, Franz hadn't said anything.

He wanted to go home. Davey squeezed his eyes shut tight so the tears wouldn't come out. He wanted his memmi. He wanted Cap. And his kitten. And Jethro. Uncle Wilhelm had been in such a hurry to leave that Davey had forgotten to go say goodbye to Jethro, his own little lamb. What had Jethro thought when he hadn't come back to visit him? He had been gone for such a long time, the little ram might not even remember him.

Davey sniffed and wiped his nose on his sleeve. He could leave. He could walk down the road until he reached home. If he stayed on the dusty, sandy road, it would lead him back to Memmi and Cap. He stood up, then slumped down again. His chest, and his bag with the memory stone. Uncle Wilhelm kept the chest under the wagon seat. He couldn't leave without it, and it was too big for him to carry. He wiped his eyes with his sleeve again. He would have to leave it behind.

Except for Ma's lace shawl. He couldn't leave that with Uncle Wilhelm and Aunt Greta.

Once camp was set up, Aunt Greta went into the wagon to lie down. Franz went to find a fishing hole, and the girls lay down under the lean-to. They talked for a while, then all was quiet. The afternoon was hot. Davey heard the other children playing somewhere. Splashing and shouts drifted through the trees. A locust started buzzing in the trees, and then another, and another. A small breeze stirred the leaves hanging over the barn wall.

Davey crept to the wagon. He peeked into the lean-to. Both girls were asleep. He climbed up the wagon wheel to the seat. Aunt Greta was on her back on the big bed in the back of the wagon. Her eyes were closed but her mouth was open, making funny noises. Davey let himself down into the wagon behind the seat and lifted the lid of his chest. He pushed some papers aside until he found Ma's shawl. He held it to his face and breathed deeply, but the scent had faded. She was gone. Davey took his bag from the hook where it rode during the day and thrust the shawl inside. He climbed out of the wagon.

He stopped, waiting to see if anyone saw him, but nothing had changed. No one was there. No one could see him. He walked toward the road, turning around once to look at the cabin and the barn. Ma and Pa were gone, but Memmi wasn't. Even if she thought he wasn't coming home, she would be glad to see him. She loved him. He started down the sandy road toward the west.

Shem leaned back in the kitchen chair, his feet crossed on the table. Cutting a slice of apple, he popped it into his mouth and sighed. With Priscilla off to a work frolic at the Gingeriches', he could relax for once.

At least Priscilla was happy. The church division had come about so smoothly that she purred every time she brought it up in conversation.

"It's a good thing I came west," she had told him just that morning. She smiled at him as he poured her coffee. "We now have a church we can be proud of. And you know what Mary told me . . ." She leaned closer to him as he took his seat at the table, speaking in a conspiratorial tone even though no one else was around. "She said that Tall Peter said that the men had decided to ordain you as preacher at the next meeting instead of waiting for fall."

Shem cut another slice of apple. When Priscilla was happy, he was happy. Ja, for sure, everything was working out fine.

He had even managed to ignore Susan's attempts to talk to him alone at the church meeting on Sunday. That was too bad, but it couldn't be helped. Now that Priscilla was here, he knew better than to give any attention to the lovely girl.

Popping another apple slice into his mouth, he sighed again. He would miss Susan, but he had a church to run. As much as he hated to admit it, Priscilla was right. The two of them together worked much better than he had managed by himself.

"Shem!"

The screeching call from outside startled him so much his chair tipped over backward and he crashed to the floor with it. He picked himself up and straightened the chair, ignoring his sore elbow and the bump on the back of his head. Priscilla was home, and she sounded angry.

Shem scurried to the front door and opened it just as Priscilla reached the porch. She glared at him as she stomped past him and into the parlor. His stomach turned to jelly. She wasn't happy anymore.

"Is something wrong?"

Priscilla dropped to the sofa, fanning her face with one hand. "Is something wrong? Of course there is something wrong. What did you tell those LaGrange County folks when you went over there on Sunday?"

Shem tried to remember, but he couldn't think with Priscilla staring at him. "I . . . I said we would welcome any of them to come here and join our church."

"Anything else?"

Shem felt his face heat as he thought of the exchange with Cap. But no one would know about that. Word couldn't have gotten back to Priscilla.

She pointed to the chair across the rug from the sofa and he perched on the edge of the cushion. Sweat trickled down his back.

"What else would I have said?"

"There's a rumor that you made sure that little boy would leave the community."

Shem swallowed.

"And it's said that you did it because of

471

your feud with Cap Stoltzfus."

"But you told me to do something to hurt him." Shem shifted forward. "Remember? We agreed that I needed to do something to get Cap out of the way." He grinned as he remembered how broken Cap had looked. "And it worked. Your plan worked. Finding someone to take that boy away was perfect."

He waited for Priscilla's self-satisfied smile, but she only glared harder, her eyebrows pointed down in a dark V.

"You fool. I didn't tell you to brag about it."

"But I didn't —" Shem stopped as details of his conversation with Cap on Sunday afternoon came back to him. "How did someone find out about that? Cap wouldn't have told anyone."

"He must have, because now everyone has heard the rumor."

Shem slid back in his chair, trying to look nonchalant. "No one will believe a story like that."

"At least one person does, and she sounded pretty convincing." Priscilla rose from her seat and headed toward her bedroom. "Pack our things, Shem. We need to leave."

"What?" Shem scrambled after her, stumbling over the sofa. "Leave? Where are we going?"

Priscilla stopped in the doorway, her eyes sharp as knives. "It doesn't matter where we go as long as we leave here before the damage spreads any further. I have a reputation to keep up and you are ruining it with every word you speak."

Shem shrank away from the hatred in her eyes.

"I'm giving you one more chance, Shem Fischer. The Iowa settlement is far enough that perhaps the rumors won't follow us there. If you don't make a success of yourself there, then I'm leaving you."

His mouth dry, Shem sank to his knees. What would happen to him without Priscilla? She was the smart one, not him. She was the one who planned ahead. He had been fooling himself when he thought he had done well without her. He couldn't let her leave.

She tapped her foot, still holding the door half open. "Well?"

"I understand."

"Good. Pack everything into my trunks and load them into the wagon."

"Everything? Now?"

"Everything. We'll leave as soon as you're ready."

"But we need to sell the farm . . . the furniture . . . we can't just leave it all behind."

She started closing the door. "We can and we will. We have to get as far away as we can before anyone decides they need to question you about those rumors."

The door closed with a firm snap of the door latch, with Shem still on the floor. Shut out again.

He shuddered as he remembered that Priscilla had closed herself in the room with everything that she wanted him to pack in the trunks. When he brought the unwieldy things down from the spare room upstairs, he would have to —

He swallowed. He would have to knock on that door and face her again.

Rising to his feet as quietly as he could, Shem headed toward the kitchen and the back door. He would hitch the horse to the spring wagon. At least that would give him a few minutes' respite before enduring her displeasure again.

Shem caught himself at the back door and clung to the doorframe. Iowa was far away, and he would travel every foot of it in the buggy seat next to his wife. How many miles would they have to travel before she stopped taking out this disaster on him?

Burying his face in the crook of his elbow as he leaned against the wooden frame, Shem groaned. There had to be a way out of this. There had to be.

"Shem! Where are those trunks?"

Shem straightened and headed back into the house to the stairs. "I'm getting them now, dear. I'll be right in with them."

Pounding up the steps, he knew the truth. He was stuck with Priscilla all the way to Iowa, and then wherever she wanted to go after that. For the rest of his life.

24

On Wednesday, Jacob hammered the last nail into the boards on the roof of the low shelter. "That should be sturdy enough. And once you put shingles over the top, it will be a dry shelter for your ram."

Cap looked up from the willow fence he was weaving. The strong fence posts combined with the interlaced willow branches would give Jethro a safe pen.

"That looks fine, Jacob. Denki."

While Cap finished the fence, Jacob gathered his tools in his bag. Cap wove the last end into the weaving and joined him at the well.

"Those boards we used for the shelter were easier to work with than trying to build with logs."

Cap took a drink of the cold water from the bucket Jacob had brought up from the depths of the well. "I had them cut at the mill in Goshen earlier this summer." He ran his thumb along the edge of the dipper. "I had planned to build a loft in the cabin, but now that will wait until Davey comes home."

Jacob took the dipper and got himself some water from the bucket. "Plans don't always work out." He tapped the empty dipper against one leg, his face blank as he stared at the ground. Jacob knew about plans not working out.

Cap rubbed at a sore place in his elbow. "We leave them in God's hands."

Drawing a deep breath, Jacob straightened and thrust the dipper back into the bucket. "Ja, in God's hands."

"How is Mattie doing?"

"She will be all right. The days are hard, though." Jacob ran a hand over his face, wiping at the sweat that beaded on his nose. "I find her at the window often, looking out at the grave."

Cap nodded. "Ja. I did that too."

Jacob looked at him. "Does it ever get better?"

"Not better, but easier. The pain fades, but you never forget. And then things happen to stir up the grief all over again."

"You miss Davey, don't you?"

"Ach, ja. Like my arm has been cut off."

Jacob grasped his shoulder. "He'll be all right."

"I just wish I knew for sure." Naomi had told her parents about Shem's confession, but he hadn't told anyone else. Without proof, and without a witness, it would serve no purpose. "I have this feeling that something is wrong. That he is in danger."

"The Hinklemanns will take good care of him, won't they?"

"If I thought they wouldn't, I wouldn't have let him go with them." Cap shook his head. "I shouldn't have let him go, anyway."

"Like you said, we leave him in God's hands." Jacob leaned down to pick up his tool bag. "We will continue to pray for him, though." He hefted the leather bag in his hand. "Daed wants to go talk to Yost this afternoon. We want to see what he has to say about this division in the church. Would you want to come with us?"

Cap looked around the neat farmyard. Everything was ready for his departure in the morning. "Ja, for sure. I've been wondering how things are going under Shem's leadership. I'm going over to the Schrocks' after dinner, so I'll meet you there."

As Jacob headed down the road toward his farm, Cap got the bar of soap from the cabin and a towel. While he washed up, questions about Shem kept pestering him. He splashed the cold water over his face and hair to rinse off the soap and grabbed the towel. Never mind. He had to leave Shem in God's hands. If only it was that easy to turn his worries about Davey over to God.

After dinner, he walked through the woods to the Schrocks. Eli was just coming out of the house, heading toward the barn. There were lines in his face that hadn't been there a week ago, and he walked with a shuffle that Cap had never seen before.

The older man looked up when Cap met him on the path near the chicken coop. "Cap. It's good to see you." He smiled as he took Cap's hand and shook it.

"Good to see you too. How are you doing?"

Eli ran his thumbs along his suspenders. "Truth to tell, we've done better." He shook his head. "I never thought I'd miss that boy so much. It's like all the life is gone from our home."

Cap gripped Eli's shoulder. "Ja, I know. I keep expecting Davey to come bursting out of the woods. He almost always came over around midmorning to help with chores."

He fell silent, remembering the first time Davey had emerged from the forest into his clearing.

Cap mentally shook himself. "Jacob is taking Christian over to Clinton Township to visit Yost. Christian has been wondering what is going on in the church over there since we haven't heard anything. I'm going with them, and I thought you would like to come too."

Eli's eyes took on a spark of interest. "Ja, for sure. Yost can tell us what folks are saying over there. I would still like to see this breach closed, if possible."

"I want to say hello to Naomi before we go."

"Ja, do that. She looks forward to your visits." Eli patted his arm, then continued toward the barn.

As he walked toward the house, Naomi stepped out the door, the rag rugs from the kitchen in her hands. She smiled at him as she shook one, then the other. She finished by the time he reached the porch and hung the rugs over the porch rail.

"It's good to see you."

He scanned her face. She didn't look as pale today. "How are you? Did you sleep better last night?"

"I did." She sat on the top step and he joined her. "I had a talk with Mamm yesterday about forgiveness and new sleeves."

Cap felt his eyebrows rise. "New sleeves?"

She laced her fingers in his. "New hearts,

actually. How God takes away our old hearts that are stained with sin and gives us new hearts."

Cap cleared a tickle from his throat. He knew what that felt like, that surrender to God's work. "And your heart?"

She gave his hand a squeeze. "I finally understood what Mamm meant last night, after you went home. I have never felt so much at peace. Even though I miss my boy." Tears filled her eyes.

Cap put his arm around her shoulders and pulled her close. "Even though we miss Davey, there is a joy also, ja?"

Naomi nodded, smiling even though tears trickled down her cheeks. "Joy in knowing that God is watching over him and keeping him safe."

Cap's stomach clenched. God was watching over Davey, but he still had a feeling that their boy was in danger. He pushed the worry away and tried to replace it with the peace Naomi felt. "I'm going to try my best to find him."

Naomi nodded. "But even if you don't, God is still good."

He pressed his cheek against her kapp, then turned and gave her a quick kiss on her cheek as he heard the Yoders' spring wagon coming down the road. "Your daed and I are going over to the Clinton district with Jacob and Christian this afternoon."

She stiffened. "You will see Shem?"

"I don't know. We want to talk to Yost."

She turned to him. "If you do see him, tell him that I forgive him."

Cap's clenched stomach released. "Ja, ja, ja. I will."

Naomi wasn't the only one who needed to forgive the man. As he walked to where Jacob was waiting for him, the conviction that he had never forgiven Shem washed over him. Through all the years, ever since he was a boy, he had considered Shem his enemy. But now? Now when Shem had done his worst, Cap needed to forgive him. He gave Naomi one last look before he climbed into the wagon. If she could forgive Shem, then he could too. And now, before another minute passed, was the time to do it.

Cap stepped out of the spring wagon as Jacob stopped by Yost Bontrager's farm, then turned to help Christian down from his seat. Yost waved to them as he came out of his barn.

"This is a welcome visit, brothers." He stopped in front of them and ran his thumbs up and down his suspenders. "Turn your horse out with the others, Jacob, and let's go up to the house. Mary fixed some cold sassafras tea at dinnertime, and I'm sure there is enough for everyone."

Cap helped Jacob unhitch the horse while the older men went ahead of them to the house. "Yost looks like he's in a good mood."

Jacob grinned. "That's one thing about Yost. His house could be falling down around him, and he'd still have a smile on his face. His son, Daniel, is a lot like him. Always pleasant to be around."

Once the horse was settled, Cap and Jacob joined the others at the house. Cap took the glass of tea Mary had poured for him and drank half of it without stopping. It tasted good in the hot afternoon.

Eli turned to Jacob. "Yost says that Shem is gone."

Cap swallowed his tea. "Gone? Does anyone know where he is? Could he be hurt or something?" The memory of the look on the faces of the Smith gang gave him an uneasy feeling.

"No one knows where he went," Yost said, "and no one I've talked to really cares. Our Sunday meeting with the church divided unsettled a lot of people, and most of the folks who Shem had talked into it weren't so happy about it anymore."

"Do you think he might have gone back to Canada?" Jacob asked.

"He might have. But a few weeks back he was asking me a lot of questions about the Iowa settlement. Since Daniel moved his family out there a couple years ago, he thought I might have some recent news."

"Iowa?" Eli pulled at his beard. "That would be a new area for him. No one would know about the shenanigans he pulled around here."

Yost grinned. "Don't worry about it. I've already written a letter to Daniel. Besides, from what Daniel says, the Iowa settlement is even more conservative than we are. If so, they won't listen to Shem."

"So do you think we'll worship together again this coming Sunday? The meeting was to be here at your farm," Christian said. He still used a cane to support himself when he walked, but most of the other effects of his apoplexy had slowly fallen away, and he looked comfortable sitting in the chair on Yost's porch.

"Could be," Yost said, his long beard waggling as he nodded. "Could be. I'll talk to my neighbors, and we'll make sure most of us are here. Do you think the folks from your end of the district will make the trip?"

Eli nodded. "The congregation was grieved the week we were parted. I know everyone will be glad to come."

The three older men changed the subject to talk of the weather and the condition of their crops, but the discussion about the temporary church split had ended on a note of hope. Perhaps the whole episode was finally over.

They visited with Yost for a couple hours. Eli and Christian were in no hurry to leave, but when the sun passed midafternoon, they slowly got to their feet.

"It's been a good visit, Yost," Eli said.

Christian nodded, using his cane to help him navigate the two steps from the porch to the ground. "It certainly has been. There's nothing like brothers who are in agreement, taking counsel together."

Cap and Jacob made short work of hitching up the wagon and they were soon on their way home. The drive was quiet, each man tired from the afternoon and lost in his own thoughts.

Cap's mind flew ahead to Naomi. If he hadn't had her strength to lean on in the days after the Hinklemanns took Davey away, he might have sunk into a mire of despair. But her faith had become even stronger while his had faltered. That was one aspect of marriage that he had missed since Martha died. A partner who could share the events of life with him. Even the most disastrous events. Sharing the grief with Naomi . . . sharing his life with Naomi . . .

He straightened up on the wagon seat, startling Jacob out of his reverie.

"What's wrong?"

Cap shook his head. "Nothing. In fact, I think things are going to be right." He looked ahead, over the horse's ears. "That's the ford over the river up there, right?"

"Ja, for sure."

He couldn't sit still any longer. "I'm going on ahead." He jumped off the wagon seat onto the ground.

Jacob called after him. "We'll be home in just a few minutes. You can still ride with us."

Cap waved as he trotted toward the river. "You're too slow!"

The river was low and he splashed through the shallow water. Then he ran up the slope toward the Schrocks' farm. It was nearly suppertime, but he could still take Naomi off to the side to speak to her.

He pushed himself to run faster. Or he could invite her to his house, where they could talk without being disturbed.

His footsteps pounded on the back porch when he reached the house, and both Naomi and Lydia jumped.

Naomi's eyes widened. "Cap, what are you doing?"

Now that he was here, and she was standing right in front of him, Cap had second thoughts. His breath came in gasps.

"Hello, Naomi." He took another breath and let it out, then nodded in her mamm's direction. "Lydia."

"Have you run all the way home from Clinton Township? Where is Daed?" Naomi set the stack of plates she was holding on the kitchen table and started toward him. "There isn't anything wrong, is there?"

He shook his head, still trying to get his breath back. "Nothing is wrong. I just wanted to . . . to ask you to come to my house for supper." He took another deep breath and let it out. "Would you?"

Her face had a pretty, puzzled frown on it. "Ja, for sure. I would like to."

A sudden thought crossed Cap's mind. He had some leftover corn cake from breakfast, but that was all the food he had in his larder. The greens Lydia was cooking in bacon grease smelled wonderful.

"Maybe you could bring some greens, and maybe a couple early potatoes?"

Naomi smiled. "I'll pack a picnic for us. Does that sound good?"

He nodded and grinned at her. Lydia's shoulders shook as if she was laughing at them.

"Come in." Naomi stood back so he could take a seat at the table while he waited for her. "I'll get some things together, and then you can carry the basket."

Lydia poured a glass of water for him while Naomi packed a basket with a loaf of bread, some lettuce from the garden, and a piece of cold ham. He took the basket as she gave Lydia a hug goodbye and they left the house.

Jacob waved to him from the wagon as he pulled up in the road to let Eli off before going on home, but Cap paid him no mind. He and Naomi walked along the path between the farms arm in arm. The summer evening was golden as the sun lowered toward the treetops, and the locusts buzzed in the trees.

Cap set the basket on the bench on the east side of his cabin, in the shade but catching the slight northerly breeze that had risen.

"It's so much nicer this evening. This afternoon was hot," Naomi said, taking the bread out of the basket.

They ate the simple meal, talking about sheep and gardens, but Cap's mind wasn't on their conversation. He watched Naomi as she talked. The sharpness of her grief had passed, but it still shadowed her eyes. He would be with her to watch time ease those shadows.

"Cap, did you hear what I said?" Naomi had packed the leftovers from their meal back in the basket and had stood to go.

He took the basket from her and pulled at her hand until she was sitting next to him again. "What did you say?"

"It's getting late. I should be getting home."

Cap looked at the dusky sky above them. "It isn't dark yet."

"It's midsummer. The sky doesn't get dark until long after my bedtime, and that's getting close."

"I want to ask you something."

As she turned her attention toward him, her beauty made his mouth go dry.

"I never thought I'd find you." Her face took on that puzzled frown again and he cleared his throat. "I mean, I never thought I'd find a woman to love like I love you."

She lowered her gaze and he took her hand.

"Naomi, I want to build a life with you.

The two of us together. I want us to have a family. Davey, when I find him and bring him home, and then more children."

A smile started and she raised her eyes to his. "I would like that, Cap."

"You'll wait for me? I don't know when I'll find him, but you'll wait? You won't marry anyone else?"

She didn't say anything, but leaned over and kissed him. He wrapped his arms around her and deepened the kiss. Now he was home.

Davey had spent the night under a shrub by the side of the road, but his sleep had been short. His stomach pinched.

Uncle Wilhelm had ridden by him last night, when it was almost dark, but Davey had hidden behind a tree when he saw the horse coming. Uncle Wilhelm's fat face had looked happy. He must have sold the farm like he wanted to. Then Uncle Wilhelm had ridden on to the east, and Davey went west until it was too dark and he was too tired. When he couldn't walk any farther, he found a bush and curled up to sleep.

In the gray light of the morning, he crawled out from under the bush and stood by the side of the dusty road. The chilly air made him want his jacket, but he could only hug himself to try to stay warm as he walked.

The light grew stronger and Davey looked for food. Crow Flies had taught him what plants were good to eat, but he couldn't find the cattails or dandelion greens along the road. He found some berries, though. They looked just like the currants that grew behind the house. Grossmutti made jelly out of them. They were sour, but good. Davey stood by the bush and ate all of them.

He was beginning to get hungry again when he came to a road leading south. The road he was on continued in a straight brown ribbon under the trees, but this one was filled with tree stumps, just like the road at home. He took a step down it, then another. Had Uncle Wilhelm come this way? He couldn't tell, but the road looked right. Davey went on south.

There were no berries on this road. The trees crowded in on either side and everything was in shadow. Davey stumbled, and then fell once. But he got up again. He was thirsty and his stomach ached. Bad. If he was at home, Memmi would give him medicine for his stomachache.

One foot in front of the other. The road narrowed until it was only a trail winding through the trees. He caught his toe on a root lying in the dust and fell again, but he didn't get up. Sitting in the dirt of the trail, he watched the darkness under the trees grow. He tried to swallow, but his throat was too dry.

He wanted Memmi. He tried to imagine her arms holding him. She would bring him a cup of water and tuck him into his bed. She would cover him with the smooth, cool sheet as he laid his head on the soft pillow. Uncle Henry would come to bed later, and with him sleeping in the second bed in the loft, Davey was never scared. Never alone.

He looked up at the branches hanging over the road. A screech owl's call made him jump. It was almost dark, but he could walk a little farther. He wanted to get home. He pushed himself to his feet.

Davey hadn't walked for very long when he heard hoofbeats behind him. The noise was loud, and as it came closer, he could hear saddle leather creaking. The horses were trotting, even though the road was rough. The man riding the first horse pulled up when he saw Davey.

"What do we have here?" The man spoke English, like Crow Flies.

Another rider pulled his horse to a stop next to the first one. "A boy?" The man said a word Davey didn't know. "We can't stop for a boy."

The first man turned his horse in a circle as the rest of the riders crowded up, surrounding them. "What's a boy doing out here alone?" He glared at Davey. His hat was black and pulled low over his face, almost to his nose. "Where are your folks, boy? Nobody lives along this trail."

Davey's knees shook. None of the faces were friendly. "I want to go home, but I can't find the way."

One of the other men spit into the bushes at the side of the road. "He's just a lost kid. Forget him. We can't stick around here."

The first man looked back down the way they had come, as if he was expecting to see someone. "Yeah. We need to keep moving. Forget the boy."

He reined his horse around and started down the road again, and the riders followed him. Davey had to jump back to keep from being bumped by the horses.

The last rider stopped next to Davey. He looked at Davey, and then down the trail at the riders disappearing in the twilight.

"You really alone, boy?"

Davey nodded.

The rider reached a hand down and Davey grabbed it. He lifted him up and on his saddle quicker than Davey could think.

"We can't leave you here to tell the posse where we've gone. You can ride with me."

The horse started off at a gallop when the man leaned forward, dodging the trees and twisting back and forth until they reached the rest of the horses. The horse slowed to a trot. Davey sat in front of the man on his saddle, encircled by strong arms. The man smelled like sweat and smoke, but the smell from the horse was pleasant. Like the horses at home.

"You got any folks, boy?"

Davey nodded. "I don't know where they are. I thought this road would go there, but it didn't."

"You a runaway?"

"I didn't run away. Uncle Wilhelm wanted to take me with them. He said I could be his son, but then they didn't want me. They only wanted Pa's farm." Davey sniffed. If he cried, maybe the man would hit him the way Uncle Wilhelm did.

"So you're lost." The man rode without saying anything more as the darkness grew thicker. Even when it was so black that Davey couldn't see the riders in front of them, they kept traveling down the trail.

Davey's head waggled on his neck until it fell back against the man's chest. He was held tight in the saddle as the horse slowed to a walk. The rhythm of the horse's steps was like sitting with Memmi in the rocking chair. He could almost hear her voice singing to him.

When Davey awoke, the sun shone through the leaves above with a green light. All of the riders were lying with their heads on their saddles or sitting on a fallen log. Some of them were eating pieces of dried beef.

"You're awake. I thought you was gonna sleep until nightfall." The man who he had ridden with held out a piece of beef and Davey took it. In the daylight, he looked a little like Uncle Henry.

"Are we home?"

"I don't know where home is, boy. You got any idea?"

Davey looked around. All of the trees looked the same. "We live by the Yoders. Do you know where their farm is?"

The man looked around. When he saw that none of the others were watching them, he scooted closer to Davey. "Yoder? Bischt du Amish?" He looked around again, and then asked in English, "Are you Amish?"

Davey nodded. "Are you?"

The man plucked a blade of grass. "I used to be. But I ran away." He looked around at the other riders again. "I think I know how we can get you home."

Davey rose up on his knees and threw his arm around the man's neck. "Memmi will be so glad to see me."

"What is your name?"

"Davey Schrock."

"I'm Hans Borntreger. It's good to meet you." He shook hands with Davey, just like they were both grown-ups. "The men in the gang call me Johnny, so you had better too."

Davey nodded.

Johnny gripped his shoulder, then stood. "Eat your breakfast, and stay here. Don't go wandering around. I'm going to talk to Bill."

Davey took a bite of his beef. It was tough and dry, so he chewed slowly. Johnny picked his way around the riders until he got to the one with the black hat. He said something to the man, but the black hat wagged back and forth. One fist hit his other hand. The black hat wagged again. Johnny pulled something out of his pocket, and then the black hat bobbed up and down. Davey tore off another bite of the dried beef.

"It's all right. He'll let me take you home." He rolled up the blanket Davey had been curled up in and tied it on his saddle. "I'm going to saddle up, then we'll ride for the Amish settlement north of the Haw Patch.

"The Haw Patch, ja. That's where we live."

Johnny tousled his hair. "Good. Then let's ride."

By the time Davey was sitting in front of Johnny in the saddle again, most of the other men were awake. They watched Johnny ride out of the camp, but no one said anything. When they reached the trail, Johnny leaned forward and the horse started trotting.

"We need to be quiet. There might be men in these woods looking for us."

Davey peered in between the trees as they rode through the forest. "For me?"

"Naw. For me and the rest of the gang. No talking, you hear?"

Davey leaned against Johnny's chest and watched the trees go by. Maybe when he got home, Memmi would let him have a pony. He dozed in the safety of Johnny's arms.

"Wake up, Davey. We're here."

When Davey opened his eyes, the sun had set again. But in the summer twilight, he saw Jonas Plank's house. "Ja, ja, ja. I know where we are."

Johnny lowered Davey to the ground, and then dismounted. He knelt so they could see each other eye to eye.

"Listen to me, Davey, and listen good."

Davey nodded.

"I made a bad decision when I ran away from home. And a worse one when I got mixed up with this bunch. Once you get home, you stay there, you hear?"

Davey nodded. "You could come with me."

Johnny stared at the Planks' house. Lanterns were lit inside, and through the window Davey could see the family at their evening prayers. Johnny stared for a long time. "I don't know if I could. I've done some pretty bad things."

"Doesn't God forgive you if you're sorry? That's what Memmi says."

Johnny looked at him. "Your memmi's right, but . . ." He looked back at the soft light filtering through the window.

"But what? You can take me home and meet my grossdatti. He'll let you stay with us. He lets lots of people stay with us." Even Uncle Wilhelm.

Davey's nose itched. All he wanted was to go home.

"Please, Johnny? Please take me home."

Naomi rested in Cap's arms. His kisses had been tender, but with the promise of a lifetime of love.

The evening breeze had picked up just

enough to keep the mosquitoes at bay, and they had sat together, talking of the future, until darkness fell.

"I'll be leaving in the morning," Cap said, tightening his hold on her.

"How long do you think you'll be gone?"

He shook his head. "I don't know which way the Hinklemanns have gone, so I might have to try several directions before I find their trail. I'll find Davey as soon as I can."

"But you don't know when that will be."

Cap sighed and pulled her closer to kiss the top of her head. "I don't want to go. I want to marry you as soon as possible. But until our boy is back with us, we can't make any plans."

A stream of cold water passed through Naomi and she gripped Cap's hand. "What if . . ." She swallowed. She didn't want to give a voice to the possibility. "What if you don't find him? What if he's gone forever?"

Cap groaned. "I've thought of that. But we need to trust God. We need to trust that he is watching out for Davey and will bring him home."

Cap stilled as the sound of hoofbeats echoed from the road.

"Someone is coming. Only one rider." He stood and Naomi rose with him. "Ne, stay here."

She sank back down on the bench as Cap walked toward the road. The moon hadn't risen yet, and the open space in front of the cabin glowed in the starlight. But the road was dark under the shelter of the trees.

"Hallo the house." The voice was a man's, speaking Deitsch.

"Ja," Cap answered. "Who is there?"

"It's Johnny Borntreger. We've met before."

"Come on in. We have a bit of supper left."

The man and horse turned off the road and moved toward Cap. "Good. Because I have one hungry boy here." The rider stopped and dismounted, then reached up for a bundle on the saddle.

"Cap?"

It was Davey's voice. Naomi stood, then paused. Could it really be her boy, or was she only imagining it?

Cap took a step toward the boy, now standing on the ground. "Davey, is that you?"

Naomi flew past Cap and grabbed Davey in her arms, paying no attention to the horse or the stranger.

She pulled back and turned his face up toward the starlight. His dirty, grinning face.

"Hallo, Memmi."

Cap gathered them both in his arms as

Naomi laughed, tears streaming down her cheeks. "Davey, ach, Davey, you're home."

"Memmi, you're squeezing too tight. I can't breathe!"

Naomi loosened her grip but didn't let him go. "Are you all right?" She brushed the hair back from his face.

"I'm hungry, and I'm tired. Awful tired."

Cap lifted Davey in his arms, then turned to the stranger. "Denki. You don't know how much this means to us."

The man took a step back. "Ja, well, when I found out Davey was Amish, I thought you might know where he belonged. I didn't know he belonged here."

"He belongs at the neighbors'." Cap glanced at Naomi. "And here."

The rider gathered the reins in his hand and turned to mount.

"Wait," Naomi said. "You don't need to leave so quickly. Come with us, and we'll fix some supper for both of you."

"Johnny, come meet my grossdatti. Remember? I told you he'd let you stay with us."

Cap took a step closer. "You don't have to go back to the bandits, do you? Why don't you come home?"

Johnny looked at Cap for a long minute, his foot in the stirrup and his hands on the saddle. "I can't. I've turned too far away." His voice was muffled, strained.

Naomi looked from Johnny to Cap. Bandits? They were talking as if she had come into the middle of a conversation.

Cap took a step toward him. "You can always come home. At least have some supper. Stay the night. Decide in the morning."

Johnny cleared his throat. "You're sure you want me?"

Cap nodded. "Of course. You don't fit in with the Smith gang, do you?"

"But will I fit in here?"

"Come and see."

Naomi took Davey's hand until they reached the edge of the woods at Daed's farm, then he ran to the house. It was dark and the family was sleeping, but they wouldn't mind being awakened by this news.

As Naomi and Cap came into the kitchen, with Johnny behind them, Davey ran to the bedroom door and knocked. Cap lit the lantern in the middle of the table while they waited.

Davey knocked again. "Grossmutti! Grossdatti! Come out!"

Mamm rushed out, her hair hanging down in a braid. "Davey. Our Davey is home."

She folded him in her arms as Daed joined her.

Henry clattered down the ladder. "Davey is here?" He looked from Naomi to Cap, and then caught sight of Johnny. "Daed, we have a visitor."

Daed walked into the kitchen where Johnny stood next to the door, his ragged hat twisting in his hands. Daed didn't hesitate, but held out his hand. "Welcome to our home. My name is Eli Schrock."

Davey ran over and grabbed Johnny's other arm. "He brought me home, Gross-datti. This is John —"

"Hans," Johnny interrupted. "My name is Hans Borntreger, from Holmes County."

Daed grinned as Naomi held Davey close again. "Welcome, Hans. We are grateful to you for bringing our boy home."

Naomi squeezed Davey, ignoring his protests. Cap circled both of them in his arms and pulled them close. He bent his head to whisper in her ear.

"He's home. Everything we have hoped and prayed for has come to pass."

She smiled as she looked into his eyes. "Everything."

EPILOGUE

Naomi set the basket of rolls on the table Cap and Henry had put together the day before and looked around Cap's farm. Men from both parts of the district were hard at work already, framing the walls of the new barn as Daed set the ridgepole.

Davey set his basket next to hers. "Is Crow Flies here?"

The old Pottawatomie had returned to his winter camp the week before, and Davey had invited him to the barn raising.

"I don't see him. Maybe he's coming later."

Davey tugged at her sleeve. "Then can I go play now?"

"Instead of playing, why don't you go see what William and Mose and the other boys are doing to help?" She turned Davey's shoulders so he could see the work site. "See? There is Mose, helping Hans carry a board. You can do the same with Cap."

"Can I?" His blue eyes sparkled and Naomi hugged him. He had grown tall over the summer and his head was nearly up to her shoulder.

"Ja, for sure."

He took off and Naomi heard laughter behind her. It was Mattie, walking beside Hannah as she made her way to the table. Hannah definitely had a waddle in her step.

"He is in a hurry, for sure," Mattie said.

"Isn't he always?" Naomi pulled a bench out from the table for them.

When they had taken their seats, Naomi leaned close to Hannah. "When did you say you expect this baby?"

Hannah rubbed her swollen stomach. "Any day now, but I couldn't miss Cap's barn raising. I've been looking forward to this day ever since Jacob and Cap started organizing it."

"I wouldn't miss it," Mattie said. She bit her lip and laid her hand on her own stomach. She had confided to Naomi two weeks ago that she thought another little one might be making his appearance in the spring, and she was feeling the same all-day illness that she had with her first.

Naomi didn't answer but watched the men hammer nails into the newly sawn boards. Cap had made the trip back to Ohio last month to retrieve the proceeds from the sale of his Ohio farm from his brother-in-law, and had invested most of the money in lumber for the barn and improvements for the house. He had also purchased some more ewes from a farmer in Holmes County who raised Leicestershire Longwools to strengthen their flock and Jacob's. But the most exciting purchase, as far as Davey was concerned, was a pony, already broken to pull a cart.

"I was so happy for you when Preacher Abe announced your coming wedding in church on Sunday." Mattie smiled, in spite of her pale face. "I just knew you and Cap were going to get married one day."

"Only a couple more weeks." Naomi couldn't help but watch Cap as he swung his hammer.

Hannah nudged her. "You must think Cap is pretty special."

Naomi rested her chin in the heel of one hand. "Ja." He was coaching Davey on how to hold a nail with one hand and manage the heavy hammer with the other. "Ja, he's pretty special."

Mattie and Hannah giggled and Naomi felt her face turning red. "I remember you, Mattie, going all moony over Jacob a few years ago."

Her sister glanced at Jacob, working alongside Hans Borntreger. "Ja, well, he was worth being moony over."

They all watched the building until Hannah sighed and Naomi and Mattie turned to her.

"I was just thinking. Our children" — she waved her hand toward the dozen or so little ones and the older boys and girls like Davey — "will all grow up together here in Pleasant Prairie. Just think what it will be like twenty years from now."

Mattie smiled. "Henry will be married by then, with his own family."

"All of these children could be marrying and setting up housekeeping for themselves by then," Hannah said. "Even my own James and Maria."

"I wonder what kind of man Davey will be by then," Naomi said.

Hannah squeezed her hand. "With a father like Cap, he will be a fine young man. The father of his own family."

"Each of them will need their own farms." Mattie looked at the trees all around them. "And more trees will be cleared."

"Josef said that the county is planning to improve the roads, and build schools."

Naomi shook her head. "As long as the

507

progress doesn't happen too fast."

"I know one thing, though," Mattie said. "It will be everything we have hoped for, and more."

When dinner was ready, the men took a break from their work and the whole community gathered together to pray. Cap found Naomi and stood near her. Christian Yoder, with Annalise and their younger children beside them, prayed for the meal, for the safety of the workers, and for blessings for the barn that was being built.

"And Lord, as we have many times before, we give thanks to you for bringing us to this full and fruitful land. A land that sustains us through your blessing, and will continue to sustain our families for years into the future."

Cap slid his arm around Naomi's waist and drew her close.

"We thank thee, and give thee all of the glory. In the name of our Lord, Jesus Christ, we pray. Amen."

The men formed into a line for their food, but Cap took Naomi's hand and led her toward the barn. "Come see what we did this morning."

"I was watching you. You've made a lot of progress."

He drew her into the interior of the barn.

Walls had been built part of the way up on three sides, providing a secluded spot for a few minutes. He put his arms around her and kissed her cheek.

"How many more weeks do we have to wait?"

Naomi snuggled close to him. "Only two. Two weeks from Thursday."

"And then you'll be my wife. My very own."

He leaned his forehead against hers and she gazed into his golden brown eyes. Cap was more than she had ever hoped to find. He was her friend, her partner, and soon to be her husband. She lifted up her lips and kissed him.

"What are you doing in here?"

At the sound of Davey's voice, Naomi pushed away from Cap. She could feel her ears burning.

Cap held out a hand to Davey and he joined them in the corner of the barn. "What do you think we were doing?"

"I saw you." Davey crossed his arms and frowned. "You were kissing."

Cap shrugged. "That's what mamms and daeds do. They kiss."

"When you get married, you'll be my real daed, right?"

Naomi grasped Cap's hand. "That's right.

509

Cap will be your real daed."

"Not pretend anymore."

Cap grinned. "Ne, Davey. Not pretend anymore. When I marry your memmi, we'll be a whole family."

"When do I get brothers and sisters?"

Naomi ducked her head to hide her laugh, waiting to see how Cap was going to answer this question.

He pulled Davey into a hug. "We'll leave that up to God, all right?"

Davey nodded. "Ja, for sure."

AUTHOR'S NOTE

Arriving at the last book in a trilogy is just as bittersweet for an author as it is for a reader. I hope you feel the way I do, that you aren't quite ready to leave the world of Pleasant Prairie.

The events in this story are based on facts, with a lot of literary license employed. The Amish settlement in northern Indiana did have its problems in the 1840s. The two halves of the district were divided by the swampy area around the two forks of the Little Elkhart River and traveling from one end of the district to the other was difficult.

Added to that is the fact that the Amish didn't drive buggies on the Sabbath in those early days. Modern Amish have both buggy horses and work horses, but one hundred seventy years ago, they would have had only one team. The Sabbath was a day of rest for the horses as well as the farmers, so the families walked to church. The long distances they needed to travel on some Sundays (as much as five miles one way) was a strain on the members of the community.

Another factor that the early Amish settlers in northern Indiana dealt with was the slight doctrinal differences between the families who had come from Pennsylvania and the families who had come from Ohio. The tensions between the tradition-minded settlers (generally from Pennsylvania) and the change-minded settlers (mostly from Ohio) of the church were a microcosm of the unrest throughout the Amish church at this time, leading to a division in the denomination in the second half of the nineteenth century.

There was a temporary split in the northern Indiana church in the late 1840s, but no one is quite clear on what caused it. Shem Fischer, the instigator of the split in my story, is a creation out of my own imagination. His role in the split is what *might* have happened — always the case in a work of fiction.

Thank you for reading *Naomi's Hope*. I hope you enjoyed her story!

And I love to hear from readers. You can contact me through my website, www.Jan Drexler.com, or on Facebook at www.face book.com/JanDrexlerAuthor.

ACKNOWLEDGMENTS

The more books I write, the more I am indebted to all the people "behind the scenes." Without them, we would have no stories to read!

Thank you to my agent, Sarah Joy Freese of WordServe Literary. Your encouragement always comes at the right time.

Thank you to the editors at Revell who keep me on my toes when life gets chaotic —Vicki Crumpton, Barb Barnes, and many others who make sure all of the *i*'s are dotted and the *t*'s crossed.

Thank you to the publicity and marketing people at Revell and Baker who get the word out so well. Karen Steele and Michele Misiak are tireless in their work!

And a big thank-you to our daughter and new son-in-law, Carrie and Josh, who scheduled their wedding with the deadline for *Naomi's Hope* in mind. I so appreciate it!

ABOUT THE AUTHOR

Jan Drexler brings a unique understanding of Amish traditions and beliefs to her writing. Her ancestors were among the first Amish, Mennonite, and Brethren immigrants to Pennsylvania in the 1700s, and their experiences are the inspiration for her stories. Jan lives in the Black Hills of South Dakota with her husband of more than thirty-five years, where she enjoys hiking in the Hills and spending time with their expanding family.

The employees of Thorndike Press hope you have enjoyed this Large Print book. All our Thorndike, Wheeler, and Kennebec Large Print titles are designed for easy reading, and all our books are made to last. Other Thorndike Press Large Print books are available at your library, through selected bookstores, or directly from us.

For information about titles, please call:
(800) 223-1244

or visit our website at:
gale.com/thorndike

To share your comments, please write:
Publisher
Thorndike Press
10 Water St., Suite 310
Waterville, ME 04901